The Wolves Of Satan

By

Richard Cozicar

Richard Cozicar

Calgary, Alberta, Canada

Copyright © - 2018 Richard Cozicar

First Edition   - 2018

ISBN

Paper back - 978-0-9950946-8-0

E-book   - 978-0-9950946-6-6

Hardcover - 978-0-9950946-7-3

1. Mystery, Thriller

This book in its entirety is a work of fiction. People's names, characters, locations and incidents are the product of the author's imagination or are used fictitiously and any similarities or resemblances to real persons, events or settings are wholly coincidental.

Richard Cozicar

Author

Contact information:

Twitter: *@RichardCozicar*
Www.facebook.com/RichardCozicar
richardcozicar@gmail.com
www.Richardcozicar.com

To my son Dan and daughter in-law Heather

Circumstances allowed the time for me to start this endeavour.

The book is finally finished, Heather.

The Wolves Of Satan

Chapter 1

"Well, you shore ain't gonna believe this one, boys…" old Jerry set his beer on the table. The bottle wobbled and drops of the golden liquid spilled from its mouth. Unfazed by the mishap, the seasoned fishing guide straightened the bottle and continued his story. His Maritime accent becoming more pronounced with each drink.

With a hook clamped in the vise, and the thread base laid down, Brand cinched the black thread tight, capturing the brown turkey biots for the tail. He reached for a couple of strands of peacock herl to form the body. His hand in mid-air, he paused. A smile tugged at his lips as he mockingly shook his head at the start of Jerry's now famous but often repeated fishing stories.

Brand had known Jerry for close to five years. The two guides crossed paths over the summer months at the river while launching or loading their drift boats. From friendly exchanges at the boat launch to an occasional drink after a day on the river, the frequent meetings building into a mutual friendship.

With the temperature swings of late spring and the early June rains, booked float trips on the rivers were postponed. The men took advantage of the breaks in their schedules. Days spent drinking coffee in the local fly shops and evenings idled away with impromptu fly tying sessions mixed with beer and friends.

Brand, like the rest of the fishing community, welcomed the short breaks, using the time to replenish the depleted inventory in his fly boxes. The collection of streamers and dry flies, nymphs and wet flies lost to fish and snags in the water by clients on previous trips.

With the passing of time, Brand selfishly looked forward to these opportunities away from the business to drink a few beers and spend time with his friend. Jerry had to be crowding seventy, he realized. How much longer would the old guide be able to participate in the strenuous grind of life on the water? How many more rainy evenings, he wondered, remained for the two to spend carefree, drinking beer and tying hooks?

With a relaxed smile on his face, Brand studied his friend. The older man's animated speech growing louder with each pull from the beer bottle.

Jerry wore a grimy ball cap pulled tight over his forehead covering his sparse white hair. As was his habit whenever he began a wild tale, Jerry would lift his hat and rake his reed-like fingers across his scalp. The features of his face set in a mask of leathery skin wrinkled by too many years of sitting in a boat on the river. A pair of pale green eyes peered back from the darkened skin separated by a nose that betrayed Jerry's fondness for alcohol, the nub bulbous and veined.

Brand set the herl down next to his vise and grabbed his beer. He tested his drink and shot a knowing glance at the old guide, a smirk lifting the edges of his mouth.

His friend's slurred Maritime speech underlined by a gravelly voice. Jerry used his hands as props and paused for dramatics, the size of the catch ballooning with each re-telling of the adventure.

Brand raised an eyebrow and glanced across the table. Dave Halperson looked up from behind his vise shrugging a 'here we go again' look in Brand's direction. Where Jerry maintained the gruff look of an old and wizened man who'd spent a lifetime outdoors, Dave was the polar opposite. The younger guide was on the lower end of the age spectrum, maybe a few years removed from school at best, but had worked doggedly to become one of the better guides in the Calgary fishing community.

Compared to Jerry's weathered features, Dave's age highlighted by the lack of wrinkled skin. Light brown hair leaked from beneath his ball cap and draped awkwardly over a sun-reddened face and onto the collar of his plaid shirt. The lights from above the table reflected in the younger man's face. His brown eyes and sharp nose mounted beneath thick eyebrows and framed by a dark, burly beard. Again, Brand wondered at the young man's attire. Even with the warmth in the room, Dave remained in a light jacket. The sleeves pulled up to his elbows.

Dave leaned back in his chair and lifted the warming beer to his mouth. A mischievous glint reflected in his eyes from the effects of the alcohol. The younger man smiled politely prodding Jerry on with disruptive comments.

"You mind your manners," Jerry quipped at one of the young guide's snide remarks. "This here is the honest to goodness truth."

Dave threw his hands in the air in surrender. "Sorry." He said trying hard to control his laughter.

Brand looked between the two men. Over the last few months, he couldn't help but notice the close bond developing between Jerry and Dave. The guides had become nearly inseparable. The two, even with the age difference and different interests, hung out more often away from the banks of the rivers. It was nice to see Jerry mentor the younger guide, Brand mused.

Jerry paused his tale and pushed away from the table. The bobbin in his hand banged off the table leaving the thread trailing up to the unfinished fly clamped in the vise.

"How your beers doing, fellas?" He asked and walked to the kitchen. "Always time for one more," Jerry judged as he rounded the island and bent to look in the fridge. A sigh of mock disgust warned of his frustration.

"Some kind of friend you are," Jerry called over his shoulder to Brand. The man's mumbled words changing to laughter as he reached to grab the remaining bottles. "There are only two lonely soldiers left."

Brand swallowed the remainder of his beer and looked at the clock. Quarter to eleven. He paused and mulled over the tragedy. The forecast called for heavy showers spread over the next few days, the lack of sunshine leaving the three men with empty schedules.

"You guys have them. I'll make a quick run to the liquor store." Brand said. He rose from the table and carried the bottle over to the island adding it to the growing collection of empties staggered around the opened pizza boxes spread across the counter. "Besides, I've had the privilege of hearing this story at least a thousand times." He ribbed Jerry. "You can wow Dave with the details while I'm gone."

"Oh. That's not necessary," a blurted response came from the kitchen. Jerry's turned head highlighted by the open fridge door, a tinge of panic flitted across the old guides face. "We're good. It's late, and it's still pouring like a bastard outside."

Brand lifted a confused smile at his friend. The few beer he consumed did little to alter his judgement and Jerry's show of concern for his wellbeing struck him as odd. Jerry was never one to refuse more booze, especially when someone else paid.

Brand shrugged off Jerry's words and walked to the back entrance. Slipping on his shoes, he grabbed the key for his truck and swung open the door on his way to the garage.

"Well, be quick about it then," He heard Jerry call before the door slammed shut.

Chapter 2

Torrents of rain lashed across the truck's windshield. Late Friday night and the lack of cars on the road shortened the drive to the liquor store. With a two-four pack of beer safely on the seat, Brand shifted the truck into reverse and backed from the alley into the dry interior of his garage.

A sharp flash of light reflected off the truck's rear view mirror. Brand twisted in the seat looking past the window in the wall of the garage. His brows knitted in confusion, his sight focused on the larger panes of glass on the back of the house. He hesitated while his beer-addled brain pieced together what his eyes and ears told him.

Loud snaps of gunfire drifted across the deck. The unexpected sounds greeted Brand as he opened the small door leading to the house. His eyes traveled back up to the large picture window. More pops of light lit up the blinds followed closely by loud claps of thunder, the sound reverberating in the backyard.

A sickening feeling swept over Brand, the case of beer in his hand slipping from his fingers. The sound of shattering bottles ignored as his body and feet pivoted along with his racing thoughts pointing back the way he came. Long strides carried him through the garage door. With one hand, he flung open the rear door on the truck; his other hand dove under the back seat, his fingers feeling for his rifle.

Spinning, he ran out of the garage, gun in hand. Water splashed under his boot when it hit the first tread on the steps of the deck. Breathing heavily from exertion and adrenaline, he paused outside the back door. Brand's heart sped with anxiety at the sound of Dave's raised voice leaking outside the house and then another gunshot.

Brand tilted his head. His eyes lined up with a slit in the blinds covering the window cut into the top part of the door. Brand's friend, the young fishing guide, lay slumped over the table. Dave's eyes stared blindly back at Brand. Blood pooled on the table mixing with strands of hair. Dave's outstretched hand rested on the table. A pistol clutched in the death grip of his fingers.

A stranger stood behind the young guide, the gun in the man's hand still smoking, the stranger's eyes turned away from the dead man toward the middle of the room.

Brand fought back the urge to rush through the door. He drew a deep breath and waited with his left hand on the doorknob.

The stranger's eyes turned away from the dead man at the table and looked toward the middle of the room.

Brand slowly eased the door inward. His right hand held the rifle, its barrel levelled at the intruder's chest.

The gunman swung his head in Brand's direction. Before the man's eyes traced the sound of the opening door and brought his weapon in line, Brand barged through the opening, his finger squeezing the rifle's trigger. The bullet slammed into the stranger's chest, raised the man up and tossed him back into the kitchen counter

Working the lever action on the rifle, Brand ejected the spent shell. A second bullet nestled in the chamber. Two quick steps carried him further into the house. With his back pressed tight to the partition wall separating the back entrance and the open interior, he stopped and listened. His ears searched for sounds of movement hidden from his sight.

Richard Cozicar

A bullet tore a chunk out of the drywall as Brand edged closer to the open corner. The repercussions of the gunshot echoing in the confines of the house, acrid clouds of blue-grey smoke stung his nostrils and choked the air

Bullets lodged themselves into the wall Brand used as cover. One pierced the drywall, nicking his leg, the chunk of hot lead leaving a ragged furrow below his knee. Brand winced, pushed the pain from his mind. He calculated the direction the bullet traveled. A second gunman would have to be standing at the far end of the table, a position blocked from his view by the partition wall. From where he stood, the shooter had the advantage. A situation Brand needed to change.

Eyeing the table, Brand paced his breathing and dove from his shelter. Plastic boxes filled with assorted sizes of tiny hooks crushed under his weight and dug deep into his side as he bounced awkwardly on the table. Spools of tying thread rolled underneath, and sleeves of feathers and dried fur scraped across the wooden surface caught in the motion of his slide.

He tucked his head and rolled his shoulders. The momentum carried him over the edge of the table. A chair brushed from his path. A sobering jolt of physics recoiled through his body. The result of his awkward slide suddenly halted by the stationary bank of cabinets separating the kitchen from the dining room.

Hitting the island at an awkward angle, Brand scrambled to swing the rifle barrel toward the far end of the table. Through the tangle of chair legs, he spotted a second gunman turning in his direction. Brand fired at the man's legs. The bullet struck the man's thigh, spoiling the intruder's aim.

Scrambling to his knees, Brand worked the bolt action on his rifle. A live cartridge replaced the empty shell. Rising clear of the table, he fired a round at the gunman when the man

8

attempted to stand. The bullet sank deep into the soft flesh of the straightening body and knocked the man back down to the floor.

Brand's right arm jacked the rifle's lever. Another shell slid into the chamber while the spent casing flew into the air. He stayed still allowing his breathing to fight down the adrenaline spiking in his veins. He waited, body tense and nerves firing while he scanned the room. Unsure how many intruders invaded his house, he relied on his hearing to warn of the sound of moving feet or chambered bullets.

The steady roar of blood pounding in his ears, the only audible sound in the eerie quiet that followed the gunshots, Brand remained wary. His feet planted, his body tensed, he cast his eyes about the smoke-filled room. Bloodied bodies littered the room. The first man he shot lay sprawled on the floor close to his feet.

A moan intruded on the silence. Brand followed the sound to the end of the table. Jerry's crumpled body twitched from under an overturned chair, a broken bottle of beer clutched in one hand and a pistol, on the floor, just beyond his outstretched fingertips.

Brand scooped the guns lying near the gunmen, stooping down to check pulses as he went. Stepping over the prone body of the second shooter Brand's eyes returned to the young guide, who only minutes ago, was politely listening to Jerry's fishing story.

Brand winced as he moved closer, his mind rebelling against what his eyes proved true. Blood had already begun to thicken against the side of Dave's face, the dark red liquid congealing and turning his light hair dark. The bullet punched a gaping hole in the back of the young guide's skull quickly ending his life.

Richard Cozicar

Brand lingered over Dave then cleared a path to check on his other friend. Bending, he rolled Jerry onto his back. A dark stain bloomed on the front of old guide's shirt. Brand's fingers slipped as he gripped the wet cloth and tugged against the hold of the buttons. The fabric tore open and he peeled the blood-soaked material away to expose Jerry's body.

Small, dark red pools bubbled on the man's chest. Fears for his friend's survival hammered the edge of his mind as he climbed to his feet. The late hour, an evening of drinking and the coming down from a sudden flood of adrenaline caused him to pause before deeply ingrained instincts kicked in. A dying man with blood pumping from chest wounds lay at his feet. Voices screamed in his head pleading for him to hurry and save the man.

A few quick steps carried Brand into the kitchen and to a drawer where he removed a stack of towels. Kneeling down at Jerry's side, he dabbed at the rising blood, wiping the wounds dry before he layered clean towels tight to his friend's chest and back. Using his knee to elevate Jerry's upper body off the floor, Brand tore strips of cloth and wrapped the bandages tight to stop the flow of blood.

He worked feverishly to comfort his friend. Several minutes passed as he struggled to trap the escaping blood. The stack of soaked rags grew on the floor before the bleeding slowed. Satisfied at the bandaging, Brand slipped his arms under Jerry's limp body, slowly lifting the old guide.

On unsteady legs, he carried Jerry to the couch and propped a cushion under his friend's head. The slight rising of Jerry's chest told Brand of his friend's weak but still beating heart. He prayed the temporary dressing would slow the loss of blood and prolong the old guide's life until medical help arrived.

The Wolves Of Satan

Red, wet stains ran the length of Brand's arms and chest. A slick, sticky hand dug into the pocket of his jeans and retrieved his cell phone. His fingers slipped on the glass screen as he dialled 911.

"I need an ambulance…" The exertion and adrenaline of the last handful of minutes tearing deep, ragged breaths from his lungs as he spoke to the operator. His voice barely contained the urgency drumming inside his mind while he explained the emergency.

Brand focused on slowing down his breaths and regained his composure at the dispatcher's volley of questions. He glanced around the kitchen, his eyes studying the trail of destruction. The quick tap of keyboard strokes on the opposite end of the line grew quite. The dispatcher reaffirmed his address and assured him that the police and ambulance were already on their way.

Refusing to believe the young fishing guide was dead Brand stared at Dave's lifeless body. He let out a sigh and sidestepped around the corpse of a gunman, calculating every placement of his feet, careful to not disturb the scene more than he already had. He retrieved his rifle and carried it to the front door. Leaning the gun against the doorjamb, he walked onto the front deck to wait for the ambulance.

Fishing a cigarette out of its package, he lit the smoke. His mind drifted while he listened to the raindrops. The ordinarily soothing rhythm the rain played on the porch roof added an eerie soundtrack to the unsettling turn of events that erupted on this chilly Friday evening.

Brand sat hunched over and contemplated the surreal scene that played out in the house behind him. The men who entered his house obviously confused his address with another. The local news was rife with likewise stories of home invasions in the city lately. The illegal drug trade fuelled a majority of the incidents, but those attacks centred on criminals involved with the drug business.

Sitting on the veranda, he recalled segments of the evening news, reports of shootings with a similar M.O., gang bangers who targeted houses and shot up the occupants in some form of perverse street justice. Wouldn't be the first time the perpetrators confused the address and involved innocent people.

What other explanation would fit, Brand rationalized, although his years of experience railed against this reasoning? The men lying dead in his kitchen didn't have the usual markings of local gangbangers? Not the type that he'd crossed paths with during his career in law enforcement or the criminals commonly shown on the evening news.

Brand took a pull from the cigarette. Happier feelings seeped into his mind as his thoughts travelled halfway across the country to his girlfriend, Sara Monahan. The image of Sara he pictured in his mind faded with reality. The momentary break from the shooting in his house, fleeting. He said a silent prayer that Sara had left earlier in the day for a business trip to Ottawa, far removed from the events that shattered the evening.

Sara, unfortunately, had witnessed enough horror to last anyone a lifetime. The blatant disregard for human life caused by the ideologically corrupt ideals of society. She still struggled with bouts of anxiety since a group of religious zealots abducted her a year earlier. The actions of the kidnapping pulled the couple into the midst of a home-grown terrorist plot south of the Canadian border.

Brand was sceptical of Sara's constant assurances that the events were behind her. He knew the tragedy still visited in her dreams. Her words betrayed by changes in her attitude.

The Wolves Of Satan

As the cigarette burnt down, the recollection of Sara's unwanted nightmare replaced the evening's shootings if only offering a brief respite. The heinous plot of a zealous religious cabal intended to rain terror on the United States and force the American President's hand in deploying nuclear weapons against the group's rivals.

The brutal ordeal was a bit more than a computer analyst of Sara's stature should have to endure. Brand's involvement in exposing the Cabal and thwarting their reprehensible plan resulted with him breaking several American laws. His tactics were deemed necessary, but legal problems persisted

He waited for the day of his return to the U.S.A. to answer for the charges filed by the American government. Whenever the subject of his impending court appearance surfaced, he noticed a change in Sara's mood.

The mitigating factors surrounding his conduct were out of his hands, placed with overworked bureaucrats, mostly south of the border. His day in court was looming ever closer. A technicality, the lawyer's assured, but political matters had a way of dragging on.

The Canadian government currently handled the backroom details to exonerate him of charges, but until the final verdict, the repercussions of his actions still weighed on both of their minds.

Chapter 3

Brand wondered back onto the deck after returning from inside the house and a check on Jerry. He lit a fresh cigarette. The night erupted with the wail of sirens closing in on his block. The mechanical warning signalled the imminent arrival of a black and white. Flashing blue and red lights perched on the car's roof pierced the darkness seconds before the cruiser roared into view. The car screeched to an abrupt halt in front of his house, the blur of rubber wipers slapped against the windshield's glass to drive away the falling rain.

Rising in his seat, he leaned on the metal railing at the same time the doors of the cop car flew open. Brand tracked the officer's movements through the wispy tendrils of smoke drifting upward from the cigarette pinched between his fingers.

A pair of uniformed officers stepped out onto the slick pavement, their bodies protected behind the open car doors, guns in hand, heads swivelled while searching the front of the house for danger.

"In here." He shouted down to the officer over the high-pitched wail of the siren. He stood and waved an arm beckoning the pair toward the house. The officers edged from behind the safety of the metal doors and cautiously crossed to the sidewalk. The no-nonsense barrels of their revolvers held ready in outstretched arms. Brand stuck both hands in the air, not knowing what else to do, showing the officers he was unarmed.

An older policeman, light reflecting off Sergeant bars pinned to the man's lapels, climbed the stairs. A younger officer, the driver of the car, walked close behind. The Sergeant stopped on the deck, his eyes switching between the open door and Brand. The gun in the sergeant's outstretched hand held firm, the barrel unwavering.

Brand glanced at the nametag stitched on the Sergeant's chest as the officer stepped past the square column on the edge of the deck. The man's last name, Whitly, was embroidered in blue thread on a white rectangle patch on the front of the man's uniform. Brand crushed his cigarette in the ashtray, nodded toward the open door and began summarizing the shootings from only minutes earlier.

In a voice tainted by years of smoking, Sergeant Whitly interrupted Brand. "Mac…" Whitly called to the younger cop. "Grab your notebook and record the man's statement. I'm heading inside to have a look around."

The Sergeant turned his attention back to Brand. "You stay put and fill officer McLennan in on the details." Finished with his instructions the Sergeant eased into the house, his arm extended, his service revolver leading the way.

A second set of flashing lights and the added noise of another loud horn announced the arrival of a city ambulance seconds before it rounded the street corner. Like the police car, the ambulance screeched to a halt behind the parked cruiser about the time the Sergeant entered the house. A pair of attendants jumped to the street with medical bags in their hands. Officer McLennan waved them to the house and called inside to the Sergeant.

"How you doing in there Sarg? The paramedics are here."

The Sergeants raspy voice echoed through the open door. "Tell them to get their asses in here. Got a weak pulse in need of attention."

Staying out of the way, Brand sat in his chair, his fingers absently reaching for a fresh cigarette from the package sitting on a table. His thoughts followed the responders into the house. Concern for his friends foremost on his mind.

Additional police cars steered onto the street along with an extra set of ambulances. The deluge of vehicles accumulating on the crowded, narrow road. The quiet, rain-soaked evening in the neighbourhood echoed under siege of the deafening sirens. The flashing lights from the vehicles lighting the block in a melding of red and blue strobe lights.

Brand looked around from his seat and watched as his neighbours ventured outside to the sounds of emergency vehicles. Porch light after porch light flared into the night as people poured onto their decks curious to find the reason for the disturbance to their sleep.

In the ensuing minutes, the pavement swarmed with first responders and onlookers alike. Brand stepped toward the door eager to check on Jerry's condition, but the young officer McLennan held up a hand. With a shake of his head, the policeman motioned Brand back to the chair.

Brand sat down. Paramedics climbed from their vehicles, gathered on the wet pavement collecting their equipment before climbing the sidewalk and entering the house. Fishing another cigarette from the pack, Brand cupped the lighter in his hands and blocked the light, chill breeze. He bent his head, touching the cigarette tip to the waiting flame and drew on the cigarette until it smouldered. Straightening, he lifted his head to peer across the deck rail, his thoughts in disarray. He stared off into space. Concern for his friends flowed deep inside as he once again contemplated the bizarre turn of events the evening had taken.

He sensed, rather than saw a man step past the young policeman and walk over to stand beside his chair. Looking up,

The Wolves Of Satan

Brand saw a balding, heavyset man gazing back down at him. The buttons on the man's rumpled shirt strained to hold the stretched fabric closed over the man's girth. A brown blazer sagged over the man's slumping shoulders. Tan slacks hung loosely below a large belly and ran down to a pair of scuffed loafers.

The large man stood blocking the porch light, his face obscured by shadows. Brand's gaze followed the man's hand as he dug inside his jacket and produced a wallet. Flipping it open, the man waved a CPS detective badge. Brand read the name stamped on the ID, Walgreen, detective Frank Walgreen. Raising his eyes from the wallet, Brand stared into the detective's face.

"Mind if I sit down?" Walgreen asked. Brand motioned to a chair with his head. "Looks like you've had a busy evening?" The detective said, worming his portly frame into the narrow deckchair.

Brand shook his head absently, half listening to the detective's words. Walgreen sat silent for a couple of minutes before speaking.

"You feel up to telling me what happened?" Walgreen asked. "Start from the beginning… when you're ready." He added, as he removed a notebook from an inside pocket of his blazer, then sent his hand back inside to recover a pen.

"Find out how the old man on the couch is doing first." Brand said.

"A friend of yours?" Detective Walgreen inquired. Brand nodded his reply. "Hang tight for a minute. I'll be right back." A grunt escaped the detective's mouth as he lifted from the chair and wandered into the house. Several minutes passed before Detective Walgreen returned to the deck and sat down.

"The paramedics tell me the guy on the couch is stable." Detective Walgreen studied Brand's face. " You apply the bandages? Seems that your handy work probably saved your friend's life." The detective squeezed back into the deck chair. "They're about to wheel him out. He'll be on his way to the hospital in short time."

Brand nodded his head. "Good. From the beginning then." He sorted his thoughts then explained that he and his friends were local guides who gathered for the evening to tie flies and drink a few beers. Followed by his impromptu trip to the liquor store and got to the part of describing the gunshots he had heard upon backing into the garage when the paramedics wheeled Jerry Kartman from the house, down the steps, and into a waiting ambulance.

Brand paused his narrative. His thoughts interrupted by the first-responders lifting the stretcher supporting Jerry into the back of the emergency vehicle. He stared after the flashing lights as the ambulance disappeared down the block before turned his attention back to the detective and continued his story. Detective Walgreen jotted notes in his book, occasionally interrupting for clarification as Brand walked him through the shootings.

Another man, a second detective Brand assumed, joined them on the deck before Brand finished his statement. The second man stood behind Walgreen, the porch light shining on his face revealing a full head of short red hair and the stubble of a five o'clock shadow clinging to man's pale face. A blue sports blazer covered a pale yellow shirt and dark, sharply pressed slacks finished the look. The new detective's attire a stark contrast to the shabbily dressed Walgreen.

The Wolves Of Satan

When Brand got to the end of his statement, the second detective showed Brand his badge and ID, Detective Darcy O'Brien. Detective O'Brien asked Brand if he carried I.D. Brand looked at O'Brien quizzically, and then slid his wallet from his pocket and opened it, showing his driver's license. The detective removed the offered I.D. and moved closer to the exterior light.

"Brandon James Coldstream," O'Brien said out loud and continued reading the specifics. "Born, May twenty-second, nineteen sixty-nine." The man droned on. "1.82 metres, ninety kilos. Brown hair. Brown eyes." The detective glanced at the picture on the license and then matched the face with Brands.

"That your rifle leaning inside the door?" The detective asked.

"Yes."

"Is it registered?"

"Yup."

"And you arrived back to your house from a liquor run to find these men already inside and shots being fired, is that right?"

"Pretty much like that."

"Couldn't be that you guys had too much to drink? A beer or three too many when a wrong word or two is spoken, a heated disagreement and suddenly a flare up of testosterone among a room full of armed men. Not unheard of." O'Brien's eyebrows furrowed as he regarded Brand. "There is an awful lot of empty bottles and guns lying scattered about inside the house. Maybe your quiet evening turned violent, and friends became enemies?"

The comment was a slap in the face for Brand. He looked up at the man, anger mixed with shock. "You're kidding…right?" Brand braced the detective.

"Just asking." Detective O'Brien said defensively, throwing his shoulders and hands up in a questioning fashion.

"You and your friends aren't in the habit of using recreational drugs, are you? Maybe the shooters were a message sent by a pissed-off associate." Detective O'Brien drifted to a different train of thought. "A sort of, even things up, kind of deal?"

Brand glared at the man and shook his head. The detective remained silent for a minute then continued his tirade. "This is the way I see it. Those two men came to your house, invited, not invited, doesn't matter," the detective shrugged, "and you and your friends had some previous trouble with them. Business disagreement, I don't know, whatever.

The two show up unexpectedly and pull their guns. Luckily you all were armed. What next. A wild west free for all." O'Brien turned and glanced back into the house. " These men you say attacked your house, they're unknown to us, but shit like this is pretty unusual in a quiet neighbourhood like this one." O'Brien paused. "I sent pictures of the men to our gang unit for identification, so far nothing," he clarified.

"How do we know you three didn't plan to shoot those men when they arrived, but things escalated out of your control" Again O'Brien paused. "You want to know what I think. Something doesn't smell right. Three dead inside the house, another man, rushed to the hospital, barely breathing, and here you sit, feet up, smoking cigarettes on the deck, enjoying the evening air. What's your take on this, Frank?"

"I have to agree." Walgreen looked from his partner back over at Brand. "You'll need to come downtown." Walgreen paused and read over his notes. "You're right O'Brien. The story doesn't add up."

"Bullshit." Brand replied and started to stand up. "I'm the one who called 911. My friends were shot, and my house is a crime scene, for god's sake. If I was going to kill someone, I could sure in the hell think of a better place to do that than where I live." Brand stared from one detective to the other.

Brand made a step to leave. "You guys believe what you want, I could care less, but I'm driving to the hospital to check on my friend."

"Whoa. Sit back down." Walgreen warned. "You've got a lot of explaining to do. There will be plenty of time for you to visit your friend."

O'Brien called into the house for Sergeant Whitly. The three waited in awkward silence until the sergeant appeared.

"Sarg. We're going to run this fellow downtown for a chat. Make sure the crime scene is buttoned up when forensics are done and have a pair of uniforms remain behind to guard the house?"

The sergeant nodded and returned inside. "You coming along peacefully or…" Detective Walgreen asked, a pair of handcuffs dangling in his hand. The detectives waited for Brand to stand up.

"Turn around," Walgreen commanded. The cold metal handcuffs bit into Brand's wrists before the detectives marched him down the deck stairs. The three climbed down to the street, Brand walking between the two detectives.

Walgreen's partner, O'Brien, opened the back of the squad car, waited for Brand to climb inside. The detective closed the door and circled the vehicle for the driver's seat. Walgreen flicked off the siren while O'Brien steered the car away from Brand's house. The three rolled out of the suburbs and headed for police headquarters.

Chapter 4

Brand shifted uncomfortably in the back seat of the cruiser. The metal cuffs dug into his wrists with each bump in the road. The seatbelt strung across his chest chafed his skin and added to his discomfort. The ride downtown to the police precinct was slow and silent. Quiet chatter on the car's radio mostly involved the shooting incident at his house.

Brand seethed inside. His arms tugged the short chain binding his wrists tight in anger while he bit his tongue holding back a string of angry words, which repeatedly crossed his thoughts, aimed at the detectives in the front seat. Having spent years on the other side of the equation, he reminded himself the cops were only following protocol. The handcuffs and the stink of the cruiser's back seat did little to reinforce his reasoning.

Armed men broke into his house. One friend laid dead and the other critical in the hospital, and the detectives, Walgreen and O'Brien, deemed it necessary to drag him downtown like one of Canada's most wanted. Bullshit! The fire and anger barely subsided by the time the squad car rolled to a stop in front of police headquarters.

The detectives led Brand past the booking sergeant, through a room lined with desks and into an interview room. Brand stood by the table while O'Brien released the cuffs off one wrist and pulled Brand's arms to the front, running the restraints through an anchor bolted to the tabletop.

"Have a seat," O'Brien barked.

"Do you think this is necessary?" Brand growled, raising his hands, yanking the chain joining the cuffs tight against the anchor.

"Four men were shot at your house. Yeah, I think the chains are required." O'Brien spat back.

Without another word the detectives left the interview room. Fatigue began replacing the shreds of anger Brand felt. His focus waned as the minutes passed. Resting his head on his hands, he struggled against closing his eyes. Each time he gave into the impulse the sight of Dave bleeding out on the kitchen table and Jerry wounded and writhing on the floor replayed in his mind.

Exhaustion consumed his body blocking all other thoughts until Walgreen and O'Brien returned and resumed their questioning. The next couple of hours ticked by slowly. A head-numbing tactic by the detectives where they asked a question and then with subtle rephrasing asked the same thing again kept Brand bobbing off balance. The investigators accomplished nothing by the redundant questioning and Brand, fighting monotony and lack of sleep tired of playing the game.

By four in the morning, the adrenaline and beer, combined with a lack of sleep, took its toll on him. His eyes closed and he dozed off. O'Brien slammed his fist on the table, startling Brand awake. His eyes snapped open as he sought out the source of the interruption. Detective O'Brien raised his voice.

"Frank, can you believe the nerve of this guy. We're trying to solve multiple murders; one he claims is his friend, and all he wants to do is sleep. If my friends had gotten shot, I know that I'd be eager to help any way I could."

Through sleep heavy eyelids, Brand lifted his gaze catching the detective glaring back down at him.

"I bet Mr. Coldstream thinks we're just a couple of simpletons, what do you think, Frank?" O'Brien continued.

Walgreen looked at his partner and then back at Brand. "Yeah. No doubt. I suppose that shooting that many people in one evening is tiring. Not to mention the stress of remembering the lies concocted to convince us he's a victim." The detective's words dripped of sarcasm. "And the bogus claims of concern for his friends. Seems all he's concerned about is taking a nap."

"Can we find him a bed in the basement? When he's rested, I bet he'll be more cooperative," O'Brien replied. "We must have some space downstairs for him to lay his head, don't we, Frank?"

"What the hell is going on?" Brand shook his head clear and straightened up. The direction the detective's conversation headed causing worry to seep into his mind.

A smirk curled O'Brien's lips while he stared at Brand. "I think the action at your house is a lot more complicated than you're letting on." O'Brien paused. "Tell you what. We'll find you a bed to sleep in for a few hours. That should clear your head. Then we can get back to investigating the shooting at your house. How does that sound?"

"Hey wait a minute. Since when do the police lock up innocent people?" Brand came fully awake with the realization of what was about to happen. "I haven't been charged with a crime. This isn't some lawless third world country. There are procedures to follow. What in the hell is going on! Where's my lawyer, a phone call, stuff like that?"

O'Brien glanced back at Walgreen. "Shit. Did we forget to log our guest in at the front desk when we arrived, Frank?"

Walgreen sat hunched over the table playing with a token from a casino. The hefty detective gave the coin a spin and nodded at his partner. "I'm afraid we might have overlooked that." He looked at Brand. "According to the log at the front desk…you're not here. We haven't charged you so you're here as our guest."

Brand looked between the detectives in disbelief. "I guess my calling a friend is probably out of the question then?"

"A comedian and obstructing an investigation…a couple hours in the tank should improve your respect for the law." O'Brien scowled. "Give you some alone time to think over your situation," O'Brien said, cuffing Brand's arms behind his back.

The two Calgary police officers marched Brand to the back of the precinct and down a set of stairs to the basement. The pungent, musty odour of unwashed bodies, urine and soiled clothing floated in the air assaulting Brand's sense of smell as he descended to the bowels of the police building. Holding cells lined the sides of a grey, poorly lit hallway.

Walgreen and the uniformed officer guarding the entrance huddled together in a hushed conversation. The night guard slid a key across the desk to Walgreen. The detective stepped in front of Brand, leading deeper into the lockup area. A few cells down the hall, Walgreen unlocked a door.

"I hope you're a God fearing Christian?" O'Brien spoke quietly to Brand. "You may want to say a little prayer." The detective pulled the handcuffs off Brand's wrists and pushed him into the cell. To the men already detained in the chamber, O'Brien raised his voice.

"Gentlemen, got someone to keep you company. Clear some space on the floor for this lost soul and maybe let him use one of those mattresses to kneel on." O'Brien stopped. His lips close to Brand's ear, he mumbled, pointing with his finger, "Enjoy your stay." Then in a louder voice he said. "I believe East is that direction. I know you missed your evening prayer."

In the raised voice, O'Brien spoke to the other lockups. "You boys be accommodating. I'll be back in a couple of hours to check in on you."

Brand stumbled a couple of steps into the cell when the detective shoved him from behind. He stood facing his cellmates. His ears registered the clanging of the cell door slamming closed and the sliding of the bolt locking the door. He accessed the situation. This won't be good, the thought slogged into his tired brain.

Remaining by the door, Brand studied the faces of the men in the cell. Three men sat crowded on a bunk in front of him, and two more sat across the short space on a thin, stained mattress. A couple of the guys were scrawny drug types. Another looked to be working off a hangover, and the last two glared at him, their heads shaved. The shaved-heads sported scraggly beards and tattoos, both clad in filthy wife-beater t-shirts, typical, skinhead, white power types.

The first three, Brand dismissed. The other two sat with their eyes locked on him. Brand watched their features darken, the pair apparently bothered by the detectives parting words.

Moving back and to the side, Brand stopped when his back contacted the iron bars. He waited to see what the two skinheads would do. The men glanced in his direction but remained seated. He slid down the bars and squatted on the floor. His leg throbbed from the bullet crease. The fatigue from earlier returned.

He averted his eyes and focused on his hands. The dried blood caked between his fingers sent him back a couple of hours. Christ, he thought. He must look quite the sight. He tugged at his shirt. Dark patches stiffened the fabric. He gazed at the stains on his jeans, and then over his discoloured arms. The blood dried a dark black and smeared from when he lifted

Jerry to the couch earlier in the evening. A large splotch covered the tear in the lower part of his pant leg, circling the wound from the gunman's bullet.

Movement from across the cell caught his attention, forcing him to lift his head. The skinheads mumbled between themselves and then with built up bravado, stood up and glowered in his direction, working up the nerve to approach. Brand's mood went from bad to down right pissed off.

"You guys are better off sitting back down. Things will go a lot easier for all of us," he said by way of warning.

"Is that a fact?" One of the skinheads, a big guy, at least thirty pounds heavier than Brand, spoke. The man's partner was shorter, maybe five and a half feet tall and no more than one fifty soaking wet. The smaller of the two puffed up his chest in an attempt to look intimidating

"I figured we'd oblige the detective and help put you close to the floor. Could be we'll even turn you east so you can pray." The bigger of the two growled.

Brand flexed his shoulders, easing the soreness from his dive across the kitchen table a few hours earlier. The leg with the bullet wound was stiff, but he doubted that it would hinder his movements much.

Staying crouched against the metal bars, Brand's body tensed as the skinheads edged closer. His eyes locked on the advancing men, the shorter of the two men a full step behind his bigger partner. Brand tracked the men's movements. His mind working through possible defensive moves if the pair insisted on pushing.

"Sit back down guys. Really. This won't end well for you." He repeated his warning.

"Did you hear that, Harv. The bum's concerned about our well-being." The larger of the men shouted.

Brand slowly filled his lungs and tensed his muscles in anticipation. The pair crowded closer. The larger shin head's foot swept off the floor when he walked within kicking distance. Brand launched off the floor, his legs pushing upwards like pistons, the boney point of his shoulder spearing into the big man's chest.

A gust of foul breath washed over Brand. The larger skinhead, taken by surprise, stumbled back under the thrust of Brand's charge. The metal cot along the far wall stopped the man's movement. The skinhead fell backward. Brand followed with a combination of blows to the man's jaw. When he heard bones crack he vaulted off the beaten man, spun and faced the second skinhead.

The smaller man stood frozen, his face a confused, unbelieving mask, his eyes wide as he gawked down at his buddy. Brand anchored his weight on his wounded leg, rotated on the ball of his foot and allowed his free foot to slice through the air. The hard leather toe sank deep into the pit of the smaller opponent's stomach. The man doubled over and sagged to the dirty concrete floor.

Spinning around, Brand faced the remaining inmates in the cell. He waited, fist clenched, his body positioned for another attack. Hangover looked like he was sleeping and the two druggies cowered on the bunk, avoiding his eyes. Taking a step toward the cot, he bent over the big, moaning skinhead. Brand grabbed a handful of t-shirt around the man's neck and slid the skinhead to the floor. With the cot clear, he disregarded the condition of the mattress and sat down, the short spike of adrenaline failing to offset his fatigue. He sat hunched over with his head resting on his hands, lost in thought when the guard from the desk and Detective O'Brien rushed to the cell door.

Chapter 5

O'Brien shook his head in disgust. "You're a walking magnet for trouble, aren't you?"

O'Brien unlocked the cell door and motioned for Brand. "And a miserable cuss, at that," the detective commented securing the handcuffs on Brand's wrists. A quick yank on Brand's arm started him toward the stairs leading from the holding cells.

"You know the routine." O'Brien prodded behind his back.

Once Brand's hands were secured to the ring on the interview table, Detective O'Brien began his redundant line of questioning. "Let's start at the beginning," the detective stared across the table. "What happened at your house...unless, of course, you still need more time to think? I know a few other guys in lockup, men who think they're pretty tough, too. I imagine they could provide you with hours of entertainment."

Brand stared up at the detective. Fatigue and concern for his friends peeling away his restraint, exposing a thinly veiled temper.

"You're a grade 'A' jackass, O'Brien. They vote you the head clown in this ragtag circus." Brand's resolve waned. The two men locked eyes and squared off across the steel table, both falling silent.

The door to the interview room swung open breaking the stalemate. Walgreen's elbow pushed the door aside as he entered, three Styrofoam cups of coffee squeezed precariously in his hands. The detective shuffled toward the table setting a cup within Brand's reach. Vapours of the hot dark liquid steamed from the top.

Brand nodded his thanks, his tension toward Detective O'Brien still bubbling just beneath the surface, ready to vent again. Instead, he focused his attention on the steaming cup. He sniffed the coffee before raising the Styrofoam lip to his mouth. The coffee smelled old and burnt, the forgotten dregs that linger in the pot hours longer than necessary. The liquid tasted like shit, but Brand welcomed the break, holding the cup up to his mouth. He took a second, longer sip, the distraction helping to calm his emotions.

Brand concentrated on the coffee cupped in his hands and enjoyed the few moments of silence. Lowering the cup to the table, he organized his thoughts. His sight fell on a manila folder lying opposite him. The file was upside down, but he had no trouble reading his name printed neatly on the label of the folder's tab.

"What's going on here fellas? A random shooting at my house, one friend dead, another wounded and you're busting my chops like I'm some underworld kingpin?" Brand raised his eyes to the two men across the table.

"Calm your heels hot shot!" O'Brien replied. "You and your friends screwed up. You know that. Got yourself in too deep and now you play the victim card. Maybe shift the blame, maybe even have us coppers take care of your enemies. Well, bullshit!" O'Brien shouted.

"This department has investigated a rash of home invasions over the past year, same M.O., same sad story. You three aren't the first to fail at pulling a fast one over these drug gangs.

Little league traffickers, like you, or whatever the hell you guys think you are, all eventually screw up. What was it? Got caught trying to cheat your suppliers, or maybe you were using too much of the products or skimming profits? The bottom line is, fellows like you and your friends are at the bottom of society for a reason. You guys aren't that smart.

What do you have that puts you three on the biker's radar? Come clean, and we can work out a deal, offer you some protection even," Detective O'Brien threw in.

Brand swished the Styrofoam cup in his hands. The remains of the coffee swirled around the inside stirring the grounds hiding at the bottom. "I think this shitty coffee is rotting what little brain cells you have left." Brand shot back. "I'll tell you again. We are simply fishing guides just taking advantage of some unscheduled time off. The weather's been too shitty to float the rivers, so we met to have a few beers and tie some flies."

"Tough guy and a storyteller. Boy, that's original. With an imagination like yours, you should write a book." O'Brien looked at Brand, his face a mask of disappointment. O'Brien's eyes remained on Brand while he spoke to his partner. "Frank. Those bikers brought into booking earlier, they still in lock up?"

"Yeah. Pretty sure." Walgreen mumbled.

"You think the boys would mind listening to Mr. Coldstream's sad story? He could probably cry on their shoulders retelling this piece of shit he's trying to feed us." O'Brien smirked, "You might like these guys Coldstream. They're not pansies like the skinheads in the other cell."

"You two are making a huge mistake. Instead of wasting your time with me why don't you concentrate on finding the person responsible for sending the gunmen to my house? How many different ways can I explain that I have no knowledge of, nor am I involved with illegal drugs or biker gangs?"

The Wolves Of Satan

The room fell silent. Brand and Detective O'Brien glared at each other. Walgreen slipped a file from under the one containing Brand's name. The large detective tapped the manila envelope with his fingers.

"Okay. Look. I'll come clean. We identified the gunmen." Walgreen glanced up from the manila folder under his fingers. "We found a match in the system. The two guys you shot at your house are a pair of hired guns from the coast.

Those men are, excuse me were employees of a South American cartel, an outfit from Colombia that set up shop on the west coast. The story is that the gunmen were under contract as enforcers for the Devil's Apostles, an outlaw gang of bikers that operate on the city's west side. Until a few years ago, the Apostles were small time, and by the look of things, with the Colombian's help, the bikers are making a move to expand their territory."

Walgreen paused in his narrative, his eyes falling back to the folder. "The drug unit has been keeping an eye on this gang. They believe that the bikers are doing the heavy lifting for the Cartel. The Apostles use their businesses to aid in the distribution and collections for the Columbians."

Brand cocked his head at Walgreen's words. "That would explain the suits worn by the gunmen as opposed to gang colours. But, why my house, why shoot a pair of innocent men?" Brand calmed by the detective's candour. "Unless, I guess, they hit the wrong house?"

He stopped to ponder the possibilities searching his memory for signs of drug activity in his neighbourhood, "I know most of the people on my block, but I can't imagine any one of them involved with outlaw bikers or the drug trade. No. Can't say I've spotted any increased traffic."

"No, I imagine not. Unless you and your friends are the reason for the visit to that neighbourhood." O'Brien interjected "Here's what I'm thinking. You either work for the Apostles, or you tried to rip them off. Right now it doesn't matter.

When push came to shove, they attacked and you guys…" O'Brien flashed his fingers to emphasise his words, "had to defend yourselves. Right. We understand. And now, here you sit. Let us help. Tell us what we need to know." Detective O'Brien leaned over the table and rested on his arms, his face crowding Brand. "We deal with small operators like you all the time. You piss the wrong people off, and now you need to be saved from the big boys."

"You guys are funny. There is no…" Brand raised his fingers mimicking O'Brien's actions. "Wrong people or bikers or Colombians. No one is looking to even the score!" Brand's anger returned. "And I'm quite capable of watching my own God damn back, thank you."

"Yes, so we've found out. Three men shot dead in your house. You do know your way around guns." O'Brien conceded.

Brand motioned toward the file with his name printed on the label. "You guys should take the time to read. I used to be one of you."

"Yeah. I skimmed the report. Crazy isn't it. Who would believe a retired officer of the law would go rogue and work with the very people he used to throw into jail. Na, that's never happened before, has it, Frank?" O'Brien sneered at Brand.

"I'm going to level with you since we're all being honest here." Detective Walgreen tag teamed with his partner. "The men you killed at your house were very dangerous. The

Colombian backed Apostles have surfaced in similar attacks, like the one at your place.

In the time since they joined forces with the Colombians, the Apostles have killed or driven out most of the competition." Walgreen stated, pausing to let his words sink in, his fingers busy twirling a casino chip. "We figure that if these men showed up at your house...well, I'll let you draw your own conclusion."

"Maybe the only conclusion to fit the crime is the shooters made a mistake. Right house number, wrong street. I don't know," Brand confessed, his patience running thin after having to repeat himself. "A mix up involving the wrong address."

"We are dealing with professionals." Walgreen slammed the chip on the table. "They don't make mistakes. They are, if nothing else, a very well run organization. They shoot first and ask questions later if anyone is alive to answer. I suppose that's to discourage people from cheating them." Walgreen's eyes locked on Brand's face. "We'll give you one more chance to come clean and make a deal. What do you have that's so important that the Apostle's would send imported professionals to collect?"

"I think you're as crazy as these bikers. We're fishing guides. I don't know what else to tell you. The weather's been shitty lately, and we got together to tie flies and drink beer. Jerry's retelling of his fish stories was the only criminal activity happening at my house."

Brand leaned back in the chair and looked between the detectives. " This talk is over. It's about time I got my phone call and a lawyer."

"I was wondering when you'd get around to asking," Walgreen said.

Detective O'Brien interrupted his partner. "Coldstream, you know that we are well within the law to hold you for a few days before charging you. After all, you did kill two, three men. But, I think," The Detective tapped his fingers on the steel tabletop pausing for effect. "The smarter move is to let you go and see what climbs out of the shadows hunting you."

I could care less which way this story ends. Eventually, we will catch those bastards and shut them down." The detective let out a forced sigh of air. " What's your opinion, Frank? Lock him up or send him outside to the wolves?"

"No use holding him in a cell. The man is obviously disruptive. Sure, why in the hell not. Let his biker buddies or the Colombians put the heat on him. Who knows? He might be more cooperative after they take a few runs at him. And, if they do succeed in killing him, maybe they'll screw up, and we can be there to catch them."

"Alright." O'Brien conceded. "I'll have a patrol car drive you home. Good luck Mr. Coldstream. We'll keep an eye on you, but honestly, the next time we see you, it'll probably be your death we're investigating."

Chapter 6

The smell of bleach struck Brand as he climbed into the passenger side of the patrol car. The harsh cleaning substance used to mask the smell of vomit, and other foul odours left by the myriad of back seat occupants collected during nightly patrols. He nodded to the patrolman, his eyes sweeping across the name, Waldron, stitched on the man's uniform.

Neither man spoke during the ride. When the streets of his neighbourhood appeared, Brand switched his gaze from the car window to the clock on the dash. The cruiser neared his house. Six a.m. Saturday morning. He sat silently fighting to keep his eyes open, his body wracked with fatigue from the long night.

Constable Waldron repeated the Detective's orders and reminded Brand to use the brief opportunity to grab some personal items. Until further notice, the house was to remain an active crime scene while the investigation was ongoing.

Bright yellow crime tape flapped in the morning breeze, the plastic strung around the deck posts and draped across the yard. The front door blocked by a stretched, yellow X pulled diagonally across the frame.

Desperately wanting a shower and a clean set of clothes, Brand sighed, resigned to the fact his needs would have to wait until he checked into a hotel. Waldron followed him from the car to the front door.

"You'll have to be quick," the patrolman apologized.

Brand hesitated on the front deck, thinking through a string of arguments so he would be allowed to stay long enough to shower and change. Even as he rehearsed the unspoken excuses in his head, his reasoning sounded weak. He nodded instead and waited for the door to be unlocked.

Brand took a step inside and hesitated. His gag reflexes tested as the soured air from the combination of gunpowder and drying blood rushed to greet him at the doorway. Nausea mixed with disbelief roiled his stomach as the smells brought back snapshots of last evening's nightmare. A disconcerting vibe, no, more a feeling or intuition, rendered him motionless.

He hadn't stopped to reflect on the attack yet, but a voice in his head screamed for attention. A lot of the pieces failed to connect, starting with shooting, the oddly dressed assailants and indeed, the timing.

For the first time since the incident, a sliver of doubt tugged at the back of his brain. Could the detectives be right? Was there a slim possibility that Dave was the reason for the attack?

His movements frozen by the raw memory of his friend lying face down, the young guide's life ended. The image of blood pooling on the table from the head wound, and then he pictured Dave's outstretched fingers, and the handgun. Could Dave have been expecting the gunmen?

Years of investigative work forced him to question everything. How much of what O'Brien and Walgreen told him was fact and how much was assumption?

"Grab your things. I'm sorry, but we can't stay long." The policeman's words brought Brand back to the present. He hesitated a second longer.

The house welcomed him silently, the interior, dark, except for a few weak strands of light sneaking in through the closed blinds. He moved a few steps to the right improving his line of sight into the dining room. Shadowed pools of dried blood stood out on the dark hardwood, an image of his friend's sprawled bodies lying lifeless, burned into his mind.

A hand grabbed his arm. Waldron interrupted his thoughts, warning him against entering the area and nudged him toward the stairs. A couple of steps up, Brand turned to the patrolman.

"I'll need my truck keys." He pointed to the back of the house. "They're hanging by the back door. Would you mind? I'll walk around the outside to the garage and my truck," he promised.

Rummaging through the bedroom drawers, Brand collected a handful of clothes, stuffed them into a travel bag and returned to the main floor, thanked the officer for the truck keys, and walked off the deck, around the side of the house and entered the garage. He turned back to glance at the house and paused. The next time he'd be able to step foot back inside his house, he had no idea.

*****

Brand locked the hotel door, tossed the key on a nearby table and dropped his bag on the floor. He looked toward the bathroom and the promise of a hot shower. His eyelids drooped, forcing him to change course and wander toward the freshly made bed. Out of sheer exhaustion, he dropped, fully clothed, onto the bed. As tired and worn out as he felt, his mind refused to let go of what the detectives had told him. What the pair had accused him and his friends of doing.

He hadn't known Dave Halperson long, but he found it hard to believe the young guide was mixed up with a group of outlaw bikers. Jerry, he did know well, and there was no doubt in his mind that the old guide was an innocent bystander. He admitted to himself that Jerry liked to drink a little too much, but Brand never had once suspected his friend of taking illegal substances. So, the question remained. What, if anything, did the cops have on Dave to make them so sure the attack was a targeted and drug-related affair?

The number of guns found at the scene troubled Brand. He had no idea that Dave or Jerry carried concealed weapons and why they would. With that train of thought, he struggled to make sense out of the attack. Namely, what brought the gunmen to his house and what occurred while he was gone that caused the shooting of his friends?

He focused on the gun in Dave's outstretched fingers. Was Dave able to wrestle the pistol free from one of the attackers? Brand couldn't be sure. And the handgun that lay on the floor beside Jerry? Whose was that?

Too many questions with no answers, unless the police were correct about Dave's involvement and he came to the house armed and expecting danger.

The unrelenting line of questioning by the detectives about the attack and the bloody scene at his house made no sense. Something troubling played at the back of his brain. Lying on the bed staring at the ceiling, Brand replayed the problem over and over, the missing pieces just out of reach for his exhausted mind.

The only decision he settled on before drifting off to sleep was that right after he visited Jerry, Brand planned on driving to Dave's apartment to disprove the detective's accusations. Dig into Dave's life and see if the young guide had any skeletons hiding in his past.

The Wolves Of Satan

Brand woke up mid-afternoon. A long, hot shower and a cigarette in the hotel's parking lot gave him a renewed boost of energy. Searching information on his phone, the second hospital he dialled confirmed Jerry as a patient. He inquired about the visiting hours, climbed into his truck and left in search of a restaurant and lunch before making the drive to the hospital.

A couple of black coffees down and halfway through a greasy burger, his phone rang. Brand glanced at the caller I.D. A local number, one he didn't recognize.

"Hello?" He answered tentatively.

"Coldstream, O'Brien." The detective's voice broadcasted from the phone's speaker. "Just checking to see if you are still among the living." The detective fell silent. "Have you thought more about our conversation? I can still offer you a deal and protection."

"Detective O'Brien, I believe this call borders on harassment."

"Not harassment, yet," the detective replied, "but soon it may well come to that. This time I am calling as a concerned public servant worried about your wellbeing. Okay then. Seeing you're still able to answer the phone, you're still in the land of the living, so all's good…you have a great day now. We'll talk soon."

Brand shook his head and stared at the phone wondering what type of disorder occupied the detective's mind. He pulled a couple of bills from his wallet and slid them under the plate for the waitress and walked to his truck. The hospital was halfway across town.

The nurse at the information desk gave him the number for Jerry's room and directions through the labyrinth of corridors.

He wound his way around hallways crowded with gurneys, found the bank of elevators and pressed the button for the 3rd floor. A few steps from the elevator, he checked with a nursing station. The on-duty nurse walked him to the room.

Brand stopped just outside the door. Standing beside his friend's bed was a woman he hadn't seen for a few years. Brand waited in the opening. Flashes of better times in the past froze him in his tracks. Jerry's only living relative, his daughter, sat hunched over the bed holding her father's hand; her back turned to the partitioned entrance. Moving a couple of steps into the room, Brand spoke quietly.

"Susan. How's your father doing?"

Susan Kartman, or rather Susan Bowles, he corrected himself, she had married since the last time they met, but Brand still thought of her as Kartman. He studied her as she turned away from her father's side and self-consciously wiped a hand across her face, smearing a tear into a smudge of mascara on her cheek.

Susan's face was a little heavier since he'd last seen her. Wrinkles guarded her eyes and the corners of her mouth. Traces of white highlights streaked the hair surrounding her face. Susan's eyes were swollen and red, her features haggard and etched with worry. A tired smile played across her lips as she tilted her head back to meet his eyes.

He waited patiently. Susan's smile faded as she stared into his face. With a few quick steps, she crossed the gap to where he stood and threw her arms around his waist hugging him tightly. Brand reciprocated. His arms circled her body as he felt her weep on his shoulder. Minutes of silence passed before she backed away and rubbed her face with the back of her hand in an attempt to dry her eyes.

"Have you been in town long?" He asked. She shook her head, swallowed back more tears, her reply quiet and uncertain.

"No. I arrived this morning. I drove straight from the airport." She explained. "What happened Brand? The police won't tell me much. Only that dad suffered a gun-shot wound in a home invasion."

"I'm still trying to figure that out." Brand said sadly. His eyes focused on his friend lying in the hospital bed. "Have you talked to the doctors...what do they say about his condition?"

"Only that he's in a coma, but resting easy." She swallowed again. "The doctors are not sure how long he will remain unconscious. A bullet tore some arteries and caused internal bleeding." Susan stopped, fought back the tears that insisted on pooling in her eyes, composed herself and continued. "The doctor did comment on dad's drinking and the toll it has taken on his body. The excess booze thinned his blood and made it much harder for them to stabilize his wound."

Brand listened to the monitor's hum and beep in the background. His friend's breathing, even and shallow. "Yeah." He agreed with the doctors. " He has been hitting the bottle a little harder lately."

Changing the subject, he gently put his hand on Susan's arm. "Let's walk downstairs. I'll buy you a coffee. We can talk."

In the hospital cafeteria, the two discussed Jerry's fragile condition. Brand did his best to assure Susan that her dad would be all right, while, at the same time trying to convince himself.

He recounted the attack at his house, glossing over the grislier details. Telling Susan of the two gunmen and the death of another friend, again skipping the specifics. His account was short, and he finished with his belief of the attack being unprovoked.

"The gunmen probably confused my address with some other. The pair mistakenly showed up at the wrong address and stormed into the wrong house. What transpired once they entered and confronted your dad and our friend…no one knows yet." He explained. He held back his fleeting suspicions about the young guide and the detective's insistence that the hit on his house was not random.

"I can wait until you're ready to leave. Give you a ride to a hotel if you need?" He offered.

"I rented a car at the airport. I'll stay at dad's house." She replied, her expression one of uncertainty.

Brand grabbed a napkin off the table and fishing a pen from his pocket began scribbling a row of numbers. "Changed cell numbers since your last visit," he explained pushing the paper across the small table. "I've got some things to do, but I'll check in with you later," he promised.

He walked across the parking lot toward his truck, his mind occupied by thoughts of Jerry and his daughter and his dead friend, Dave. He found it was becoming easier to accept the detective's far-flung theory and maybe Dave had gotten mixed up with this biker gang. He hoped to find the answers waiting at Dave's apartment.

Guilty or not, Brand wouldn't stop until he dug to the bottom of this tragedy.

Chapter 7

Late afternoon. Brand re-joined the flow of traffic, his truck pointed in a northwest direction. The spray lifting off the wet road from the tires of the passing vehicles and the constant slap of the wipers swiping at the heavy rain went unnoticed. Brand navigated the route distracted. Snap shots of last evening's shootings played across his mind bringing with them questions in search of answers. He found his thoughts lingering on the young guide's short life.

He had only been to Dave's complex once before. That time, he dropped the young guide off outside the building but never went inside. His mood darkened further as he realized that in the couple of years the two had been friends he had no idea what floor Dave lived on, not to mention his apartment number.

Parking in an empty stall, he shut the motor off and looked at the building through the rain-streaked windshield. Brand ground out his cigarette and dug into the glove box for a pair of leather gloves.

Regrets of a lost friend settled deep in his soul as he leaned against the steering wheel. He absently traced the path of falling raindrops outside the truck windows. Pushing past the guilt, he jumped from the cab and raced for the large roof sheltering the building's entrance and the chore of locating Dave's home.

Most of his working life had involved tracking people for CSIS, so the menial task of discovering an unknown apartment number shouldn't prove too difficult to locate.

The door leading to the labyrinth of apartments refused to open when he tugged on the handle. Glancing at the intercom panel, he randomly selected a numbered button. His finger lingered over the depressed button while the wires connected and transmitted a notification somewhere deep within the building informing the occupants that a visitor waited by the front door. A woman's voice replied from the small speaker asking for his name. Brand ignored the query and repeated the process until finally the lock on the front door buzzed open allowing him access to the lobby.

A bank of mailboxes lined an inner wall. Brand walked across the small room and scanned the list of names until he located Halperson beside apartment number 403. Wandering away from the front doors, Brand followed a brightly lit hallway deeper into the building. A pair of elevators waited where the corridor branched away in opposite directions. Pressing the button for the fourth floor, he waited for the elevator doors to close.

An unmarked police car pulled up to the curb across the street from the apartment complex, Brand's parked truck in full view on the paved lot. The driver waited until Brand entered the building before he slipped from the car and pulled the back of his coat over his head to protect against the falling rain. The man hurried across the street weaving among the parked vehicles, rushing through the rain for the glass doors and the dry comfort of the entrance.

The elevator doors opened. Apartment 420 sat on the opposite side of the hall. Brand stood in the open doors and glanced one way and then the other noting which way the apartment numbers climbed. Glancing at each door number he passed, Brand moved down the hallway toward apartment 403.

The Wolves Of Satan

He faced the door and hesitated before twisting his hand behind his back, fishing for the pair of gloves stuffed in his jeans pocket.

Once he worked his fingers into the gloves, he reached for the doorknob expecting a locked door. Surprise was quickly replaced by caution habitually slowing his actions when the solid metal door guarding the apartment from the rest of the building, noiselessly opened.

As far as Brand knew, Dave lived alone; still he hesitated at the opening. The thought of knocking surfaced then passed. He would rather apologize for intruding then issue a warning to anyone in the unit.

Standing to the side, Brand pushed the door clear. His eyes tracking the doors swing and automatically scanning the small entrance before shifting to the darkened interior of the suite. Pausing quietly in the doorway, he listened for movement. Silence floated in the apartment as stale, musty air rushed from the sealed interior and escaped through the opening into the hallway. The hall lights from behind faded into the shadows a few feet from where he stood.

Brand crept in further. One hand swept the door closed leaving his vision waning while the other hand rubbed along the wall in the gloom feeling for the light switch. He took a calming breath, instincts borne from years of training subconsciously controlled his movements, his body tensed, prepared for the unexpected. His finger nudged the plastic toggle switch upward.

Ceiling mounted light fixtures flared to life, their dull yellow glow stretched into the darkened corners. A few feet inside the door, the main room lay visible. The apartment was in shambles. Scattered furniture covered the carpet at the end of the short hallway. Weaving deeper into the unit, Brand sidestepped the contents strewn across the apartment floor. He placed his feet carefully to avoid disrupting the mess. If anyone remained in the apartment their presence would be easy to detect considering Dave's belongings covered every square inch of floor space.

Brand slowed by the entrance to the kitchen. Here, the scene was the same. The interior of the cupboards laid exposed, drawers were pulled from their frames and dumped, even the fridge door hung open. Doubts of Dave's innocence began nudging against Brand's conscious. The homes of innocent people were rarely the target of extensive searches like the one he was witnessing.

The utter disregard for the contents of the apartment told a disturbing story. Brand surveyed the destruction from the kitchen. Someone was desperate in their search, but for what?

If the detective's assumptions were correct about Dave's involvement with the bikers and the drug trade, Brand could effectively rule out the act of Dave carrying a large quantity of drugs up to his apartment, four floors up, without the other tenants noticing. Whatever lay at the source of this break-in had to be something small, an easily concealed item.

He ran his eyes over the floors and then over the apartment walls. White outlines showed against the darker staining of the paint and revealed where pictures must have hung. From his point of view, the search of the interior appeared thorough. Every possible hiding spot uncovered and exposed, many of the spaces much too small to conceal drugs of any quantity.

It was quite obvious that whoever conducted the search spent a good amount of time inside the apartment and was very intent on finding whatever Dave had in his possession. The question, did they find what they were looking for?

m the kitchen turning to the rest of the
ᴩu ., cursory glance in the bathroom and then a
surveying the bedroom. Empty handed, he
ᵤₜₚₚₑᵤ from the pile of trash that remained of Dave's bedroom. He had only just crossed back into the kitchen when the slight whisper of door hinges made him freeze. The crunch of footsteps on the tile floor of the apartments entrance followed.

Brand waited. A wall stood between him and the front door. The slow scuffle of feet accompanied by laboured breathing and then the unmistakable, metallic click of a gun's hammer cocking, echoed in the silence.

Shit…Brand swore in his head. The shock and fatigue of the past day's events made him sloppy. The thought of carrying a handgun for protection had never entered his mind. What the hell was Dave up to? The side trip to the apartment only an endeavour to ease his mind of his friend's guilt. It never occurred to him that he would be facing armed adversaries.

He moved, snugging his back tight against the wall, inching slowly to the opening at the end of the hallway. There, he listened. The footsteps crept from the tiled entrance and disappeared into the cushioned carpeting covering the main floor. Brand waited, his breathing shallow and silent. Even with the intruder's footsteps absorbed by the soft carpet, Brand tracked the loud breathing as the person edged closer.

Soon the black metal sheen of a handgun extended past the end of wall. Then came the wrist holding it. Brand acted instinctively. His hand sliced downward, chopping at the extended wrist. His actions sent the handgun plummeting to the apartment floor. In the same fluid motion his right hand shot out and gripped a clump of fabric. Twisting at the waist, he jerked the intruder past the wall. The body attached to the end of the arm, tumbled out of control, awkwardly stumbling into the scattered furniture littering room.

The heavy body of Detective Walgreen blurred past. B heard the detective curse as he struggled to regain his footing. Walgreen glared at Brand, swore again and grunted as he bent to retrieve his service revolver.

"You nearly broke my GOD DAMNED wrist!" Walgreen yelled. The detective's face reddened, spittle flying from his mouth while he rubbed his sore arm.

"What the hell are you doing here?" Brand replied, surprised by the detective's unexpected appearance.

"I think I should be the one asking you the same question?" Walgreen answered. "What are you looking for? Your buddy's hidden stash of drugs. Was he stealing from you, too? Is that why you shot him?

This certainly doesn't look suspicious, Coldstream." The detective's words dripped with sarcasm. "You were released from custody only a few hours ago. You definitely don't waste time."

"Cool your heels. This is how I found the apartment." Brand explained. "I've only been here a few minutes for what it's worth. I was at the hospital before this," he said defensively feeling the need to explain his whereabouts to the detective. "Check with the staff. Someone at the hospital should remember me."

"Looks like you still had plenty of time to," Walgreen swung his arm over the scattered furniture, "redecorate."

Walgreen studied Brand. His eyes peering from beneath drooping eyelids, his breathing still ragged from the surprised welcome.

"Why are you here? Really." Walgreen twisted his upper body; his movements slow as he surveyed the condition of the

The Wolves Of Satan

ravaged apartment. "What are you looking for? Finding you combing through your buddy's apartment certainly reinforces our theory of you holding key information from us. Are you positive that there's not more to this story that you'd like to share?"

"Detective, I have no idea what kind of strange thoughts circle in that small brain of yours, but honestly, try using that round ball above your shoulders for more than just supporting your ugly face." Brand snapped at the detective.

"By the way. What are YOU doing here? Are you following me?" Brand tracked the detective's movements as Walgreen massaged his sore wrist. A twitch of pain flitted across the man's face.

Walgreen swung his attention back to Brand. "Three men shot dead by your hand…"

Anger flushed Brands face. "The gunmen were attacking my friends. They left me little choice. Dave, he was shot before I entered the…"

"Matter of semantics, really." Walgreen interrupted. "Three men are still dead. So yes, I'm keeping you on the radar until I figure out what type of game you're playing. Those shooters weren't at your house by mistake."

Walgreen shifted his bulky body. A breath of stale air rushed forward. A noxious combination of coffee, cigarettes and spicy food washed over Brand. "I'm curious to know what the three of you are hiding?"

The detective inched his face closer. "What are you afraid to you tell us? In time, you know we'll discover the truth."

"I told you everything back at the station. We're not..." Brand thought about his reply. Doubts about Dave's involvement becoming unclear in his head, "I'm not involved with any drug gangs."

He took a step toward the door. "Unless you're going to arrest me and drag me downtown. I'm leaving."

"Oh. And a little free advice. Next time we meet, think about announcing your presence." Brand continued. "Sneaking up on people is a bad habit. Could get you seriously hurt."

Walgreen continued glaring. He dug a card from his pocket and shoved it in Brand's direction. Brand grabbed the card and without taking his eyes off Walgreen, he stuffed the card in his pocket. Turning, he left the detective standing in the apartment.

Let the cops deal with the mess, he thought, as he waited for the elevator. The fact that Dave's flat lay in shambles, uneasy on his mind. Back in his truck, Brand sat staring out the windshield. How well had he really known Dave, he found himself wondering for a second time?

The detective's wild accusations were leaving him with traces of doubt. Their seemingly outrageous theories were gaining substance.

Chapter 8

Susan Bowles paused at the end of the curtain and glanced back down at her father. The strong man she had known all her life appeared small and fragile lying in the hospital bed. Still, in a coma, he lay partially hidden beneath blankets.

She followed the variety of tubes and wires leading from his arm and chest over to monitors that stood like sentinels posted beside the bed. She listened to the machines quiet beeping and studied the monitor's changing displays of her father's vitals. Turning to leave the room, thoughts of her father lying helpless in the hospital bed brought fresh tears welling in her eyes.

Her reluctance to leave his side battled with her needs of food and rest. The doctor's insistence that if Jerry's condition changed she would be contacted immediately lacked the reassuring effect. With a sad smile, the doctor pleaded with her to go home and get some rest.

She climbed into the rental, navigated through the crowded parking lot before being consumed by the midday traffic on her drive west to the community of Bowness. She rolled the car to the curb in front of her father's house, her mind preoccupied. Rain drummed the roof of the vehicle. Digging through her purse, she found the house key Jerry gave her years earlier when he first purchased the place.

Susan wiped a single tear from her cheek. Swinging the car door open, she stood on the street. Water soaked into her hair and clothes while she looked up at the house. The wood siding desperately needed paint; the grass in front was long and dead from lack of attention. The shingles on the house were well past their due date, and sections of the sidewalk, leading up to the front step, had sunk over the years. The concrete broken and crumbling, showing clumps of grass growing wildly through the voids in the cement.

Her father had never been much of a handyman. She almost smiled with the brief respite of normalcy. He would never change. The man would sooner crack open a beer than fire up a lawnmower, or open a can of paint. Her father, a man she idolized, would never be one to trouble over the maintenance of his house.

Susan dreaded going inside. On her last visit, the interior of the house suffered worse neglect than the exterior. Drawing in a deep breath, she tentatively stepped forward on the sidewalk, steeling herself for what waited inside the house, the dishevelled realm of an old, single drunk. She carefully wove her way across the crumbling sidewalk, careful to avoid rolling an ankle on one the several holes in the disintegrating walkway.

Her lips drooped as she neared the front door. The faintest of smiles brought on by happier memories disappeared at the trepidation she felt before entering. She raised her purse over her head to block the rain. Sucking in a deep breath, she tentatively climbed the first step steeling against what waited inside the house, the dishevelled realm of an old, booze-loving bachelor.

Standing at the front door, she waited. A worn and weathered rocker sat to the side of the step, empty beer bottles lay scattered at its base. Happier images of her father, rocking away the evenings on the front step, while enjoying his favourite brew tugged at her memory, a stark contrast from the pale old man she witnessed lying unconscious in a hospital bed minutes earlier.

Pulling back the torn screen door, she inserted the key and swung the front door inwards. Susan froze in the opening.

Shock turned to confusion as she glanced over the interior of the house. The open room, beyond the front door, resembled the devastation one viewed after a tornado tore its path of destruction. Her father being a slob, she could accept and expect, the sight that she now witnessed, was utterly bewildering.

She called out before stepping foot inside the house. Why, she wasn't sure, except for a feeling that she wasn't alone. Pushing past the door, she halted, her breath caught in her throat. Unusual sounds filtered from the back of the house. For all she knew, her father probably took to letting neighbourhood cats live with him. The only problem, stray cats couldn't have possibly left this horrible mess.

She removed her cell phone from her purse and pressed Brand's number. Susan stood among the vandalized room, waiting nervously while the line connected and he answered. Disturbed by both the sight and the sounds, she whispered into the phone, fighting back hysteria, as she waded further into the house.

"Brand…this is Susan. Something awful happened to dad's house." She exclaimed, walking deeper into the catastrophe, pushing furniture out of her way as she explored. "The house is ransacked…" Before she finished the sentence, she felt a hand brush against the back of her head, knocking her off balance, the phone falling from her hand.

*****

On the other end of the line, Brand called her name several times. He had just left Detective Walgreen at Dave's apartment and was heading east when she called.

Brand cranked the steering wheel and sent the truck veering across three lanes of traffic, cutting off a line of cars, aiming for the exit to Nose Hill Drive. He wove his way in and out and across the lanes. He wasn't far from Bowness and Jerry's house. The abrupt ending to Susan's distressed call spurred him on as he ignored a red light and sped through traffic. With one eye watching the road, he fumbled with his phone and distractedly typed Detective Walgreens number. Impatience led to anxiety as he waited for the call to connect.

The detective's raspy voice echoed in his ear. "Walgreen."

"Detective Walgreen this is Brand Coldstream." he blurted out. "I just received a call from Jerry Kartman's daughter...I think she may be in serious trouble."

"Who? Jerry who's daughter?"

"Kartman. One of the men shot at my house, the one lying in the hospital."

"You think I have nothing better to than rush around the city, stomping out your fires and rescuing your sorry ass!" Detective Walgreen exclaimed. "You're unbelievable. All tough talk until trouble finds you, and now, I'm suddenly your best friend." The detective vented.

"Look, we're not...never mind...she's at her dad's house. Sounds like someone was lying in wait for her." Brand gave the detective the address, ending the call with an angry stab of his finger. More horns honked as he continued to cut his way through traffic, speeding in the direction of Jerry's house.

A half-dozen blocks away, Brand ran another red light and narrowly avoided t- boning a delivery truck lumbering through the intersection. At well over the speed limit, he raced around a corner. His eyes were searching ahead, identifying the peeling paint on the exterior of Jerry's house perched at the far end of the block. Pulling his foot off the gas, he crushed the brake pedal to the floor. Wafts of black smoke rose, and the high pitched squeal of overheated metal brake pads poured from the wheel wells as the soft rubber tires skidded over the wet pavement.

Brand rammed the gear selector into park. The truck lurched as he threw open the driver's door, and abandoned the vehicle in the middle of the street. He ran up the sidewalk, all pretence of caution tossed aside. His actions were single-minded. One friend was already dead, and Jerry was clinging to life in the hospital, so as he crossed from the street to the house, he promised Susan would not be another name on that list.

Long strides carried him up the concrete step. The gaping opening of the front door greeted him. He burst into the house.

His lead foot cleared the threshold. In the act of raising his trailing foot, the back of his head exploded with pain. An unexpected blow sent him tumbling toward the floor. Fireworks went off in his head as he rocked on wobbly legs attempting to remain upright. He felt his shoe slide on a stack of books scattered on the floor.

Awkwardly clawing at the air, Brand's legs crumpled, the weight of his body pulling him down to join the ranks of discarded contents covering the floor.

A chair leg broke under his back shifting his fall into a tangle of furniture and restricting his movements. Instinctively, he twisted to the side. A second strike flashed by his face. A balled fist brushed past his turned head and thudded against the hardwood floor.

Brand grabbed at the passing arm trying to subdue the attacker. Gripping tight, he partially rose off the floor before the cloth covering the arm slipped through his fingers. He fell back to the floor, his head cracking against the unyielding edge of an overturned table. Tears of pain swam in his eyes.

Through the mist, he caught the blur of another fist aimed for his face. Raising his arm, he slowed the downward swing. The attempt weakened but the force of the blow jolting as it glanced off the side of his head, the jolt to his skull momentarily stunning him.

Shaking the grogginess away, he blinked rapidly to clear his vision. His addled brain mired in fog, slow to react. Frozen to the floor, unable to rise, two blurry silhouettes step away from where he lay and slipped out the open door.

Brand struggled to his feet then sank back to one knee. Dizziness and nausea overwhelmed his senses. He gulped a couple quick, deep breaths forcing his mind to clear. Seconds passed before he was able to gain his footing and move out the door. The men from the attack a couple of blocks away by the time he stepped outside. They moved quickly, running down the rain-soaked sidewalk, the distance too far for him to be able to catch up.

A wave of anger pushed against the mush in his brain. More for the stupid mistake of rushing headlong into the situation than from the blows he received. His head ached, and his ears rang. He was in no condition to pursue the men. Under his breath, he cursed at his stupidity while the pair turned and disappeared around a corner at the end of the street.

Concern for Susan's safety battled aside his desire for pursuit and urged him back inside the house. Disgusted by his blunder, he stepped from the rain, his thoughts switched from the unexpected attack and returned to the vandalized interior and the safety of Jerry's daughter.

Using a hand to steady his body, Brand staggered across the littered floor and entered the hall. A door of the back of the house hung open. Susan's ragged sobbing drifted from the room. Brand flung the door fully open. Susan lay on the bed, her face swollen and bruised, tears ran down her cheeks, her body quivering.

Brand knelt down beside her, his voice, quiet and soothing, while he calmed her.

"The men who attacked you are gone," he whispered. "You're safe now."

Reluctantly, he left her side. In the bathroom, he found a towel and ran the taps, warming the water. With the heated towel, he returned to Susan's side. Carefully, he wiped her tears, and then pressed the warm cloth against her bruised face. His other arm circled her shoulders for comfort. The two sat on the bed, quiet sobs rising from Susan as her head rested on his chest.

Using the breather to think, he was no longer under the illusion that the attack at his house was random. Maybe the detectives weren't blowing smoke. Something serious was brewing. The shooting of his friends was not the end of this story. Whoever was behind this was hunting for something valuable, and they weren't wasting any time.

Brand held Susan tight, gently whispering to her. The minutes passed while she struggled to rein her emotions under control. He helped her walk into the living room. Leaving her standing, he pushed at the mess to clear a spot on the floor to set a chair then urged Susan to sit down. He stood by her side, his eyes roaming over the chaos that transformed Jerry's house. He realized that the thoroughness of the search resembled the same destruction he walked into at Dave's apartment.

He bent down and knelt at Susan's side. "Are you okay?" He asked watching Susan's reaction.

Swiping her cheek, she lifted her eyes to his face. "I'll be alright." She answered.

"What happened?" He coaxed softly.

Susan took a deep breath. "I drove straight here after leaving the hospital." She explained. "I was such a fool. I knew something was wrong the moment I opened the door. I should have got back in the car once I discovered the front door open. Instead, I wandered in, and that's when I called you. One of the men grabbed me when I was on the phone.

I must have walked in on the men, surprising them while they were still searching the house. The men dragged me into the bedroom..." She paused and dabbed at her eyes, her breath catching in her throat as she relived her ordeal.

"...They sat me on the bed and repeatedly asked me where "it" was hidden. I told them I had no idea what they were talking about, and that's when they started to hit me...they told me I was lying and said they had no qualms about beating the location out of me..." Susan fell silent. Tears welled at the bottom of her eyes.

"Did they give you any indication of what they were hunting for?" Brand asked quietly.

Susan shook her head, the word "no" barely escaping her lips.

From where he was kneeling, Brand looked around the trashed room. This time he ignored the contents lying haphazardly across the floor, he studied the walls of the room, his examination narrowed to include the smaller niches left exposed by the vandals. In all the wanton destruction, the search was meticulous. He paid closer attention to the nooks built into the walls and the discoloured patches of paint where Jerry's pictures once hung then down at their broken frames and slashed backs.

The search of both Jerry's and Dave's homes led to the same conclusion. The hidden object had to be much smaller than a cache of drugs. Papers maybe, or a key, or even some digital device, like a thumb drive. Whatever the hell it was, it had to be of a size easily concealed from sight.

He tried to concentrate. He couldn't be positive, and after being hit, his vision was a little blurry, but the men running from the house appeared to be empty handed. If he interrupted the assault on Susan, then the two probably never found what they were looking for. That would mean, they or somebody else, would be back to search again. Susan's safety was going to be a problem as long as she remained in the house.

Brand was still debating this line of reasoning when sirens bleated from the street out front. He waited by Susan's side, watching the front door. A pair of police officers climbed the crumbling concrete step. The officers shouted their arrival, and then, with guns drawn, cautiously entered the ransacked house, closely followed by Detective O'Brien.

The uniform officers conducted a room-by-room search; O'Brien stood in the doorway, his head slowly turning as he studied the displayed vandalism. With a grunt of disapproval and a shake of his head, he waded through the mess stopping beside Brand and Susan.

"Coldstream…what in the Lord's name is going on? It hasn't even been 24 hours since the shootings at your house. Does trouble always travel with you, or are you the most unlucky bastard on the planet?" O'Brien asked. The detective spoke while he continued eyeing the contents scattered across the floor.

Glancing down into Brand's face, the red-haired detective rubbed his trimmed beard then checked off his talking points on his fingers. "Gunmen storm your house. I receive a call from Detective Walgreen after he talked to you. He filled me in on the meeting you two had at your buddy's apartment. And now, here we are.

You and your lady friend look a little worse for wear," O'Brien glanced at Susan. "You okay, ma'am? Do I need to call an ambulance?"

Susan ran the back of her hand across her face smudging her makeup with tears. "No. I'll be fine." She said shaking her head. "

"Alright. If you change your mind, let me know." O'Brien replied.

Turning around, he whistled. "Somebody is a horrible decorator. This place resembles a garbage dump."

His eyes sought out Brand. "I'm not sure what kind of trouble you're involved in, but it must be some serious shit. You still want to continue this façade while your friend's safety is in question. Before anyone else dies, let me help you, what do you have that's so important."

"Detective. If I had any idea, I would talk your ear off, but I've already told you, I have no idea what this is about."

"Well, that is too bad ain't it?" The detective said disappointedly. His eyes resumed surveying the trashed room while he slipped a notepad from inside his jacket pocket. Shrugging, he remarked to Brand.

The Wolves Of Satan

"Play it your way. It's your funeral?"

Chapter 9

Brand stood by Susan's side, briefly talking with the detective then standing silent while O'Brien patiently walked Susan through the confrontation. The detective wrote furiously in his notebook with each answered question. When O'Brien finished, Brand placed his hand at the small of her back and steered Susan away from the house and the scene of the attack.

Lighter grey clouds hung low in the sky blocking the midday sun. Random drops warned of the impending rain preparing to fall as the two crossed the overgrown sidewalk and stepped onto the street. Police cars lined up behind the truck's bumper, red and blue strobe lights coloured the smattering of raindrops. The vehicles nosed tight behind one another plugging the street out front.

Brand took Susan's elbow and led her around the vacant police vehicles. His truck remained parked in the middle of the street. The driver's door wide open from when he rushed the house, the key in the ignition, the engine running.

"I'll drive you to a hospital," Brand said helping Susan into the truck. "Let the docs check you over then we can think about what to do next."

Susan raised her face. Traces of tears and smudged mascara marked her cheeks. "I'm fine. A little shook up but…I'll be okay, honest."

Brand watched the police cars and Jerry's vandalized house grow smaller in the rear-view mirror. He steered the truck with no destination in mind, only to put distance between Susan and her father's house and the memories of the attackers. He drove in silence, his thoughts on where to take Susan, one where this nightmare wouldn't touch her again. His house was of no use, and he questioned the security of his hotel.

Driving aimlessly through the streets, Brand mulled over the problems this latest situation brought with it; his eyes instinctively made careful sweeps of the streets ahead before pausing on the truck's mirrors, studying the afternoon traffic for tell tale signs of pursuit. His mind sorted through different possibilities to keep his friend's daughter safe. With the police convinced of his involvement, counting on their protection for Susan's safety was doubtful. Where did that leave him? He shrugged as if the answer was inevitable. If the men and women paid to protect the innocent were of no help, then maybe the solution lay in the opposite direction.

All of his reasoning circled back to the single option that remained open, one he would have preferred to avoid. Leaving the community of Bowness, he steered the truck east, his destination the outskirts of the city, the far eastern edge. The journey started off in silence, both he and Susan lost in their thoughts. Susan was the first to speak.

"Those men at dad's house. They kept asking me where it was. I begged them to tell what "it" was. They told me to quit stalling. Said I damn well knew what they wanted and I should quit playing them for fools.

I tried to tell them that I had recently arrived in the city and had no idea what they were talking about." She went silent again. After a couple more minutes she resumed. "I was afraid they were going to kill me. What do they want? What are they after, Brand?" She glanced across the seat. Tears rimmed her eyes.

Brand was slow to reply. He checked the mirrors, then looked at the street ahead. He thought through his answer. At a red light, he looked Susan in the eyes.

"The police believe that your dad and I, and a friend of ours, are involved with a local bike gang. These bikers are heavily involved in the local drug trade." He said the words out loud more to hear how ridiculous they sounded than as an explanation to Susan. "When you called, I was at the apartment of this friend, the one I told you about; the guy killed at my house the night your dad took a bullet... his place, like Jerry's house, was trashed too."

"The drug angle the cops are chasing, I don't buy. I have my doubts that our friend was involved in the drug business, no more than your father or I am, but after visiting his apartment," Brand averted his eyes, " I'm not so sure anymore.

None of what's been happening the last few days makes sense, though. If these bikers were looking for stolen product, the intensity of their searches was off the charts. Anyways, that being what it is, I've got to get you somewhere and keep you safe. I can't keep you near while I figure out what's going on."

The traffic on Glenmore Trail grew heavier and slowed as he approached a train crossing. Flashing lights on the track's barriers brought the volume of cars and transport trucks to a halt. Brand's focus drifted as he sat behind the wheel. The honking of a car horn urged him to drive. The train had passed, and the road in front was emptying.

Driving further east, he signalled a few lefts and a right into an industrial area spread out in a desolate part of the city. The crowd of old warehouses gave way to empty, unkempt tracts of land.

He brought the truck to a stop on the shoulder of a secondary road alongside a heavily fenced acreage. Susan's eyes widened as she looked out the window. The roof of a house appeared hidden behind a tall, reinforced fence built more for security than curb appeal.

As the truck rolled toward a wide iron gate, Susan caught snatches of the yard and building inside the perimeter of the fence. The property was not overly inviting. An older stuccoed house stood back of the road. It's windows guarded by rusted shutters. The yard sat barren. No trees or shrubs occupied the space, and the ground was brown and muddy, void of grass.

As she looked over the property, her breath caught. Men milled about the barren yard, some with large dogs at their sides, others leaning against motorcycles.

She glanced over at Brand, her brows knitted in confusion, her mouth open in disbelief, waiting for an explanation.

Brand stared out the truck window at the house. A large banner hung over the door, the words 'Mahihkan Manito' printed over a picture of a pack of wolves, the beasts' eyes a fiery glaze, the saliva dripping from their snarling mouths a blood red.

Brand's knowledge of the Cree dialect faded over the years, but the words on the banner rang with familiarity, easily translating in his head, Wolves of Satan.

Many years had passed since he last drove down this road, and after that trip, he had sworn never to return. He glanced at Susan. Instead of explaining why they had driven to the property, he curtly told her to stay in the truck with the doors locked.

"I won't be long," he said and opened the driver's door, his eyes drawn back to the hanging banner. He reluctantly climbed out and stood beside the open door, quiet and unmoving while contemplating his decision.

Dark grey clouds hung from the sky. The rain had abated on the drive across town leaving the air humid and thick with the promise of more showers to follow. The odd drop fell from the threatening sky while Brand stood alongside the truck. He tilted his head looking at the clouds, then down the short, paved approach and the security gate before glancing back at Jerry's daughter.

"Keep the doors locked." He repeated, slammed the door shut, and moved toward the reinforced gate.

Men stepped out from both sides of the gate. Bikers dressed alike in leather vests. A colourful crest sporting a wolf's head with fiery red eyes stitched to the fronts of their vests. The guards stepped to the front of the gate, challenging, as he approached.

"Private property, mister. You'd be better off to climb back in your truck and drive away." A large biker warned. Brand studied the man and then took stock of the other bikers in the group.

"I'm here to see Roy." Brand spoke, undaunted by the warning.

"Roy's busy. He doesn't have time for unannounced visitors. Leave a card; I'll book you an appointment." The man said for the amusement of his friends.

"Geez…I didn't know Roy began hanging with comedians." Brand commented sarcastically to the biker. "I need to speak with him. Tell him Brand Coldstream is here."

The bikers moved threateningly in his direction. Brand stared at the men. He held his ground as the group tightened around him. He hoped this gamble paid off; he wasn't in the mood to

The Wolves Of Satan

get into a slugfest with a group of greasy, leather-clad bums with tattoos.

The large biker's face lit up. Days of hanging around the clubhouse led to boredom. The unexpected arrival of this man might provide a little entertainment for the lot of them.

Brand waited while the bikers circled him. None of the bikers seemed inclined to contact the house and speak to the man he drove out to see. Brand assessed the situation. The mouthy biker would be the first one he dealt with, the man seemed to fancy himself as somewhat of a leader. Brand watched the biker edge closer, tracking the remaining men with his peripheral vision.

Realizing his only chance of getting to the house may be through this group, he prepared himself. His breathing slowed, muscles tensed, ready to release a sudden world of hurt on the men standing in his way. The last few days had been bad. The frustration and anger that built up inside his chest like a loaded weapon with a hair trigger ready to be released at the slightest indication of pressure.

The bikers walked closer, glancing from one to another, smirks plastered on their faces as they sized Brand up as an easy target. Anxious seconds passed.

Brand backed against the hood of his truck, his patience draining. The bike members crowded each other closing his escape.

"Jimmy. You and the boys back the hell up and leave that man alone." A harsh, growling command rose from the now open gate calling an end the standoff. The bikers stopped, their confused faces collectively turning toward the entrance and voice. Brand's eyes followed the bikers turned heads toward the sound.

Richard Cozicar

Standing with one hand holding a section of gate open stood a bear of a man, nearly a foot taller than Brand's six feet and surely twice the weight. The man glowered as he walked closer. His clean-shaven face pockmarked with scars. Furrowed eyebrows wrinkled the broad forehead and a pair of intense black eyes locked on Brand. An arrow straight nose centred the giant's face above a mouth outlined by thin lips frozen in a vicious snarl. The top of the man's head crowned with crow black hair pulled tightly to the back and tied in a ponytail at the nape of the neck.

The leather vest the man wore bulged across a massive chest. A t-shirt stretched past its limit, partially covered tattoos on his upper arms and black leather motorcycle chaps draped over lace-up leather boots finished the man's attire.

Brand stood, unfazed, regarding the giant staring back at him. The massive biker pushed through the gate and ambled onto the asphalt driveway. To Brand's eyes, the man had grown in size since the two had met last. Time measured in years had passed since then, Brand recalled. All by the wayside, since he had last met with his foster brother, Roy Thundercloud.

"How are you, Roy. It's been a while." Brand looked up at the man, his right hand extended. Roy Thundercloud grabbed Brand's arm and pulled him close. A mixture of emotions rushed over Brand as his brother's massive arms wrapped him in a crushing bear hug.

Chapter 10

Memories of a long past childhood embraced Brand with Roy's crushing show of affection. Memories, some buried since a young age, deep in the recesses of his mind floated to the surface.

As a six-year-old kid, his life changed dramatically. His parents died tragically, the victims of a horrible house fire. Fragments of that fatal night surfaced. He saw the little boy, standing in pyjamas, barefoot in the snow packed yard, on the street in front of the burning building. With a tear-stained face, he recalled looking up at the burly firefighters, grown men returning the little boys stare, their soot covered faces streaked by emotion, as he cried for his mother and father.

A heavyset woman with frizzy hair and a scrunched face arrived and walked him away from the house, his parents, and even the brave firefighters who pulled him from the burning home. At the young age of six, he was an orphan. With no extended family to care for him, Brand was alone in a world he was too young to understand. Social services took responsibility for him, and he became a ward of the province, then from the government shelter to an older couple and a foster home.

His new family was a childless couple, a hardworking husband and caring wife, decent, God fearing, but not ones to spare the rod. His foster parents taught him to follow the rules; sometimes the lessons were learned the hard way.

Brand was the only child in the couple's care, and through tough, emotional times, the orphaned kid and the kindly couple grew closer as Brand dealt with realization of his parent's death. Slowly, the three became a family.

Richard Cozicar

A few years down the road, the hard working couple accepted another foster child. Another orphaned boy with the same pain that darkened Brand's soul. Roy Thundercloud came into his life.

Roy was younger than Brand, an easy-going kid with a rebellious spirit and the type of personality that allowed him to gravitate through trouble with a smirk and a shit-eating attitude. The years passed and a bond developed between the orphaned boys. Roy referred to Brand as his big brother, which Brand, even to this day, found funny. Roy, since a young age, towered over him. With only each other to rely on, the two became inseparable. Fights at school, trouble with the police, the duo helped each other out of the many tribulations that followed them through adolescence.

Brand felt a stab of guilt in his gut when he recalled the look of betrayal and sadness on Roy's face when he decided to join the R.C.M.P. and left Edmonton to attend the police academy in Saskatchewan, the first time since primary school that the two were apart. As the years marched forward and Brand moved up in the Royal Canadian Mounted Police and then into the intelligence service of his country with the Canadian Security Intelligence Agency, Roy's future ventured in the opposite direction. It soon followed that wherever Roy went, trouble wasn't far behind.

Roy had a terrible temper, which Brand was witness to over the years. On the outside, Roy was as gentle as a teddy bear, until someone would push or cross the man. Then a streak of violence would rain down on that person. The only ones spared Roy's violence were Brand and their foster parents. Everyone else beware.

The Wolves Of Satan

After several minor run in's with the law, Roy became involved with a local bike gang. Roy already had a growing sheet of misdemeanours and found his name on several police watch lists, so Brand tried to steer Roy away from the seedier side of the law.

The difference of opinions drove a wedge between the inseparable brothers until Brand backed away from being his brother's keeper.

Reluctantly, but out of love and respect for his brother, Brand turned a blind eye to Roy's outlaw life and only occasionally the two talked. The lifestyles the two men had chosen marched them in different directions.

After serving a short stint in jail, Brand convinced Roy to join the Army with hopes the change of venue would convince his brother of a better life. Roy enlisted and served several tours overseas before being honourably discharged. Roy settled in the southern Alberta city of Calgary. Medals adorned his uniform signifying the valour he portrayed in the face of combat plus an injury he would carry the rest of his life

The switch back to civilian life proved a bumpy transition. Lack of employable skills left him disillusioned. The draw of motorcycles and walking on the wrong side of the law became too powerful to ignore. After a short while, Roy founded his own gang.

Brand, through connections in the law community, kept tabs on his brother. Even against his morals he could never abandon the only family he had left. He refused to intrude in Roy's lifestyle choices, but watched from the background, adopting the attitude that where Roy was concerned, what he pretended he didn't know wouldn't hurt his brother.

Even after his retirement from CSIS, Brand maintained his distance. Once a cop always a cop, he felt, so he stayed away from the biker life Roy adopted, never voicing his concerns. The two rarely talked, never associated over the years because of Brand's law career and Roy's illegal activities.

With each morning newspaper and every evening newscast, Brand expected to hear Roy's name, either of his arrest...or worse. When it came to his brother's well being, Brand's self-imposed ignorance of Roy's activities acted as a thinly veiled façade.

Their different lifestyles aside, Roy was still family. With that bond, Brand would go to his deathbed watching over his foster brother. But now, in a time of need, he drove east of the city filled with recrimination for the years of self-imposed separation. With reluctance, Brand stood outside the fence of a place he once vowed he'd never visit, seeking help from a brother he avoided for his own asinine reasons.

The only person he could trust, without reservations, happened to be the very same person he willingly avoided, and now, here he was.

Chapter 11

Roy let Brand go and stood back to look at his older brother. Brand took a moment to regain the breath squeezed from his lungs. Smiling like a kid on Christmas morning, Roy turned to his men and introduced his older brother.

"Any of you ever lift a finger against this man, I will personally tear you apart," Roy told them, his face briefly losing its smile. "Now what in the hell do I owe this visit to?" He spoke to Brand, the smile returning.

Brand motioned toward his truck and waved Susan to join him. He waited as she hesitantly made her way to the group. Brand watched her approach. When Susan stood at his side, he looked up at his brother.

"I need a favour, Roy." He said. "Is there somewhere we can talk a little more private than the driveway?"

Roy laughed. "Sure, follow me." Roy turned and led the way to the clubhouse. A few strides in he stopped, shouting orders to his men. "Jimmy, get a few men to watch Brand's truck, and make damn sure no one is snooping around."

Brand followed Roy, his eyes wondering over the yard. Any grass had long been trampled, and the yard lay barren, mostly packed dirt dotted with puddles of muddy water. An assembly of motorbikes sat close to the house, parked on the higher, drier spots. Lone trees randomly scattered throughout the front yard provided the only touch of green. An uneven walkway of sidewalk blocks led up to a large desolate looking bungalow. Sun faded siding wrapping the exterior. Brand took note of the newly installed metal shutters standing sentinel on the sides of the barred windows obstructing the view into the fortified building from the exterior.

Approaching the front door, Brand made note of the reinforced hinges and doorframe. Where the average front door was composed of wood or a light metal this one consisted of heavy steel plating.

"Quite the fort, Roy." Brand commented as the small group crossed the threshold.

"It's a tough neighbourhood." Roy responded.

Brand let Susan walk ahead as the pair followed Roy through the house to an office occupying a back room. The interior of the house was surprisingly neat and well maintained. A baseball game showed on the TV in the front room, and a scattering of leather-clad bikers lounged in chairs, beers in hand. The members in the place looked up curiously as Brand and Susan walked passed them.

Roy stopped at an open door and motioned his guests inside before closing the door. Roy walked to a cupboard behind a cluttered desk and returned with a whiskey bottle and three glasses. Setting the glasses down, he poured the drinks, sliding two glasses across.

"So how you doing these days, Roy?" Brand inquired.

"Oh. You know. Just trying to survive in the white man's world." Roy said with a smirk on his face.

"You're still playing the sympathy card. Don't you ever get tired of your own bullshit?" Brand smiled back, returning the sarcasm.

Roy erupted with laughter. "You would be surprised at how many bleeding hearts still fall for that line, brother."

"Yeah. No shit." Brand replied.

The Wolves Of Satan

A feeble attempt at small talk lasted only minutes, both men wary of the unusual circumstances of the meeting. Roy Thundercloud spoke in monosyllabic sentences, waiting for an explanation, the reason his brother suddenly appeared at the gate of his compound.

Brand scrutinized his brother. The man he purposely avoided, now sitting across the desk. He sat silent, debating how to word his thoughts.

"Roy." Brand nodded toward Susan. "This is Susan Bowles. Her father and I are fishing guides. Her father, Jerry, is a good friend…"

With a short, detailed summary, Brand told of the events leading up to the drive to the clubhouse. A professional description of the shooting at his house, a quick flyover of his trip downtown, and the accusations by the police, then the discovery of Dave's trashed apartment, and finally about the attack on Susan, at her father's house. When Brand finished, he fell silent, giving Roy time to digest his words.

"A bit of a situation has come up." Brand explained. "I'm sure it will amount to nothing, but still." He motioned with his head toward Jerry's daughter. "I need you to keep an eye on Susan? I need to follow this through. I won't be able to protect her."

Locking eyes with his foster brother, the silence in the room intensified. Susan, realizing what Brand was asking, and afraid to be left with a gang of bikers, in a place like a clubhouse, began protesting. Roy glanced over at her and then, unexpectedly, started to laugh.

"What's so damn funny?" She asked Roy, her face colouring.

"First. Yes to your request." He nodded at Brand then turned back to Susan. "Don't worry, you won't have to stay here," he said, the grin still lighting his face. "I have a much nicer place, one I know you'll be much more comfortable in." Roy let out a booming laugh, "but by the look on your face, that must be what you're thinking." He continued laughing. "This is our clubhouse, a place of business. Some of the boys live here, not me.

My good fortune has afforded me a few luxuries. I've got a place a short drive from here. You think this place is set up like a goddamned fort, wait until you see my house." He winked at Susan before turning his attention back to Brand. "So, what are you thinking?"

"Talk to Dave's friends. If he was involved in the drug business, they might know something."

"You're saying the cops believe the Devil's Apostles are part of this. Some definite badass boys are running with that group. We've had our share of run-ins with the bastards. Hell, been checking out rumours that the Apostles have hooked up with some Colombians from the West Coast.

Things are changing in the city. After years of sticking to our territory, the Apostles have begun throwing their weight around, hassling my people, pushing into our turf, selling to our customers. We've had some skirmishes breakout with the Apostles lately and the way things are building, I don't think it will be long before a war tears this city wide open."

Roy's large frame sank back into his chair. The leader of the Wolves leaned his head back and stared at the smoke-stained ceiling. "A bloody war, of that I'm certain. Worked out an agreement years ago, we did. Divided the city. They took the west side, we ran the east, and our members respected the division, but things have changed. Those assholes are crossing the boundaries, forcefully moving east into our territory. They've grown way past annoying, and bad for business."

"What type of shit are they into?"

"Everything. You name it the Apostles have got their hands in it."

"Big into drugs too?" Brand prodded.

Roy shook his head. "Not at first. They pushed bad product. Not sure who their supplier was. But not any longer."

Roy sipped his whiskey, anger building at the thoughts of his rivals. "The Apostles were small fry. They run a string of nightclubs, mostly around the northwest and a bit of prostitution. A few of the boys branched out into racketeering and extortion. I don't know how successful they were. Sissy things the cops usually went easy on." Roy's thoughts drifted away. Slamming his fist on the wooden desktop, he sat up straight. "Teaming up with the Colombians. That changed things. The buggers began parading about town with a whole new attitude and money flowing from their pockets."

"If the Apostles were so small, why did you agree to split the city?"

Roy shrugged. "Too many headaches. Didn't want to spend my efforts chasing after them. The buggers would pop up every now and again and disrupt shit. Hell. The city's a big place. I let them have a piece of the action so they'd leave my business alone."

"Why not remove them? Chase them out of town?"

"Would have drawn too much attention from the cops. Didn't seem worth it at the time." Roy leaned his forearms on the desktop. "Now in hindsight, it was a mistake to leave them kicking.

Rumours started filtering to us a while back. Whispers at first and then…bang. The Apostles suddenly owned a casino, and along with the gambling, they plunged feet first into hardcore chemicals. Designer drugs, pills, crack cocaine. You name it they push it. Started with that big ole casino on the trail to Banff."

Roy leaned back in his chair and clasped his hands behind his head. "Took me a while to figure out where they got the cash or the balls to follow through. The change to their operation came quickly.

Heard of customers being hoodwinked by the house and manipulated into muling product from the other side of the mountains in lieu of debt owed. Overnight it seemed the Apostles became a significant player in the city's supply of illicit drugs."

"The detectives figure these South Americans for a nasty bunch." Brand interjected.

Roy nodded his agreement. "I've had run-ins with Cartels over the years. Don't know these particular ones overly well yet, but I'm betting that changes soon.

Brand, if you're thinking about tangling with those boys, you better be damn careful. Those are some seriously bad people. They give us bikers a bad name if you can believe that."

Roy snatched his drink off the desk and drained the glass. "The Wolves won't back down, and we won't surrender. Smaller bike crews have either hitched their wagon to the Apostles or rode out of town. We're the only ones left to stand against them, and I've got to tell you, I'm growing damn tired of the Apostles and their new way of doing business.

One other thing." Roy added. "Some of the local law boys are in their pockets. It's getting confusing out there as to who are the good guys and who aren't. You watch your step. Don't do anything stupid."

Brand sat, his head bent low, absorbing Roy's warning.

"You just make sure she's safe." Brand brushed aside his brother's advice motioning at Susan.

Richard Cozicar

Chapter 12

Sunday morning. Brand watched the rain beat against the restaurant window while he toyed with his breakfast. The rain had increased as the morning wore on. Pushing the plate of half-eaten food to the side, he wrapped his hand around the steaming mug of coffee, raising the hot cup to his lips. The flavour of the coffee, black and fresh, unnoticed, as he blankly stared out the window.

With Susan safely out of harm's way, he puzzled over the attack at his house. He struggled to accept the detectives reasoning that the hit was drug-related. Still. How well had he known Dave? Doubts about the young guide began filtering into the scenario. Could Dave have been involved and was he the reason for the attack at the house?

Trying to keep an open mind Brand revisited the scene in his mind, especially the image of the handgun in Dave's limp hand. Why would an innocent man bring a concealed weapon on a rainy night of fly tying and drinking? The easy answers lost when Dave died. How did the thugs know to hit Brand's house? Why choose that moment to make a move? Too many unanswered questions surfaced and each new discovery only added to the list.

Brand pulled his head away from watching rivulets of water wind down the outside glass and stared at nothing somewhere across the room. Questions he wouldn't find the answer to sitting inside a restaurant, he concluded. He gulped the remnants of his coffee and waved for the waitress.

The fly shop, the one where he, Jerry and Dave ran guided trips out of, was open Sundays. He planned to talk to a couple

82

of the boys at the shop who also knew Dave, both at work and away. Whether they were at the store or not, he could at least get their numbers.

Parking, Brand pulled a hat from the back seat and settled it on his head. He flung open the door and jumped from the truck, quickly closing the door against the sheets of rain. Small streams snaked across the asphalt melding into large pools where the parking lot dipped. Swiftly, he skirted the building water, weaving around parked cars, his hand holding his hat to screen his face from the wind-driven deluge.

Reaching for the door, he paused. A customer with a rod case tucked under his arm, and a plastic bag bearing the shop's logo arrived on the dry side of the glass door. Brand stepped to the side allowing the man to leave before stepping into the sheltered interior.

Standing just inside the doorway, he removed his cap, shaking it dry, then brushed beads of water from his coat. The stormy weather hadn't impeded business. A number of customers crowded the aisles. Fishermen taking advantage of the leaden rain filled skies to restock depleted fishing supplies in preparation for sunnier days ahead.

The first person Brand noticed was the store's owner, Jay Welds, busy behind the counter. Jay dealt with a customer; one of his hands filled with fishing accessories, the other, busy punching numbers on a debit pad. Sliding the readied machine to the customer, the bell from the opened door caught the owner's attention. A slight nod of his head greeted Brand. Walking over to the counter, Brand leaned his arm on the glass top, waiting for Jay to finish the sale.

Brand watched the old man deal with another customer. The two had been friends for several years. A memory of the first time the two met surfaced, occupying Brand's thoughts while he stood idle. Mid-September, more than a ten years ago, he was in town holidaying while still employed by the government agency. He wandered into the store and booked a fishing trip. Jay was at the till then, too. The day Brand wanted was scheduled because of a shortage of help, but Jay agreed to guide him down the Bow in search of Rainbows and Brown trout.

The random trip down the river, which started as a getaway between missions to balance a chaotic lifestyle, grew into a love of fishing and soon left Brand well versed in fly-fishing. During a shore lunch, Jay commented on the problems of finding reliable fishing guides and jokingly offered Brand a job should he tire of his current employer.

A couple of years later, Brand retired from the agency and pondering his future, reminded Jay of the offer. Since that time, the two worked closely together. With Jay booking the trips in the store and Brand guiding fishing enthusiasts from across the globe on the rivers in the Southern part of the province.

Brand fondly watched the old man work the till and the store's customers. When the two first met, Jay looked much younger than the man Brand now observed. Where Jay was once thin with a dark, full head of hair, now he was several pounds heavier and moved about slowly, hunched over. The hair, the little that still clung to the fringes of Jay's head, was now snow white.

His face was no longer taut and rugged, but puffy, with an unhealthy pallor. Discoloured bags of skin hung under the old man's light grey eyes with bushy white eyebrows arched in a permanent scowl. Now, a pair of thick-framed glasses perched on the end of Jay's nose causing him to peer over their top whenever he talked. Brand shook his head at his observation.

The Wolves Of Satan

The ravages of age, he thought, old age will catch us all eventually.

Jay's voice woke Brand from his musing. The till clear of customers for the moment.

"What brings you out on such a miserable day?" Jay inquired before another customer sauntered up to the till, hands full of fly tying material.

Brand waited as Jay punched keys on the till then scooped the bought items into a bag.

"I've got a couple of questions if you can sneak away for a few minutes?" Brand answered, his eyes probing the store to see who was working. Jay called one of the floor staff over to operate the till; finished ringing in the customer's purchase then motioned Brand to follow.

"How well did you know Dave?" Brand asked.

A puzzled expression clouded Jay's face. "Why? What's bugging you?" Jay stopped in the aisle and turned to look up at Brand before resuming the route through the maze of aisles to the back of the store and a small office crammed into a corner.

"Close the door," Jay called as he walked behind his desk. His attention fell on a pile of invoices lying on the top. Pushing the papers to the side, he raised his head and looked over the rim of his glasses, his eyes curiously searching Brand's face. "Does this have something to do with the trouble at your house?"

"Just trying to put the pieces together." Brand shrugged. "Thought you might know Dave better than I did." Before the store owner replied, Brand added, "How about Brian or Phil, are they in today? I didn't see them on the floor?"

"Brian has the day off. Phil, he's somewhere around. Helping a customer re-spool some reels...as to Dave, I don't know…you've known him as long as I have. Never talked to him outside of the store. Seemed like an all right fellow and his clients were happy with his services.

"Not much else I can tell you?" Jay fell quiet. His eyes locked on Brand's face. "How about you? How are you doing?"

Brand shrugged his response. Jay changed the subject. "I checked in on Jerry yesterday. He's still in a coma, but the doctors are optimistic."

Brand nodded. "Jerry's a tough old boy. He'll pull through."

"Jay. Do you mind if I talk to Phil?" Brand asked. "The two seemed to chat a lot whenever Dave was in the store. Maybe they hung out after hours. I need to know more about how Dave spent his off hours."

"What's this about Brand? Was Dave in some kind of trouble? I mean, the men who shot up your house? You thinking it was something he was involved in?"

"I don't really know. The cops believe the attack at my house had something to do with drugs and gangs."

The storeowner shrugged at the news. "Huh. Doesn't sound right." Jay started to rise from his chair. "You wait here, and I'll find Phil and send him over when he's finished up with his customer."

"Don't bother, I can find him." Brand left Jay standing in the office. Winding his way around shelves stocked with fishing supplies, waders and boots, past aisles of assorted feathers and small bags of multi-coloured, multi specied patches of fur displayed on revolving racks, he crossed the shop floor. Near the back wall of the store, Brand stepped around a stand of fly rods, single and double handed, walked past the bins stocked with assorted tied flies and stopped in an aisle. The man he sought was seated behind a glass counter, a spool of floating line in his hands. Brand waited while the store clerk finished.

Brand watched the transaction, the customer struggling to wrap his hands around his purchases. Phil had the generic look of a lot of young men in their early twenties to Brand's way of thinking. Shaved head with a full, bushy beard, gaudy, oversized earrings stretching his earlobes and numerous tattoos showing on his arms and around his neck with thick-framed glasses that hid what little face not covered in hair.

"You got a minute Phil?" Brand asked. Phil was turned toward a shelf straightening out boxes of fly line. The man stopped and looked at Brand, his hands busy arranging the products on the shelf.

"Yeah, you bet. What do you need?" Phil stopped and twisted in Brand direction.

"You and Dave. You guys hung out away from the store, right?"

"Sure. We did a lot of stuff together. Why?"

"What kind of interests did Dave have aside from work?"

"The usual, I suppose. Video games, beer, the odd movie." Phil stated and shrugged. "Most weekends we'd head out meet up with a few other fellas and hit some of the clubs downtown. Mostly on seventeenth, there's always lots of women there."

"Did Dave like to gamble?"

"No…not really. Dave always said the gambling bored him, and none of us made enough money to piss away at the casinos."

"Are you sure? Did Dave…" Brand chose his words carefully. "Did Dave ever complain about any debts he owed to a casino? Something that haunted him?" Brand recalled Roy's words from the day before about the Apostles hooking unsuspecting gamblers to use as mules to move their drug shipments, an angle he now considered, one that might explain the late night visit to his house.

"No," Phil repeated adamantly. "I told you. We never gambled. Dave especially hated that shit.

"Did he ever say why? Religious reasons, old addiction…" Brand tossed his hands wide in search of an answer.

"Yeah. I don't know man. He never said, and I never asked."

"Okay. I needed to ask." Brand switched his questioning with a different approach.

"I know it's none of my business…but did you guys, did Dave do drugs?" Brand regretted asking, but he watched Phil's face for a reaction.

"What?" Phil exclaimed. His eyes narrowed, his manner cooled as he suspiciously stared at Brand. "What the hell man. You a cop, what's going on?"

"No. No, I'm not. At least not anymore." Brand hastily rummaged for words to ease the situation. "It's nothing to do with you. The police think that Dave's death may be gang involved."

"Not Dave. No way, man. None of us touched that shit. Hell," Phil stammered, flustered and red-faced, his voice growing pitchy with indignation. "Dave barely even drank. The guy was a pretty boring dude. I can't believe the cops think that he is messed up in that type of garbage. That's ludicrous. No. Impossible. Doesn't make any sense."

"Yeah…I don't know. I'm trying to get a handle on this mess. A lot of things that I've heard don't add up." Brand confessed and searched for other questions that might shed light on the shootings and his friend's death.

"You know…there were a couple of times," Phil interrupted, "he told me that he and old Jerry would get drinks in a bar down in Bowness. I can't remember exactly which one, but I know he met Jerry there several times. That always struck me as odd, considering Dave drank very little, but …well…you know how Jerry likes his drinks." Phil stared at the floor trying to command the memory to return to him. Brand waited a few beats.

"And you don't recall the name of the bar?" Brand prodded.

"Esmeraldas, maybe." Phil shrugged. "I'm not sure, but it sounded like a popular biker hangout the way Dave described it." Then he added, "Hey, are you going to his funeral. I hear the police are releasing his body already and allowing his family to make arrangements."

"You bet." Brand said and stood up to leave. "I'll see you there." He said as he moved down the aisle toward the cash register and the door. At the counter, he asked Jay to cancel his booked trips for the near future.

Pausing for a moment at the door, he pressed the key fob unlocking the truck door hoping to avoid spending unnecessary time in the open. Tugging his hat back down into place, he hurried past the puddles, sprinted the last few steps to his truck, then swung onto the seat quickly closing the door, shutting out the continuing rain.

Brand fired up the truck's engine and sat in the parking lot alone with his thoughts. His breath fogged the windshield. He spun the defrost dial to high then removed his phone. His thumb pressed the camera icon. A photo gallery materialized. Sweeping through the long line of photo's, he stopped at a picture he had taken only weeks before.

Richard Cozicar

Dave and Jerry smiled back at him. The Bow River, at McKinnon's Flats, flowed across the background, the end of a long day on the river. The two guides stood by their boats, tired smiles on their faces, paying customers from the days float, captured at the edge of the picture. Brand stared at the picture, memories of better days running across his mind.

"What the hell happened, boys?" he muttered to himself in the isolation of the truck's cab.

Letting the happier times from the past slip away, he refocused on the picture of the guides and took a screenshot. Saving the image separately, he switched it to the phone's screen saver, an easily accessible picture to use when he located the biker bar in the older community on the northwest section of the city.

Chapter 13

The lack of bars, especially ones frequented by bikers, in and around the community of Bowness, narrowed Brand's search. He had little trouble locating the particular establishment Phil described.

On the edge of a rundown strip mall, on a street seemingly forgotten during the neighbourhoods revitalization, tucked away from the steady pace of the northwest community's busy business district, a flickering sign, half its neon bulbs long dead, stood guard above the front entrance. Esmeraldas Bar and Grill.

The parking lot was next to empty. Brand pulled the truck into a stall close to the door. A few motorbikes sat dripping water, mixed among a scattering of half-ton trucks. The rain continued lashing down. He rushed from the dry confines of the heated cab to the awning drooping over the front door. Shaking off rainwater that collected on his coat, he crossed the sidewalk, hesitated, and then pushed into the dimly lit bar.

The smell of stale beer and even staler air assaulted his nose. An old Skynyrd song played above the din of the bar. A Southern man didn't need him around anyhow, the words floated toward the door.

He stood in the entrance and looked around the interior of Esmeraldas. In the seventies, even early eighties, this bar was probably a happening place. Now, it was run down and dated. The atmosphere was depressing. Stained wood trim and discoloured paneling covered the majority of the walls. The cracked, faux leather booth seats had seen better days and the Formica tabletops were peeled and pitted. The carpeting was mashed with gravel from the parking lot and looked like it needed changing more than cleaning.

Straight ahead stood a long wooden countertop, shelves of bottles displayed behind it. Brand brushed more rain off his jacket sleeves and sauntered over to the bar, He moved between empty tables on a worn path deeper into the room. Slight turns of his head allowed his eyes to soak in the interior layout and the few customers enjoying a mid-day drink

A couple tables to the side of the door and near the pool table were occupied with men in biker colours. Cigarettes smoke drifted among the patrons and bottles of beer covered the tables.

Signalling the bartender, Brand ordered a rye and coke, no ice. He dug a twenty out of his wallet while the bartender fixed the drink. Laying the money on the counter, he looked over the selection of liquor displayed on the glass shelves rising behind the bar, the bottles reflecting off a mirrored tiled wall.

The bartender set the drink down and took several steps back toward a cash register to change the bill. Brand lifted the glass for a sip of the drink, his head forward, his eyes casually checking the room behind him, the mirrored wall conveniently allowing him to observe without turning around.

Further down the bar, an older gentleman sat flipping a coin and mumbling into his beer. Brand watched the man twirl the coin on the top of the bar. Something about that coin struck him as familiar. Brand stared, his glass half lifted to his lips. He'd seen a coin like the one the gentleman toyed with only recently, and unable to grasp why the coin piqued his interest, he hesitated with his drink in mid air trying to conjure the memory hidden somewhere in his consciousness.

When the bartender returned with change, Brand asked the man if he knew a Dave Halperson. The bartender stared blankly back. Brand pulled his phone out and showed the picture on the screen, repeating the question. A slight change in the bartender's eyes betrayed the man. Digging in his wallet, Brand removed another twenty and slid it toward the barkeeper. When the man still refused to answer, Brand parted with another twenty.

"The older guy in the picture, Jerry, I know. I don't recall the younger guy, though." The bartender spoke while pocketing the money.

"They've come here together I'm told." Brand said. The bartender shook his head.

"Nope. The face doesn't ring a bell, but Jerry, he's a regular. Knows most of the staff here by name." The man volunteered and turned to pour draft beer for a waitress standing at the till. The bartender lifted a rag from behind the counter and wiped the top of the bar, the forty-dollar conversation obviously over. Brand turned his attention back to the coin flipper.

Brand drained his glass, signalled the bartender for a second, and then moved down the bar toward the man twirling the coloured coin.

"Excuse me. Where's that coin from?" Brand asked. The man ignored the interruption and continued toying with the coin. Is everyone in this bar deaf Brand wondered? He was of no mind to pull more cash out of his pocket to get an answer to his question, so he waited.

Timing the coin spinner's movements, he watched the man touch the side of the coin to the dark wood counter and waited while the man snapped his fingers sending the coin twirling. Brand shot his hand forward and snatched the coin off the counter. Lifting it to his eyes, he scrutinized the coin, flipping it front and back. Millennium Casino, the lettering stamped in embossed gold ran the perimeter on both sides of the coin, the number, one hundred, stamped in the middle.

Brand set the coin back down in front of the man, mumbled an apology and lost in thought, stepped away, stopping in front of his drink. He raised his glass, absently sipping the rye, his eyes naturally returning to the mirrored wall behind the assorted spirits.

Movement from the far tables brought his mind back in focus. A group sitting across the room pushed back their chairs, looked in Brand's direction and after a hushed discussion, ambled across the floor. The men walked with their chests puffed out and their heads held back, pushed past the few tables blocking their path and spread apart from each other as they strode closer.

Brand studied the bike patches on their vests. The writing appearing backwards in the mirror but one word was easily decipherable. The capitalized "D" for devil then the letter "A" with its halo beginning the word Apostle became clear. Signalling the bartender, Brand ordered a shot of tequila then went back watching the mirror as the bikers approached. The bartender glanced at the advancing group of men and then back at Brand, hesitated a moment and then poured the shot as requested.

Brand reached for the shot glass as one of the bikers spoke to him.

"You a cop, buddy." The speaker asked. Brand remained watching the men in the mirror.

"Nope." Brand answered.

"We're wondering what business you got coming in here and harassing people?"

Brand shrugged. "I'm just a curious guy I suppose."

"Well you know what curiosity can get you."

The Wolves Of Satan

"I suppose you're going to tell me." Brand replied carelessly. Built up frustration and lack of sleep putting an edge on his words. He lifted the shot of tequila to his lips and felt the burn as the fiery liquid slid down his throat. He pulled a ten out of his wallet and laid it on the bar in payment for the shot. "I suppose I had better leave then." He said as he waited for the bartender to return with his change.

"You'll leave when we say you can leave." Another of the other bikers joined the conversation. Brand pivoted away from the bar to face the group, looking each man in the eyes, the shot glass still clutched in his hand.

Brand gave the speaker a once over. Thinning speckled hair crept from under a discoloured bandana tied around the man's head. Dark eyes peered back at him from a grizzled, scarred face tanned red by the sun. A grimy t-shirt stretched behind the leather fighting to contain the man's protruding beer gut that drooped over an ornate belt buckle strung though the loops of a pair of faded jeans.

Brand found his attention returning to the capital "A" circled with a red halo. The stamp of the Apostles stood lonely on the front of the man's vest. He no doubt was in Apostle territory.

Brand concentrated on the man. If trouble started, he decided to deal with the speaker first.

His chest rose as he breathed deeply, his fingers playing with the thick shot glass in his hand.

"We should teach him to mind his manners, Ike." A younger man with a greasy ball cap screwed backwards on his head spoke up.

"Shut your trap, Tommy." Ike muttered. "You and Lloyd watch so he doesn't get it in his mind to leave before we finish our conversation."

Brand's focused divided. He followed the grizzled speaker's movements while gazing over the man's shoulders at the pair moving to box him in. On the left, Tommy adjusted his hat while he settled into position. He stood half a head taller than the older biker. Tommy's jaw muscles flexed, his features clenched in anger as he glared back at Brand. Acme scars blended with patches of facial hair. The sleeves of his t-shirt taut over flexed biceps, his massive arms twitched as they lay restlessly folded over a bulging chest straining the fabric of his vest.

The second of the pair, Lloyd, skirted right, his weathered face passive. Brand noted the man's glossy eyes and the strong waft of weed that drifted with each step he took. How stoned the man was Brand couldn't be certain but relegated the threat of the man lower on the scale.

The last of the group remained further back. A skinny, nervous kid with an angular face that reminded Brand of a weasel, the kid's eyes busy darting about avoiding Brand's scrutiny.

Ike turned his attention back at Brand. "So Hoss. What are you doing here?"

Brand watched the leader's eyes, his body tensed for the inevitable.

Ike telegraphed his intentions by tightening his hands into fists; his eyes breaking contact with Brand's face as he stepped closer.

Brand closed his hand around the shot glass and pushed off the bar to meet the threat. He rammed his fist under the man's chin, the force of the blow staggering the biker. Ike's hands flew to his throat, his breath gurgling through a collapsed windpipe while he gasped for air. The viciousness of Brand's strike sent the man floundering back into a table.

The pair waiting on the sides, rushed. Brand spun on his heels, grabbed the guy with the screwed on ball cap, throwing him heavily into the bar. The collision upset a tray of glasses and rattled the bottles perched on the counter. He then drove his hand, palm first, the shot glass still clutched tightly, into Lloyd's jaw; bones crunched and blood seeped from the torn flesh where the glass entered.

A bottle crashed behind him. Brand spun. The nervous kid stood waving a broken beer bottle, the kid's arms twitching with spasmodic tremours, the jagged edges of glass pointed at Brand's head while the remnants of liquor dribbled from the bottle. Brand jerked back as the biker swung the broken bottle at his face. The bar impeded Brand's retreat, the brown, sharp edges of the broken bottle crowding him as it sliced through the air.

Twisting his head clear, the glass slashed into the portion shirt left exposed by his open jacket. Brand winced as the sting from the glass bit through the cloth and into his skin leaving a trail of torn fabric and blood across his chest.

Brand rolled to the side. A table behind him stuttered along the carpet as he stumbled against it. The table tipped sending Brand to the floor. A boot dug into his side. A second foot stomped down hard on his stomach. The broken bottle in the kid's hand blurred downward. Brand rolled, the slash of glass nicking his cheek.

Reaching with one hand, he got a firm grip on a loose chair and pulled himself off the floor. He clamped his hands around the padded metal back and turned, the chair gaining momentum as it lifted from the floor. He felt a jolt travel the lengths of his arms when the chair made contact.

The kid straightened. His face twisted with confusion as air rushed past his teeth while it emptied from his lungs, the jagged remains of the broken beer bottle in the kid's hand clambered to the floor. The force of the blow sent the young man staggering backwards where he collapsed onto a nearby table.

Brand filled his lungs and took a quick tally of his attackers. Three of the group were down. One gasping for breath from a crushed larynx, another moaning while trying to stop the bleeding where the shot glass penetrated his cheek and the third lying in the middle of a table, holding his ribs and sighing from the impact of the chair. The only one remaining in the fight was Tommy; the one Brand threw into the bar.

Brand spun to face the biker. Tommy swung for the bleachers. Brand threw his arms up to block the man's swing. A surprisingly powerful fist sent Brand backward and off balance. His motion carried him into an overturned table, his feet tangled in the legs of an errant chair, his body lurching haphazardly as he fought to stay off the floor.

The biker growled and yelled as he lashed out with a foot aimed at Brand's head. Brand scrambled his arms to block the foot from connecting and causing serious damage. Desperately, he gripped the man's boot and shoved back. The sudden transfer of power knocking the large man off balance and back into the wooden bar. Tommy roared with pain as the edge of the counter crushed into his side.

The men faced each other. Tommy threw a reckless fist aimed for Brand's jaw. Using the big man's own motion, Brand grabbed the outstretched arm and jerked the biker forward. Instinctually, Brand raised his knee and drove it into the man's stomach. Once, twice, on the third strike the biker doubled over, his breath rushing from his lungs.

The Wolves Of Satan

Brand clasped his hands together and brought them down hard onto the back of Tommy's neck. The combined strength of his coupled hands drove the man head first into the gravel packed carpet. The biker hit the floor, the last bit of air whistling as it escaped through his lips.

Brand bent over with his hands on his knees, breathing deeply. He surveyed the four downed men. Two things came to mind as he breathed deeply to fill his burning lungs. One, he could use another drink but probably wasn't going to get served, and two; the image of another coin similar to the one he watched the customer at the bar twirl earlier, surfaced. Where he had seen the previous coin eluded his grasp but the memory led him back to Roy's warning about the Apostles bike gang operating the casino. The coincidence would make the Millennium Casino an obvious next stop.

Catching his breath he straightened up, told the barman to keep the change from the ten he set on the bar before the fight started and walked out into the pouring rain. He stood by his truck letting the steady downfall of rain wash over the gash across his stomach, the water feeling cool and refreshing after the tussle in the bar.

Barely a half block down the street from the bar, Brand watched through the intermittent, wiper cleared windshield as a car rushed past his truck. The revolving strobe lights of red and blue on the cars dash warning others to clear a path. Brand caught a glimpse of the two detectives, Walgreen and O'Brien, partially screened by the police car's own rain-splattered windshield, as the pair raced by. Slowing, he kept an eye on the trucks mirror. The unmarked sedan skidded off the street and into the parking lot of Esmeraldas bar.

An odd thought pinged Brand's brain. The dynamic duo certainly arrived on the scene quickly. The detectives were sticking very close, lately. Was that because of him or was there some other reason behind the extra attention?

What was everyone searching so hard for, he pondered, glancing back at the road and stepping on the gas?

Chapter 14

Brand stood in front of the hotel room's mirror. The broken bottle had left a nasty little cut, not bad enough to require stitching, but a nuisance none the less. He unrolled a bandage purchased at a drugstore on the way back to the room and dabbed at the bleeding wound. He dried a small amount of blood before carefully centring the bandage's padding over the nasty red streak. Pulling a clean t-shirt off the bed, he dressed and left his room, walked to the elevator and rode down to the lobby where the hotel's restaurant waited.

Seating himself, he pondered the casino chip the old man at the bar played with and tried to place where he would have seen a matching coin. He shifted, trying to sit comfortably without aggravating the wound on his chest. The waitress returned with a cup of steaming black coffee interrupting his thoughts. A rye would have been preferable but an alcohol-dulled mind didn't fit with his plans for the evening.

The coin occupied his thoughts through the meal. The last few days were a mash up of memories. Draining the last of his coffee, he let his mind drift away from the coin and to other memories. The break helped. The answer flickered in his mind. He traced his movements back to the police precinct the night of the shooting, the interrogation room and repeated questions by the detectives, the redundancy of his answers. One of the detectives seated by the table, but which one? Spent adrenaline from the attack on his house mixed with alcohol and lack of sleep combined to mask the memory. Was it O'Brien or Walgreen but his best guess was that was where he saw the coin originally. And what of its significance?

How personally involved were the pair of the cities finest. Gambling was by no means illegal so for a cop to have a coin meant little. Unless. The detectives were assigned to investigate the shooting at his house. Was the investigation on a professional level or were there underlining motives at play?

Something Roy had said about the casino trading gambling debts for favours hung with him, as did the warning about members of the police department working for the Apostles. He wondered if one or possibly both of the cops were tied to the biker's because of the casino, and if so, was it because of gambling debts. He filed that thought away for later reference. This line of thinking could explain the detective's fascination with him.

Brand sat for one last cup of coffee loading up on caffeine to stave off the weariness coursing in his veins. As tired as he felt, the evening hours held loads of possibilities.

Back in his room, Brand removed his t-shirt, exchanging it for a button down western shirt. Tucking his shirt into his jeans, he crossed to the front closet and slipped his feet into a pair of scuffed, dusty cowboy boots. Removing a Panama hat off the closet shelve, he left the room for the parking lot and his truck.

Only mid-afternoon, the sky remained overcast and dark. The rain lashed down with no signs of ending. Traffic was light as he threaded his way across town. 16 ave. flowed easily and the lights worked in his favour. A string of green escorted him through the intersections and pointed him toward the mountains.

The Millennium Casino stood on the west edge of the city, just beyond the city limits, at the bottom of a hill, on the north side of Highway One. Finding a stall in the crowded parking lot, Brand studied the outside of the casino from behind his windshield, his truck still running, the defrost fighting against the excess moisture coming down outside.

The Wolves Of Satan

He watched a group of people huddled around each other trying to enjoy their smokes while hiding under roof of the casino's extended portico and out of the rain. Not being a big fan of gambling, Brand rarely had reason to visit any casino. This particular one he had been in before. He and Sara had taken in a concert by an old rock and roll band a few months back. He thought back to that night. There were no obvious signs of the casino being overrun by outlaw bikers.

He watched the comings and goings of patrons for a few minutes before locking his truck and rushing across the parking lot for the protection of the front entrance. Brushing raindrops off his jacket and slapping his hat against his leg to remove the water, he opened one of the double entrance doors and headed for the bells and lights of the gaming room.

Pulling the brim of his hat down to partially screen his face, Brand walked past a security guard at the entrance and stopped a few steps inside the door while slowly looking over the interior. Rows upon rows of gaming tables ran the length of the brightly lit room. A large bar was situated in the middle of the vast space, shelves in the centre held myriad bottles of liquor and TV's suspended from the ceiling, ringed the bar.

He turned his attention to the banks of slot machines stacked back-to-back to the side of the floor, lights flashing and bells ringing, people standing and sitting in front of electronic bandits, feeding a supply of coins and bills. The rain was good for business he assumed. Middle of the day and the floor was filled with customers eager to loose their money. He had imagined the casino would be fairly dead this early in the day. The crowds of people surprised him.

Brand walked straight to the bar and waited in line to order a drink. Passing the girl behind the bar a ten, he told her to keep the change when she handed him a drink.

Reaching into his pocket for his phone, he brought up the picture taken of his friends at the river and lifted the screen in front of the bartender.

"Any chance you recall seeing either of these guys before?" He asked.

The bartender took the phone from Brand's hand for a closer look. "Sure...the older guy...Jerry...he comes in here quite a bit. He usually sits at the bar, watches the action while he enjoys a few cocktails before wondering off to test his luck." Her lips curled into a smile. "Some nights Jerry wins and stops back here to celebrate." The smile widened. "He leaves me a nice tip on those nights."

The smile disappeared and worry seeped across her features. "Why, did something happen to him? Is he in trouble?" She asked as she returned Brand's phone.

"No." Brand replied quickly shaking his head. "Jerry's a friend of mine." And led with another question, "how about the younger guy? Have you ever noticed him in here?"

Taking the phone again, the bartender studied the picture closer and then looked back at Brand passing the phone back. "Don't recall seeing him before." She said and turned away to serve another customer putting and end to Brand's inquiries.

Brand slipped his drink off the counter and walked toward the gaming tables. He knew that you had to have cash to play the slots, thus eliminating anyone from running up a huge debt. He strolled down the line of Black Jack tables, stopping every now and then to watch a few hands being played. In all honesty he didn't know exactly how he would be able to discover any more information but he came prepared to spend a few hours and see what presented itself.

The Wolves Of Satan

Nursing his drink, he wondered from one game of luck to another studying peoples faces. Most had blank looks as they concentrated on the games of chance. Every now and then a scream or a whoop floated up and filled the room as some lucky gambler hit it big.

Mingling among the crowds, Brand alternated between wearing his hat and carrying it by his side for a change of look. Less suspicious he hoped, making it harder for the casino security to notice him loitering while he roamed among the gamblers. Another drink ordered and hours later he continued to watch the throngs of people and the endless exchange of money at the tables.

His reconnaissance of the gaming floor proved fruitless. Unless it was an off night, nothing among the roulette tables or blackjack, even the craps table failed to turn up anything he would deem attention worthy.

Strolling to the side of the large, noisy floor, he turned his attention to a room partitioned at the side of the casino. Large stencilled letters on dual glass doors separated the noisy main floor from the 'Poker Room'. Brand sauntered past a bouncer stationed at the door and stopped to lean against a glass wall to watch the action at a table only a few steps inside the room.

He studied the players. The stack of chips growing in front of some gamblers, shrinking in front of others. With each loss, he studied the card player's faces looking for tell tale signs of anxiety. Remaining at the table while a couple rounds were dealt, he moved to a different angle and a second table fell under his observation. He noted the player's manners as they placed bets, waited for new cards and either folded or pushed more chips into the pile.

Watching large amounts of chips flowing back and forth across the table it was pretty obvious that this could be the one place a person, under the right circumstances, could end up owing the casino a small fortune. He was too far away to read the small writing on the poker chips, but the colours matched the chip he had seen at the biker bar earlier.

Brand watched the table for a short time before walking back into the main floor. He altered between trying his luck at the higher risk games blending with the gambling crowd. A few spins at the roulette wheel, a run of bad bounces at the craps table mixed with intermissions of wandering back into the poker room to study the players.

Brand began focusing on a middle age man parked at a poker table. Brand studied the card player. The guy had occupied the seat at the table since Brand began walking the floor hours earlier. The only time the guy looked up from the cards in his hand was to summon a hostess and have a new stack of chips to replace his losses.

Curious, Brand stepped among the busy tables to camouflage his interest. Moving to different vantage points, he let his eyes return to the man. Brand scrutinized the gamblers attire, the tattered ball cap pushed high exposing a balding forehead, the plaid shirt with sleeves rolled up past the elbows, the material clean but showing spots of wear. On one pass, Brand glanced down at the man's shoes, scuffed leather boots with frayed laces.

If the man had the resources to sustain losses at the table, his grooming didn't reflect any type of fortune.

As the evening wore on, the gambler's face showed the kind of night he was having. The man's wife, if he had one, would not be impressed by the losses being incurred at the poker table, Brand reasoned. Was the evening's run of bad luck a one off or could this be the type of gambler Brand was had set out to find.

The Wolves Of Satan

After spending numerous hours among the bells and whistles of the crowded casino he had discovered little else to aid in his investigation. His night's search hinged on a big if, if his reasoning was sound and if the guy's fortunes remained going down the toilet.

Brand walked away from the poker tables and sat at a slot machine with a view of the door to the walled off room. Gazing past the machine he noted the people coming and going. Time marched past. Down several dollars to the electronic game, he pushed away, bought another drink and returned to the poker room. The gambler Brand marked looked like he was sweating money. The man twitched in his seat, his mouth moved, his words silent as he stared down at his stack of dwindling chips.

A little after midnight, a sizeable, uniformed man broke from a cluster of security guards in the corner of the room and crossed the crowded floor stopping to stand beside the card player. Bending low, the guard whispered into the gambler's ear then waited while the man stood up.

The much bigger employee stared down at the smaller poker player then up at the dealer. Unspoken signals passed between the two casino employees before the guard tapped the gambler on the shoulder and nodded toward a back door to the room. The colour drained from the unlucky gambler's face. With a knowing glance at his dwindling fortune, the gambler grabbed the remaining chips, pushed away from the table and moved in the door's direction.

Brand sipped his drink while his eyes followed the two men as they wound a path to the back of the room. With his concentration trained on the door where the men disappeared, Brand failed to notice a different security guard approach him from behind. A finger tapped Brand's shoulder.

"Buddy, I've noticed you spending a lot of time eyeing the people at the tables. You're not here to gamble are you?" the guard stated. "So what ya doing. You waiting to see which ones make some extra money so you can fleece them in the parking lot?" The guard gripped Brand's arm tightly and shoved him toward the glass doors. "I think you've seen enough. Time for you to leave."

Brand twisted his head and looked the man in the eye. Anger and boredom almost forced a challenging insult for the guard before second thoughts made him bite his tongue. Placing his hat back on his head, he let the guard escort him off the gaming floor.

Setting his unfinished drink on a table at the exit, he walked outside and stood under the casino entrance. Cupping his hands around a cigarette, Brand sucked the smoke deep into his lungs. He watched the puddles flooding the low spots on the wet asphalt dance with the rhythm of the falling rain while he thought through his next move. Shrugging deeper into his coat to fend off the cold and damp night air, he stepped from the sheltering casino entrance and walked through the chill rain to his truck.

Firing up the engine and turning the defrost fan on high, Brand sat behind the wheel. From where he was parked, he had an excellent view of the casino doors. He dialled the trucks exterior lights off hiding the running vehicle among the parked cars. The rain pounded off the truck's roof, as he waited, his vision strained as he focused on the entrance doors through the raindrops splattering the windshield. With nowhere to be, he settled in to wait with hopes of spotting the poker player when the man left the building. The thin possibility of catching the Apostles in one of their illegal endeavours the only thing to he had to show for his wasted hours.

The Wolves Of Satan

Brand lowered the driver's window a crack and then fished in his pocket for his pack of smokes, dug one out and found his lighter. Blowing a mouthful of smoke toward the opening at the top of the window, he turned his gaze back to peer through the steady beat of rain. The cab of the truck warmed, the defroster winning the battle against the dampness, the building heat bolstering the fatigue that flowed through his body. Tired eyes trained on the casino entrance caught a movement at the side of the building. Brand pushed away the exhaustion and forced his mind alert.

Dragging his eyes away from the front of the building, he watched two people exit a side door and slowly walk toward the parking lot. As the pair ventured closer to his truck, Brand studied the men's faces. Walking in front, was the unfortunate gambler, hunched over against the rain; the lack of fortune lady luck refused him this evening etched on his face, the second person unfamiliar to Brand.

The second man walked with his head held high in the rain, and a serious, mean look about him. The man was obviously the muscle bound brute assigned to babysitting duty. Tiny and the lonesome loser, Brand dubbed the unlikely duo.

The gambler's escort was just smaller than enormous. The complete opposite of tiny, times two. The girth of the man's upper body barely restrained by a sports coat and shirt, arms the size of tree limbs swung at the man's side as he slowly moved through the parking lot.

Brand watched the two stop at an old Ford pick-up truck parked a couple rows in front of where he waited. Tiny dug in his pocket and retrieved a keychain. The men climbed into the truck, the large man climbed into the driver's seat and started the truck's engine while the down-on-his-luck poker player hesitated at the passenger's door, probably weighing his options before conceding and climbing into the passenger seat. The old ford left its parking spot.

Brand cursed. He had planned on talking to the gambler, but seeing that wasn't going to happen, he backed his truck out of its spot. Keeping a safe distance away from the older truck, he followed as the lead vehicle entered the late evening traffic.

Chapter 15

Brand switched the wipers on high to remove the deluge of rainwater. He hesitated at the exit, letting cars merge into his lane between his truck and the men from the casino. He pulled in several car lengths back. He figured the extra space combined with the pouring rain should help mask his truck while he matched his targets route through traffic.

The old Ford turned left off Highway One onto Sarcee Trail. Brand ignored the changing traffic signal, running across the intersection on a yellow in his attempt to keep the unsuspecting vehicle in sight.

At the next intersection he was five-car lengths back, the wipers on his truck struggling to clean the windshield. Red turned green. The car in front of Brand slowly jerked ahead before coming to a complete stop almost catching Brand off guard. He crushed the brake pedal to the floor in order avoid rear-ending the stopped vehicle. The car stalled, his path forward blocked, four-way flashers began a slow red pulse.

Frustrated, Brand let a car pass, clearing the neighbouring lane before he was able to manoeuvre around the prone car. He wheeled back into the right lane behind another automobile, this one slamming on the breaks as the light turned to yellow then red. Frustrated, Brand slammed his palms into the steering wheel. Through the streaked windshield he watched the taillights from the old truck disappear into the night.

On the next green he continued driving east. Knowing full well the other truck would too be far ahead to catch he decided to play a hunch. If he were right, he would meet up with the men from the casino, if not, he would write the evening off and try a different approach.

Winding his way down the rain slicked highway, Brand followed behind the traffic, taking the overpass onto Sarcee Trail as it crossed back over 16 Ave and the river valley. Sheets of rain splashed up from the tires of the cars in front, the trucks wipers working furiously to remove the spray building on the windshield. Traffic crawled as the downpour continued. The cab of the truck rattled with each roar of thunder. Flashes of lightning bolted to earth briefly lighting the overcast skies. June in Calgary, the wettest month of the year was holding true to form.

Blocks short of the Bow River and Bowness Park, the streets became deserted. Brand slowed his speed to just above a crawl.

He watched out the driver's side window. The neighbourhood slipped by. Most houses too dark to read the numbers bolted to the fronts. The address Brand searched for wouldn't need a number to distinguish it from the others in the area.

Slowing the truck, he gazed out the windows. Certain he was in the right vicinity he looped street after street increasing his search. On the edge of the community, where residential properties began to mix with commercial, his persistence paid off.

Shingles glistened in the rain marking the roof of squat bungalow. Below the eaves of the roof, a couple of feet of stucco showed. The rest of his view limited by a tall wooden fence lining the backside of the sidewalk and shielding the property. The solitary house on the enclosed lot the home of the Devil's Apostles.

Not unlike the Wolves clubhouse, the Apostles property consumed two huge lots. The high fence discouraged the outside world from spying on the private and mostly illegal matters that took place inside the cordoned off area.

Studying the wooden structure surrounding the lot as he drove by, Brand noted the solid construction of the perimeter fence. He arrived at the house with no immediate plans to access the house or the property, but he couldn't help notice the work and reinforcement of the structure. A small army would be needed to try and breach the compound. Considering the type of activities the bike gang was involved in, the extra security made sense.

Parked out front the gate, blocking the entrance to the biker's property, the old truck sat next to a grey a SUV. Brand had almost come to a complete stop by this time and was surprised by the sound of a car horn. He looked in the trucks rear-view mirror. The shadowed silhouette of the car's driver gesturing for him to get out of the way and quit blocking the road.

Brand pressed the gas pedal and signalled for the next turn. A quarter block away he pulled the truck to the curb and stopped to consider the situation. Roy was right about the west end bikers operating out of a casino. In the few hours Brand observed the poker games, the card player escorted from the table had accumulated a sizeable loss. One he obviously didn't have the cash to cover. And now, the gambler was escorted straight to the Apostles clubhouse.

Brand set the thought aside. Looking at the surrounding buildings, he searched for a suitable spot to park. Somewhere close enough to watch over the compound but allow him to avoid detection.

A yawn escaped his lips. The thought of settling in to wait for tiny and the lonesome loser to leave the clubhouse battled against his need for sleep but the hours inside the casino left him more than curious. An evening already wasted with little lcarned strengthened his resolve to remain outside the clubhouse. The gambler inside might prove to be a valuable source of information, one that he shouldn't risk losing. He decided to wait and talk with the man and discover how much of Roy's story rang true.

Shrugging deeper into his coat, he placed his hat back on his head, then left the shelter of the truck and stepped out into the evening rain. The fence surrounding the biker compound, while working to keep prying eyes from peering into the yard, also worked the other way and blocked the view from inside the house as well. So unless tiny was standing guard at the gate, the chances of the presence of a solitary figure standing on a street corner were probably slim.

He walked to the end of the block and leaned against the bricks of an old building trying to hide from the wet weather under a ravaged overhang. His eyes roamed over the biker property, his attention never straying long from the solid gate leading into the yard.

The tattered canvas of the overhang did little to shelter him from the falling rain. If he remained where he was, the moisture would soak through his clothes in a short time. He spent the next few minutes scoping out the streets and buildings in the surrounding area hoping to locate a better place to hide his truck and still allow a decent vantage point to continue watching the front gate.

Chapter 16

The leader of the Devil's Apostle bike gang, James, "the Manager" Cartwright lounged on a couch in the front room of the fenced off clubhouse. A replay of an earlier UFC fight broadcast from the TV.

The front door of the house opened. An average sized man in a drenched coat and ball cap stumbled into the house. Cartwright's trusted lieutenant and the head of security for the Millennium Casino, Don Bakker, following closely on the soaked man's heels. The two men stepped out of the rain and into the house.

Cartwright watched with amusement as Bakker seized the smaller man by the jacket collar and pushed him further into the house. He regarded the pair. His focus settled on Bakker. The man was the size of any two average people put together. The huge man damn near had to turn sideways to enter the front door. A smirk flitted across Cartwright's face when he thought about the big man's capacity for the job. Rarely did Bakker have to resort to violence to get his way; most people cowered and were instantly subservient in the giant's presence, no threats necessary.

Out of the corner of his eye, Cartwright caught movement back in the room. One member of the group who gathered earlier to watch the live fight, rose from his chair and hurried down the hall. A bedroom door closed screening the man from the scrutiny of the stranger Bakker escorted into the house. The detective was still touchy about outsiders seeing him among the gang members.

The detective would surely come around to accepting his fate like all the others who've found themselves in similar situations. The bike gang owned the detective now. The member of Calgary's finest owed a sizable debt to the casino and by association to the Apostles.

Cartwright chuckled to himself. So, maybe the tables on the casino floor were rigged, so what. The man was a bloody detective, after all, if he was stupid enough to be played, too bad. At the casino, Cartwright encouraged the staff to push a line of credit on the detective to feed the man's gambling addiction. Over time the detective's losses accumulated and terms of repayment resulted in a growing stack of incriminating evidence. The casino added another member of the Calgary police force who had little choice but to offer his services as collateral, reluctant or not.

Normally he handled casino business in his offices atop the Millennium but tonight he needed a break. Things at the casino were growing out of his control and he soured toward his partners, the Colombians. The familiar feel of the gang's head quarters often helped him refocus.

Turning his attention back to Bakker and the new mark, Cartwright left his seat on the couch and motioned the two men to follow. He led the pair down the hallway toward the back of the house where the back rooms were converted into his office.

Cartwright walked through the door and left it open. He walked over to the desk and sat on the front corner waiting for the two to enter, eyeing the smaller man with both disdain and amusement.

"Close the door." He ordered. He waited several more minutes, then stood back up and walked behind his desk, seating himself. "Don. Why don't you fix us all a drink," Cartwright nodded toward the corner of the office. A makeshift bar of old cupboards and a plywood top held an assortment of liquors. A small fridge holding up one end of the plywood contained soda and ice cubes and finished the illusion.

"What you drinkin'?" the Manager smiled at the gambler.

"What...whatever you're drinking is fine," the gambler rushed out the words aiming to please his host.

"Two rums," Cartwright instructed Bakker before turning back to the gambler. "Watch this evenings fight?" the Manager eased into small talk. The evening proved to be boring and he wished to prolong the interruption. The three men chatted, eating away at the slow evening, two speaking confidently and the gambler nervously smiling and saying little.

After exhausting several avenues of conversation, mostly between the two bikers, the Manager's lib manner grew serious.

"Well, Chad. I thought we worked out an understanding relating to your gambling, but yet; here you are, once again. What in the hell am I supposed to do with you?

Instead of learning your lesson, you end up back at the Casino. What? You think you're smart enough to enter our facility and...win your money back?" Cartwright shrugged his shoulders, shaking his head. "Did you run up another loss?" The Manager looked at Bakker for confirmation.

"I...I. I'm sorry Mister Cartwright. I tried to do what you told me but I needed a way to raise the money, and I was feeling lucky...I honestly thought that this time would be different...." Chad Worenko stuttered and wilted in front of the boss of the Apostles piercing eyes.

"How much does he owe us now, Don?" Cartwright asked. Although he suspected the amount to be enormous, he wanted to stress the large amount of debt owed making the man standing before him easier to manipulate.

"Little over two hundred k," Bakker responded, looking first at his boss and then glancing down at the unlucky gambler cowering by his side.

Cartwright whistled for dramatic effect, "You drive a truck, don't you Chad?" He asked the rhetorical question feigning a display of ignorance. The gambler had played into his plans perfectly but why let on.

The gang's largest source of income came from the distribution of illegal drugs flooding the city from across the mountains. Drugs smuggled out of South America and into Canada by a Columbian Cartel that set up shop on the west coast a few years back. After the Apostles were brought in to distribute the Colombians shipments, they looked for new ways to recruit mules to carry the products.

Cartwright's plan was to avoid the usual types of transport. Methods the police were well aware of and especially good at ferreting out. The secret to the Apostles success was the way they tricked hard working, law abiding folks to transport the drugs, the very same people who rarely registered on the radar of law enforcement and thus were able to move the product out in the open.

Unfortunately, law-abiding people didn't readily volunteer to carry illegal substances across borders, so Cartwright, as the manager, sought new methods. The Millennium Casino filled that part. People were attracted to the bells and whistles of the gaming floor, so potential clients walked through the door every hour of every day.

Some. The unluckiest gamblers who never knew when to cut their loses were marked by the establishment. Lines of credit for these unlucky few offered them a chance to recoup the accumulating loses. Few came out ahead. Most sunk deeper in debt owing the casino.

The scheme worked well. Now, volunteers were almost begging to turn a blind eye and skirt the law in order to repay the casino's kindness. For some, a trunk or two full of contraband was favourable compared to the alternatives they faced.

The plan was hugely successful. The Apostles controlled people from all walks of life. Police, lawyers, and even a few judges in their pockets to help smooth legal problems, which ran hand in hand with the operating of illegal enterprises. Volunteers from the justice system were certainly useful in keeping the law off his back, but Cartwright would never consider using them as mules to transport his goods. No, losers like Chad came in handy for errands like that.

Cartwright paused as if he was struggling to find an alternative solution to the gambler's problem.

"Well, lucky for you, I do have a job that would be perfect for a man with your particular skill set. Your cooperation will be looked upon kindly in regards to repaying your debt, but if you can't help us, I will understand. Don has other methods of collecting on those in debt." He finished. The answer was a foregone conclusion, but why not let Chad believe he had a choice. Cartwright looked up at the giant standing behind the despondent gambler, an evil grin spreading across his face.

The truck driver looked up at Cartwright, nervously glanced over his shoulder at the giant towering over him and gulped before blurting out his answer afraid that the manager might rescind the offer.

"Yeah…sure…whatever you need." Chad squeaked out.

"Good. Good." Cartwright beamed a smile.

Richard Cozicar

"I need a shipment of…shall we say, produce, picked up from a warehouse in Castlegar the day after tomorrow? You know where Castlegar is, right?" The gambler nodded his head in confirmation. "Someone will call ahead and make the arrangements. The men at the warehouse will load your trailer and give you further instructions. Any questions?" He asked as he wrote down the address of the warehouse and passed it across the desk to his newly enlisted driver.

Chad reluctantly palmed the slip of paper and turned toward the door. Cartwright spoke from behind. "I don't need to remind you to not talk to anyone about our deal, do I?"

Chad nodded his head in agreement.

"Don. Give our friend a ride back to his vehicle. Thanks." He then turned his attention to some papers on his desk dismissing the two.

When the door to the room closed, Cartwright stood and walked around his desk, over to a bar sitting in the corner of the office. He poured himself a Jack on the rocks and stopped to gaze into a mirror hanging above the liquor cabinet.

The reflection showed a middle-aged man, grey hair starting to mix at the edges of dark brown locks. Steely blue eyes, red veined and tired sunk in a scarred, weathered face peered back from the mirror. Hours of sitting around and too many drinks added puffiness to the cheeks and sagging skin on his neck. Not the most handsome but probably not the homeliest face either, he judged. His hand brushing the stubble on his face, the five o'clock shadow thickening to a scruffy, careless look.

He flexed his arms. He still spent hours pumping iron in an attempt to fight off the ravages of the advancing years. The tight t-shirt he wore still showed a well-muscled body. Until he was ready to ride off into the sunset and leave this life behind, he had no choice. To remain on top of this gang of outlaws, he had to be the toughest, meanest man in the room all the time or yield to a stronger, younger member.

Nobody in his gang had the balls to challenge for his spot. Not yet any ways, but the day would come. He was no fool. The world was changing. Time was an enemy. Age was beginning to make it harder to stay prepared and stave off threats to his authority. His men knew he was still able. He had fought hard to stay on top and he sure and the hell wasn't opposed to doing it again.

The only man in his crew that caused worry was the big man, but he was fiercely loyal and if that loyalty ever faded. Cartwright pondered the thought. Bakker would be dealt with like others before. In this business nice guys didn't finish first, they died and were never heard of again.

He took his drink and left his office. In the hallway, he stopped outside a closed door and rapped lightly.

"You can come out now. Our guest has left." He said sardonically. He had little respect or regard for the detective who had ducked into the room, but the man proved helpful at times, and for this reason, Cartwright put up with the man's quirks.

Cartwright leaned against the wall as he waited for the detective to emerge.

"You know I can't be seen hanging with you guys." The detective whined.

Cartwright rolled his eyes at this statement; maybe the guy's helpfulness had almost run its path. He'd be glad to deal with this asshole personally.

"So you were telling me where your investigation was in regards to the missing phone." Cartwright pushed off the wall and headed back to his office, the police detective in close pursuit.

"Well, there's very little to tell. When the shooters attacked the house, they didn't have time to search the place before they were gunned down. What a fucking mess," the detective whined. "All those assholes managed to accomplish were to involve the whole damn police force. One of the three men at the house died, an old fishing guide is critical in the hospital, he's still in a coma, by the way, and the third guy, the home owner, the one who killed our guys, is not cooperating. I confiscated the cell phones from the house before forensics could bag them, but none contained the recordings or videos. Long story short, we haven't found the one we need, if it even exists."

Cartwright focused on the man's face. "You've searched the other men's homes?"

"My guys tore apart one and got surprised at the other. The guy who walked away from the house attack, this Brand Coldstream, keeps getting in the way. We had the old guys daughter, but the son of a bitch showed up. There was nothing the boys could do, they had to leave her behind before they could learn what she knew." The detective pleaded his case.

Cartwright turned in his chair and faced the window watching the rain worm paths down the glass. He remained quiet for several minutes before spinning back to face the detective.

"Excuses are not going to find that phone, and you know what will happen if," the Manager glared at the detective, "say, some real police officers get their hands on the information locked in its memory."

"The old man could have been blowing smoke about the recording for all we know. He might have concocted the whole damn story get us off his back." The detective answered locking eyes with the leader of the Apostles.

"If my Colombian friends are worried about this phone, then we're worried about it. One of those three men stole it, and the Cartel wants us to get it back. So why don't you pretend that you are a competent detective and find the damn thing just in case the phone recording does exist and before it falls into the wrong hands?" Cartwright slammed his fist on the top of the desk to emphasize his growing anger on the subject. "Get your ass out of here and do what you're paid to do."

The detective glared, his face red with pent up rage.

"Sayonara." The Manager said pointing to the office door.

Chapter 17

A chill from the rain and a rumbling in his stomach tore Brand away from his vigil. Leaving the truck hidden, he stuck to shadows and jogged the few blocks down the road to a convenience store for a pack of smokes, coffee, and a protein bar to suffice as supper. Back under the awning, Brand bent back the plastic lid and sipped the hot coffee.

The darkened skies had eased their assault on the city, the rain growing lighter. A shiver passed through his body. The coffee brought warmth to his hands and comfort as it heated his mouth and throat and warmed his stomach, renewing his resolve to play the night out to its conclusion.

The narrow doorway he stood in, under the torn awning, belonged to a deserted business, diagonally across from the steel gates protecting the biker's clubhouse. Rain slipped past the torn canvas roof protecting the doorway. The drops tapping a rhythm on his hat and coldly sliding down his back.

He wished for the comfort of his truck that he reluctantly left behind. The risk of a lone vehicle's engine idling so close to the biker's compound, a decidedly bad idea, but with no heat and his warm breath in the moist, cool cab the windshield repeatedly fogged over. He gave up on the shelter of the truck for the darkened doorway and a better line of sight.

A few sips later, movement at the house caught his attention. The same duo he had followed to the clubhouse appeared at the gate, squeezed through the opening and walked to the old Ford. Brand waited in the doorway until the pair climbed into the cab before following the shadows back toward his truck. He waited while the Ford backed onto the street then turned and rolled away.

Quickly, he jumped inside the cab, twisted the key in the ignition and rammed the selector into drive. The old ford had driven away in the opposite direction his truck faced. Brand sped down the block for the next intersection, wheeled a U-turn at the crossing and eased on the gas passing back in front of the biker's clubhouse. Half a block later, his foot heavy on the gas pedal, he raced to keep the old Ford in sight.

Brand retraced the route taken earlier when leaving the casino, his worry about keeping the truck in sight dwindling. With a change of tactic, he played his hunch and raced ahead using the few vehicles to act as a buffer while he watched the old Ford's headlights in the mirror. He drove, his eyes constantly checking the rear-view mirror on the off chance the men deviated from a return to the casino parking lot.

The darkness and the persistent drizzle made a chore of maintaining sight of the Ford's lights forcing Brand to slow and let the other vehicle close the distance. Within blocks of the casino, he raced ahead, blew through a yellow traffic light before making the turn into the crowded casino grounds.

Stopping near the back of the lot, he reversed into a stall, the view out of the windshield covering the length of the area. With a twist of a dial, the truck sat in darkness with only the engine running. He waited.

A few short minutes, just as predicted, Tiny turned into the lot, wound past lines of automobiles sitting under the casino lights, and drove to the far side of the dark asphalt before stopping alongside a row of cars. Brand strained to see what type of vehicle the gambler drove. The gambler climbed from the cab of Tiny's truck and hunched against the late night chill, squeezed between a pair of parked cars and stopped beside a truck. The distance and positioning of the vehicle too far from where Brand sat to make out the model or colour in the rain obstructed lighting.

Very slowly Brand crept his truck closer, the headlights still off. Two rows short of where Tiny sat in the old Ford, Brand found an open stall, backed in and continued watching. Brand studied the area until an interior light appeared on the far side of the old Ford. Brake lights went off as Tiny rolled his vehicle away from the spot.

The big man from the casino drove past Brand's idling truck. A couple rows of vehicles separated the two. As Tiny passed, Brand noticed the big man turn his head and even in the darkened cab of Tiny's truck, Brand had the notion of the big man's eyes crossing the gap between the two trucks and peering straight at him. Impossible, Brand thought, for the man to have marked his presence from that distance but the truck seemed to slow as it drove past.

The last thing on Brand's mind was to tangle with the monstrosity driving the old Ford. Hell. He would have to run the man over with his truck just to soften the big oaf up and give himself a chance. Unaware he was holding his breath, Brand let a sigh escape as Tiny sped up and continued driving. He watched the taillights disappear before swinging his attention back in the direction of the second vehicle.

While the man wedged his ride out of a tight spot, Brand remained in his truck with the lights off. The gambler drove a late model Chevy pick-up. Missing chunks of rusted metal around the rear fender gaped like a black hole in the overhead lights and the side of the truck's box facing Brand displayed an array of dents. In the artificial lighting of the lot the colour of the truck could have been anything from dark green to black.

The beaten half-ton stopped reversing and then began inching forward. Brand let the gambler gain some distance before slowly creeping along the lines of parked cars heading for the same exit. He drove slowly, allowing the man time to merge into the late night traffic. Brand waited another moment before switching the truck's lights on and pulling onto the street several car lengths behind.

The gambler had left the parking lot in a south direction. Brand glanced at the time on the dashboard. The small LED numbers glowed in the dark cab, quarter after one in the A.M.

The trip south lasted twenty some minutes before the gambler pulled into a subdivision in the deep south of the city, a community only a couple of years in the making. Newly paved streets twisted among recently constructed houses. Some blocks featured partially ready structures while other streets were basically empty. Piles of dirt sat where future homes would be built. Security fences on other lots signalled freshly dug basements waiting their turn for the construction crews.

The gambler rounded a curve then steered the Chevy onto a driveway. Brand slowed and stopped his truck on the street behind the driveway, blocking the Chevy. He swung the door open and stepped outside as the gambler stood on the concrete drive fishing through his keys.

"Hang on a minute." He called to the other man.

The gambler jerked around nervously at the sound of Brand's voice.

"What do you want?" The gambler asked, his voice edged with desperation.

"Business." Brand said.

"Hey, give a guy a break, will you. I might have a gambling problem but I don't have a problem with my hearing." The gambler's voice grew bitter. "I understand your boss's orders, so Jesus, what else can he want?"

"He ah…" Brand thought quickly. "He just wanted to make sure you're clear on…the …plan?"

"It wasn't complicated. I leave Tuesday morning for Castlegar and pick up his shipment of…produce." The gambler almost choked on the thought of what he had to do. Scared or not he was tired and prayed for this nightmare to end.

"Uh. Yeah…" Brand ad-libbed. "Uh…the boss wants me to accompany you, help smooth any problems."

"Yeah…like I need this shit. Whatever." The gambler grumbled. "I'll be leaving bright and early Tuesday morning. If you're not there when I'm ready to roll, I won't be waiting. Goodnight." The gambler said turning to insert his key into the lock before swinging the front door open.

"Wait a minute." Brand growled. "Where in the hell am I supposed to meet you?" The gambler looked at Brand for a few seconds, fighting down the desire to tell this intruder to go to hell and then, with a sigh of resignation, gave up the address. Brand refrained from asking for a name. If Brand's story of working for the casino were right, he would obviously know already.

"I need your cell number too, don't want any misunderstandings because of lack of communication, do we. And your driver's licence, too" Brand pushed his luck.

"Why in the hell do you need my drivers licence?" The gambler asked.

"Just give me the damn thing." Brand snapped. The man read off his cell number, dug a worn leather wallet out of his pants pocket and passed the licence to Brand. Brand quickly memorized man's name, Chad Worenko, then shoved the card to its owner. The gambler snatched the plastic card, left Brand standing in the driveway, and stormed into his house, the front door slamming against its wooden frame.

Walking down the driveway, Brand noted the Chevy's licence plate number. Added insurance. Luck and lies only lasted so long.

Chapter 18

Morning came quickly. Brand roused his tired body out of bed. Phoning the front desk, he ordered a pot of coffee and headed for the shower. He had a few tasks that needed attending, items he needed to address before meeting his new driving partner the following morning.

The hot water in the shower rinsed the sleep out of his brain, pulsing a soothing stream over his head, freeing his mind while he reviewed the stray threads of information gathered the previous day.

One question he found kept circling in his thoughts. Could Dave be the main factor in the gunmen's attack at his house? The evidence certainly pointed in that direction, but intuition told him that this investigation got started on the wrong foot. He began to see errors in his judgment and views. Dave was not a gambler and drank little. Still, Dave's apartment was ransacked and the shooters that targeted his house put a bullet in Dave's head.

Things didn't line up. Dave's actions differed from the typical marks the Apostles sought at Millennium. What was missing? Was Dave just an innocent bystander after all? Unlucky enough to be in the wrong place at the wrong time, Brand wondered.

While dwelling on a half assed plan for the next day's adventure, his mind wandered over to Jerry. He had a few questions he'd like Jerry to answer, but the word from the hospital had his friend still in a coma. Dave and Jerry had been palling around a lot lately. What did the two talk about? Maybe the old guide had an inside tract on what Dave was into or maybe Dave talked out of turn and told Jerry things. The kind of things only close friends shared.

After breakfast, Brand decided to swing back by the Wolves clubhouse and have a chat with Roy. Pick Roy's brain on whatever Intel he could share on the Apostles operations, then a quick drive to the hospital and look in on Jerry.

The hotel restaurant was empty by the time Brand entered. He seated himself, and once the waitress stopped at his table, he ordered a black coffee and eggs benedict with toast on the side. The chocolate bar and coffee from last nights stakeout did little to quell his hunger and since he awoke, his stomach grumbled incessantly.

While he waited, Brand stared into the mouth of the coffee cup. Likely scenarios of tomorrow's trip across the mountains played on his thoughts. He mulled the situation over for a couple of minutes before moving on, his lack of information leading to more conjecture then factual planning. This adventure wouldn't be the first time he's had to improvise for an operation.

He mowed his way through the eggs and toast, stopping briefly to wash the meal down with sips of the scalding black coffee.

Sliding his plate aside, he picked up a deserted newspaper from an adjoining table and scanned the news stories. He slowly read an article on the police and the accumulating gang troubles brewing in the city. The chief of Police released a statement. The city was under siege from the escalating violence from organized crimes. A rash of drug related incidents declared the number one concern of Calgary's finest, the bold letters of the headline screamed from the front page.

Sipping the cooling coffee, Brand flipped to the sports section. The Eskimos lost a preseason game the night before,

Richard Cozicar

and the Jay's were sliding down in the standings. At least the sunshine girl was pretty enough, a pleasant distraction from the bad news the paper bore.

Setting down the cash for his meal on the table, Brand headed for the door. First on his list the Wolves clubhouse.

Pulling out of the hotel parking lot, Brand suddenly realized a whole new problem. He dug out his cell and working the phone as he drove, checked for missed calls. Damn. Sara's number appeared several times on the screen.

Brand signalled out of traffic and into the nearest parking lot. He shoved the truck into park and reluctantly dialled her number. A smile twerked the edges of his mouth. It had been nearly a week since he last saw Sara. Memories of her face and the longing to hear her voice temporarily refocused his mind and with the longing came trepidation.

He would face a crazed grizzly without second thought if he had to, but forgetting to call this five foot four woman made him nervous. The phone rang a third time. Maybe he should try later he told himself. While he contemplated leaving a message, Sara answered.

"It's about time you called." Her voice tinged with concern and annoyance.

"Yeah...I suppose..." He stalled trying to think of a suitable explanation for the last couple days without causing her more worry.

"Brent heard about a shooting at your house...you alright."

"Pretty good. I'm staying in a hotel until the police are finished dusting my house. I don't suppose you're interested in helping me do some late spring cleaning?" he said to lighten the mood. "How are things in Ottawa?" He asked, hoping to avoid

132

questions about the shooting. Sara worked from her house in the city, but often had to fly to Ottawa on business.

Brand listened patiently for a few minutes as Sara spoke of her current assignment before she wound the conversation back to the shootings. Briefly telling Sara of the attack at the house, he glossed over the unpleasant details consuming the last few days.

As the conversation drew to an end, she added. "Don't go getting yourself killed; I'd like to see you again." She said jokingly, but he detected a tremble in her voice.

"I promise." He reassured her.

Brand resumed driving, deciding to change course and go past his house. He wanted to see if the police presence and crime scene tape were still there. The hotel was decent, but home was home, besides he needed a new change of clothes if he was going to continue living in the hotel.

Pulling the truck up to the curb, he noticed the front door sitting ajar. He climbed out of the truck and cautiously looked over the house, walked up the sidewalk and climbed the stairs to the front deck. Hesitating at the door, he pushed it open and called out while examining the broken doorjamb. From the entrance, he could see clear to the back of the house. The interior bore the brunt of unwanted intruders.

Brand stepped a single foot onto the floor and studied the interior. Either the police were getting awfully careless when they conducted investigations nowadays, or he had had other visitors. It could have been vandals, although it was more likely associates of the two gunmen. Either way he decided, somebody spent some time alone in the house and conducted a thorough search of the inside. The depth of the search made Brand think that the intruders were not worried about being discovered while they went about their business.

He crossed deeper into the house. His eyes checking shadows and corners, his ears strained to detect unusual movements as he walked past the kitchen and into the living room. Carefully he set his feet down, checking their placement to avoid the overturned furniture.

The contents in his house were strewn about, upended and scattered. Cushions cut and white cotton stuffing tossed across the floor. The paintings yanked off the walls, the paper on the backs peeled, the frames smashed. Everything in the house had obviously been subjected to an intense search, a scene that had recently become all too familiar.

Brand walked the entire house from basement to the bedrooms on the second floor. Each room, like the one before, disassembled. His belongings scattered across the floors, bed frames broken apart, mattresses slit and gutted, and everywhere, the items that hung on the walls removed and laying broken on the floor.

He shook his head, disappointed and outraged. He kicked at some of the mess on the floor. Whatever the bastards who ransacked his house were looking for, it sure and the hell wasn't a stash of drugs. This time he was a hundred percent certain. But, the meticulous search of the smallest hiding spaces ruled that theory out, again.

Walking down the stairs, Brand hesitated. When his foot touched the last step, a thought occurred. Brand turned and raced back to his bedroom pushing aside the mess left in the walk-in closet. Lying on the floor was his metal gun safe. Somebody went through a lot of trouble to get the safe open. The nine-millimetre Browning he had kept from his days with the government was no longer there. Also missing were the extra thirteen round magazines.

Brand swore under his breath and bent down to examine the box. He had bought the box to comply with federal gun laws. It was not meant to keep out an over anxious thief. Brand remained crouched over, thinking about the ramifications of the stolen firearm. The best he could hope for was that the missing gun wouldn't show up at some crime scene and cause him undue problems. The police had already confiscated his rifle, and now his old service piece was stolen.

Brand realized the need to call the police and report the theft. He made a mental reminder to file a report about the missing 9-mil once he returned to the hotel.

Standing by the front door, he punched 9-1-1 on the keypad of his phone, waited scant seconds before the call connected. The dispatcher on the receiving end of the phone asked him a barrage of standard questions. Brand stood with the phone held tight to his ear. The sounds of computer keys clicking filled the silent line until the officer typed a report.

"Okay, Mr. Coldstream. I will direct a unit to your address. The officers will take your statement and walk through the damage with you."

"The door will be open." Brand responded. "Tell the patrolmen to feel free to enter the house. I won't be here when they arrive."

Brand ran his eyes over the house's interior one last time and walked down to his truck. Slamming the door, he stared back up at the house shaking his head in frustration. He needed a second to calm down. Digging in in his pocket he retrieved his package of cigarettes, lit one, and after a long drag, drove away.

Chapter 19

"I need to know everything about the Apostles and their Colombian partners you can tell me?" Brand asked. "I was down at the Millennium last night. Wandered around the floors checking out the action. For the most part, the casino looked legit, with the exception of the poker tables. I watched one guy lose his shorts." Brand explained. "Took me a while to figure out how the Apostles recruited runners into the system. Simple I suppose when you consider people's fascination for gambling and the promise of a large payoff that most never find.

Having a feeling about that guy, I kept an eye on him. Sure as shit, after several calls for more funds and a mean streak of bad luck, security pulled the man from the table and escorted him from the building. You'll never believe where I followed them to?"

"The Apostles clubhouse," Brand continued.

"Not surprising." Roy agreed.

"I had a chat with the guy. He drives transport truck. Seems he's making an unscheduled run into B.C. tomorrow. Figured I'd go along for the ride."

Brand caught Roy up to date on his findings over the past day, the fight at Esmeraldas he left out. He didn't need Roy thinking he was overly violent.

The two men sat across the desk in Roy's office, a bottle of whiskey perched between them. Brand watched his brother's face for a reaction. Brand flushed out the pieces of info and how he began piecing them together. His request for detailed information on the Apostles casino and their connection with the Colombians caused Roy's features to darken.

Roy broke his silence. "You know as much as I do. The casino rigs the games. The scam is simple. When a potential mark joins the tables, the dealers shuffle the cards accordingly. Once the losses accumulate, the house offers a loan, a show of faith and the chance for the mark to recoup his money. That never happens, of course, and the casino owns the debt, making the marks easier to control.

From there, a heavy-handed approach in some backroom, either cough up the cash or...an option of debt forgiveness for favours" Roy locked eyes with Brand. " These are some very dangerous vermin, brother."

"Crazy white men backed by a ruthless cartel that cares little about who they roll over building their distribution empire," Roy emphasized. "The Apostles have cops and lawyers, even judges protecting them. And now with the Colombians backing them, they roam the city like they're untouchable. You're up against a wall of trouble if you go after them."

"No worries..." Brand brushed off his brother's concern. "I'm only taking a ride tomorrow. Get a feel for the way this organization operates. See what flaws I can use to my advantage.

Brand paused. The image of blood flowing from the bullet hole in Dave's head haunted his memories. "I need to play this out, Roy. I can't stand on the sidelines while the cops play with themselves pretending to care and then head on to other unsolved murders. I need to figure out what the Apostles are up to and what they are searching so desperately for. I want to find the item before they do. Gain some leverage. Get them off our backs. And unfortunately, the only person who might be able to help is laying in a hospital bed in a bullet induced coma."

Brand changed the conversation. "Susan out at your hacienda, I didn't see her when I walked in?"

"She's fine. She's at the house. Some of the boys escorted her to the hospital earlier today."

"You take good care of her, Roy. She certainly didn't ask for this bullshit. She shouldn't have to suffer." Brand reiterated and thanked his younger brother before leaving. The hours were passing and he still planned to stop by the hospital and check on Jerry before the day was over.

*****

The hallways were barren of visitors when Brand strolled into the hospital. Walking past the information desk, he caught the elevator to the third floor. There he stood at the nursing station waiting to inquire about Jerry's condition before heading into the room. Lunchtime and attendants were scurrying about hallways crowded with carts and equipment while nurses wove around the choreographed calamity attending to their duties.

When a nurse returned to the station, Brand asked about his friend. The nurse lifted a chart from the desk and after a quick reading reported Jerry was still in a coma, his vitals were stable, but he hadn't woken up yet. The situation was all wait and see. Nothing anyone could do for now.

Brand thanked the nurse and walked the short distance to Jerry's room. Opening the door and sliding the curtain out of his way, he moved a chair close to the head of the bed and sat quietly watching the old man sleep. Brand remained motionless for a time, and then he started talking out loud, explaining his thoughts on the shootings and even though he knew Jerry couldn't hear the words he said, he sorted out the few facts he had, mixed with his speculations on the matter.

"...when I first started looking into the shooting, I was certain Dave was the target, but now, as I dig deeper, I no longer believe that to be true. My way of thinking was wrong. I don't know. Even with all the damning evidence I can't help think that Dave may have been an innocent bystander.

The more people I talk to, the more pieces that come together, as strange as this sounds, I find myself wondering if you're not responsible. I know. I'm tired and the situation has kept me off balance so I'm probably not thinking straight. I can't put my finger on anything in particular but it could just as easily be you instead of Dave who got into money troubles.

Staff I talked to at the Millennium casino recognized you." Brand paused, pondering this train of reasoning. "Crazy. I know. I can't wrap my head around why you'd be involved with drugs or even somewhat friendly with a group of asshole bikers, but I suppose stranger things have happened, old friend."

Brand let his words fade as his thoughts surged into different directions. "...I wish you could help me out...why would some asshole bikers, or a Colombian Cartel target us. They wouldn't do that on a whim. They must have had a reason. I mean, the way they've torn apart our houses, it's a lot more serious than a cache of drugs, whatever they're looking for...it has to be something that can really hurt them...something a hell of a lot smaller, something important enough that they're forced to take rash actions. But what?"

His words faded into the background. The room fell silent with the exception of the beeping and humming of the medical equipment monitoring Jerry. Brand sat staring at the machines. His mind occupied, hunting for some small shard of information he might be missing.

"Dave's dead. Susan was accosted at your house and my place has been turned inside out. Something. I'm missing something, but I can't seem to put my finger on it. DAMN IT, Jerry. What. What the hell am I missing?" Brand's voice rose with frustration. Sucking in deep breaths he calmed, glancing down at the prone figure of his friend wrapped in the hospital blankets.

"Anyway, I've got a lead. Spotted him sitting at the poker tables at the Millennium. This guy drives truck. Gambled his ass away and now, is in debt to the Apostles." Brand paused. Did Jerry know who the Apostles were? "A gang of outlaw bikers who've tied their fortunes to a cartel from Colombia." He explained before realizing he was talking to a coma patient. Shrugging, he continued his line of thinking. "Big into drug running I'm told. Anyways, they've got this guy driving over to Castlegar tomorrow to pick up…I presume a shipment of drugs destined for our city.

I'm going along for the ride. I'm going to get to the bottom of this one way or the other…" Brand stood up and returned the chair back by the door.

"Get better, old friend, I'll stop in when I get back." He said as he turned to leave.

"It wasn't supposed to happen this way…" Came a weak voice from behind him.

Brand stopped, his hand on the door. Several thoughts rushed through his head. Slowly, he looked back at the bed. Jerry laid prone, his eyes still closed. Was his mind playing tricks, Brand wondered? Turning at the door, he softly walked back to the head of the bed.

"What wasn't supposed to happen?" He asked quietly, then waited, hoping he'd get a reply.

"Nobody was supposed to get hurt...I thought I had it all figured out." Jerry mumbled in a strained voice, his words barely a whisper. Brand leaned close to his friends face. Tears began rolling from beneath Jerry's closed eyelids.

"I had lost scads of money, and they promised if I hauled their shipments, that over time my debt would be repaid and I would be free of them. That never happened, my debt hung over my head, and I was in too deep to get away." Jerry's chest heaved while the tears slowly ran down his cheeks.

"One day I decided to get my life back," Jerry choked out, "so from then on, whenever I met with those bastards or picked up new shipments, I recorded the conversations and recorded videos with my phone. I bought one of those new phones, the kind that you can do pretty much anything. A kid at the mall store showed me how to use the features.

After months, I knew I had enough evidence to incriminate them so I warned them to leave me alone or I'd take the recordings to the cops, and I'd sing like a pigeon. I wanted to retire. Head home to the Maritimes. But I couldn't, not with their threats hanging over me. They had me by the balls, Brand. You have to believe me." Jerry quit talking. Tears continued to roll down his cheeks and gather on the pillow beneath his head. Brand waited for his friend to finish his confession. Jerry remained quiet.

Brand stared at his friend, dumbfounded. A flood of emotions rendered him speechless. The steady beat of the monitors underlined the silence. Rage became replaced by empathy for the old guide. The seconds dragged by until Brand thought himself calm enough to speak. "Where's the phone now

Jerry?" He asked quietly. "Apparently, neither the bikers nor the Cartel have located it or they wouldn't still be searching."

Jerry released a short laugh, or maybe a cry, Brand wasn't couldn't tell.

"That's...kind of a funny story," Jerry mumbled. "I don't rightly know...I ...lost it."

Brand waited for Jerry to explain. When no words came from the old man's mouth, Brand prodded.

"Can't it be found...if your phone is new, it must have one of those tracking features, right?"

"I turned the app off. I didn't want the damn Apostles to track its location." Jerry answered.

"But you have a phone. I called you the other night."

"I bought a new one. I couldn't let the buggers know my phone was missing, that I'd lost my only bargaining chip, could I?"

"No idea where you lost it?"

"I've been laying here wracking my brain, trying to remember exactly where I had it last. I keep thinking, if I could find the phone and surrender it, the Apostles could leave all of you alone. I vaguely recall the last few places I might have left it. I was...well...I had been drinking at a bar one night, and the next morning I couldn't find the damn thing." Jerry admitted.

Brand found a piece of paper on a desk and coaxed Jerry into providing the locations of the places he visited when he last had his phone. The two talked a bit more before Brand left. At least now he knew why the bikers were desperate. Another piece of the puzzle fell into place. When he returned after the trip west, he would busy himself with finding Jerry's lost phone.

Chapter 20

Five A.M. Tuesday morning. The rain had relented, but the clouds remained, low and threatening more precipitation, as Brand drove past the Foothills Industrial Park to the address where the gambler's 18-wheeler waited. Brand roamed the east side industrial park, past the meeting place, then circled back and found a spot on the street a block from where the truck sat. He was early, not wanting the trucker to leave without him.

Half an hour later he noticed the beat up Chevy pull along side the tractor-trailer unit. Brand waited as the man loaded a duffle bag into the cab and then watched him walk around the truck checking the tires and equipment. Brand grabbed a ball cap off the truck seat and stuck it on his head, the cigarette he was smoking, he threw to the ground and squashed under his foot as he walked from the street, across the lot and made his way down the block.

In the opposite direction from where Brand's truck sat against the curb, a grey Toyota SUV idled. The detective inside sipped his coffee and watched the trucker before he noticed a man walking down the block in the direction of the semi. It took the detective a couple of seconds to recognize the man walking down the sidewalk. Damn. It was that bastard Coldstream. What was he doing here? How did he know about the trucker? He was sure that this wasn't a coincidence. Not certain what to do, he sat and observed the two men.

Approaching the tractor-trailer, Brand called a greeting to the driver. Chad Worenko looked in his direction and glared. Not going to be a pleasant trip, Brand decided. Waiting for the driver to finish the inspection of his rig, Brand opened the passenger door on the big truck, stepped on the saddle tank leading to the cab and settled into a comfortable bucket seat.

Shortly, the trucker joined him inside the cab. The powerful engine rumbled. The tractor-trailer unit crawled out of the parking compound; turned on the street and drove past the grey Toyota.

Traffic was light as the driver wove his 18-wheeler through the nearly deserted industrial area and onto the busier city streets toward Highway 22 before merging onto Highway 2 south. The four-lane highway was starting to fill with vehicles at the early morning hour as they passed the city limits, the occupants in the cab silent. The driver, scowling, his eyes never leaving the road and Brand's thoughts occupied with the destination at the end of the trip.

Gazing out the windshield, Brand watched as the 18-wheeler rolled passed Okotoks and then High River. At the south end of Nanton, the driver turned onto a secondary highway crossing the Porcupine Hills. Soon they were headed south once again to the Crowsnest pass and then west into British Columbia.

The skies had cleared, bright sunlight streamed into the cab of the truck when they neared Fernie. Cranbrook lay an hour to the west and south. There, the route snaked its way down to Creston before the road climbed over a low mountain pass and on toward Castlegar.

At points, the highway came close to the U.S. border. Brand began to understand the reason the Cartel and the Apostles chose the southern B.C. city for their staging warehouse to store drugs. Access from the shipping waters off the B.C. coast and the near proximity to the United States made the city a perfect transitioning point, small and off the beaten path without the usual police presence of a bigger centre.

By mid-afternoon, the town of Castlegar appeared on the horizon. Brand idly watched as the trucker shifted gears steering the semi past the final overpass into town. The two hadn't exchanged more than a half dozen words on the eight-hour trip.

"Where's the warehouse located? Here in town?" Brand asked.

Chad Worenko glanced at Brand but continued to ignore his unwanted passenger. The lack of conversation on the trip Brand appreciated. He spent the quiet miles devising a method for a reconnaissance of the warehouse. The start to all his plans involved bypassing the undoubtedly tight security, something he needed assistance with. The time for cooperation was fast approaching. It would be essential to have the trucker pull his head out of his ass and play along.

"This little jaunt of ours is going to go either one of two ways." Brand stated, breaking the silence. He studied the driver as the town of Castlegar unfolded before them. "You can play along and maybe, just maybe you will come out of this alright, or you can sit and sulk, and I'll leave you to your own devices. The state of your health is not a big concern to me, so decide which way you want this to go."

"The warehouse is a few miles west of town, a small industrial area off by itself." Worenko spat out his reply refusing to look at his passenger. Finally the odd nature of the question flipped a switch in his brain. He looked at Brand. His furrowed brows telegraphed his confusion. As the truck neared its destination, his mood soured.

Brand studied the driver and watched the change come over the man's features. The guy was no idiot. How long until he realizes that I'm not working for the Apostles, Brand wondered.

Worenko cleared his throat and summed his courage. "What are you up to? Is this some kind of a test? It's your guy's warehouse. Your boss has got me by the balls and now I'll have to haul this shit until my services are no longer needed. Which, I'm sure, will be, never," Chad spat out sarcastically. " Or I suppose, at least until the cops bust me and throw me in jail so what are you trying to pull?" He went back to staring out the windshield as sections of highway disappeared under the front of the truck while it motored on. His head sagged in defeat.

Brand chose his next words carefully. He wanted an ally when they arrived at the Apostles warehouse. Time to tell the truth, besides, the trucker would find out Brand didn't work for the bikers soon enough. By that time, if the trucker was scared shitless of the Apostles he would most likely try to save his skin and turn Brand in when confronted by the truth.

"I lied to you the other night." Brand decided to take the chance. "I don't work for the Apostles. They sent men to my house a couple nights ago, two men with guns. Killed one friend and sent another to the hospital." Brand shared a short version of the shootings and the path that led to his sitting inside the west bound truck.

"What the hell are you going to do?" Worenko asked. "I'm not looking to get myself killed. They said if I haul their goods, they'd scrub my debts. I don't need to shorten my life by getting tangled up in some crazy scheme of revenge."

"Do you honestly think the bikers will let you make one delivery and then …what." Brand snapped back. "You will all become best of friends. Give your head a shake. They've got you by the short and curlies. You make this trip, and then they'll ask for another, and another, because then they'll have enough evidence of you hauling illegal cargo that the only way out is death or jail."

Brand watched the truck driver. The man's eyes grew moist; his head sunk lower on his chest.

"What else can I do? All I've got left is this truck," Worenko mumbled, his voice shaky with fear and desperation.

"Help me out. Maybe I can make this go away. Find you a way out." Brand replied. His plan was weak, mostly involving timing and a fair share of luck, but he'd dealt with worse.

Brand swung his head toward the window, letting his words sink in. He gazed at the countryside rolling by outside. Chad Worenko anchored his eyes on the twin lanes of asphalt being gobbled up by the rolling 18-wheeler. Both men fell silent.

"What kind of help?" Worenko asked.

"Tell whoever is in charge that I'm your swamper. Keep suspicion away from me. All I require is a small opportunity to snoop around the warehouse. Get a feel for their operation and then we can leave. You just do what they say. If they catch on that I'd invited myself, I don't think that either of us will be able to leave." Brand looked at Worenko as he spoke. The trucker's features became drained, his skin glistened a sickly white.

"Do you know how long they'll take to load the trailer?" Brand asked.

"I have no idea. My instructions were to show up at a certain time, wait for the trailer to be loaded, and not ask questions. Somebody at the warehouse will provide me with a return address to deliver the cargo."

Chapter 21

Worenko swung the 18-wheeler onto a deserted lane of blacktop and followed the short side road past ditches lined with cedars and pine trees. Asphalt gave way to gravel as the semi rolled through a gate. A one-story building appeared inside a tightly fenced yard.

The warehouse a few miles drive past the outskirts of Castlegar. The compound sat on a piece of land carved from a thick stand of trees, the dense bush sheltering the business from unwanted attention. The property, a gravel parking lot, and a relatively obscure one-story building crouched in the clearing safeguarded by a chain link fence.

To one side of the building, a scattering of personal vehicles gleamed under the midday sun. Four large overhead bays faced the property's entrance waiting to receive trailers, three of the doors occupied.

With trained ease, the trucker shifted into lower gears, slowing the speed of the truck then expertly began turning the large tractor-trailer unit, lining the back of the truck with the empty overhead door. Slowly he inched the 54-foot trailer until it made contact with the rubber bumpers protecting the dock.

Dust rose from the gravelled lot when the truck's air brakes released. Brand remained in the cab letting the dust settle.

Worenko flicked off the ignition, sitting with his hand on the keys. Moments had passed before he glanced in Brand's direction. "What now?"

The Wolves Of Satan

"Do what you're told," Brand replied. The trip allowed him a lot of time to think about this moment. His original idea was to ride along, have a look around and gather Intel to use at a later date. Those thoughts seemed to fall by the wayside once the forest road opened up revealing the biker's compound. Flashes of memory from the night of the attack at his house and his friends lying unconscious after being shot, surfaced, along with a smouldering rage. What exactly it was that he planned to do, he didn't know. The men inside the building would determine today's outcome.

He pushed open the cab door and jumped to the ground. Stretching, he looked skyward at the blue sky, and bright sun then gave a cursory glance at the exterior of the building. Tucked under the eaves, the tell tale lens of high tech security cameras. Made sense, he thought, considering the type of products the warehouse stocked.

The day was warm. The sun beat down into the lot, the surrounding trees blocked the wind allowing the heat to build.

He walked around the cab to the driver's door as Worenko stepped onto the running board and then down to the ground. The trucker's boots crunched on the gravel as the man stepped from the truck and walked toward a set of metal stairs leading into the warehouse.

Brand grabbed the ball cap tucked in his back pocket, flattened the brim as best he could and pulled it low over his head. He then slouched to make himself seem less imposing, put a big grin on his face and loped behind, projecting the impression that he was a few litres short of a full tank.

A blast of cold air greeted the pair. A man in jeans and a t-shirt layered under a vest displaying his biker colours met them at the door with an automatic rifle cradled in his hand. He stood in their path and stared, unmoving. Loud words poured onto the concrete dock from behind the biker. Brand peered from under the brim of his ball cap.

A copper skinned man, small in stature with a headful of slicked back, black hair appeared at the biker's side. South American, Brand noted, no doubt Colombian. The Latino's expensive suit and polished footwear, noticeably out of place in the warehouse, and a stark contrast to the biker's casual attire.

"Who are you?" The Colombian demanded, the words rolling rapidly off his tongue, his accent heavy.

"The Manager gave me the address. Told me to be here today." Worenko rattled nervously. He shoved a crumpled piece of paper at the men with the warehouse's address. "Said you would have a load of produce destined for Calgary."

The Latino ignored the paper in the trucker's hand and glared up at Brand. "This is...my swamper...Duane." Worenko stammered.

"We weren't informed there'd be two of you." The Latino scowled. "Search them." He instructed the gun-toting biker.

Brand giggled as the biker patted him down. The biker finished and looked at Worenko. "Your buddy here...he's seems kind of special." The biker said through a malicious sneer. The trucker nodded and glanced at Brand, his skin paler under the close scrutiny of the armed biker.

The Latino walked over to a closed door at the side of the loading dock, and pushed it open, barking orders to the men sitting in the room.

"Get off your butts and load this truck." He shouted through the open doorway not waiting for the workers to respond. "You two wait outside," he said to Worenko. "I'll let you know when they've finished loading your trailer."

The Wolves Of Satan

Keeping the stupid ass grin on his face, Brand let his eyes roam the interior of the building before exiting behind the truck driver. Two men at the front door, three from the other room and he only spotted one other guy deeper inside the building, among pallets of vegetables lined up in rows on the dock. The man guarding the front door held the only visible weapon, but Brand had no doubt the Latino was probably packing a concealed gun, but with only a quick glance at the others, he had know way of telling if they too were armed.

Outside, the men walked to the cab of the truck. Brand turned his back to the warehouse, dropped the grin and lit a cigarette. He thought about the building sitting in the clearing of trees, private, and no witnesses around for miles. Only a few men on the premises, at least a couple guns and a building constructed mainly from wood. These things he could work with.

He continued leaning against the cab of the truck as the men inside busied themselves with loading the trailer. The whining of propane powered forklifts filled the still afternoon air, the solid rubber tires mucking across the concrete floor and then echoing in the tin interior of the trailer. The rig rocked and bounced as pallet after pallet was transported inside and placed carefully against its neighbour. Following Brand's lead, Worenko leaned against the trucks chrome bumper. The trucker stood silent, his face a sickly grey from fear of the unknown and worry about what the stranger who rode to the warehouse with him, would do.

An hour and a half later, the man in the suit and the armed biker walked from the building and met the two at the front of the truck. The Latino handed the truck driver a slip of paper.

"Drive straight to this address. No dickin' around." He warned and turned away, the biker following.

"Wait here." Brand mumbled to Worenko. Putting the stupid grin back on his face, Brand rushed after the retreating men. "I gotta use the can." He called out.

The boss turned and looked at him. "There are three acres of woods, pick a spot."

"No." Brand whined. "I need a seat, badly." He protested.

The suited man sighed. "Escort him to the bathroom." He left the duty to the biker before climbing the metal stairs into the warehouse.

"Hurry up." The biker growled walking inside the building. "Over there." he pointed with the barrel of the gun at a room partially hidden in the back corner. Brand loped in the direction indicated, his escort following close behind. Brand moved slowly. Under the cover of his cap's brim, he ran his eyes across the open concrete floor searching for the three men who loaded the truck.

The loading area was quiet except for the ringing of boot soles echoing off the cement floor. Brand increased his speed, passing behind skids of stacked produce boxes, the biker forced to increase his stride to remain a close step behind. At the bathroom door, Brand planted a foot and abruptly stopped.

Brand felt the large biker's knuckles dig into his back when the man, not anticipating the sudden stop, collided with him.

With an unexpected quickness, Brand twisted, focused the weight of his body and drove his elbow back into the biker's face. The larger man hesitated, his hands rising awkwardly to block the blow. Brand spun, his fingers reaching for the weapon in the biker's hands.

The surprising move and a knee placed to the man's groin allowed Brand to wrench the long gun out of the biker's hands.

In the shelter of the pellets, Brand swung the gun, and using the rifle's solid stock as a club, drove the end into the biker's head until the man fell unconscious.

Brand paused, hidden behind the boxes of produce wary for signs of running feet or any indication the commotion may have attracted the attention of the other warehouse employees. The building remained quiet, so he crept from behind the cover and made his way to the rooms near the entrance. Muffled voices of relaxed talking met his ears, the men evidently unaware of his presence.

He skirted past the partially open door and hesitated at the side of the entrance of the small Latino's office. Taking a deep breath, he held the gun, his fingers wrapped around the stock, his finger hovering near the trigger; his free hand on the doorknob.

Flinging the door opened, his head followed the metal gun barrel as it swept across the room's interior. His eyes and the barrel stopped at a desk behind the door. The small man was slow to act. When Brand met the Latino's eyes, the smaller man already had his hand reaching for the handgun hidden inside his coat.

Brand steadied the rifle and fired. The bullet struck the Latino in the chest driving the smaller man back into the wall. Without slowing, Brand stepped away from the office door and moved to the opening of the second room. The workers looked away from a television in the corner, caught off-guard by his appearance. He raised the rifle, bracing the men as they began to rise out of their chairs.

"Hands on your heads." He shouted motioning the workers out. Brand held the gun on the men as he cleared the room. The rifle held in one hand, Brand patted the men. No weapons, only keys, wallets and cell phones. He pocketed one of the phones, throwing the rest of items in a stack on the floor.

Glancing around the loading dock, he spotted a short roll of poly, the type used to wrap boxes securely on the wooden pallets for shipping. He spoke to the men. "One of you, grab that roll of plastic. You other two," he pointed to where the biker lay unconscious. "Drag your buddy over here." Brand held his finger on the rifle's trigger covering the men as they obeyed his orders.

"Stand him up." Brand instructed the men carrying the biker." To the third man holding the roll, "wrap him tight. I don't want him moving." With the job finished, Brand barked new orders. He wanted the biker and the roll of poly taken outside. He followed a few paces behind the dockworkers as they struggled to move the unconscious biker out into the sunlight.

He marched the small group past the tractor-trailers, and away from the building while he called to Chad. In the middle of the parking lot, he stopped the men, instructing them to stand facing one another with their hands hanging by their sides, the biker, held up by the three men, in the middle.

"Take this roll and wrap them tightly," he ordered Chad. "Stop when the roll is empty. We don't need any surprises."

Brand watched until Chad was well into the roll, confident that the men couldn't move and then headed back into the warehouse. He slowly approached the office where he had shot the boss and peered in. The man was lying on the floor behind his desk. Brand grabbed the man's gun and then checked for a pulse. The boss was still breathing.

The Wolves Of Satan

Grabbing the man under one shoulder Brand drug the wounded Colombian from the building to where the others were bound and asked Chad to put a couple wraps around him as a precaution. Chad showed Brand the empty roll. Brand shrugged.

"Keep an eye on them. I won't be long." He said and hustled back into the building.

Checking the office first, he scooped up the Latino's laptop. He wasn't talented enough to crack passwords, but what the hell, he'd take it anyway, it might come in handy down the line, and he had friends who could make short work of the computers security system.

Rifle in one hand and laptop in the other, he searched the warehouse. A quick look through the wrapped pallets on the dock floor revealed nothing but produce, so he explored the far end of the building. In the back, he found a false room hidden discreetly inside a large drive-in freezer. Opening the door carefully, he entered, the barrel of the gun leading the way.

Two men, their backs to the door, headphones covering their ears, sat hunched over a table. The men worked methodically stuffing plastic pouches into partially empty boxes of vegetables. A handful of the pouches were laid into the open boxes followed by bags of fresh produce. Taking a careful step closer, Brand studied the little baggies, each stuffed with a white powder sealed inside.

Brand stepped behind the men, tapped them with the barrel of his gun before pointing to the open door leading out of the freezer.

Brand marched the two men outside, stopping long enough to have one of the men grab a second roll of poly. He watched Chad bind the two before walking back into the warehouse for the last time. Taking his time, he removed the propane tanks from the pallet jacks and stacked them beside the freezer with the hidden drugs. While gathering the tanks, he kept a clear path to the front door. As soon as he finished, Brand poked his head out the door, shouting a warning to Chad to start the truck and drive it away from the building.

Brand waited as the truck rumbled across the gravel lot. He turned his attention to the bound men. "You might want some distance between you and the building," he warned and watched with a bitter amusement as the group waddled like penguins, scrambling toward the perimeter fence.

Brand took a final look around. Satisfied, he walked toward the wooden structure. In view of the cameras, he lifted his hand, the middle finger raised. Climbing the metal stairs, he focused his attention back to the warehouse interior. Raising the rifle's stock to his shoulder, he sighted down the gun barrel aiming for the stack of propane tanks. He drew a breath, tightened his finger on the trigger and prepared to launch out the door to safety.

The bullet raced from the barrel striking the centre of the closest tank. A thundering clap rocked the small building. The air in the warehouse heated with the explosion of the ruptured cylinder. A chain reaction followed igniting the remaining propane tanks sending a wall of rushing air toward the open door.

The wave of hot air from the initial explosion blew Brand off the top step leading out of the warehouse. The force from the following eruption split the building apart from the inside, debris flying skyward and outward.

Brand dragged himself to his feet, and with an arm sheltering his head, ran for the cab of the truck. Carrots, potatoes, jagged pieces of lumber and tin from the roof of the building rained down over the gravel parking lot. Jumping onto the step of the truck, he flung open the door and scrambled in.

"Drive." He hollered across the cab.

Chapter 22

Brand brushed the dust off his clothes while gambler shifted gears. The tractor-trailer unit picking up speed, the burning warehouse shrinking in the truck's mirrors as they rolled over the tree-lined road back toward Castlegar. Waiting until they were safely south of the small B.C. city, Brand dug the confiscated cell phone out of his pocket, dialled 911 and left an anonymous tip regarding the blast at the warehouse. Ignoring the dispatcher's questions for his name and location, he abruptly ended the call, tossed the phone into the passing ditch and lit a cigarette.

*****

The Latino drug boss roused from his stupor and stared at the smoke covered sky while consciousness slowly crept through the fog in his brain. Struggling to sit up, shock and then a sickening realization seized his thoughts as he stared, mouth agape, at the destroyed warehouse.

Ignoring the piercing pain of the bullet wound, he dug his hand into his pocket, his fingers clawing for a cell phone. Loyalty to his bosses and the Cartel's business came long before he would worry about his own safety.

A call went out to the Apostles clubhouse in Calgary, then a second, more urgent call to a similar clubhouse on the southern outskirts of Castlegar. At the second location, all available members and associates rushed to their bikes, the attack on the supply warehouse a matter to be dealt with swiftly and without prejudice. The Latino was finishing the second of the calls when the sounds of screaming sirens filled the air.

The first motorcycle that passed the rig escaped Brand's notice. Caught unawares, he watched the B.C. landscape unfold outside the truck's window. The ramifications from his demolition of the warehouse he knew would indeed produce a loud and angry blowback from the Apostles and their Colombian business partners.

Brand accepted the challenge. The Apostles fired the first shots; the loss of the building and the shipment were a small price for them to pay for the killing of his dead friend and putting Jerry in the hospital. The destruction at the warehouse would work two fold. Cripple the Cartel's drug distribution and focus the eyes of the local law on the out of the way location.

Brand pulled out of his reverie and watched the highway signs. The pair had recently crossed the short mountain range, slowed through the streets of Creston and joined the Crowsnest highway traveling in an eastern direction. The twin ribbon of asphalt traversed the lower end of the province, winding among forests of pine and cedar trees, scattered farms, meandering rivers, and kilometres of green meadows and thick forests.

A short drive up the road and Brand noticed the biker for a second time. Parked on the side of the road. The man lounged against his machine, a phone held to his ear, the man's eyes locked on the moving truck as it passed.

Brand's mind snapped to the present. The patches on the biker's vest, colours of the Apostles bike club. A disturbing but not unexpected thought ran through Brand's mind. A scout for the Apostles reporting back on the truck's whereabouts. Brand glanced at the truck's speedometer. Worenko sat stoically in his seat, his hands covering the wheel and the gear shifter. The man was not relaxed, his face still a strained pasty shade, but his whining had stopped.

The highway straightened out. The B.C. city of Cranbrook, the next major population, was less than an hour ahead. A short distance after spotting the lone biker, a roar from behind the truck drew Brand's eyes to the side mirror.

A pair of bikes raced up behind the 18-wheeler. Brand watched the bikers and looking above the pair, studied the open road to the west. Small black objects began appearing in the distance. Soon the lanes behind the trailer were filled with two wheeled hellions.

"Theses two lanes should widen into four shortly, correct?" Brand looked across the cab. Worenko returned his gaze and nodded.

"A few more kilometres, why?"

"How about hills. Any large enough to slow our speed?"

"No. Not really." Again the trucker asked why.

Brand continued watching out the side mirror, the reflection filled with motorcycles and men wearing biker colours.

"We have company."

"The bikers from the warehouse? Oh, shit." Worenko exclaimed glancing at the mirror.

"Probably. But we'll know for sure soon enough."

The lanes around the truck became flooded with the roar of motorbikes.

"I don't care if you run the bastards over, but do not even think about slowing down." Brand ordered, his voice stern. The truck driver checked the side mirrors, the bikers now swarming around the cab. Worenko's hands clawed for the gear shifter.

"I...I can't. I'm not going to run anybody over." The trucker protested.

Brand stared at the man, his mind racing.

"Fine. Get out of your seat, just keep a hand on the wheel until I can grab it."

"Are you crazy. We'll hit the ditch."

"When I tell you to." Brand repeated leaving no room for argument.

Brand watched the bikers crowd the truck.

"Move." Brand shouted jolting Worenko into action. Brand stood and squeezed in between the seats leaving an awkward path to the passenger's seat. The trucker hesitated, frozen with doubt. Brand grabbed a handful of Worenko's shirt and tugged. The truck driver glanced from the scene on the road up to Brand, his face white with fear. Reluctantly, he removed his feet from the petals; one hand gripping the steering wheel as he clumsily rose.

Brand pulled harder on Worenko's shirt speeding the exchange, brushing the driver past. The trucker stumbled in the cramped space, bumping Brand as he reached for the wheel. Brand's hands shot forward to gain control the truck. The powerful engine whined and lurched from lack of fuel before veering toward the ditch. The trailer swung into the opposing lane forcing bikers to scatter. Brand settled quickly into the driver's seat, one hand clutching the wheel, the other working the gearshift, fighting to straighten the rig.

The bikers crowded the front of the truck; brake lights flared as they reduced their speed. Brand didn't. The reinforced, chrome truck bumper nudged the rear wheel of the closest bike.

The front tire of the bike bounced up, and the rider flew off to the side of the road. The bikers in front revved their engines giving the larger vehicle more space.

The group of bikes behind the truck kept growing. A smaller group separated, lining up in the second lane, ready to pass the truck.

"How hard is it going to be to straighten this rig when it starts swinging?" Brand's attention split between the highway and the growing number of obstacles lining the lanes in front of the truck.

"A bit of work, but why, you've got it back under control? We're alright?"

Brand quickly cranked the steering right, and then just as quickly, to the left as he tapped the brakes. The trailer slowly started to pivot behind the tractor.

"You're crazy," The trucker screamed from the passengers seat. "You trying to get us killed."

Brand ignored Worenko's words. He cranked the wheel and tapped the break. The trailer skidded left; the sliding metal container forcing a group of bikes into the ditch and then, the trailer began a haphazard arc to the right. In the side mirror, Brand watched as the thirty or so thousand pounds of cargo in the trailer added to the momentum, cutting a swath through the passing bikes, the riders scrambling to get out of the path of the large rubber tires. .

The trailer swung back and forth several more times, each time jerking the tractor along with it. Brand fought it back under control. He risked a quick glance across the cab, the trucker's face drained of colour, and the man's fingers dug firmly into the soft cushioning of the truck's dash.

The Wolves Of Satan

The group of bikers kept growing making daredevil rushes past the truck, crowding the lanes in front of the 18-wheeler, the bikers attempting to slow the semi's speed. Brand pressed the accelerator. No time to be timid. Would the tires of the big rig hold up after rolling over the bikes? It looked like he was about to find out.

A glance at the road ahead revealed a wall of black lining the highway in the near distance. Shit. More bikes and this group didn't look like they were prepared to move. The stationary row of bikers numbered in the hundreds. The Apostles buzzing around the front of the truck noticed the waiting party too. They began clearing the lane ahead of the truck, falling in beside and behind.

Brand calculated the trucks forward momentum. He might crush a few of the metal bikes but there was no way possible the large tractor could make the entire path, so he started to down shift into lower gears slowing the revving engine.

As the distance closed, the line of waiting machines split in the middle, clearing a lane for the truck to pass. The lead biker stood out from the rest of the group. The man was huge. A smile of relief snuck onto Brand's face. The leader of the group loomed large. A Wolves of Satan patch adorned the man's vest. Roy Thundercloud sat leaning against his bike watching the pursuit as it drew near.

The Apostles dogging the truck slowed, nervous by what confronted them. Roy nodded as Brand continued down shifting, steering the long rig through the open gap, slowly rolling past the waiting line of Wolves.

Roy waited until the truck safely passed then signalled his men to close the gap. Brand ground through the lower gears bringing the loaded truck to a stop. He jumped from the cab and raced back toward the line of bikers. From several feet away, he watched Roy push off from his bike and walk to meet the pursuing Apostles. Roy's large hand lifted to his neck, his massive fingers grabbing a length of logging chain looped over his shoulders.

Roy began swinging the chain in the air as he moved toward the now cautiously approaching rival bike gang. The first Apostles to arrive straddled their bikes, creeping closer to the Wolves leader. When the leading two rival members came within striking distance, Roy let the end of the chain fly.

The helmet of one biker shattered under the chains force, the man falling to the pavement. The second biker leaned with his bike to avoid the bite of the steel links, sending his machine sliding sideways across the pavement. The bike stopped. The engine roared as the back tire spun freely in the air.

On Roy's cue, the Wolves advanced against their rivals. The riders at the front of the Apostles charge unable to avoid the onslaught, the members further back, slowed, quickly realizing they were out numbered, retreating away from the battle, waiting to fight another day.

Cars and trucks approaching the scene from both directions on the highway slowed, noticed the fight blocking the highway, turned around and sped away from the area.

Brand stood watching as the two gangs clashed in the middle of the four-lane highway, the Wolves relentless in the fight against the out-manned Apostles. Roy stood his ground in the centre of the road, the large man swinging the logging chain, knocking opposing bikers to the road.

The thrashing of the Apostles lasted minutes. Members that were able to move climbed on their bikes and drove back the way they had arrived; the others were left writhing where they fell. Roy left the dying fracas and walked over to Brand.

"War was in the making." He said. "I guess this will just hasten it a bit."

"Yeah…thanks for coming. How did you know where to look?"

"Like any good business, we have moles planted within the competition." Roy smiled. "I put the word out after we talked. I thought about your idea of visiting the warehouse and remember, I know how you operate. The fellows and me, well, we figured we'd go for a ride. Haven't seen this beautiful province in years."

The highway lay littered with smashed motorcycles and bleeding men. The battle was over. Roy ordered his men to mount up before the place started to smell like a pig barn. The cops couldn't be far behind. Roy chose a group of the men to ride with him and escort Brand and the truck back to Calgary, the other members he told to disperse.

"We're heading back in that direction anyway." He said.

"You got a family in town?" Brand asked when he and Worenko were back in the truck.

"Nope. The wife and I divorced year's back, something about me being on the road all the time and then, of course, my luck in the casinos. She took the kids and headed back to Ontario." He stated.

"Any other ties to hold you back?"

"No. None."

"Good." Brand continued. "When we get back to the city, call your insurance company and report your truck missing. Then I suggest you leave town. Drive east; a long way east. And buddy. You would be wise to avoid your house. Chances are good the Apostles or the Colombians will be looking for redemption. Don't become an easy target. Those boys are going to be pissed with their warehouse destroyed and this truckload of drugs about to disappear."

Chapter 23

James " the Manager" Cartwright stared at the Colombian. The Cartel underboss, as was his custom whenever he came to town, had taken Cartwright's chair behind the desk at the Millennium Casino's back office. The diminutive man acted like he was twelve feet tall and king of the world, secure in his roll as the liaison for the Cartel with his three armed bodyguards always close at hand.

Cartwright caught his reflection in a glass display case to the side of his desk. The skin stretched tight across his cheeks weather-beaten from years of riding his bike, around his eyes, wrinkles from the constant exposure to the sunlight. His once handsome face beginning to sag with age. Every day, the fight against middle age weight grew harder, the pounds slowly adding.

How long can a person continue this lifestyle was a question that lingered in his thoughts more and more each day? Nearing the age of fifty, he was a little on the old side of the game. Younger and tougher men rose through the ranks. Their actions and thinly veiled contempt a daily challenge to his leadership. Will I live long enough to ride off into the sunset, he wondered, or die like so many others in this cutthroat business.

Cartwright considered himself as tough as they come, but even he was paled by the savageness of the Colombian Cartel. The Manager set his conscious aside while ordering the punishment or deaths of others, a gene he believed these Colombian's were born without.

On his rise to the top of the Apostles criminal organization, he'd undertaken crimes of unspeakable nature and continued to show little mercy for others that forsaken his rules. A hard line to maintain but needed to rule without question knowing full well that one simple moment of weakness shown and his life would end in the rugged mountain wilderness in the foothills of the Rockies west of the city limits. His body left to the ravages of the wild animals to pick his carcass clean. Would that be where his legacy died?

This city veered from the stereotypical scene of Hollywood movies. The mighty Bow River flowing through the centre of town was too shallow to dispose of bodies. Instead, a short distance away was a vast mountain playground where he, himself, had vanquished several unlucky victims, their bodies never recovered.

The way the short Colombian leered, the lack of respect the man showed toward others made Cartwright wonder how long his services would be needed? With the Apostles help the Colombians had their hand in the local market. How long until they turned the tables and decided to eliminate their partners.

Narrowing his eyes, the Manager steeled his nerves and turned away from his reflection. Until that time came he still ran the city, and he would act accordingly. A deep, quiet sigh left his lips as he turned to face his business partner.

The meeting with the Colombian underboss to discuss the future expansion of their burgeoning enterprise from the west side of town and into Wolves territory on the east side, a golden opportunity now attainable with the money and product streaming into the city with his partners. A business position which both the Apostles and the Colombian's planned to exploit to grow their market share in the lucrative drug business.

Cartwright's cell phone rang interrupting the discussion. Listening to the caller, Cartwright waited before asking questions, the fingers holding the phone squeezing the plastic frame tight. His other hand balled tightly, fingernails digging into the soft flesh of his palm as he fought down the anger rising through his system.

"The whole damn warehouse is gone? How the hell did this happen?" He breathed deeply, struggling to maintain his composure.

"Let me see if I understand. The mule I sent to pick up the product beat your men and burned down the warehouse?" He asked incredulously. "The man's a loser, he can barely stand upright, so how in the world is this possible? One man slips past all of you and blows up the damn building?" Irritability crept into the Manager's tone. He paused, his anger rising.

"What!" "No. I only sent one guy," he shouted back into the phone. "I have no idea who this other guy could be. What did he look like?" The unmistakable sound of wailing sirens bleated across the phone line. The Latino manager of the now destroyed warehouse informed Cartwright of a call already dispatched to the boys at the Apostles clubhouse in Castlegar and the orders for the capture of the truck, and the death of the men responsible.

"I'll take care of it from here," Cartwright told the caller and ended the call. He remained silent, his mind reeling. The skin on his arms stood with the awareness of the underboss glaring in his direction waiting for answers. He processed the implications of the information before relaying the negative news to his visitor.

"That was Diego...the warehouse came under attack. He took a bullet, and our building, it's destroyed..." The Manager looked at the wall behind his desk, repeating the phone conversation verbatim.

"And your men. Have they caught the fuckers who did this, Parcero?" Quintin Rojas, the underboss asked, using the

Colombian slang word for partner, his face emotionless. "I want those men alive...I will deal with them," Rojas said staunching any argument. James Cartwright typed away at the keys of his cell phone, the Colombian's instructions relayed. The two men dropped the unwanted interruption and resumed discussing the expansion into the Wolves side of the city.

"I have met with big Roy, the leader of the Wolves, but he refuses to partner, so I propose we put Satan's Wolves out of business once and for all...I just hope the boys are up to it." He snapped, his anger still visible from the bad news. The underboss stressed the importance of the forthcoming hostile takeover along with delivering a promise to send reinforcements when the Apostles moved against their rivals.

A couple of hours later, the meeting interrupted again by Cartwright's phone. The Manager's face drained of blood as he listened to the caller's report. He hung up the phone and sat motionless until Rojas broke his reverie.

"You don't look well, Parcero?" The Colombian stated, urging the gang leader to talk.

"Our men failed to retrieve the truck and our shipment. It seems the boys ran into Thundercloud's men outside of Cranbrook." Cartwright said slamming his phone onto the desk.

"Maybe we are backing the wrong gang...I am beginning to wonder if the misfits under your leadership are man enough for the task." The underboss retorted. Wounded by the lack of faith the Colombian showed, Cartwright busied himself typing a text message. '**All eyes be on the lookout for our stolen shipment.**' Several minutes had passed before a reply pinged on his phone.

'**Have the truck and Wolves in sight. Following east on Highway 3**.' Came the response.

James Cartwright stared at the Colombian, the sting of the man's words and the underlying threat palpable. He glanced at the phone in his hand, checked to make sure it still worked and then placed a call to the Apostles clubhouse. When Bakker answered, Cartwright spoke loudly and angrily belting out new orders to counteract the Wolves' actions; he had to regain control over the situation fast. A means of saving face and preventing the Colombians from losing faith in his abilities as a leader which could prove very hazardous to his health.

"Don, round up the men. We've got a problem, and you need to move now. Right now." Cartwright explained about the stolen shipment of drugs and the destruction of the warehouse. "Roundup every available man. Tell them to be ready to ride. When the guys are ready, call me back. I'll have the route the shipment is taking."

Ending the call, the Manager then dialled a number associated with the text from the biker following the stolen shipment.

"What happened?" Cartwright quizzed his man. The biker told of the battle on the highway west of Cranbrook and how he alone was tracking the shipment of stolen drugs, along with the Wolves biker escort as they drove east on Highway 3 toward the Alberta border.

"Keep me updated on the route those bastards are taking," Cartwright barked into the phone. "I want to know their every move and which highway they use in returning to the city." He paced the office. The conversation of the take over was forgotten while he fumed about his men's failure to recapture his shipment of drugs.

Quintin Rojas sat behind the desk and watched the leader of the Apostles pace back and forth. Cartwright ignored the Colombian, making several calls to his men, leaving little room for doubt as to what he expected. A large contingent of bikers from Calgary hustled to their bikes and headed for the southwest corner of the province anxious to intercept the stolen shipment and the Wolves of Satan.

When he completed his calls, the Colombian broached another serious problem. "What happened to the phone? Have your men located it yet?" Rojas asked.

"I had a cop at the house before the smoke from the guns cleared," Cartwright told the underboss. "My man retrieved all the phones at the scene." He took another long breath. Locking eyes with the Colombian perched behind his desk; his mind briefly flitted over the thought of how his world was spinning out of control. Be strong; he steadied himself. "None of the cell phones contained the video. I think the old man either hid the phone and or was bluffing. My guys have checked other locations connected to the three at the house, but so far we've come up empty."

"Do you think the old man was…how do you say… jerking our chain, perhaps?" Rojas asked.

"If he was, the old boy has got mega-sized gonads," Cartwright answered, glad for the change of topic even if it shed light on another problem he had yet to resolve.

"I don't think I need to remind you of the importance of getting our hands on that phone." Then Rojas started to laugh.

"What the hell is so funny?" Cartwright asked, the laughter grating on his already dour mood.

"The manager…isn't that what your men call you. Hell, if you worked for me at a Wal-Mart, I'd have to fire you." Rojas' laughter stopped, his eyes narrowed. "If this situation continues, Parcero, being fired will be the least of your worries, comprender."

Chapter 24

Brand worked the pedals and gear shifter slowing the truck as the caravan rolled through the Crowsnest Pass. He idled through Coleman then Blairmore, past the Franks slide and across Bellevue before pulling into a rest stop on the side of the highway. He climbed out of the truck and stretched. His joints sore from the long drive and built up tension. He turned his head at the roar of bikes. Roy, leading his men, followed Brand's lead and signalled off the highway following the semi.

Leaning against the side of the truck Brand fished in his pocket for a cigarette, cupped his hands to his face, blocking the southwest wind from blowing out the lighter's small flame, and waited for Roy to walk over.

"What are you planning on doing with the truck?" Roy asked.

"Calgary is a big city. It covers lots of ground. Probably hide it among a few truck stops. Out in the open." Brand tossed out the idea. Now, confronted with the reality, he required a solution. The destruction of the warehouse and highjacking of the drug shipment was an audible, a last minute decision. Originally, the trip west was to gather information, find flaws to exploit against the Apostles. The anger that took hold once he was standing in front of the biker's supply warehouse changed all that.

Now, faced with the scenario, he turned his thoughts to deal with the problem.

"Any suggestions?" Brand asked, knowing full well that the Wolves had locations scattered around the city for hiding vehicles appropriated in their line of business. Roy thought about his answer before replying. The tractor-trailer unit was a lot bigger than the average automobiles they came across.

"There's a barn off Highway 2, comes in handy every now and again. Should fit this rig." Roy described the place and gave Brand directions.

"Sorry you had to get involved," Brand apologized. Another unfortunate circumstance, he realized, brought on by his rash decision and the burning need to exact revenge against the men who shot his friends. The situation was quickly growing out of hand, and now, he brought his brother and the Wolves into a battle they had not asked for. He had to put a stop to this before more people ended up on the wrong side of a shovel.

Roy scuffed the gravel with his feet. "A war for the city was imminent. The Manager and his Colombian brethren have already pushed into our territory. Might as well give them the finger and declare our intentions." Roy offered.

*****

The lone Apostle biker following the truck lost site of the caravan. The group in front crested a large hill blocking his view. He had been traveling close to a mile behind to avoid being detected. Driving through Bellevue, tourists driving rented R.V's cut him off and slowed his progress. The crawling motor homes forced him to fall farther behind and to lose sight of the Wolves and the stolen shipment.

Panicking, he snuck past the slow moving vehicles, riding the shoulder of the pavement and raced up the steep incline. He crested the long hill, his sight focused on the road far in the distance. Too late he noticed the bikes and truck pulled off on the side of the highway. The lone biker realized there was nothing he could do to avoid discovery. With no choice remaining, he revved the bike's engine and hurled down the highway.

A yell of recognition rose above the conversations in the rest area. One of the men happened to be looking toward the highway as the loud rumble of the revved engine from the single Apostles bike roared past. The colours of the biker, he spotted immediately and ran over to where the brothers stood. The two men turned their heads and watched, the back of the rival gang member shrinking in the growing distance.

"Take a couple of the boys, and hunt that bastard down. "Roy yelled to his men. "Don't need our moves telegraphed." His words spread among the resting riders. Excited talk and the rumble of exhaust pipes from igniting engines tore through the afternoon air. Members of the Wolves straddled their bikes. Twisted throttles set the bikes rolling, and gravel flying as the powerful machines thundered onto the highway.

"Probably on our trail since the attack." Roy thought out loud. "There is going to be hell to pay if he's reporting our movements back to his boss. I imagine every Apostles wanna-be in the lower part of the province must be racing in our direction by now." He added. "We better get moving."

"Hang on a minute." Brand interrupted. "Give your boys a chance. See if they can catch up with him. If they do, tell them to bring him back here." He reasoned. "Besides, if the Apostles are heading this way for a showdown...this place is as good as any to deal with them."

The Wolves Of Satan

20 minutes later Roy's phone rang. His men had run the opposing biker off the road and were waiting for further instructions. He cut short his initial response, thinking about Brand's request.

"Drag the man and his bike back here," Roy conceded.

Brand talked to Roy about the difficulties that would arise from the Wolves aid in helping him avoid the Apostles attempts at reclaiming the drug shipment. The supper hour had passed; the sun was starting its descent toward dusk. The two men sat atop a wooden picnic table, cold beers in their hands bought from the local bar a few kilometres back in the Pass.

Four bikes slipped off the highway and rolled into the rest stop. A stranger wearing Apostle colours boxed in the middle of the returning group. The man's face stern, indifferent, but a close glance displayed signs of concern. The man looked slowly around his enemies then dropped his eyes to the ground.

"What are your plans now brother." Roy looked from Brand to the captured biker. "This little *ominiw*, pigeon, has probably burned up the phone lines informing his Colombian bosses."

"I'm not sure. I suppose we could ask the man, see what their plans are…if he knows anything."

The tractor-trailer unit sat parallel to the highway, blocking the view of the evening traffic. Brand sat idle watching Roy's men escort the rival biker behind the semi and out of view. Crushing out his half smoked cigarette in the parking lot gravel, he pushed away from the bench and with his foster brother in tow walked around the trailer to talk to the man.

Two of Roy's gang stood beside the rival biker, the man on his knees in the gravel.

"Nice evening for a ride." Brand said to the Apostles. "You got a name kid?" Brand asked. The man glared back up at him,

177

his lips clamped tight. Looking over the scrawny young biker kneeling on the ground, Brand waited for a few seconds for the man to answer. When no response was forthcoming, he spoke again.

"This is the part where I say this is going to hurt me more than it's going to hurt you...but I would just be lying to you." He finished, searched the biker until he found the man's phone and then nodded to the bikers standing guard.

"Do what you got to do." He said and stepped back giving the small group some room.

The two Wolves took to the task enthusiastically. Other members of the group drifted toward the conflict joining Brand and Roy. The tired biker's egging on the one sided assault. At one point, the Apostles pleaded for the men to stop, promising he would answer any question they had. Roy's men looked at Roy and then Brand. Brand shook his head declining the wounded man's pleas. He motioned for Roy's men to continue.

"Reinforce with him what will happen if he tries to bullshit us." Brand's thoughts flashed back a few days to the shooting of his friends; this man was getting off lucky with only a severe beating Brand reasoned. "Leave him the use of one hand; I might need him to make a call before we leave." Brand stood back and lit a cigarette, slowly smoking while he watched the beating continue before he raised his hand to stop the assault. Bending at the knees, he squatted beside the trembling, bleeding man.

"See those falls behind us." Brand pointed to the Lumbreck falls south of the roadside rest area. "The water at the bottom swirls and is deep enough that no one will discover your dead body for a hell of a long time. Thought you might want that information if you plan on being a hero." Brand drew lines in the gravel as he waited for the reality of his words to sink in.

"What have you reported back? What is your Manager planning on doing about this high jacked shipment?" He asked.

The beaten man looked up at Brand, his face bruised and bleeding. The man swallowed, raised himself up onto his elbow and told Brand about his phone calls to the Apostles boss.

"My instructions are to follow you guys and call it in when the truck turns north toward the city. The Manager will have a group of riders waiting and ready to leave Calgary, driving south to intercept all of you." The man swung his arm around to include the group of bikers.

"Where. Where are the Managers men supposed to meet us?" Brand implored.

"I was told to report on your route back, let them know which roads you take." The biker answered avoiding Brand's eyes.

"Good. We shouldn't keep you from doing your duty then, should we." Brand replied as he stood up and looked at Roy, an idea forming in his head. He smiled upon seeing the look of confusion displayed on his brother's face.

Brand put a hand on Roy's arm and led him away from the crowd. He thought out loud as the idea morphed into a workable plan.

Chapter 25

Chad Worenko worked the gears of the big rig. The caravan began its journey toward Calgary. The 18-wheeler climbed from the roadside turnout and lumbered onto highway 3. A fleet of motorcycles flanked the truck and trailer. Brand traded his seat inside the cab for the captured Apostles' bike and rode ahead with Roy by his side. The captive biker traveled locked in the trailer, bound to a pallet of produce.

James Cartwright paced the floor in his Millennium office, a generous amount of rye sloshed in the glass clutched in his fingers. The Manager walked off his tension, his mind racing ahead to the forthcoming showdown between the rival bike gangs. Bakker left the city with fifty plus hardened Apostles riders. But, would that be enough to crush Roy and his men.

The call he received a little under an hour ago placed the truck and the stolen shipment of drugs at the intersection of Highway 22x. A route that traveled from the Crowsnest and ventured north toward the city. The two-lane road, less popular than Highways 3 or 2, rolled over hills along the edge of the Rocky Mountains, cutting through several small communities south of Calgary.

The Manager went from one call, the update from his lone scout to ordering big Don Bakker to hasten his exit from the city. Time was short and the miles, long. The idea was to ambush the Wolves among the tree covered hills south of the town of Longview, the long hills forcing the tractor-trailer unit to climb in lower gears. Other than a few tourists this time of

The Wolves Of Satan

year the highway would be deserted, the perfect place to end this conflict, far away from the prying eyes of law enforcement.

The large contingent of bikers roared down the highway. Motorists encountering the swath of motorbikes hurtling over the asphalt smartly pulled to the side of the road and let the pack pass. With car doors locked, families waited nervously as the cacophony of bikes and the leather clad bikers riding the metal two wheelers roared past allowing the gang to cruise unimpeded as they rushed to greet the Wolves of Satan.

Sitting astride the motorbike, the wind battering his t-shirt and whistling past his helmet, Brand dwelled on the captured biker's words to his boss. Was the man convincing in the lies he was forced to tell? A lot depended on luck for Brand's impromptu plan to have any chance of success. His thoughts swung between hope and forming an alternate course of action should the ruse fail. The biker's misinformation to his boss included a false route back to the city.

When signs of High River lit the horizon, Brand blew out a sigh of relief. The short distance to Roy's property consisted of open country mostly but included less chance of being surprised or attacked.

Dusk settled over the prairie landscape when the caravan left the paved highway for the last few kilometres of gravel road. Dust lifted into the air blanking out the darkening countryside. The convoy rolled through a bush littered gate and onto an abandoned acreage. A deserted farmhouse stood silhouetted in the weed filled yard against the moonlight. Roy led the procession on a flattened grass path past the decaying building to a rusted, oversized building hidden at the back of the acreage.

The night air roared with the sounds of powerful engines. A queue of bikes lined the grass path behind Chad Worenko and the tractor-trailer unit while the massive doors on the metal building slid open. Roy motioned the truck inside and then followed. When every machine rolled onto the concrete floor, the doors closed, blocking out the night.

Brand removed his helmet, and from the seat of the bike he looked around the brightly lit interior. Leather vested men spread across catwalks ringing the upper level of the building. Apostles ready to battle, hardened men unafraid of conflict standing with assault rifles covering the lower floor.

Brand stepped from the bike and worked the stiffness from his legs and arms before crossing to Roy. "You know there is going to be hell to pay for today's antics. Are you sure you want me and this truck around?"

Roy smiled and shrugged. "Things were happening before you got involved. Shit was already starting to bubble up; a little stirring to make it boil over is irrelevant. Better we begin the dance on our terms as opposed to theirs." He said.

The opening of the doors at the back of the trailer caught Brand's attention. Two men climbed up and in the darkness deep within the long trailer. Minutes passed before the same men walked to the edge of the trailer, the blindfolded Apostles struggling between the two. Aiding the prisoner to the concrete floor the men forced the captive the short distance to where their boss stood.

"Drive him and his bike to the outskirts near the ski hill and leave him bound in a ditch. His buddies will stumble across him in the daylight." Roy instructed the men.

"What are you going to do now?" Brand asked.

Roy glanced over the inside of the building; he met the eyes of his men. The tired bikers waited silently for their boss's response.

"The next move is up to the Manager, I guess. I'll wait and see how he responds. I don't think it will be long before we know how this is going to play out." "How about you?" his eyes returned to Brand.

"The old guide, Jerry, Susan's father. I visited him at the hospital yesterday. We had a good conversation. Apparently he had a phone containing incriminating video of the Cartel's business. Meetings he secretly recorded." Brand found his thoughts shifting from the current problems of the stolen drugs to the search that lay ahead. "Problem is, Jerry, misplaced the phone. Lost it a bar he'd been drinking at or so he thinks. If I can locate the videos before the Apostles get their hands on it." Brand shrugged at the long shot. "Who knows?

"Jerry's known to be full of shit, but if he's telling the truth, the video would go a long way in bringing down the Apostles and the Cartel right along side them. Give the cops some solid evidence. That way, this shit goes away." Brand paused; the memories stirred the rage seeping through his body once again. "At least the men who ordered the shooting of my friends won't go unpunished."

"The Manager will find out who you are. Between his boys and the Colombians, you are going to have a lot of men gunning for you." A look of concern grew on Roy's face as he thought about Brand's safety. "You can hang out here for a while. Let things cool."

Brand put his hand on his brother's shoulder. "I'll keep that in mind. I need a ride to my truck. It's a hell of a walk from here, and it has been a long day." Brand noticed the truck driver standing to the side. "Bring one of your boys along to drive

Chad's truck back here, would you. He won't be safe in the city." Brand began to walk away then stopped abruptly. " Oh, I need one more favour." The two men left and walked into a small room at the side of the building. Brand remembered his promise to help the trucker disappear and needed Roy's assistance.

When Brand returned, the gathering at the centre of the Quonset began breaking up, the riders mingling with the guards in the Quonset or climbing on their bikes and leaving the property. Brand wandered over to the trucker, his hand outstretched. "You took a big risk today. Thanks." In Brand's hand, a thickly folded wad of dollar bills.

"One of Roy's guys will drive your pick-up back here within the hour. Don't linger and don't look back. And no matter how far you put this province behind you, don't talk about what happened today. The Apostles have chapters across the country. Okay."

Chad Worenko nodded his understanding. "Yeah. Thanks," he said holding the cash up.

Brand looked past the trucker at the parked semi. "It's far less than what your truck is worth. Maybe when this trouble ends, I can get it back to you."

"Don't worry. The bank owns it more than I do. But I appreciate the offer."

*****

Quintin Rojas had returned to the Manager's Casino office when Cartwright received the call about the truck and the

Wolves bikers and how the convoy never showed. Cartwright sat silent, digesting the news. Rojas watched with mild interest for a brief moment before uttering words dripping with a lack of respect for the other man, asked the question he already knew the answer to.

"They slipped past your men?" He uttered out loud, his mouth forming into a deadly grin while the Apostles leader fumbled for an answer. All Cartwright could do was nod.

The Colombian stood and walked over to the lone window in the office and gazed at the lit parking lot several floors below, a scattering of patron's vehicles remained at this early hour. Rojas thought over the situation before turning his attention back to the Manager.

"Do you know this guy that destroyed the warehouse and stole our drugs?"

"The trucker?"

"No. The asshole riding with the trucker?" The Colombian replied with more than a little annoyance.

"Not yet. Diego sent a picture from the security cameras. I've forwarded the file to a contact in the police department. We will know soon enough."

"What about the big Indian running the Wolves. How can we get to him?"

"Won't be easy. We don't have enough men to confront him." Cartwright replied. His thoughts currently mired in shame and defeat from the past few hours lifted with the talk of the looming war against his cross-town rivals.

"I'll bring in extra manpower. You tell me what you need to accomplish this feat. You concentrate on finding the identity of the asshole who stole our shipment." Rojas paused. "If these men want to play with fire, then we need to increase the size of the flames, Parcero. Don't you think?"

Chapter 26

Business at the Cat's Eye lounge was busy for a Wednesday night. The supper hour came and went, and the exotic dancers were grinding for dollars on the centre stage. Of the men who frequented the nightclub and filled the tables enjoying the show, most were several drinks past the legal limit to drive.

Wednesday night, the wings were cheap and the beer cold from the tap. The combination pulled in a decent amount of business on an otherwise slow weeknight. The Cat's Eye lounge, located in the northeast part of town, blended in among other one-story businesses in a smattering of malls that made up the local areas retail section.

While the dancers and patrons in the main part of the club gave the place an air of legitimacy, in the back rooms, a different type of business took place. One that the cops suspected, hell, they full on knew about, but for various reasons they never raided. One designated room served as a distribution centre for illegal narcotics. People in the know made weekly or nightly treks to the back room, depending on their drug of choice. A knowing knock, the right password and a steady exchange of cash took place there every night of the week.

A small group of Wolves alumni operated from this back room. One of many such businesses scattered over the east side of the city, and under the Wolves control. It was a type of Wolves retirement plan, easy money, easy women, and a reward of easy living after years of dedicated service to the pack.

Shortly before midnight, five well-dressed, dark haired, bronze skinned men entered the bar, and sat at a back table ordering drinks and enjoying the scenery on the stage. The group took advantage of the cheap hot wings, washing away the lingering burn of the hot sauce with glasses of dark rum, quietly idling away the passing evening.

Around one in the morning, two of the well-dressed men dabbed their faces clean of the sauce from the wings and crossed the floor to the washroom at the back of the building. From this position they were only one locked door away from the room containing the illicit drug trade. A lone biker in Wolves leathers sat guarding the locked door, his gun hidden, his fingers occupied, busy pressing keys on a cell phone.

As the two men ventured to the washroom, a third man from the table walked the opposite direction, passing tables littered with empty beer glasses and paused at entrance to the strip joint, the man, stationing himself just inside the door. The last two at the table finished the plate of wings before leaving their chairs and sauntering to opposing sides of the small club.

The first pair stopped inside the washroom door and removed powerful automatic pistols from under their coats. A nod to each other signalled their readiness, and one of the men backed out of the washroom door, blocking the guard's view of the gun.

The biker sitting in the chair noticed the man loitering and looked up from his phone.

"Hey, buddy. Get a move on," the biker warned, stashing his phone in a back pocket. The man blocking the bathroom door stepped aside, his partner filled the vacant space and fired three quick bursts into the guard. The pair stepped over the fallen guard, made short work of the locked door, and used the automatic weapons to rapidly send a searching fire into the room.

The Wolves Of Satan

At the sound of the gunfire, the accompanying men spread through the lounge, pulled out matching guns and sprayed rounds of bullets indiscriminately at the patrons and dancers. Screams of terror and pain flowed above the canned dance music.

The assault lasted several minutes. The Wolves associates, running the drug operation out of the room deep in the back of the building, grabbed for their guns. The bikers put up a valiant but short-lived fight before they dropped like the their fellow members in the front of the club. One of the Wolves, hidden behind a thick, wooden desk, pushed the buttons on his phone in a panic. The call to Roy Thundercloud was cut short when another series of bullets found the hidden man and ended the conversation.

The two members of the assault team carefully stepped around the fallen bikers gathering handfuls of cash, reefs of paper, and bundles of drugs into a pile before setting a flame to the stack. Satisfied the fire would burn, the men moved back toward the front of the club. There they reunited with their partners, the five men stacking tables and chairs and starting a second fire.

Just over an hour had passed since they had entered the Cat's Eye Lounge. The five men exited through the front doors. Careful to sidestep past the bouncer they shot on the way in, they climbed into waiting cars, and casually drove away from the scene.

Roy Thundercloud swore repeatedly. The walls of the room appeared to close in on him. In every direction, men sat watching his mood darken, concern growing on their faces. He had no clear outlet to release the rage building in his massive body. Anger from the attack and anguish at the loss of lives gripped his body, threatening to paralyze his thoughts and movements.

Roy fought past the haze of red blocking his vision; his large fingers jabbed punishingly at the small buttons on the phone pad. The attack was not the first one this night.

"How in the hell…" He said to no one in particular, letting the sentence die off. He paced in a tight circle; his leather boot slammed into a footstool that dared stand in his way. Realistically, he prepared for signs of retaliation from the Apostles but obviously, the brutality the Colombians brought to the fight ranged well above his line of possibilities.

Several of his men were either killed or injured, and this was the second nightclub that had fallen this night. Calls went out to all Wolves gang members to flood the streets. Extra firepower rode to the more vulnerable establishments. The cowardly ambushes would meet return fire.

Struggling for a calmer demeanour, Roy clutched his phone reissuing warnings to his men stationed at the clubs various establishments. Operations he was certain were well known to the Apostles. Other businesses, ones operated on a different level, he reasoned would escape this type of treatment, or so he hoped.

Calls rang throughout the early hours, men reporting on the damage sustained in the early morning attacks, others on the watch for suspicious activities. Scouts began tracking the Apostles and searching the streets for the cars of Colombians. By the time the calls quieted, the sun had begun its climb, lighting the eastern horizon. Roy grabbed a bottle of his favourite tequila and took several long pulls to calm the burning rage pumping through his veins.

The Wolves Of Satan

The Apostles fired the first shots of the turf war, and he needed to re-evaluate the addition of the Colombians. Depending on the number of Cartel men added to bolster the Apostles, he began to think of bringing in reinforcements. Tonight's attacks stung, but he held the upper hand in manpower, but how persistent were his enemies. How long could his men fend off the attack until his forces were worn down.

Roy stood staring at a blank wall; in his mind's eye he foresaw a bleak future. With the Cartel helping his rivals, this war had the makings to tear the city apart while one gang destroyed the other.

Chapter 27

Detective Frank Walgreen awoke in the middle of the night. The cursed bleating of his cell phone broke into his troubled sleep. The device rattled on a table next to the couch the detective lay after falling into a drunken stupor the evening before. To add to his troubled sleep, the irate voice of the Manager raged across the line.

"I'm texting a picture to you," the Manager roared dispensing of all pleasantries. "The picture is of the man responsible for the destruction of our warehouse near Castlegar."

"I need you to find out who this man is. I want his name and all the information you can dig up!" The Manager bellowed. Walgreen waited until the photo appeared on his phone and stared at the picture. He was surprised to recognize the man, even with a ball cap covering a portion of the perpetrator's face, but held off telling the Manager. Instead, Walgreen agreed to match the face with a name and call back once the identity was confirmed.

"I'll get on it in a couple of hours. The minute I clock in at the precinct," Walgreen reassured the Manager. "If I show up before my shift, too many questions will be asked."

James Cartwright spewed a few curses over the phone and then abruptly ended the call. Walgreen stared at the silent clump of plastic in his hand and without turning on the apartment lights, strode to the kitchen and poured a couple ounces of vodka into a glass. If gambling wasn't a bad enough vice, he had taken to drinking himself to sleep, his conscious consumed with the threat of exposure that hung over like a threatening cloud. His tension brought on by the vast amount of debt owed to the damn bikers and their casino.

His will to live diminished daily as he was forced to do errands for the outlaw bikers under thinly veiled threats of being turned in for the illegal actions he had undertaken on their behalf. Coming clean to anyone who could help him out of the situation only ensured the remaining years of his life rotting in jail cell or worse, a slow and painful death by the same outlaw gang for betrayal.

Sitting in the dark, he slowly nursed the vodka as he tried to get his alcohol-numbed brain to make some sense of this current predicament. He decided to spend a few hours at his desk at work before going to the Apostles clubhouse and surrendering the name of the man the Manager asked for. By five in the morning, he found the ambition to shower and then searched through a pile of clothes spread across the bedroom floor trying to find his cleanest, least wrinkled suit.

His partner, Detective O'Brien was picking him up again this morning. Walgreens piece of shit Chevy was broken down, and with no extra money to fix it; O'Brien had kindly offered to drive him to the precinct in his SUV. O'Brien even allowed Walgreen to borrow the Toyota when he had personal errands to run. He knew that O'Brien wouldn't be too pleased if he were aware that some of those errands involved driving to an outlaw bike gang's clubhouse on occasion.

Walgreen's life had gotten so shitty lately that even the booze was starting to have little effect in drowning out the unpleasant memories of day-to-day life.

"You look like shit," O'Brien said by way of greeting as Walgreen climbed into the passenger side of his partner's SUV.

"Been a long night" Walgreen scowled at his partner hoping to put an end to another of O'Brien's sermons. Walgreen rode the remainder of the way to the station in silence wrapped up in his thoughts of how life became so unfair.

At the station, Walgreen grabbed a coffee on his way to his desk, fired up his computer and sat staring at the screen. He searched for all the information on Brand Coldstream the net had to offer. Finding very little, he put his password in and searched through police network. Neither place had any relevant information on the guy. After several tries and numerous avenues of checking were exhausted, he looked across his desk at O'Brien.

"Can I borrow your car, I want to head to a garage and see if I can get a price to fix that piece of crap I'm driving." He lied.

"You can book out an unmarked off the lot you know."

"Yeah. I don't like driving one when I'm on personal business. You know that." He further lied. The thought of being discovered at the Apostles clubhouse with an unmarked car was something even he wouldn't risk.

O'Brien tossed him the keys as he stood up and grabbed his jacket off the back of his chair. He nodded to O'Brien as he made his way out of the precinct building.

"This is the same guy who shot the Cartel's men at the house." The manager grilled the detective as he stood in front of the desk. The Manager never offered him a chair. "Why didn't you tell me that this morning when I sent you the picture?" Cartwright said as he glowered at the dishevelled detective.

"I see a lot of faces in my line of work. I can't be expected to remember them all." The detective lied again. It seemed like all he did these days was lie. He wasn't even sure if he could remember how the truth went anymore.

"Do you still have that gun you found at the house?" The Manager asked.

"Yeah." He answered hesitantly not liking where he saw this conversation heading. "I'm sure and the hell not going to kill this guy if that's what you're getting at." He added beating the Manager to any thoughts of the sort.

"No. That's not what I was thinking, but leave it with me. I might use it to teach this guy a lesson." Pausing, the Manager flipped through some papers on his desk then turned his gaze back to the detective. "What I need you to do is arrange a meeting with this guy. See if he has any information that could hurt us. He doesn't have any idea about our...association. I mean, you, working with us. Does he?"

"I doubt it." Walgreen blurted out.

"Good. Tell this, Coldstream, that you have info about the shooting at his house then. That should be believable. Make something up, just get him to meet with you.

What did you say this guy does? He's a fishing guide, is that right?" The Manager stopped in his train of thought. His mind reeled back over the past day and the amount of trouble the fisherman caused. "His actions seem out of place for somebody who wields a fishing rod." The Manager scowled at his words. "Anyways, pump him for information with out him getting wise."

"Sure." Walgreen agreed and motioned to leave. The manager stopped him before he exited the room.

"I want to know when and where you're planning to talk to him." The Manager said leaving no room for disagreement. Detective Walgreen wondered at the Managers request. Did he plan to have Coldstream killed while the two met?

"I'll let you know when we're I've got a place set," Walgreen promised then added. "Have one of your men meet me at my house in a bit, and I'll pass along the gun."

Brand's cell rang. He looked at the number before answering. Not recognizing the number, he connected the call and waited. A few seconds passed before he heard Detective Walgreen's voice.

"Coldstream, Detective Walgreen." Walgreen sat behind the wheel of his partner's SUV outside the biker clubhouse.

"How can I help you, detective?" Brand asked.

"Can we meet?" Walgreen asked. "I've got some background on the men who shot up your house." Walgreen ad-libbed. His alcohol dulled brain unable to conjure up a better reason for the two to meet. The detective evaded Brand's searching questions and quickly searched his muddled brain for a suitable location to rendezvous.

"The hotel in the strip mall off of Deerfoot and Heritage. There's that breakfast joint behind the sports club. Jim's or Harry's…whatever the hell the name of the place is. Say, later this afternoon. Does that work for you?'"

"Yeah. I know which one you're talking about." Brand replied.

"Meet me in the parking lot adjacent to the hotel. I'd like to talk in private before we go inside and eat."

Reluctantly, Brand agreed. Suspicions entered his mind. He already figured that either Walgreen or O'Brien or even both were working with the rogue gang of bikers. Usually, cops liked the sanction of the police station to conduct queries, not at some obscure destination, definitely not parking lots.

Chapter 28

With the meeting set for the afternoon, Brand turned his attention to Jerry's missing cell phone. The palm-sized device would be difficult to locate, and the possibilities of finding it would require a lot more luck than good detective work. First, he wanted to stop at the hospital and talk to Jerry. See if the old-timer had remembered any other details about the phones possible location. Maybe narrow down the search area for Brand.

Stepping out of the elevator, Brand noticed a bustle of activity in front of his friend's room. Police officers stood at the curtained entrance talking to the hospital staff. At the nursing station, Brand confronted a nurse, his curiosity mixing with a rising tide of unease settling in his gut.

"Can I help you," the nurse asked, her eyes traveling between the charts in her hands and Brand, a look of annoyance reflecting off her face at the intrusion.

"The patient in that room," Brand pointed to the cluster of cops outside the curtained wall. "Jerry Kartman. Is he alright?" Brand asked.

"Mr. Kartman is gone," the nurse replied, anxiety mixed with a tinge of concern underlined her words. "When the attendant checked on him this morning, the bed was empty." She explained.

"Did the doctors release him?" Brand inquired. "The other day when I visited he looked to be in rough shape still."

"His clothes and his items are still in the room." The nurse set her charts down and dug through the second stack of files lying on the raised counter. She pulled out a file and quickly skimmed the pages. "Mr. Kartman had only shown signs of recovering from his coma. The doctor's report states that Mr. Kartman remains weak and disoriented, so it seems unlikely that he'd have the ability to leave under his own power." She paused, glanced toward the police officers wondering if she should be divulging this information.

She turned her gaze back to Brand and continued in a confidential voice. "We are checking the hospital and the grounds. He may have wandered off, but that seems very doubtful. Everyone we can spare has been searching since morning. We finally agreed to bring the police in, and one of their detectives appears to be particularly interested in Mr. Kartman." She confided to Brand. Before he had a chance to ask the nurse which detective showed the interest, another nurse interrupted their conversation.

Brand left the station walking up to the crowd gathered outside Jerry's room. A police officer watched as he approached. The officer left the group and asked Brand's name and purpose at the room before abruptly telling him to leave.

Brand returned the nursing station. His mind raced with possibilities of Jerry's disappearance while he watched the police interrogate the hospital staff. Could Jerry possibly have wandered away from his room in his condition or...more worrying thoughts began troubling Brand's mind? If the Cartel knew about the missing phone, would they have the balls to snatch Jerry from his hospital room?

From the corner of his vision, a movement from across the hall caught Brand's attention. He recognized Detective O'Brien at the same time the detective spotted him. Veering away from the room, the detective changed course and stopped beside Brand.

Brand began to ask about his missing friend when the detective cut him off, O'Brien ignoring Brand's questions.

"Time to come clean Coldstream. This shit you and your buddies have dug into is starting to pile up. Why don't you tell me what the hell is going on before I find another of your friends dead?"

"What makes you think that he didn't just wander off?" Brand questioned the detective hoping to pry some relevant information out of the cop.

The detective snorted in disgust. Grabbing Brand by the shoulder, O'Brien moved away from the nursing station.

"Let's take a walk?" Was all the detective said as the two squeezed their way past the throng of police and hospital staff and moved down the hallway toward a steel door marked stairwell. Once the door closed behind them, O'Brien stopped and leaned against the faded white cinder block stairwell.

"I'm still not certain how you and your friends are tied up with those mothers in the Moreno Cartel," the detective raised his hand to staunch Brand's reply, "and I'm sure you're about to feed me a long line of bull, but I'll make you a deal. Tell me the truth. How are the three of you involved, off the record of course?" The detective hesitated. "In fact, come clean and name names and I'll even guarantee you immunity from prosecution…and I'll fill you in on what we believe has happened to your friend." The detective sweetened the deal then tapped his foot impatiently while waiting for Brand's response.

"Detective, I don't think I can be much help to you. I tried to tell you before; I'm not involved in what happened at my house. Not until I came back and saw my friends under attack, at least." Brand shrugged. "Sorry. I honestly wished I knew more."

Detective O'Brien snorted disgustedly again and spun, grabbing the handle of the stairwell door and flinging it open. Almost through the door, he turned back to face Brand. "Security tapes show a pair of Latino men escorting your friend out on a gurney. I think your Colombian buddies may now have him. Back on the coast, I've seen what they do to people who cross them...I don't think I'd want to be your friend." He said then let the door close behind him.

Brand sat motionless on the dimly lit stairwell. If the detective was telling the truth, Jerry's story about losing the phone with the incriminating videos wasn't going to convince the Colombians to leave them alone, and with Jerry's condition, he would never stand up to any strenuous interrogation.

Brand was left wondering what he should attempt first. The odds of finding either Jerry or the missing phone both had the same odds. Not good. With Jerry's disappearance, at least the bulk of Calgary's police force would be out searching for the time being. The phone was something he alone knew about. The decision hard but one he had to see through.

Checking the time on his phone, he discovered his decision would have to wait. He was out of time to start searching for either before his meeting with Detective Walgreen. Taking the stairwell down to the hospital lobby, Brand left the building and ran to his truck. At the curb, he stepped around a grey Toyota SUV.

A few steps farther, Brand stopped in the middle of the street and glanced back at the SUV. He had seen the vehicle before. Suddenly, it dawned on him. He recalled seeing the same Toyota parked in front of the Apostles' clubhouse, and then, once again when he climbed in the cab of the tractor-trailer on the trip to Castlegar.

Son of a bitch Brand cursed. No wonder he was always running into the detective. O'Brien had be on the Apostles payroll. That explained why the detective was so eager to befriend Brand. He was looking to recover the missing phone for the Cartel.

Chapter 29

Brand arrived at the mall with time to spare. He parked along the side of the large super centre near the location Walgreen designated for their meeting, walked around to the front of the building and followed a group of women, kids in tow, into the box store. Mid afternoon and the store was doing a brisk business. There were a handful of products he required and taking advantage of the few free minutes, he walked the aisles in search of the items he wanted.

Brand spent more time than he wished combing the shelves. Glancing at his phone he noticed that the time was running away on him. Taking the items, he sped up his pace only to be stuck in a long line at the check out. Impatiently he waited as the line crawled forward. When his turn came he passed the cashier money, grabbed his purchases and rushed out of the store, walking directly to his truck. He planned to leave his purchases in the truck and then set out to find the detective.

Brand stood at the side of his truck, his fingers ready to punch the code into the keypad to unlock the door. Peering through the truck windows, he was distracted by a movement a few aisles over. Brand watched a man step from the back of a van and stop in the middle of an aisle staring over the roofs of parked cars at something in the distance. Curious, Brand followed the man's gaze. Detective Walgreen lounged against the hood of a car, the detective's attention focused on a phone in his hands.

*****

Richard Cozicar

Detective Frank Walgreen sat on the hood of the unmarked police car in the parking lot of the mall off of Deerfoot. His eyes riveted on his phone as he double-checked the latest sports scores from the night before. Unbelievable, he fumed. A sizeable amount of his money was riding on several games and it looked like he hit another losing string.

His gambling addiction had all but consumed him. It seemed like every time he placed a bet these days he went farther into debt to those damn bikers. Several times he had tried to walk away from his past, but he fought a losing battle. How much money did he owe to those outlaws, he no longer kept track.

When they first approached him to do small jobs as repayment, he balked. What little conscious he had at the time slowly dissolved with every illegal task they assigned him. At first he walked a thin line between right and wrong but now he was limboing well under that line, no longer able to even walk close to it.

He found that he couldn't care less. His story was going to end one of two ways. Spend the rest of his life in jail, if and when his illegal deeds were uncovered, or die at the hands of the bike gang when he was no longer useful. Until that time, he held little hope that his luck would turn, though that never kept him from trying.

His thick fingers were manoeuvring the small screen display through the ball scores when he heard someone yell his name. Prying his eyes away from the scoreboard, he scanned the crowded parking lot for the person calling to him. His eyes landed on Brand Coldstream, and then, as his head rotated, he spotted another man a few aisles over. This man was also looking in his direction from across the lot.

204

Several heartbeats passed before Walgreen realized that the second man stood with a gun in his hands. The black hole of the barrel pointed over the car roofs in his direction. Before the detective had a chance to react, a burning pain exploded in his chest. The impact from the bullet removed all thought from his brain, the force of the blow driving him backward onto the hood of the car. Walgreen's gambling problems ended, the detective's eyes frozen open to the blinding glare of the midday sun. His brain beyond noticing the bright light as he slowly slid off the hood and sagged onto the asphalt-covered ground.

*****

Brand turned back and looked at the man by the van. A gun materialized in the man's hand. In the seconds it took for Brand to compute the following sequence of action, while he mouthed the detective's name in warning, the roar of exploding gunpowder echoed across the parking lot. The bag in Brand's hand dropped to the ground. Brand spun his head back to where the detective had been standing earlier, his vision dropping to the pavement where fallen detective lay.

A couple, fresh from climbing out of their parked car appeared at the end of the aisle, cell phones in their hands.

"Call nine-one-one." Brand yelled at the couple as he raced in pursuit of the shooter. Leaping over a small car to gain ground, Brand closed the distance. One aisle away from the gunman, Brand squeezed between the mirrors of two closely parked vehicles and stepped into the same aisle the gunman occupied, only a few steps behind.

His breath coming in ragged gasps, Brand rushed closer and stretched an arm to grab the man's clothing when a car raced up from behind. The automobile's bumper brushed his legs, pinning them together sending Brand spiralling to the side, his upper body bouncing off the hood of one parked car and into another.

Soon the parking lot was filled with the whining and bleating of car alarms. With out stopping to check for injuries, Brand scrambled to his feet in time to see the shooter climbing into the very car that had brushed him aside.

Making a mental note of the licence plate, Brand sat on the hood of a car breathing in ragged breathes. With his heart rate slowing down, he stood to return and help the detective. His leg buckled. Pausing on the asphalt, he did a quick check on his leg, bruised not broken, and then carefully stood up. Using parked cars as support, he hobbled back in the direction of the detective.

Still some distance away from the body of the fallen detective, the noise of the busy mid-day freeway traffic passing by the mall disappeared under the growing wail of approaching sirens. Changing routes, Brand passed by the front of his truck. From there he noticed a growing crowd of people gather around the detective, some bent low attending the shot man while others talked excitedly on their phones and a couple others taking videos of the calamity.

As the police cars wove their way through the crowded parking toward the crowd, Brand bent down to retrieve his bag from the store, unlocked the truck door and threw the bag on the seat. He hobbled closer to the scene only to be pushed back by the swelling throng of onlookers. The cops arriving on the scene began assuming control of the area and moving everyone away.

The Wolves Of Satan

Brand tried to get the attention of one of the officers, but was repeatedly rebuked. As the adrenaline rush from the chase subsided, pain flared in his side. Having enough of the crowd, he wrote the plate number of the shooter's car on a business card and handed it to one of the bystanders.

"Give this to one of the police officers if you get a chance." He said without further explanation and limped back to his truck. He wasn't sure of the fallen detective's condition. He noticed a sizeable pool of blood under the man before he was forced back with the rest of the crowd. He thought of the detective as he opened the door to his truck. Hopefully Walgreen would be all right. Even an asshole like the detective deserved better.

Brand made a mental note to ask the *pain in the ass detective* how he made out the next time the two talked, besides there wasn't much he could do for the man. Backing the truck out of its stall, he merged into traffic and headed back in the direction of his hotel.

Random thoughts crowed his mind as he drove. He wondered who else knew about the meeting other than Walgreen? Brand wasn't foolish enough to believe that the detective would allow himself up to be set up and shot. The man was stupid but that would be pushing it.

The grey Toyota and its owner came to mind. He'd seen Walgreen's partner's truck at the Apostles clubhouse a few evenings earlier and then at the hospital where Jerry was recently abducted and now this. Coincidence. Was O'Brien so deeply involved with the Colombians and the criminal bike gang? And the question was would he stoop to have his own partner gunned down?

Chapter 30

Brand stood in front of the bathroom mirror and gingerly peeled his t-shirt over his head. A glance sideways in the mirror showed a large inflamed bruise climb from his thigh upwards. The muscles in his shoulder protested, the joint, tender when he raised his arm. With his hand, he brushed away a coating of dirt and gravel that clung to his skin. His leg was badly banged up, but his ribs took the brunt of the beating from being thrown into the side of the parked car. A dark purple colouring surrounded the bruises and lines of dried blood blended with the scrapes down the right side of his body.

Nothing broken, only bruised, along with his ego. He underestimated the Colombian Cartel's ruthlessness. He gave his head a shake. Age had made him careless. He was messing with a dangerous group. One, who along with the Apostles, wouldn't be troubled if they killed him and like an idiot, he stumbles in front of a car while chasing a man. Maybe he was getting too old to play this game. The thought disappeared as quickly as it surfaced. No, he justified. They had to pay. No organization was infallible. Everyone had a weak link to be exploited. He just had to stay alive to find it.

Brand soaked under a hot shower, his mind occupied by Jerry's disappearance, the detective's shooting and the supposed video on a lost phone that started this mess.

Before leaving the hotel room, he placed a call to Roy. Minutes later he left the hotel and drove to one of Roy's favourite watering holes. A bar, slash, nightclub the Wolves owned off of Sixteenth Ave. Parking behind the building, Brand crossed the dimly lit alley and knocked on a door hidden by the deepening evening shadows. A bouncer opened the door, the man's bulky frame blocking the entrance as he questioned Brand. After a few minutes, the bouncer escorted Brand down a hallway, stopping to knock on the door to a back room.

Roy and a small cluster of bikers glanced up watching Brand as he squeezed past the bouncer. The men sat on couches surrounding a cluttered coffee table. Bottles of beer and several open bottles of liquor covered the top of the table. Roy nudged the man sitting next to him, motioning the biker to vacate the seat for Brand.

"Fergus. Give the man your seat."

The other members in the room kept their eyes on Brand as he limped across the floor.

"We were just contemplating having supper. You hungry?" Roy asked, lifting a menu from the table. Turning to the man who surrendered his seat, Roy suggested the man go to the bar and grab Brand a rye and Pepsi. No ice, he stressed.

"Hell, Fergus, bring the whole damn bottle. The way he's moving, it looks like he could use it." Roy studied Brand.

"What happened to you, Kemosabe?" A smile played across Roy's face but his eyebrows furrowed with concern.

Brand passed the menu back to his brother and remained quiet. He watched as a 26 of rye and a pitcher of Pepsi loaded with ice cubes landed on the table in front of where he sat. Leaning forward, Brand ignored Roy's inquiries and mixed a strong drink. The muscles on his face twitched as he winced from the pain in his side. Leaning back into the couch cushions, he tested his drink then turned to look Roy in the face.

"It has been a first class shitty day so far." Brand began his story. "Started out by my going to the hospital. I wanted to talk

to Jerry, hoped to jog his memory about his missing phone..."
He paused. "Jerry has disappeared...his clothes and other
belongings are still in the room..." The rye glass emptied in a
couple of swallows. Brand leaned over the table again and
mixed another drink before proceeding.

"A detective O'Brien was at the hospital. He believes that
Jerry was wheeled out on a gurney, by what the detective said,
looked like a pair of Latino men." Brand paused thinking again.

"I was supposed to meet with Detective Walgreen earlier this
afternoon. That went sideways when some asshole with a gun
showed up. Almost caught the shooter but his accomplice
clipped me with a car, helping the shooter escape." Brand
downed the second drink. "I've had better days." He finished
and poured a third drink then fumbled in his pocket for his
cigarette. Stopping before he lit up, he looked at Roy.

"Do you mind?" he asked. Roy pantomimed an exaggerated
look of indignation.

"I am an Indian, and I own this place. Indian territory. White
man's rules don't apply." Roy said, side stepping the cities
public smoking laws with as straight a face as he could muster.

"Cut the crap." Brand replied and lit the cigarette.

"That Cartel is coming at us with everything they've got."
Roy turned serious. "Three of our clubs have been attacked.
Crippled a few of the boys along the way and the damage to the
buildings is extensive."

"Sorry I got you involved." Brand apologized again.

Roy set aside the menu in his hands. His brows knitted as a
look of bewilderment spread across his face. Roy shook his
head and looked over at Brand. "I appreciate your concern but
the Apostles were gunning for our territory long before you

came into the picture. This war was inevitable. This fight over the city was going to come to a head sooner than later. The Apostles have been crowding the boundaries for several months now. I guess, with their South American friends backing them, they're feeling brave."

"You got the manpower to fight them?"

"For now. There have been rumours floating that the Colombians are bringing more guys from the coast to help out. I've had talks with the leaders of some other biker outfits. We think that now might be a good time to call a truce and combine our forces. A lot of these gangs are beginning to feel the heat from the Apostles, Cartel merger."

As Roy was telling Brand about the other bike gangs, Brand's phone rang. Hitting the call button, Brand placed the phone to his ear. The caller spoke before Brand said a word.

"Coldstream. Detective O'Brien. We need to talk."

"You're already talking, keep going." The last thing Brand wanted was another meeting with a detective after today's shooting.

"Detective Walgreen was shot today. Know anything about that." O'Brien asked.

"What kind of stuff are you asking about?" Brand shot back.

The detective hesitated. "I've got video and witnesses who swear they saw you running away from Detective Walgreen after he took a bullet."

"Yeah. I was supposed to meet Walgreen." Brand defended. "I spotted a man with a gun lurking in the parking lot, his attention on Walgreen. I tried to warn the detective but the guy fired. I almost caught the bastard, but he had a buddy whack me with a car. The pair got away." Then Brand remembered. "I left the plate number with one of the bystanders. Check with your uniforms; I'm sure one of them will have it."

"That's a pretty sad story. Is that your official statement?" O'Brien replied. "We found a gun not far from the scene. When we ran the prints through AFIS, do you want me to explain what AFIS is?"

"I know what AFIS is. " Brand replied angrily. "Is there a point to this call or do you just miss the sound of my voice?"

"There's a point, asshole. We were unable to identify the prints and then I had an idea. I remembered our little sit down at the station the other day so I asked one of our guys to check the ones on the gun against your prints from that night. The gun that killed Walgreen is yours; your prints are all over the gun." O'Brien yelled into the phone. "Why in the hell would you kill him? Was he on to you and your buddies? You wanted to silence him, is that It?"

"Go get stuffed O'Brien...I didn't shoot the man." Detective O'Brien's words wormed into Brand's brain. "Wait. Did you say killed? Walgreen's dead? I didn't shoot the man." Brand yelled back and ended the call. He sat staring at the phone in his hand. The gun stolen from his house, apparently, it wasn't missing any longer. Pressing the power button, he stared at the phone's screen until it darkened. He knew how easy it was to track cell phones and he needed time to think. Time to figure what the hell was going on. The Colombians were stepping up their game. They obviously didn't care who died, and that was a bad thing. If they were brash enough to murder a police officer, no one would be safe in this war.

The room remained silent. Brand poured another drink then dug out his smokes lighting one and throwing the pack on the table. "Son of a bitch." He muttered. Speaking to Roy, he said.

"I may need a place to crash for a while. It seems that Calgary's finest think I killed one of their members." All the while his thoughts returned to earlier when he was wondering if O'Brien didn't have something to do with Walgreens death. He didn't like coincidences.

Chapter 31

Brand sat on the couch lost in his thoughts. He rejected the offer of food. As the other men ate, he kept replaying the shooting earlier in the day. Finally, he gave up. Experts, he came to admit, played him for a fool and set him up for Walgreen's death.

The cops undoubtedly checked the store video proving he was in the area at the same time Detective Walgreen took a bullet and there were a fair amount of people in the parking lot to witnesses him running, which he had, when he chased the shooter. These factors combined with the appearance of his stolen gun at the scene, which naturally would have his fingerprints on it, made any defense he claimed reasonably weak. Unless, unless he was somehow able to track down the man who shot Walgreen, and get the shooter to confess. Depending on whether the man remained in the city, which of course was very unlikely if the Colombians were smart.

No problem, he told himself. He only needed to avoid a gang of outlaw bikers and a Colombian Cartel looking to run their competition from the city. So, all he had to do was find a phone Jerry had lost while drinking and then convince the Colombians to leave his friends alone while locating the man responsible for shooting a police officer, and all this, while avoiding death Cartel fashion for burning down their drug distribution warehouse. He contemplated asking Roy's man to go back to the bar for another bottle of rye. One wasn't going to be enough.

Brand was pondering the second bottle of rye when the snapping of gunfire roused him back to reality. The door to the back office flew open. A bartender, a towel still grasped in his hand, hurried into the room. Words spewed from the man's mouth between gasps of breath.

"We got gunmen pouring in through the front door. They're shooting the place up." The bartender yelled. The men in the room stood as one, everyone's attention focused on the bartender's words. Roy hesitated briefly then rushed toward a closet at the far end of the office. He pulled the door open and flicked on the lights before sweeping hangers of clothes aside to expose a hidden panel. Roy slid a panel open revealing a hidden compartment.

Brand shook his head, clearing what he thought were the effects of the whiskey. The niche, hidden in the back of the closet, resembled a small armoury. Light glinted off a row of assault rifles. Army issues. On a bench below the rifles, a handful of 9-mm handguns spread among boxes of ammo.

Roy was the first one into the closet and started passing weapons and boxes of ammunition to his men. Along with the guns, the leader of the Wolves issued orders. The first of the men to receive the firearms moved to cover the office door.

"Boss. We'll secure the hallway. You get the hell out of here." One of the men told Roy.

"No. I don't think so." Roy quashed the man's plea. "These bastards want to shoot up my club then they'll pay dearly."

"You are not going to do anybody any good by getting killed." The man replied. Roy ignored the appeal.

"Fergus. You stay here and work the phone. See which of our boys are close and call them in. The police will be coming. Get a hold of our police contact and make certain that some of the uniforms showing up are friendly. When you've done that, hide the rest of these guns in case the joint gets searched."

Brand fought against the dulling effects of the whiskey, adrenaline from sudden attack clearing his mind.

"Can we get to the second floor from here." He asked no one in particular.

"Down at the end of the hallway, the first door on your right. Before the entrance to the bar." Someone answered.

"Toss me one of those guns, Roy." Brand demanded. The effects of the alcohol helped him push the pain in his body to the back of his mind. In a rush, he grabbed a gun from Roy's hands. Instinctively, he checked the magazine before working the rifles bolt action jacking a shell into the empty chamber and stood ready waiting for his brother. Roy motioned with the barrel of his weapon directing men to defensive positions.

"You two. Cover the back door. Vaun, take Mike and Saddler. You three," He said, "get down the hall. Block the door leading from the dance floor and hold it. No one but our guys come through."

He looked down at Brand. "You ready," he asked, then followed the three men into the hallway toward the front of the building. Roy's men spread out ahead, the three melding into niches for shelter, their guns pointed toward the door separating the main room from the back of the building, prepared to defend the exit while Roy led the way up the stairwell to the second floor.

Carefully the pair scanned the stairwell as they climbed to a mezzanine overlooking the large dance floor. Bullets thudded into walls. The echo of gunfire mixed with screams and hollering as the brothers hurried to the upper level.

Roy ran ahead. A few long strides across the balcony, he stopped behind a cluster of decorative columns, his back tight to the wood. Brand topped the stairs and crouching behind the cover of a bulky half post, he inched his face around the wooden column clearing a sight line to the havoc playing out among the tables and clients on the club's dance floor. The flickering party lights added a surreal, staccato motion to the chilling scene one story below as the two brothers searched the open room for the gunmen attacking the club.

From behind the decorative baluster, Brand surveyed the floor. The pulsating strobe lights played with the focus of his eyes. He struggled to distinguish the armed assailants from beer drinkers and the clubs staff, the dark, pulsing lights giving an advantage to the gunmen.

While Brand and Roy's men hesitated, careful to separate club's patrons from gun-wielding assailants, the intruding gangsters had no such restrictions. Their bullets aimed to provide the maximum amount of panic inside the packed building.

A group of suited men stood side by side with bikers wearing Apostles colours. The Cartel alliance walked deeper into the noisy poorly lit bar sealing off the street entrance, preventing the scared customers from leaving. The line of suited and leather-clad rivals advanced with automatic rifles held in their hands, content to fire sporadic rounds of bullets over the heads of the bars scrambling clientele.

Brand caught movement from the bar side of the room. A bartender levelled a handgun at a biker from the rival gang, the biker's actions quicker than the bartenders. Bullets from an automatic rifle tore into the bartender's upright body. Brand swore and concentrated, his eyes narrowed against the pulsing lighting playing over the crowded room. Locking on the biker, he sighted the length of the barrel of his gun.

He slowed his breathing, his finger lightly resting on the rifle's cool metallic trigger as he tracked the leather-clad biker's movements. He waited a heartbeat. The Apostles gang member raised his gun toward the side. Caught in front of the biker's sights, another of Roy's employees pinned in the open. With a gentle squeeze of his finger, the rifle bucked in Brand's hands as a trail of bullets streaked across the short distance and embedded in the rival biker's up right body. Under the pulsing lights, the body of the gunman enacted a macabre dance before his weapon slid to the floor shortly followed by the man himself.

As soon as the shots exploded from the barrel of his gun, Brand swung his head, his eyes sweeping the confusion below for a second target, his finger ready against the trigger. Brand heard the bark of Roy's gun as he strained to separate friend from foe through the flickering club lights.

A volley of bullets angled upward from the front of the bar slammed into the wooden posts on the second floor. Brand dropped to the ground to avoid the return fire. A short distance across the balcony, Roy sat with his back to the cluster of columns. Bullets sprayed upward tearing chunks of wood from the post the brothers used as cover. The columns rattled and shook. The two men trapped in the flurry of bullets, unable to move.

A brief pause in the gun battle allowed Brand to snake a look from behind the post. The flickering of the strobe lights slowed the detection of the gunmen, disguising the intruder's movements with the rapid, alternating flashes. The erratic lighting impaired Brand's vision, blurring the chaos on the lower level. Both the gunmen and club goers faded in and out of focus in a sporadic, epileptic motion.

The Wolves Of Satan

A pair of men filtered into sight from the side of the room. Brand angled the barrel of the gun in the men's direction and put pressure on the trigger. Bullets erupted, striking the floor, missing the pair by inches. A volley of shots answered his actions, forcing him to duck back behind the safety of the baluster. The brief moment he had to survey the situation below told a grim tale.

The floor littered with writhing bodies of wounded and screaming patrons and the silhouettes of rival gang members. The cries of the wounded rose up over the loud techno beat that still boomed and echoed off the walls of the bar. His rushed glimpse revealed pockets of Roy's men hidden behind the barest of cover, bravely resisting the swarming enemies.

Crouched over, a lull in searching fire allowed Brand to scuttle closer to Roy. The music and screams made talking impossible. When he neared Roy, he hollered.

"Any idea how many gunmen we're up against?"

Roy shook his head without turning to look at Brand. His neck twisted around the bottom of the post, his eyes glued to the dance floor below while he combed for the movements of either Apostles bikers or the Cartel's men.

"We need to move. Your guys on the floor won't last long." Brand yelled. Roy shook his head in acknowledgment.

Gunfire continued to crack in the confines of the bar. The repeated explosions of live ammo mixed and reverberated among the chaos of screaming, terrified customers all to a soundtrack of bass filled techno music thumping loudly off the room's walls and ceiling.

Moments later Roy tapped Brand's shoulder. "They've got us trapped. We can't do much good from here." Brand studied

Roy's face in the flickering strobes, both men grasping for a way out of the noose slowly tightening around Roy's club.

"Keep your head down and stay alive," Roy said suddenly then pushed away from the metal railing. Brand watched, momentarily confused, his brother palming a phone. Roy's huge fingers stabbed at the small numbered buttons.

"Fergus... back door... alley... hurry" Parts of a broken conversation reached Brand's ears before Roy leaped to his feet and threw the weight of his body against a second story window. The panes of glass shattered as Roy's massive body fell outward. Bullets whined past the balcony rail and thudded into the drywall, some blasting away the remaining glass left in the window frame. Over the deafening report of gunfire, Brand heard a surprised grunt spring from Roy's direction followed by a loud crash outside the window.

Chapter 32

A grunt borne from surprise and exertion escaped Roy's lungs as he hurtled backward through the second story window. Jagged edges of broken glass sliced across his body, stinging the skin on his forearms left unprotected by the leather vest that covered his upper body. A piercing, hot pain impacted his shoulder, spinning his body before he dropped behind the safety of the building's exterior wall. Another sharp expulsion of air left his lips as his body collided with a flat roof one floor above the back entrance to the nightclub.

Stunned, he lay gasping for breath. He pushed past the pain and shook off the effects of the fall. Climbing to his feet, he glanced back up at the broken window. The flash of exploding gunpowder mingled with the pulsing lights alternating inside the club.

Roy crept to the edge of the small roof and peered into the darkened alley. His eyes adjusting to the poor lighting as he watched the shadows. His hand groped for the metal bars of a ladder mounted to the back of the building. A light splayed across the dark. Roy halted his climb to the ground. He watched a man step through a door into the darkness, the glint of light revealing the man's identity.

"Fergus," The Wolves leader called in a harsh whisper. "Up here." Roy's aide glanced up at the voice of his boss. Roy slid the last few feet, his boots raising a cloud of alley dust. A check to see if his man was armed, Roy motioned for the end of the alley.

"Back-ups on the way," the biker notified his boss.

*****

Roy's sudden departure, noticed by the killers a floor below, drew a volley of gunfire. Brand rolled away from the broken window and scuttled back toward the bulky post at the top of the stairs. He peered cautiously between two metal pickets that lined the stairway. Glimpses of men appeared through the distorted lighting, the group edging their way toward the door at the bottom of the staircase.

Before Brand could swing his rifle in line, bullets sprayed upward gouging into the wooden baluster. Dropping to his stomach, Brand forgot about the approaching gunmen, pulled away from the opening and peered around the far side of the wooden post. He scanned the lower floor for the source of the sniper fire.

A solitary gunman stared up at the top of the stairs over the barrel of a rifle. The man waited, partially hidden behind an extension of the club's wooden bar. The man's head and shoulder blinked in and out of focus above the counter as the man studied the balcony. Brand lifted off the floor and shifted the gun barrel a few inches to the side bringing the man's head into his sights. The gun's movements hampered by the post and rails, his timing a second too slow.

While Brand keyed on the sniper, the Wolves guarding the back of the building left the relative safety of hallway and crossed into the bar area at the bottom of the stairs. Their assault rifles bucked in their hands as they laid down covering fire, the wall of bullets driving back the advancing assailants.

The sniper dropped the barrel of his gun. Brand watched the small explosions as gunpowder flashed at the end of the weapon. The exchange of rounds took a man down, forcing two others to dive for cover.

Brand snapped his attention back on the sniper, his finger tight on the trigger, the loud crack of exploding shells and expelled gunpowder blending with the chaos in the room. Bullets ricocheted off the solid wooden counter catching the man's upper body and driving the sniper back into the bottles of assorted spirits lining the glass shelves behind the bar.

A new volley of lead rose from the lower floor in Brand's direction. He twisted and dove back down to the floor, his bruised rib and leg painfully reminding him of the earlier events of the day. Rolling, he came to rest behind one of the decorative columns, gun up and ready. Several men snaked their way along the right side of the dance floor ducking around the confused and panicked club patrons and using overturned tables as cover.

Brand watched the group move across the room as they inched their way toward the back. With the customers scrambling and rushing the front door, he waited patiently for the gunmen to make a mistake, step away from cover and leave him a shot. From the edge of his sight, two Wolves bikers climbed the stairs, crouching close to Brand. A phone rang. One of the bikers fished the device from his pocket. The man answered, nodding while he listened.

"Roy needs us to stop the Cartel boys from pushing to the back of the bar. He's coming in the front door. Says we'll catch these buggers in a crossfire." The man yelled the conversation to Brand. Dropping the phone, Roy's men joined Brand, the three firing down into the group of gunmen spread across the floor. Time slowly ticked by while the standoff continued.

Brand swung the sight of the rifle over to a group edging along the wall keeping to the limited cover splayed around the room. Frightened customer's dove for tables as the men approached. The bar patrons panicked flight for survival leaving the advancing gunmen exposed to Brand's gun. Methodically and with purpose, he squeezed the trigger, releasing calculated bursts of gunfire. Wounding some of the advancing killers, he dropped a couple of others sending the men scrambling for cover.

The racket from the gunfire, the screams and groans of agony from the wounded and the relentless beat of the techno music rose as one, giving the interior of the bar a surreal, nightmarish symphony, one where only the devil would find comfort.

From the club's entrance, Roy entered the main room of the nightclub. Club patrons pinned by the sudden attack began rising from cover rushing past Roy in search of safety. A handful of Apostles rushed the front of the building. While his men spread across the littered floor breaking the Cartel's infusion, Roy aimed his gun at the clubs sound system. A flurry of bullets ripped into the mountain of stereo equipment. The components sparked into silence ending the soundtrack accompanying the gruesome scene.

"Put down your guns!" Roy bellowed above the din of patrons and shooters. His voice boomed through the room. "You're surrounded. Drop your weapons and live or you can clutch them in your dying hands when you join your downed comrades, dead on the floor."

"Someone, turn the damn lights on," Roy hollered before he made his way to the centre of the room.

The Wolves Of Satan

The club fell silent, the fractured lighting of the strobes replaced by the steady glow of overhead bulbs. Thick, stinging smoke clouded the air. Cries and murmuring pleas of the wounded filled the void created by the obliteration of the buildings sound system. Then the sound of metal hitting the floor as the Cartel alliance looked about at the angry Wolves members blocking any chance of escape. The Colombians and their Apostles counterparts that remained standing raised their empty hands high in the air.

Chapter 33

Brand looked down from the balcony surveying the aftermath. Roy stood in the middle of the room; members of his gang combed the littered floor herding the surrendered gunmen into a cluster in the centre of the large room.

Customers climbed to their feet. The uninjured gazing around dazed and confused as they made their way through a maze of overturned furniture and past the wounded and out into the sanctity of the open street where they gathered under the veil of street lamps.

While the adrenaline slowly released from his battered body, Brand let his rifle slip to the floor. His hand swiped the side of his face. His fingers came away wet with blood that had trickled and clung to the stubble on his face. His cheek cut when wood chips sprayed from the bullet riddled wooden posts.

A disturbing thought occurred. Actually. Two separate thoughts troubled Brand's mind. Fishing his phone from a pocket, he pushed the power button and dialled Susan's cell. If the Cartel knew about Roy visiting his club, they might also know where to locate her. Concern gnawed at the pit of his stomach while the phone slowly connected and rang.

The third ring in, Susan answered.

"Hey. How you are doing," Brand asked casually. "You're still awake?"

"I was restless," she confessed, "I couldn't sleep but I'm fine. How about you? Where are you? It's late," she asked, her words fast, suspicion creeping into her voice. Brand hesitated as the weight of the long day settled over his shoulders.

The Wolves Of Satan

"I'm at the club with Roy. Sorry to call so late." Brand apologized. The attack on Roy's club went unmentioned; the details could wait for another time.

"At the club with Roy? Is everything fine?" she asked. "Roy wanted me accompany him. Said I could use the diversion," she explained. "I was too tired, so I stayed put." She paused. "Have you found dad? Is that why you called?"

Brand's hopes that Jerry's departure from the hospital was of his choosing and by now had contacted his daughter faded with Susan's question. His disappointment added to his burden.

"No, but I'm looking. I'll find him," He assured, ending the call. He sighed, happy that at least Susan remained free of the Cartel's reach. Then, a second wave of concern replaced the first.

Was it luck that the Cartel decided to attack the club the same evening Roy was in the building or was someone feeding them information. Another coincidence that Brand added to the burgeoning stack of troubling facts.

He filed the thought and descended the stairs into the pit of the club. Staying on the outside of the roundup, he pushed across the floor, stopping beside Roy. A gash of blood and torn fabric sliced across Roy's shoulder. The big man paced back and forth, his large form towering over the unwelcome intruders, the Wolves' leader stopping periodical to stare down at the wounded and defeated rivals. The men, in turn, glared back with defiant faces.

"Who's in charge?" Roy growled, his pacing continued. Inadvertently, several of the group turned their heads toward a man near the end of the line. Roy walked over to the man, grabbed him by the collar and pulled him aside. Roy barked a question only to have the man answer in Spanish. Growing angrier, Roy lifted the smaller man off the floor, took a couple of long strides away from the gathering and slammed the diminutive Colombian hard into a wall.

"English, you asshole." Roy snapped at the man. "Why this place? What made you attack this club tonight?" He repeated. "Did your bosses know we'd be here?"

The small Colombian looked up at Roy then he pointed to Brand. The man disregarded Roy's question. Instead, he focused on Brand.

"That one. Our instructions were to find the man who destroyed our warehouse." The man spat back at Roy.

"Well, how in the hell would you know he'd show up here? I wasn't even aware that he planned to stop in. You got a weasel hiding among my men feeding you information?" Roy asked holding the smaller man by the throat as the Colombian struggled to be free. Roy turned away from the small man in his arm and searched the faces of his rivals kneeling on the floor.

"We are not so stupid as you think, Señor Thundercloud. It is hard for you to hide." Came the reply. "Let us leave with that bandida, and perhaps the disruption to your businesses will slow." The small Colombian spoke defiantly. Roy's massive hand tightened around the Colombians throat. He glanced at Brand, shook his head and turned his attention back to his men.

"Fergus, you and Saddler keep your guns on these guys until the cops arrive. Let the police deal with this trash. Make certain the wounded get treated. This tough guy is coming with me," Roy explained. His hand squeezing tighter around the Colombians throat, the smaller man gasping as his face reddened. "I've got more questions I need him to answer."

The Wolves Of Satan

The blast of sirens arriving on the street out front drifted in through the open doors.

"Let's get out of here." Roy motioned to Brand. "Where's your truck parked?"

*****

Roy gave Brand directions to a park, deserted at the late hour. Brand parked behind a grove of trees where the interrogation would be hidden from the sight of prying eyes. Roy dragged the Colombian away from the truck, pinning the man against a tree. Brand stood by the truck while Roy interrogated the smaller man. Other than providing his name, Jander Varela and the admission he worked for the Cartel, the man mumbled unintelligible answers to Roy's questions. Despite a cloud of fear ringing the man's eyes, he kept his face passive defiantly challenging the man twice his size.

Roy quickly tired of Varela's refusal to comply and several times anger overcame his emotions. The attacks on his clubs, the ambushing of his men, leaving them either wounded or dead, was too powerful for even he to remain calm and objective.

With his huge hand, he slammed the smaller Colombian into the trunk of the tree. Brand walked the few feet to where Roy interrogated the diminutive Colombian. Concern for what his brother might do, worrying him. Seeing Roy lose his patience, Brand put a hand on his brother's outstretched arm.

Jander Varela sagged from the repeated collisions with the base of the tree.

"Enough. You'll kill the little bugger." Brand cautioned. "He's not going to talk, and if he's dead, he'll be of little use."

Richard Cozicar

Brand's reasoning enough to make Roy pause. Opening his hand, Roy let the Colombian fall to the dew soaked ground.

"What should we do with him?" Brand asked. Roy pondered the question then knelt beside the beaten Varela.

"I'm going to let you live. When you see your boss, tell him I said to FUCK OFF and leave my turf alone. You inform the idiot, if he doesn't cool it, he might anger me, and I can guarantee he won't like the consequences."

Through swollen eyes, the small Colombian gazed up at Roy before smirking at the larger man's words.

With incredible speed for a man his size, Roy shot his hand forward, grabbing the man around the throat once again. In his rage, Roy straightened to his feet lifting the much smaller man three feet off the ground. Roy brought Valera's face close to his own, his dark brown eyes deepening to black with the burning rage he felt. Through gritted teeth, Roy spoke quietly to the man.

"You tell El Shitto if he doesn't leave us alone, I…will…destroy…everything he cherishes before I rip his head from his body and shove it up his ass. COMPRENDE!" Roy's finger dug tightly into the man's throat while he looked the squirming smaller man squarely in the face. The Colombian's eyes grew wide with fear.

Roy grabbed the Colombian's hand firmly. He eyes unwavering. Tears slipped from the Colombians eyes and meandered down the sides of his face as Roy applied pressure to the man's hand. With the sound of snapping bones, Roy eased his grip. "Now get the hell out of here." He uttered and threw the man several yards away from him.

230

The Wolves Of Satan

Jander Valera hit the ground and rolled several times before stumbling to his feet. With his crushed fingers securely held in his good hand, he looked back at Roy before hobbling away.

Brand watched the interaction, ready to stop Roy from going too far. He remained still as the Colombian ran across the park.

"What are you going to do now?" He asked his brother.

Roy walked over to him and shrugged. "I'll give the assholes a few days to see if my message was received. If this war escalates, the city will turn into a war zone. This turf war is still just simmering, but if the Colombians and their pet bikers persist, we'll take the fight to them." Roy swung his head sadly, his brows furrowed. "The city won't survive a full blown gang war."

"Any more clubs get invaded, if more civilians get hurt," Roy continued, "then police forces from across the country will be summoned here to help. The Calgary cops are far too few to handle a battle this big."

As the two men walked back to Brand's truck, Brand remembered the call from O'Brien earlier in the evening and piped up.

"I'll need to borrow a bike if you can spare one. If the cops are looking for me, my truck will make me to easy to track."

Roy stopped and smiled. "I'll have one of the boys fit a bike with training wheels for you?"

Chapter 34

Brand awoke late the next morning. The sun poked past rolling banks of light clouds and filtered into the room through openings in the curtains. Friday morning and a week since the two gunmen stormed his house and started the ball rolling on a bad run of luck that was quickly cascading down a very steep hill.

Leaving Roy at the acreage, Brand exchanged the pick-up truck for a motorbike and cruised back into the sleeping city looking for a small, out of the way motel to spend what remained of the night. His search wound from the east end to the northwest part of the city, well into the Apostles turf.

Lying in bed, he stared at the ceiling. The attack on the nightclub melded into his dreams disrupting the few hours of sleep his body longed for. Aches and pains ran up the side of his body prodding him awake each time he drifted back to sleep and tossed or moved.

Slowly, he climbed out of bed and stepped into the shower. The water blasting hotter than he usually preferred. He pressed his hand against the shower wall for support and let the scalding heat cascade down, soothing the tender purple and red bruises. The water easing the stiffness in his joints and allowing him to shake the dullness caused by the lack of sleep and helped focus his mind on the new day.

Swiping his hand across the steamed mirror, he caught a blurred glimpse of his face. Turning his head, he eyes paused on the myriad of scrapes and nicks from his hairline down to his jaw. Various sizes of red welts remained, a reminder of the flying shrapnel from the night before.

The Wolves Of Satan

With a towel wrapped around his waist, he strode out of the bathroom, made a cup of coffee and gingerly eased his aching body into a chair before reaching for his cigarette package. A lot had happened the past week that he needed to sort out. It seemed like a lifetime ago that the pair of gunmen shot up his house and started the chaos that ensued. So much had happened since then to send his life spiralling out of control that he had to take a step back and decide what to do and how to do it.

His thoughts narrowed to the lost cell phone Jerry had mentioned. Finding the phone had to be his top priority. A long shot but possibly the quickest way to bring a halt to the current crisis.

Brand firmly believed Jerry's sudden exit from the hospital was undoubtedly at the hands of the Cartel. Funny, he mused, the actions of the Apostles began taking a backseat to the Colombians in his train of thought. Who was really calling the shots he wondered?

Circling back to his original line of thinking, he reinforced in his mind the importance of finding the lost phone. The evidence stored in its memory would have the power to leverage a deal with the Cartel and hopefully put a stop to the mayhem overtaking the city.

Roy's warning to the Cartel wasn't going to carry far, he figured, so he'd have to find another way to end this, and now, the murder of Detective Walgreen complicated matters. Hell. Not just complicated, but the killing of a police officer would have the entire force out hunting if they believed he was responsible.

If O'Brien were involved with the Cartel, Brand knew it would be difficult to prove he wasn't the one who shot the detective.

Brand finished his coffee and stood to get dressed. Jerry was adamant about the importance of the phone and the video of incriminating evidence it contained of various Cartel members. Plus, Brand remembered Jerry's words, footage of city cops collaborating with the Cartel and bikers. If O'Brien were on the videotape, filmed alongside the Cartel, the video would carry a lot of weight in clearing his name in the death of Walgreen.

Damn, Brand shook his head. He wished he had pushed Jerry harder for the names of the cops in the video.

*****

Dressed in jeans and t-shirt with a leather jacket to ward off the cool June day, Brand stood peering through a slit in the curtains at the open motel parking lot. He smoked another cigarette while scanning the area. He started close the hotel room and the borrowed bike and then studied the area beyond the paved lot. The few vehicles in his line of sight were blanketed in the morning due, no signs of being occupied.

His stomach rumbled as he stepped from the room crossing the sidewalk to the waiting motorbike, his hand sweeping moisture from the seat and handlebars. He considered a fresh plate of breakfast, complete with coffee and a newspaper, but if the cops were hunting him for Walgreen's murder, he had no doubt the local media would be broadcasting his picture.

He decided on a breakfast sandwich from a nearby burger chain. Usually, younger people operated the drive through windows, the type that didn't spend a lot of time watching the news.

The Wolves Of Satan

A short time later, Brand sat at a picnic table eating his ham and egg burger and sipping a tolerable cup of black coffee. Distracted, he replayed his last conversation with Jerry squeezing his memory for all the small details the old guide had spoken of when confessing to where and when the phone went missing. Jerry's own memories were foggy of the night in question Brand recalled his friend admitting. The old guy vaguely remembered the evening spent drinking close to his house in Bowness at a local bar in the strip mall in the Montgomery area.

Brand finished his coffee and burger and climbed onto the bike. He wasn't far from the area, maybe twenty minutes in the mid morning traffic. Entering the flow of morning commuters, he steered the bike away from the motel and toward the southwest part of town.

His destination, a strip mall of assorted businesses sat deserted when he rolled into the parking lot. The mall contained small mom and pop specialty shops, a convenience store, a stand-alone pizzeria, sandwich shop, a few craft stores and a local pub. Business at the mall probably remained quiet most days he surmised as he scanned the storefronts and registered the lack of vehicles in the parking lot. The neighbourhood bar he was anxious to visit wasn't open for another half hour, so he drove his bike around the back of the buildings.

Several weeks had passed since Jerry lost his phone, but with a lack of leads, Brand leaned the bike on its kickstand and slowly wandered around the back of the mall. The saying of a needle in a haystack came to mind as he methodically combed the dumpsters and doorways in the alley. Starting at one end, he checked in and under garbage bins, through wind blown piles of trash and carefully combed through long tangled and unattended patches of grass that were growing against a fence on the opposite side of the alley.

The strip mall wasn't a huge complex but still ran on for thousand or so feet. At one point, Brand rousted a couple of men sitting in a doorway enjoying a bottle of something disguised in a brown paper bag.

"You fellows hang around here often?" He asked the pair. Warily, the men acknowledged his interruption. Their heads tilted down, they watched through bloodshot eyes. Neither answered, so he tried a different approach.

"A friend of mine lost his cell phone here a few weeks back. I don't suppose either of you guys has seen it?" The two continued staring at him then turned their attention back to the well-aged drink they had concealed in the brown bag.

"There might be a reward for anyone who finds the phone." Brand tossed the idea out hoping to grab the men's attention. One of the guys lifted his eyes up to Brand and slurred.

"How much of a reward?" He asked.

"Depends on the information." Brand thought fast. "The sooner I locate the phone the more the reward." Then as a show of good will, Brand pulled his wallet out and fished inside for a ten. Just his luck, the smallest bills he had were twenties. Doubting he'd ever see a return for his money, he plucked a single bill from the fold in his wallet and held it toward the men.

The quicker of the two flashed his hand and snatched the twenty before his buddy realized what had taken place.

"What about me?" The second man whined. Eyeing the pair, Brand retrieved another twenty and held it out for the second man just out of grasp.

"I'll tell you what." He paused thinking over a way to get some use from the money he was about to through away. "Do either of you guys have a pen?"

The first bum pulled open his dirty coat revealing an assortment of pens and pencils hidden inside a pocket. The man took his time deciding which pen to lend Brand as if the pens were gold. The man seemed afraid Brand would steal it. Finally, he decided on a dirty felt pen and reluctantly passed it to Brand.

Brand searched nearby for something to write on. These men would discard any paper he left with them the moment he left their sight. Figuring on this, Brand reached for the man with the pens and grabbed the flap of the man's coat. The inside pocket containing the pens remained a lighter colour then the man's stained coat so Brand quickly wrote his phone number on the man's inside pocket then released his grip.

The man looked at his pocket and grumbled briefly before turning his eyes back in Brand's direction. Brand calmly explained the rules of his deal.

"Either of you two finds a phone in this area, call and leave me a message. There will be more money involved. Don't lose my number." He said as he surrendered the second twenty and left the men to resume their drinking. Brand continued to search through the alley.

When he was satisfied he checked every possible place a phone could fit, he walked around front. He planned to speak with each business on the strip. Showing the owners a picture of Jerry and explaining about the missing phone. A long shot at best, but at the moment it was all he had to go on.

Striding toward the entrance of the first shop at the beginning of the small mall, his thoughts were on his friend. He hadn't heard a word about Jerry since his friend disappeared from the hospital. Was he being tortured or had the Colombians killed

Richard Cozicar

him. Whatever was on Jerry's phone certainly was making someone nervous. Worried enough to run the risk of being discovered while abducting a patient from a busy hospital.

Brand focused back on the task at hand. He entered a sandwich shop. A bell rang as he walked through the door announcing his presence. Behind the counter was a young girl dressed in her company uniform cleaning the large glass enclosure containing a large display of cheeses and condiments to compliment the desired sandwiches proudly pictured on the wall behind the counter.

She looked up from her cleaning and smiled a greeting. She moved behind the cash register eager to take his order. Brand showed her the picture of Jerry displayed on the screen of his phone and explained his reason for visiting the shop. She stared at the picture and started shaking her head no before telling him that she didn't recall seeing the man and she was not aware of any phone left behind by a customer. Thanking her, Brand turned on his heels and walked outside the next business just steps down the sidewalk.

After repeating this process in several other small shops, all with the same results, he found himself standing in front of the door to a small pub. Brand debated whether to skip the pub for now and check in with the owners of the convenience store on the other side or talk to the bar staff first. He glanced at the time on his phone. Too early to have a beer he decided, so he walked past the entrance and went into the convenient store.

The store was small, lined with narrow aisles and an abundance of stock. An elderly Chinese couple greeted Brand from behind the counter, the pair smiling as he approached. Brand showed the couple the picture on his phone and started to

238

inquire about the missing phone. He stopped abruptly. The couple stood with smiles on their face and nodded as he talked.

"Do you speak English?" He asked apprehensively. The woman smiled and said something to him that he couldn't quite understand. Very slowly Brand tried to break the language barrier and ask about his friend and the phone. After several attempts, he decided to move on. As a last resort he grabbed a pen and a piece of the paper from beside the cash register and wrote down his phone number and information about the missing phone in hopes that this couple would have someone working at the store who was better versed in the English language.

Pushing the paper and the pen back beside the cash register, he lifted his hand to his ear pantomiming a phone and pointed to Jerry's face on his phone screen. "If you happen to remember seeing this man?" He added.

After the frustrating exchange, he was ready for that beer. He walked the short distance back to the pub. A faded sign above a small grimy entrance proclaimed the bar the Lucky 7. Brand pushed through the door and chose a bar stool close to the till where the bartender and waitress were chatting.

Ordering a draft, he sipped the beer slowly until the waitress left and busied herself with preparing the bar for the noon crowd. Brand raised his eyes to a television above the bar. Golf was showing on the TV. Replays of Tiger Woods highlights beamed down into the room. Finishing his beer Brand waved over the bartender.

"Another beer?" The bartender asked.

"No. One is enough." Brand replied and scrolled to the picture of Jerry on his phone. "Any chance you would remember seeing this guy around here a couple of weeks ago?" The bartender took his time and studied the picture. After a momentary glance, the bartender shook his head indicating he had not.

Brand explained how his friend had lost his phone in the area a few weeks ago and was looking for it. Brand wrote his number on a coaster and slid it to the bartender.

"If somebody happens to find it can you give me a call?"

"Ya, sure. So another beer then?" The bartender inquired.

"No. But thanks." Brand slid a bill from his wallet and marched for the door. While the door was closing behind Brand, the bartender moved to the opposite end of the bar, dug through the pockets of a leather vest and reached for his phone. Stitched above the pocket, a golden halo over the emblazoned "A" of the Apostles bike club. The bartender carried the phone over to the windows overlooking the malls parking lot and watched as Brand mounted the bike and rode off.

Chapter 35

The Manager stopped at the door to his office. Quintin Rojas, the Colombian underboss's voice echoed from the room. Rojas stood on the business side of the custom crafted desk. The small man's back toward the door, strings of rapid Spanish spoken angrily filled the quiet of the room, words borne of a heated conversation. The flow of the Colombians conversation lost on Cartwright, his understanding of the language limited to a Taco Time menu.

James Cartwright, the Manager, stood in the doorway debating walking farther into the room or allowing his unwanted guest some privacy. He remained in the opening, his face impassive, his features barely veiling his dislike of the outspoken Colombian. The office, this city, was his turf and these foreign sons of bitches moved right in, set up shop and took right over.

Cartwright leaned against the doorframe. He found himself longing for the simpler life left behind over the passing years. A time before the Cartel blew into town. A time when Devil's Apostles and Thundercloud's east side gang coexisted, each group claiming parts of the city in an uneasy truce.

The Manager let his eyes roam the office interior, the headquarters of his operation floors above the noisy gaming rooms of the Millennium Casino. At one time, he lorded over the west end of the city, running his operation from a fortress-like clubhouse. Drugs, extortion, prostitution were the mainstays of his clubs activities. Occasionally, people got hurt, maybe killed and disappeared when running afoul of the Apostles but those incidents were rare. With the partnership of the Cartel, the body count climbed indiscriminately.

Richard Cozicar

When first approached by the Cartel to partner with their organization and handle the drug distribution east of the Rockies, the Manager saw the deal as a way to bring power and wealth to his followers and a way to crush his cross-town rivals.

The cash that followed the increased drug trade was more than his gang was capable of procuring. With the surge in profits, the violence escalated. The Colombian's proved they were not shy to brutally remove any obstacle in their way. His lack of understanding of how the Cartel operated soon put things in a different perspective.

It became all too evident that what the Cartel wanted, they took, and his role in the partnership clear. Another pion caught in the Cartels expanding collective. His organization's efforts to build and fight for their share of the drug trade in the city and surrounding area now in the hands of his Colombian partners. How much longer would they pretend that he was a valuable partner?

And the damn Spanish they spoke. Cartwright had no idea what the hell they were talking about, and the Colombians showed little respect, freely conversing in the language while in his presence. Nor did he trust them.

Cartwright dropped his chin to his chest. Times were changing violently, and he was becoming irrelevant. The Cartel was conniving and ruthless, and his future began to look uncertain.

Rojas slammed down the phone, the sudden noise busting through the Managers dark mood. Cartwright caught Rojas looking in his direction; the man's face dark and surly. Rojas motioned Manager into the room, pointing to a chair at the foot of the desk.

The Wolves Of Satan

"Why have we not heard from that big Indian, the leader of the Wolves?" The Colombian underboss asked angrily. "Have we not destroyed enough of his businesses yet for him to realize the trouble we bring?" The diminutive man dropped into the stuffed leather chair and swivelled facing the Manager. Rojas' coal black eyes locked on Cartwright, the Colombian's anger bubbling out in his words.

"He's a stubborn man. I don't think he scares as easily as you think." The Manager stared right back at the seated Cartel man. "I warned you against such rash actions."

"Are you scared, Parcero? Maybe you have no cojones." Rojas braced the Manager. "If you are easily frightened, I can find a real man to do your job."

"This isn't some backwoods South American country," The Manager calmly replied, "where all the cops and politicians are corrupt, and people scatter at the sight of your big scary Cartel.

Sure we have cops on the payroll, but they'll draw the line at you killing Roy's men and torching his buildings. Here the consequences are great, and the police fear going to prison more than they fear you. And Roy Thundercloud, never underestimate the man." The Manager stated. His words meant to dispel the tension in the room. "We have to plan our moves carefully."

Rojas regarded the Manager before speaking again. "El Jefe is very displeased about the loss of our warehouse and the missing shipment. He wonders why nobody has been made to pay for these atrocities. He wants, no, he demands that we end this problem swiftly and leave no doubt of the punishment that will follow further acts of disrespect.

The Indian and his pack of wolves, along with any future roadblocks that interfere in our business are to be…how do you say…removed with extreme prejudice. Our boss demands respect, and we will roll over every crook or cop to get it." The Colombians nostrils flared as he sucked in a deep breath when he finished his speech. A cold smile appeared on Rojas' face. "We will help you rid the city of these serpientes."

Rojas' thin lips curled into a smile, his tone growing friendlier.

"Call the big Indian…what was his name, Thunder…?"

"Thundercloud, Roy Thundercloud," Cartwright interjected.

"Yes. Mr. Thundercloud. What an odd name. Tell El Lobo that if he surrenders the man responsible for the destruction and theft of our property, we may leave him enough scraps to continue his way of life. If not, he can die along with his gang of mutts or get out of town! And his threats," Rojas referred to the injured Jander Valera and Roy's message, banged his fist on the desk to emphasize his words," are useless. Tell him," Rojas slid the left-hand sleeve of his jacket up revealing a diamond-studded watch, "he's got until 6:00 tomorrow night to accept."

"One more thing," Rojas added. "I want every cop under your thumb to start arresting El Lobo's men? We'll deplete his manpower, help make his decision easier."

"The cops can't hunt and arrest the Wolves without cause. Their actions will draw suspicions." Cartwright tried to reason. Quintin Rojas regarded the Manager. In the growing silence, he reached across the width of the desk and fumbled open an intricately designed humidor. Lifting the lid, the Colombian ran his fingers over the collection of exquisite cigars before choosing a thickly rolled Cuban. Beside the humidor, he slid a decorative guillotine cutter along with the cigar.

Rojas took his time inspecting the cigar before clipping the end and scratching a wooden match across the desk's surface.

The Wolves Of Satan

The match flared, burning off the sulphur, before settling to a mesmerizing yellowish flame. The Colombian closed his eyes as he touched the fire to the tobacco. Puffs of smoke escaped his mouth before he reopened his eyes.

"Tell the policìa to do what we ask. Otherwise, these men are of no use to us and become disposable. Those who stepped across the line in our service only have death or jail in their future as an escape. Remind the corrupt men in uniform why we pay them, and…of the family members they will be unable to protect." Rojas paused letting Cartwright digest the words of his thinly veiled threat. A cloud of dark grey smoke filled the air. "They take our money; they do what we ask!" Rojas banged the desk again ending the conversation, the smile no longer twisting the man's lips.

The Manager clenched his jaw, fighting down the urge to call bullshit to the Colombian's insidious orders. Threatening the freedom or the lives of the cops or worse yet, the cop's families, was well beyond any action Cartwright was willing to undertake. Where would the madness stop?

The bloodshed and loss of gang members and Cartel soldiers from the previous evening still stung the Managers pride. Without his advice, Rojas had orchestrated the attack on Thundercloud and his club. How the Colombian even knew that the Apostles leader would be there, Cartwright still didn't know. The police presence at the club and today's media coverage brought the simmering drug war into the open. Publicity that was not good for his line of business.

The Manager allowed his head to move slightly in wonder. He felt the grip on his operation, and now the war building between the rival bike gangs spinning out of control and the Cartel seemed more than eager to hasten it along.

Cartwright sat watching the Colombian. He dared not further enrage the man, but he sensed the need to rationalize with Rojas before bodies began cluttering the streets. A knock at the open office door interrupted the two men.

"Boss. I've got a bartender from the Lucky 7 on the line. He says that a man showed up this morning asking about a phone some old drunk lost. Probably nothing, but he insisted on talking to you." The man said and handed Cartwright a phone.

"Cartwright." The Manager snapped then listened as the caller updated him about the visitor at the bar and the questions asked. Cartwright grilled the bartender. The Manager's eyes widened as a picture of the man formed in his head from the bartender's description.

The snoop at the bar had to be Coldstream, and the Manager could guess why Coldstream was interested in the phone. Ending the call, Cartwright related the details of the conversation to Rojas. The man seeking the missing phone is none other than the very person they had framed in the detective's murder.

"So he must know about the video, why else would he be interested? This man undoubtedly has a death wish." The Colombian scowled at Cartwright. "We have to be the ones to find this phone. It's vital."

"Why. What the hell is so important about the video on it? So a few cops get busted for taking our money, maybe even some of your guys get arrested. What's the deal?" Cartwright failed to understand the unnecessary waste of time and the urgency of worrying about a lost phone, which may or may not contain secretly recorded videos of illegal transactions.

Rojas continued glaring at the Manager wondering how much he should tell the man. If he knew what was at stake, would the leader of the Apostles try harder to locate the phone? The Colombian sat quietly debating whether to tell the Manager exactly why the video on this phone was so important.

"The head of the Moreno Cartel has, for many years, remained anonymous to law enforcement in any country. He grows concerned that some of the videos might contain footage exposing his identity. He would very much like to remain anonymous. He finds operating with anonymity helps him travel and expand his business without the worry of the police and competitors." Rojas stopped. "Very few people know what El Jefe looks like, so, find the bandida who stole our product and locate the damn phone."

Chapter 36

In an industrial park on the south side of town, the doors to a strip club opened. A group of bikers exited the bar, the men joking with each other. Laughter erupted from a drunken joke. The men clinging to open bottles of beer huddled under the club's awning, a pack of cigarettes appeared and passed around. Lighters flared as the drunken men howled loudly from off colour jokes and tugs of strong beer.

Blast of police sirens dampened the mood. The group turned their backs to the club wall watching and wondering why the cops would venture into this section of town on a quiet Saturday afternoon. The police officers sprang from the squad cars with guns drawn, pointed at the surprised men. Beer bottles smashed on the sidewalk as the bikers raised their hands.

Roy Thundercloud had just gotten off the phone concerning a similar incident in the far south when his phone rang again. The call from the strip club in the industrial park was the third of it's kind that day. News of arrests trickled into the clubhouse all day. Roy lost track of exactly how many members were detained by the police but the count was climbing.

In between these calls, he worked the phone passing word through the city for his men to find shelter from the storm. Other calls went out to his lieutenants for a meeting at the secure acreage on the outskirts of the city.

Obviously his warning to the Apostles and their Cartel partners went unheeded. Crushing a man's hand and sending him running home with a mouth full of words rarely had an effect on serious matters. The threat levelled at the Cartel alliance after the altercation at the nightclub was his first warning, time to change course.

Roy paced away the day. A cell phone glued to his ear as he planned and talked to the vast number of gang members spread across the east side of Calgary. As the day passed, Roy recalled men to acreage. Others moved to undisclosed locations around the city with orders to remain out of sight. The acreage itself was out of the city cops jurisdiction, besides, he didn't think there were enough police in the province to mount an attack on his fortress.

He walked the floors, receiving updates on the assault of his territory, mulling over strategies for retaliation against the Apostles and their Colombian partners. The east side of the city, the territory that the Wolves had lorded over for years was slowly crumbling under the threat of the rival group.

The time for action had arrived. Roy realized the truth in this. Quick and brutal strikes against the enemies might satisfy the rising anger his fellow Wolves hungered for but at what cost? And if he proceeded in a haphazard fashion the price could be too steep. No. He had to push aside the growing fury and methodically assess the enemy and their battlefield tactics. The war wasn't the typical biker throw down. The Colombian Cartel changed that scenario.

In order to suppress the onslaught against his turf, the city would pay a huge price. The war between the city's two largest outlaw gangs wouldn't only mean dead bikers but would include unintended casualties.

Roy fought with the solution that made the most sense. He intended to let the attacks on his clubs and the police harassment die down. Ride out the storm before the Wolves would begin to reclaim the business they lost. He needed to buy time. Even with the advantage in manpower he had to tread carefully. With the appearance of the Colombians in this fight, and ultimately the increase of police presence to stem the growing danger, his gang stood a slim chance of success.

The rising number of gang related attacks was echoed by the news media causing an outcry from the city's population. Demands for the police force to quell the rising tide of violence would in turn result in added law enforcement. If he pushed back immediately, he would find that his gang would be fighting the battle on two fronts; one against the reinforced Apostles and another against a determined police force.

Too many unknown variables involved, he thought, diluting any chance at success. What he needed was an overwhelming show of force to stomp out his rivals quickly and permanently, but that meant merging forces with rival gangs from around the province and country, some friendly, some not. If the Cartel weren't stopped before they gained traction, the Colombians would roll across the country.

But his men were growing restless. The attacks were personnel. The men would rather fight in the open and take their chances with the law than hide like cowards. Roy worried that controlling their urge to take the fight to the enemy might prove to be as difficult a task as he faced in the years of heading the organization.

"What are you going to do?" Susan's voice stopped his pacing. Roy set the phone down and after hours on his feet fell into an armchair. Tiredly smiling back at her, he scratched his head in thought.

"Those boys are not leaving me much choice." He summarized his thoughts. "A strong show of force will bring the cops flocking to the city. People are scared with the recent outbreak of gang shootings. It's all over the news." He stated.

"How can you possibly stop them? United with the Cartel, the Apostles don't care who they hurt, what they destroy." Her voice grew quiet. "You could leave. Save your men. Would that be so bad?"

"I don't really see that as an option." Roy replied. He tilted his head curiously at Susan's thinking.

"What then?" Susan pushed.

Roy studied Susan's face. "A good question," he admitted then told her about possible talks with other factions of bikers. Joining forces to take back the city.

Late that evening while meeting with his men, his phone rang. The number seemed vaguely familiar. One he had seen before but couldn't place.

James Cartwright reintroduced himself to Roy.

"How's business?" Cartwright asked, the tension in the Manager's voice palpable through the phone line.

"A bit of a pain in the ass." Roy answered unperturbed. He punched the speaker button on his phone and set it on his desk. "But you know how this business can be."

"I can make this go away for you." The Manager replied. "I just need a favour."

"Now what can I possibly do for you?" Roy asked.

"The man who torched our warehouse, we want you to turn him over. The stolen truck with our shipment, that we can talk about later."

"Not going to happen." Roy replied and waited. Silence was his answer. Over the phone line Roy heard a curt exchange of words and then a heavily accented voice replaced Cartwright's.

"Mr. Thundercloud. We are not asking. We are simply giving you a chance to remain alive and still retain a small part of your operation." Quintin Rojas explained as if the deal the men were negotiating was part of any every day business transaction.

"Ah. Mr. Rojas. I'm going to speak very slowly so the language barrier doesn't screw up the translation of my words…Enjoy your last few days on this earth." Roy said very quietly into the phone. "If you continue to screw with me, I will personally introduce you to the devil."

"I'm sorry you feel that way." The Colombian underboss paused. "I have a message for you to pass on to your buddy Coldstream." When Roy failed to respond, the underboss continued. "Are you surprised that we know his name. We have eyes and ears among your local police. No one can remain anonymous for long." The Colombian gloated.

"Tell Coldstream; his friend's every conscious moment will be filled with extreme pain until he agrees to meet. Perhaps I will send him a video as a memento. He's not weak in the stomach, is he?" The Colombian laughed.

"I will leave a number for this purpose. The old guy might appreciate the cooperation. Do not forget to pass on this message…" Roy motioned to one of his men to write down the number as the Colombian deliberately emphasized the numbers.

Roy sat still, a blank wall the focus of his eyes. He punched the end button on the phone and looked at his men and shrugged.

"Anyone know where Brand is?" He asked. The men looked at each other. No one had an answer.

Chapter 37

Brand sat on the bike, the engine running. How in the hell was he going to find a phone that's been missing for weeks? The possibilities of it being anywhere in the city, from a bum's pocket to the landfill, ranged within that realm and if he found it, how relevant would the video be. The police had to have boxes of files on the ringleaders and to date have done nothing. Would the evidence urge them to act? Probably not, he reasoned.

Brand revved the bike's engine and cut into traffic. The bar at the strip mall was only the first of places Jerry remembered carrying the phone. Would it even be possible to locate such an item after it's been lost for a length of time? Brand nudged the negative thoughts aside. The search had only begun, at least where he was concerned, he reminded himself.

The sun was high in the sky when he pulled the bike into a small gravel lot fronting a stand-alone bar. The busted neon sign over the entrance flickered a name. Something like Oscars. Although between the flickering lights and the grime and dust covering the cracked plastic sign, the faded outlines were partially recognizable. The full name was hard to decipher. The name was irrelevant. The bar sat at the address Jerry had given.

The exterior of the building reflected the age and neglect of the building. Exposed areas of black building paper and wire showed against old, yellowed stucco. Rusty security bars added to the décor protecting dusty, cracked windows.

Brand rolled the bike in front of a weathered wooden rail, polished by age and splintered by the elements, the battered rail protecting an old crumbling sidewalk. Pushing the kickstand out, Brand climbed from the bike and removed his helmet, stretching the leather strap over the handlebars. Standing beside the motorbike, Brand considered the building. Nowhere near an expert on the Apostles but this seemed like the type of bar they would frequent.

A quick glance toward the back of the building eliminated the need to search. From where he stood, he doubted anyone visiting the establishment would be desperate enough to wander in that direction. A tangle of unruly shrubs crowded tight to the building separated the gravel lot from the rear of the building. The bottom of the bush packed with years of discarded garbage that collected in the tangle of stems. Brand couldn't imagine anyone entertaining the thought of attempting to squeeze through the tangle of bush.

Brushing the dust off his jeans, Brand ran his fingers through his hair before climbing the steps to the front door. Inside, the bar's interior was a slight improvement over the exterior. The dim lights hid the packed, worn carpet spread across a dirty floor. The layout was typical of these types of run down beer joints. Sets of stained circular tables surrounded by wooden chairs with torn backs sat on display under out-dated chandeliers with yellowed bulbs casting small circles of dim light.

*****

A grey Toyota SUV slowed alongside a curb half a block down from Oscar's bar. The car came to a stop, partially hidden behind a small cluster of overgrown Poplar trees. The gear selector rammed into park, the 4-cylinder engine switched off. Detective O'Brien parked with enough of the windshield exposed to allow him a view of the parking lot and the bar's entrance. He'd been on Coldstream's trail since earlier in the day, following the man at a discreet distance. O'Brien watched Coldstream enter the bar then settled in, waiting for the adventure to continue.

Ten minutes into O'Brien's vigil, a pack of bikers roared past the car and into the parking lot. He watched the group roll up to the wooden rail flanking Coldstream's bike. The men dismounted, removed their helmets and stretched, then chatted while leaning on their machines, five additional pairs of eyes watching the bar's entrance in the same manner as him. With the arrival of the bikers his boring day became a whole lot more interesting. The detective palmed the police radio, ready in case the afternoon proved too interesting. He watched and waited, his thumb hovering over the call button on the plastic mike.

*****

Like the pub before, the bartender and waitress sat huddled by the cash register. Their conversation paused by the arrival of a customer. Brand scanned the interior while walking toward the old beat up bar on the far side of the floor. Choosing a stool in the middle of the counter, he sat down and waited for the bartender to amble over. Naturally, the conversation the bar's employees were having out weighted the need for speedy service. Brand tapped a random tune on the sticky counter with the tips of his fingers waiting for the bartender to wander in his direction.

"Bud and juice." Brand called as the man closed the distance. The bartender nodded, retreated to a bank of pull levers labeled with various types of draft beer. Brand pulled crumpled bills from his front pocket and waited for the beer to arrive. Brand flattened a few twenties and shoved them toward the bartender when the man set the beer and clamato juice on the bar top.

"I've got a few questions." Brand said to the bartender, his hand holding the spread twenties flat on the bar.

The man looked back with dull eyes. "What kind of questions?" He asked flatly, no curiosity involved.

"Nothing too hard." Brand replied tapping his fingers over the bills. "A friend of mine lost his phone, and I'm trying to find it?" He toyed with the money. "One hasn't been found or turned in recently by chance?" He lifted the glass of clamato juice and poured a generous amount into the cold beer allowing the bartender time to process the question.

"Keep your money. I don't know about any lost phones." The man said and grabbed a single bill then headed for the till. "Tell your friend to buy another phone." He mumbled over his shoulder.

Noticing the waitress eavesdropping, Brand tapped his hand over the money then raised his voice so she could plainly hear his words as well.

"I told my friend that exact thing, but it seems he's partial to this phone, says all his contacts are on it, and he doesn't want the fuss of replacing them." Turning his attention back to his beer, he waited, letting his words settle. People in bars talk while they are drinking and he hoped that maybe the waitress overheard a customer discussing about such a thing. Looking back at the woman, he watched her face, but she seemed as puzzled as the bartender about the missing phone.

Pulling his phone out of a pocket, Brand scrolled the screens until the picture of Jerry and Dave appeared.

"I've got a picture of my friend. Would you two mind taking a look. Maybe you'll recognize the face. Might jog your memory? The phone is pretty important to him." Brand stood to show the picture.

"Maybe you should finish your beer and go search somewhere else?" The bartender said motioning toward the exit with his head.

Brand shrugged. How many phones were left behind in bars like this each day by drunks and why would these two remember or care about this one specifically, he wondered. Needle in the haystack.

He looked at the twenties spread on the bar. "Keep the cash." He told the bartender and swivelled in the direction of the door.

Brand squinted his eyes when he stepped into the bright sunlight as he crossed from the dark interior to the outside. He hesitated, letting his eyes adjust to the light. The loud rumble of powerful bike engines confronted him. Blinking his eyes into focus, he traced the sound to the group of bikers parked out front.

"Shit." He mumbled out loud as he looked over the parking lot. The red letter A with its golden halo stood out on the biker's leathers.

Chapter 38

The bikers stared up at Brand appearing at the entrance while he stood looking down on them. One by one they pushed up off the bike seats. By the twinkle of sunlight gleaming off the accessorized jewellery the group was wearing, knuckle busters and chains, Brand couldn't imagine that talking was going to help avoid the situation.

Like any wild animal, if you showed fear they would attack, so Brand slowly descended the steps in the direction of his bike. He had no weapons on him. Even his helmet was hanging beside the men, on his bike's handlebars. If he managed to get his hands on that, he could do a little damage or at the very least protect himself for a short time.

Brand continued moving toward his bike, his eyes shifting between the biker's faces waiting for them to telegraph their first move.

"Howdy boys. Not a bad day for a ride?" He broke the silence, getting a feel for the situation and buying time to grab his helmet. He was probably going to get a good beating at the very least, so his thoughts turned proactive, searching for a way to dish out some punishment of his own before being overwhelmed by the group.

The Apostles remained still as Brand stepped loser. When he reached across the railing for the helmet, the biker closest to him stretched out a hand to stop him. Acting on adrenaline, Brand snatched the helmet off its perch and swung it at the biker's head. The arc of the helmet surprised the biker sending him back peddling into the stationary motorcycle, the two toppling to the ground.

Feet first, Brand catapulted over the wooden rail. The bulk of his body slammed into a pair of Apostles off to one side, the force of his weight piling the men and their machines to the ground.

He twisted from the tangle and landed shoulder first onto the hard packed gravel of the lot stirring a cloud of dust upward. Scrambling to his feet, he used his helmet as a weapon swinging it at the bikers as they recovered. Catching one of the men in the face, he rushed the loose group fighting to keep the others off balance.

A link of chain bit into his back. The sting of steel and the solid impact drove him back to the ground. Moving to avoid a second bite from the chain, he rolled onto his feet and began to rise. A blow thudded against his shoulder from behind. Brand sunk down to his knees. His arms flew up to protect his head from the assault of fists and boots raining down on his body. A foot caught him flush on the side of his head sending a jolt of fire the length of his body.

Desperately, he fought to remain alert. Darkness began to push him away from consciousness when the assault to his body eased. Blinking wildly, Brand waded through the fog overwhelming his brain. Pain soared from his nerves leaving him wasted and dazed. Sirens replaced the ringing in his ears. Through blurred vision, he watched the tangle of arms and legs of the bikers pull back. Harsh voices filtered into his ears in muddled waves. Shortly, the jumbled words took form, their meanings growing clearer.

The blue attire of city police officers replaced the leather-clad bikers. Past the line of uniforms, the Apostles stood in a row. One officer bent close and looked at him. On the policeman's face, a look of surprise before recognition turned the man's features to disgust.

"Hey, Charlie. Have a look at this guy. Isn't there a BOLO out for this bastard's arrest?" The officer continued glaring at Brand. "Yeah. Isn't this the son of a bitch who gunned down Detective Walgreen? He's a god damned cop killer. Maybe we should let the bikers loose and have them finish what they started. Give this asshole everything he deserves?"

Another cop stepped into Brand's line of sight and glowered. Brand shook off the results of the biker's blows and started to rise from the gravel only to have an officer raise a foot and push him back to the ground. He lay there.

The angry tone of the officer's words sent a chill down his spine. Trapped, he looked for a means of escape, his eyes searching for the faintest sign of mercy on the faces of the cops. The bikers would have been easier to deal with than a group of police bent on revenge for the death of their colleague. Brand's thoughts raced amid shouts of the police officers urging the bikers to climb on their motorcycles and clear the area before the group was arrested and taken downtown.

The revving of the bike engines, deafening, the wheels of the bikes crunching gravel, passing close to Bands head while he remained on the ground. Before the roar of motorcycles receded, a boot thudded into his chest. One of the men in blue stood with the barrel of a gun pointed down in Brand's direction.

"We should do the world a favour and end this miserable life. Doesn't seem right to let a cop killer holiday in jail while some asshole defence lawyer tries to get him released." The cop holding the gun knelt and swung a fist into Brand's face. Soon more officers joined the dispute. A second barrage of fists and boots pounded Brand.

The Wolves Of Satan

Detective O'Brien watched in disbelief as the officer's anger increased. When the call for backup went over the radio, the fact that Coldstream was the chief suspect in Detective Walgreen's death slipped his mind. O'Brien intended to stay in the background, avoid showing his face so he could shadow his perp, but the time for discretion was over. These uniforms looked like they might finish what the Apostles had started.

Chapter 39

O'Brien flicked the siren in his car off and on to catch the uniforms attention before yelling. "You'll kill the man!"

Rushing into the uniformed officers, he pushed the angry men away, standing between them and the source of their ire. The uniforms were acting on rage, driven from a tight bond of the brotherhood of law enforcement officers and the man before them accused of shooting a fellow policeman, the men oblivious to anything else.

O'Brien pulled one officer back and drove his fist into the policeman's face, knocking the man to the ground. Then he dove into two others, the three men hitting the gravel in a tangle. Scrambling to his feet, he stood in front of Brand, daring the others to remove him.

"What in the hell are you guys thinking?" He scolded the uniformed officers, dusting off his coat as he stared them down.

"Get out of the way." An older patrolman replied. The name Carl displayed on a patch on the man's chest. "This man is a cop killer!" Then the senior patrolman screamed back. "**He deserves what he's getting**...he deserves a damn bullet, not a bed and three hot meals!"

"You back off or the next bullet I fire will be for you." O'Brien threatened. He stood facing the group of policemen, daring them to move first. After a few heated moments, cooler heads prevailed. The incensed cops reigned in their fury.

"I'll ride in the back with him," O'Brien said lifting Brand from the ground and marching him to a waiting patrol car.

The Wolves Of Satan

O'Brien escorted Brand through the process of fingerprinting, and mug shots then led to the basement and tossed him in a cell. When he asked for a washroom to clean up, his pleas fell on deaf ears. The next few hours he spent sitting on a stained bunk, dust and gravel ground into his clothing and skin mixing with the blood and bruising, before two officers escorted him to an interrogation room. With his hands cuffed to the table, the officers left him alone to stare at the walls. If this was their way of forcing him to talk, they were in for a long day.

He spent his time reviewing what had happened and what he had to do once he was released. The evidence against him was circumstantial and planted. There was no doubt in Brand's mind that he would be set free, and if not fully exonerated of the false charges, then at least with bail.

While he mulled over his misfortune and options, the door to the room opened. Detective O'Brien entered. Brand eyed the detective warily as the man approached the table, two steaming Styrofoam cups of coffee in the detective's hands. O'Brien stepped to the table setting one of the cups in front of Brand. A humourless smile pulled at Brand's lips as he looked from the coffee up to the detective.

"What's this, a peace offering…so let me guess, you're going to play the good cop now, am I right?" Brand said sarcastically. He reached for the coffee. It was unmistakably cop shop coffee. Bitter and burnt, but as he cradled the cup, the coffee tasted like a million dollars. He carefully sipped the hot liquid, feeling it burn as it passed his parched throat.

Brand kept his eyes on the detective; the man remained standing and silent.

"Look, Coldstream, we need to clear things up." The detective looked away. "I should have been upfront with you earlier," he continued, "But, in my defense, I had no way of telling how deeply involved you were in this investigation."

"Clean about what?" Brand egged the detective on. "Clean on the fact that the Cartel has you wrapped around their finger." He lashed out at the detective then relented, wondering how far he should push, after all the detective probably saved his life back at the bar. "I've noticed that grey Toyota of yours several times in my travels of late…did you gamble yourself into their debt or do you just enjoy playing on both sides of the law?"

Detective O'Brien let out a short laugh.

"Yes. I suppose I can see where you would get an idea like that." O'Brien replied. "No, I'm not in anybody's debt, and you can bet your ass that I'm on the right side of the line as you put it." Pulling a chair away from the table, the Detective sat down and proceeded to explain.

"I do not doubt that you did see my car at, shall I say, dubious haunts. I let Detective Walgreen borrow it…it seemed that his car had a run of bad luck thus resulting in repeated visits to a local garage." O'Brien lifted his cup to his mouth, blew on the steaming coffee to cool it down, then took a sip. "I have to confess. The reason Detective Walgreen's car has made repeated visits to the mechanic lately is my fault. I purposely tampered with it."

O'Brien kept talking. "I wanted him to use my car. I had it wired. I suspected he was working for the either the Apostles or the Cartel, so I needed a way to keep tabs on him." O'Brien lifted the cup back to his mouth.

"I'm new to the Calgary police department. I've only been in the province for the past few months transferring in from Surrey. I'm here on loan from the E Division of the RCMP. Part of the Drug Enforcement Branch." O'Brien paused again staring at his cup. "No one in this department is aware of this fact, so I guess you could say that I'm undercover."

Brand slowly sipped his coffee. "I am sure there is a point to all this?" He interrupted.

"There have been rumblings blowing over the mountains of the Cartel expanding their operations east into this city. Rumours surfaced about members of the local law falling under the Moreno Cartel's spell.

The upper brass preferred I didn't storm into the city and announcing my intentions. That would only put the bad guys on their best behaviour, so we managed to keep my transfer under the radar.

I think by now you are probably aware of the Cartel and the business they run. We know they came to the country from South America and we also know most of the players. The thing is, the leader of the group remains a mystery. We have a list of names and corresponding charges but can't find anyone to provide us with an identity. Because of that I've been lurking in the background, letting things unfold while I sort through the layers to discover the man's identity. Maybe even nail down his location."

"That's a pretty sad story, but I'm afraid I don't know why you're sharing this with me?" Brand asked. A drop of blood fell on the table beside his coffee. Lifting his arm, he swiped a sleeve across his chin and lips. His gaze remained on the splatter. "Why haven't you arrested some of his lackeys, guys close enough to the top to name names?"

"Yeah, we have, but no matter what we threaten or promise, they all tell the same story. No one knows who the top dog is or where the boss hides. The group has run a similar operation on the coast for years and still, no matter what we do or who we arrest, not one person can or will cough up his name." The detective set down his coffee in frustration, hard enough that the cream lightened coffee slopped over the edge of the cup. "It's like the guys a flippin' ghost."

"Dave, the guy you called your friend, he was one of us. Working undercover," O'Brien said flatly. The detective's words jolted Brand to attention. Brand pulled his focus away from the drop of blood drying on the table and met the detective's stare.

"Dave...Dave Halperson?" Brand asked disbelievingly.

"Yes." O'Brien pause. After several seconds of silent debating, O'Brien decided to bring Brand up to speed on his case.

"Dave's worked undercover for our department for probably close to ten years now. On the coast, in Vancouver, he was very successful in tracking down a human smuggling ring that brought their cargo through Washington State and used the ferries to sneak the people into the country. Part of the payment the smugglers required was that every illegal had to bring in a certain amount of contraband drugs when they crossed. If the illegals succeeded, they were free to go, but if we arrested them, well, what else. They were locked up until we turned them over to the American justice system."

"So, what are you telling me? Because of Dave, the Cartel targeted my house?"

"I got to be honest with you. When I first arrived at the scene, I presumed you were involved. You and Dave hung around a lot. So, you can see where I would conclude that you were the one he was pursuing. I believed that he had evidence that you were involved with the drugs and he was keeping you close.

Dave called the other day and set a meeting for this past Saturday. Dave hadn't been in touch for a while, and then, out of the blue, I get a call, and he wants to meet. He was very close to identifying the Moreno Cartel's top man, but first, caution was needed to make sure his path was clear before retrieving the info.

Next thing that happens, gunmen attack your house, and Dave's lying face down on your table, dead. So I ask you, what was a guy to believe?" The detective said shrugging as a way of an apology.

"So you no longer think I'm involved?" Brand queried.

"No, not any longer." The detective stood from the table, stretched, then paced in the confining space of the interrogation room. A short laugh came from O'Brien's mouth. "If you are involved, you sure in the hell are going through a lot of pain and misery to keep your cover," O'Brien said, stopped his pacing long enough to shoot a glance back at Brand. Brand sat hunched over the table, his hands in restraints, staring back. His clothes covered in dust and blood. Swollen blackish, purple bruises tightened up his facial features.

Brand watched the detective pace, confusion twisting his battered face.

"That's a good story and what happened to Dave was shitty...but I still don't understand why you are telling me this?"

"Alright. I guess I should get to the point. The point is I could use your help. The law limits my options for the ways I can gather information. You, on the other hand, don't seem to be concerned about how you come across the knowledge you're seeking. That kind of help I most certainly would appreciate."

"Whoa. I'm flattered, but if you fail to notice," Brand raised his hands the short length the handcuffs would allow, "I am currently going to be residing in a jail cell."

"Oh…that. You will be released shortly. While you were cooling your heels in the basement, I made some phone calls. The shooting of Detective Walgreen was an obvious attempt to frame you. I've talked to witnesses and studied the surveillance cameras in the vicinity. We have a picture of the Walgreen's killer. A search is underway for the man."

"How long have you known, you son of a bitch?" Brand's voice climbed an octave. "How come the patrols still thought I was the shooter?" Brand glared at the detective," Maybe you won't mind sharing that information with the uniforms in the patrol cars. Next time they stop me, I might not be so lucky."

"I have revoked the BOLO," O'Brien assured him.

"Good." Brand said raising his handcuffed arms again. "If you don't mind then…?"

Brand kept his gaze locked on the detective's face, anger adding a deeper hue to the bruising colouring his face. He watched the man's eyes break contact and travel down to his hands still fastened to the table with the steel cuffs before.

"First. Let me explain," O'Brien cleared his throat. "With Dave out of the picture, I had no way of locating the information he stashed. I needed to keep you desperate and willing to search." The detective said in a quieter voice. "And again, I wasn't sure what part you played. Dave worked for us and if you're not part of the ring, who does that leave? The old guy, the man who disappeared from the hospital?"

"That's ridiculous," Brand stammered past his ire, "The man's ancient and a drunk. When's he's sober, Jerry's a stand-up guy but most of his spare time is spent in a bottle…so…no…never."

The detective walked over and unlocked the handcuffs. "Dave stayed very close to you two. Why? Just so that he could tie feathers on tiny metal hooks with coloured string and drink your beer? Naw. He had a reason." O'Brien planted his hands flat on the table and leaned in close to Brand. "So what do you say? Will you help?"

"I don't know what to tell you. If the best plan you have is counting on me to help, then I think you're going to have a bad day." Brand replied rubbing his wrists.

Chapter 40

Detective O'Brien offered Brand a ride back to his bike. The lot fronting Oscar's bar sat vacant in the late afternoon. Brand's helmet lay in the gravel near the motorbike. Dusting the headgear, he eased it over his swollen, battered head and climbed onto the seat. A standing push against the bike's kick-start lever and the powered two-wheeler roared to life.

Brand pointed the motorcycle toward the southeast. What he needed was to clean up, change clothes, grab a decent meal and wash it down with copious amounts of rye. O'Brien left a card before he departed and let Brand know that his house was all his again, it was no longer a crime scene.

The promise of a shower and clean clothing disappeared minutes after he signalled off the Deerfoot, rerouted past a cluster of businesses and turned the corner in the direction of his house.

The front door sat ajar when he climbed the stairs to the veranda. He bent and studied the knob. Twisting it, he discovered it would no longer worked. Brand stepped inside, over and around his scattered belongings and made a careful search of the interior. The past few days made him reluctant to be complacent.

Relieved to find no surprises waiting, he grabbed a chair from the dining room and carried it to the front entrance jamming it tight under the doorknob. Time permitting, he'd have to replace the lock, but that could wait until he at least had a shower and cleaned up.

Sitting at the table, he nursed a rye and coke, working the detective's words together with pieces of information he had uncovered. A lot of holes remained that needed filling, bits of information to complete the puzzle.

Dave being undercover was a big piece to add, but how did that fit into the situation. If Dave had proof to blow the investigation open, then why would he spend the evening drinking beer and tying flies instead of meeting with O'Brien. The information had to be more important than drinking with a couple of friends. O'Brien said he would retrieve the data when it was safe to do so, but, safe from who or what?

Dave wasn't hanging around because Brand was involved in any of this...what was he missing. The only other person was Jerry and he sure and the hell wasn't the ringleader of a Colombian crime syndicate. Shit, the old boy would no doubt use the drugs personally instead of selling them. Sure. He got caught up in gambling debts to the Apostles and even admitted to making some illegal runs for them, but a drunk like Jerry sure wasn't leading a multi-national drug cartel.

Suddenly Brand's mind snapped back to Jerry. With all the excitement he had forgotten about his friend. Days had passed since Jerry disappeared from the hospital. O'Brien never said anything about locating the old guide, so where was he, and was he still alive? Would the Colombians kill Jerry once they found out that he was a hopeless drunk and lost the phone?

It seemed that everything came back to the missing phone. What had Jerry recorded on the device that could be so critical? Even video of the Cartel boss wouldn't be that big of a deal. No more than a minor inconvenience for a man hidden in some South American hideaway where no Canadian law enforcement agency could touch him. Unless, unless the head of the Moreno Cartel wasn't out of the country. Brand indulged this thought. The prospect of the drug lord lurking nearby, maybe even holed up in the city. Suddenly the phone became much more significant and would better explain the Cartel's need to get their hands on it.

Brand walked to the fridge and poured a second rye. Thinking of phones, he had his turned off and decided it was safe to power the device back on, the worry of the cops tracking him now a problem in the past. He carried his drink back to the table and sat down waiting for the phone to run its cycle.

He looked over his ransacked house and decided against cleaning up for now. The funny thing was that the fly he was tying that Friday evening was still waiting in the vice. The vice and the materials lay undisturbed through all the commotion. His eyes roamed over the devastation. Fixing the door was irrelevant, he realized. If anyone else broke into his house, there would be little else they could do to cause damage.

His phone chimed, bringing him out of his musing. Thirteen messages were waiting for him. The first hand full switched between announcing that he was a lucky winner of a free trip to the Caribbean, several robo calls from local businesses and a couple triple eight numbers from phone solicitors. Stuck near the end, a number he didn't recognize appeared several times over a short time span. The caller spoke with a thick Latin accent.

"Mr. Coldstream...you are nothing if you are not a pain in my side. I have your friend...." There was silence, and then he heard a loud, painful scream, a scream with a few maritime adjectives thrown in and a Lord Tundering Jesus, Boy. "I know you are looking for your friend's phone. A phone that you know by now is of the utmost importance to an associate of mine, so I will make you a deal...find the phone and return it and then perhaps I stop my camaradas from removing your friend's body parts. He remains alive for now, but do not take long to decide.

Your amigo will run out of appendages." The connection ended abruptly. Brand looked at the time stamp of the message. Rojas' call recorded earlier. Likely around the same time the cops had interrupted the Apostles in their efforts to kill him.

A sigh of relief blew past Brand's lips knowing that Jerry was still among the land of the breathing. Brand worked on his drink while listening and deleting the messages. The phone number from the Colombians he saved into the phones memory. Arriving at the last voicemail, he was no longer paying close attention to the voices on the phone. His mind was busy searching for a different angle to locate the lost phone. He still had one more location to check. It was to be the next on his list when the bikers confronted him at Oscar's.

"BRAND...HELP...WE'RE UNDER ATTACK. A FEW OF ROY'S MEN ARE HERE, BUT WE'RE PINNED IN THE HOUSE BY GUNFIRE...

Brand's attention shifted back to his phone. He started the recording over again and listened to Susan's frightened voice. The last time he replayed the message, he checked the time the call arrived, 35 minutes earlier.

He ran for the door and the motorbike parked by the curb, one hand busy scrolling through the contact list on the phone searching for Roy's number. He pinned the device between his ear and his shoulder while it connected, his hands occupied on the bikes handlebars working the throttle. Revving the bike's engine, he raced out of the neighbourhood.

Struggling to maintain control of the bike as he fought to hold the phone to his ear, Brand pushed his luck, precariously weaving around traffic and slipping illegally past vehicles as he gained the route to lead him east toward the outskirts of the city. Brand skirted around traffic, the speed of the motorbike climbing. He shifted in the seat, dodging in and out, around and through the two lanes of traffic, ignoring red lights and racing north first before he had the chance to swing the powerful two-wheeler in an easterly direction.

Fumbling to redial Roy's number while he drove, the front tire of the bike came within inches of contacting a merging pickup truck. Brand looked up from the phone screen with scarcely enough room to avoid a dangerous collision.

Finally, on the third attempt his call connected with Roy.

"Your house is under attack..." He yelled above the roar of the motorcycle. "I'm on my way now!" Before his brother could answer, Brand ended the call and stuck the phone into a pocket then cranked the throttle on the bike. The front wheel lifted with the extra gas, then squealed as it contacted the pavement, the bike leaping as Brand tried to erase the miles to Roy's acreage as quickly as possible.

The first thought to cross his mind was that so much time had elapsed since the message and then the reality of the situation reared its head. He was riding into a gunfight with only a bike for a weapon. He'd been in worst positions than this, but it was still a stupid idea, one he had no time to rectify.

His mind worked through a few quick scenarios, although he had to admit, a bike against a group of armed men had a low probability rate of success. He returned his attention to arriving there first; the how and why would work themselves out.

As he turned onto the highway that bordered Roy's property, lady luck toyed with him. The traffic on the busy two-lane road was substantial. Heavy traffic equalled traffic noise equalled whoever was laying siege to Roy's place wouldn't notice the roar of the bike coming. The advantage of surprise would cut the odds somewhat in his favour.

The Wolves Of Satan

The big iron gates protecting the entrance hung askew as he neared the property, the gravel driveway to the house unblocked and deserted.

He risked a glance behind. The traffic was still lined up, the loud thrum hiding the bikes roaring engine. He dropped a couple gears and leaned into the turn taking advantage of the bikes pent up motion. Gravel shot from the back tire as he careened into the deserted opening, the forward momentum carrying man and machine toward the house.

As Brand turned on to the acreage, a man surprised him by stepping out from behind one of the large posts anchoring the gate. Taking the man's appearance in stride, Brand squeezed the throttle. The bike lurched forward. Brand braced and leaned. His shoulder smashed into the waiting gunman, the collision throwing the man into the gatepost.

A short distance ahead, a collection of bodies knelt together using the metal body of a car for protection as they fired bullets towards Roy's house. Instincts took over. With the traffic on the highway camouflaging the noise from the bike engine, Brand sped closer to the gunmen. Timing his movements, he squeezed the front brake. The rear tire skidded forward. With the bike's momentum sliding in the direction of the shooters, he leaned away from the group. The bike started to lie down in the gravel driveway and skid. Brand dove, pushing away from the falling motorcycle with his feet.

One of the gunmen turned, his voice rising in surprise, echoing over the calamity of rifle fire and traffic. The man yelped as the bike and a wall of dust and gravel hurtled toward him but was too slow to react. The wall of metal and grit chewed across the driveway toward the group hiding behind the car.

The careening bike slammed the group into the side of the car with such force and awkwardness that the sedan being used as cover, rocked. Cries of surprise rose into the evening air with the dust from the impact followed by screams of pain from the unfortunate few pinned between the bike and the car.

Brand planted a foot in the gravel slowing his slide, rolled through the dust and gravel before rising to his feet. In the screening dust, he rushed after the bike with hopes of retrieving a fallen weapon or two. The air was thick and masking. Brand rushed through the veil of confusion emerging among the fallen gunmen. Disarming the few who still clutching their firearms, he retrieved a rifle with a spare magazine. Brand sidestepped the men pinned against the car by the bike and moved to take cover behind a second vehicle, cautiously scanning the yard for more assailants.

The screams of the wounded and broken men grew quiet leaving the yard silent. The chaos cut off from the highway by the wall of sound from the evening traffic. While he caught his breath, a pair of black SUV's raced into the yard kicking up more dust. The doors of the SUV flew opened. Brand watched several sets of boots land on the gravel driveway followed by the flash of weapons.

Several of the guns sighted on Brand before the bellow of Roy's voice cut through the din of road traffic. Brand waited while Roy assessed the situation in the yard and then barked orders at his men. He watched several of the Wolves leave the safety of the vehicles and moved toward the house. Some of Roy's men remained at the SUV's covering others who scattered, crouched low to the ground and spread across the yard.

The minutes ticked by as Brand sighted down the rifle's barrel at the house, his ears pricked for the sounds of gunfire. A few sporadic shots rang through the yard and then silence once again. Time passed before Roy's men appeared at the back of the house signalling that the fight was over.

Brand stood up as Roy left the SUV and strode toward him.

"You all right?" Roy's gaze stayed on Brand's swollen face. "Did you hit the gravel with your head?" He asked then looked away studying the area surrounding the house watching his men comb the yard.

Brand dusted off his clothes. "Another long story." He replied and followed Roy.

The two men walked toward the two-story building. Roy called to the men inside the house, shouting an all clear in case they were fidgety and mistook the group standing in the front yard for the attackers and shot at them as they approached.

Chapter 41

Susan ran to Brand when the two men entered the house. Roy's voice rumbled throughout the interior of the house, his words echoing off the walls and ceilings, calling his men together.

"What happened to you," she asked, her hand gently touching the bruises on Brand's face. Brand moved Susan aside leaving Roy to talk with his men.

"A long story," Brand brushed off her concern. Roy saved him further explanation by motioning the two into the living room. The three chose chairs close to each other.

Roy remained thoughtful before speaking.

"This attack makes no sense." He looked in Brand's direction. "The house was surrounded, my men trapped inside, but the Apostles remained by their vehicles, satisfied to take shots at the house…they never attempted to shoot their way inside…" Roy drifted back into silence.

"Our arrival may have cut them short. The gunmen had no way of knowing how many men were inside the house." Brand interjected. "Probably just trying to send a message." He continued the line of thought.

"Waiting in the yard to get killed is one hell of a message." Roy shot back.

"Yeah…the approach doesn't seem very smart." Brand agreed. "Didn't you tell me this place was impenetrable? The Apostles must have known."

"Probably." Roy shrugged. "But why attack at all then. Those few men would never have made it inside alive.

Whatever reason for those men to show up here, whoever decided to launch the assault, why?"

"Maybe for a distraction or to let you know that they will bring the fight right to your front door." Brand shrugged. "Who knows how these people think."

"Well. This shit is going to end." Roy rose to his feet. "I'm growing tired of the Cartel's gun and shoot tactics. Too many of my clubs have fallen; a lot of good men are in the hospital and out of commission.

Funny though, every time we've moved against them, the bastards are waiting for us. It would seem that I have a leak in my organization that needs plugging." Roy glanced away lost in thought once more. Minutes later he re-joined the conversation.

"I've started talks with gangs not involved in this skirmish," Roy talked as he paced. "Not yet anyways, smaller outfits outside the city's boundaries. Bikers not affiliated with the Apostles or us yet. I'm offering a deal, mergers with some and talk of a truce with others. These damn Colombians have brought in men from the Coast to bolster their ranks. Time to even the odds."

Roy slowed his pacing and smiled, changing the subject. "Let's get the hell out of here. Grab a bite to eat. We'll take the SUV's," he chided Brand. "Looks like your bike might need repairs."

"You want to go out?" Brand asked studying his brother's face.

"Sure. Nobody knows where we're going. Besides, I think the kitchens closed due to lead contamination." The big man laughed at his attempt at humour leading the way toward the door.

On the way back into town, Roy expanded on the details of the impending mergers under consideration. Smaller gangs from the north and east were eager to hook up with the Wolves' and share in some of the spoils of the big city boys.

"The leaders are taking my offerings to their men. I'll be contacting them in the morning. Most will become independent chapters of the Wolves. Others will join us as associates. Our," Roy held his fingers up quoting his words, "business know-how with their established connections. A win-win.

If the lot of us join forces, we'll forge a chain well into the eastern reaches of the country. And in a case like this, the combined strength of our organizations to draw manpower from." He continued, "The days of sharing the city with the Apostles is coming to an abrupt halt. If Cartwright wants to make deals with the devil and come after my turf, I think it's time I renegotiate the terms." Roy faced the window. The hum of tires rolling over the asphalt filled the quiet in the SUV.

"Time to run the Manager and his Cartel garbage all the way back to the coast and push them into the ocean." A smile marked Roy's face, but his eyes belied the fury that lay behind them.

The rest of the trip, the two rode in silence. Brand studied Susan carefully, watching to see how she fared after the gunfight. Roy's driver was entering the east side of town when he asked for directions to the restaurant Roy had in mind.

"Mescalles," Roy answered. "A small family-run restaurant on International Ave. The owners are partial to the Wolves." Roy told Brand. "Two of their boys ride with us."

The Wolves Of Satan

"They serve the best Mexican food in town," Roy bragged, adding that the eatery was locally known and discreet enough that no one should bother them.

Cars blocked the front of the restaurant. Roy pointed to a stall two businesses away. "This will do," he instructed.

The entrance to Mescalles consisted of a nondescript, windowless door bearing a small plaque with the businesses name hanging above a welcome sign. The eatery stuffed in the middle of a multi-shop strip mall. The parking lot edged onto International Avenue.

Only a handful of customers sat at tables when the three entered the restaurant. Roy led the way to a table in the back corner and pulled a chair for Susan. Brand sat facing the front door, the old instincts were running at full service and he wanted to make sure he saw trouble coming before it found them.

Talk around the table lagged. The three stared absently at the menus each lost in their thoughts. Without seeming too obvious, Brand snuck glances at Susan, worried about her mindset after the attack on Roy's house. Looking toward Roy, toying with the menu, he noticed signs of the escalating war setting heavy on his brother's mind.

"Have you learned more about the Apostles?" Roy asked Brand after the waitress retreated from taking their order. Roy glanced from Brand to Susan, resting his gaze on her face before he continued. "Received a message from our Colombian friend earlier today." Roy hesitated, his eyes darting in Susan's direction. Roy paused, wondering if he should breach the subject of Susan's dad while she was at the table. Realizing the need to push on, he told the others of the call from Rojas.

"What did he want?" Brand asked.

"He left a number and message for you. He wants you to bring him the missing phone..." Susan hid her emotions by turning her face away from the table at the spoken reminder of her kidnapped father. "If you don't agree to meet, with the missing phone in hand..." He paused again. "Jerry won't fare well."

"I don't know if this phone can be found. I've been toying with a different approach." Brand played with his drink, twisting the glass in his fingers as he organized his thoughts. "I'm going to take a run at the top guys in the organization, tit for tat so to speak. Get my hands on one of the higher-ups and use them to bargain for Jerry's release, but I will need help.

"What can you tell me about Rojas?" Brand asked. "Does he stay at the casino or is there somewhere else in town I can find him? And how about this Manager, Cartwright, any idea where he likes to hang out? Anyplace he goes to be away from the others. Does he have a wife or girlfriend?"

Roy shook his head. "You attempting to end this fight all by yourself," Laughter followed his words. "Lone Ranger type deal or what?"

"Something's got to be done." Brand replied defensively. "My friends are suffering, and you and your men are being run ragged."

"You'll have to wait until we return to my place. I can get you the information, but whatever you're planning, be damn careful. This alliance between the Apostles and the Cartel is lethal. The way they're taking to the streets proves they have little worry of being stopped. They must have most of the police force locked on their payroll, or they really don't give a rats ass about the law in this city."

Susan stood up interrupting the conversation and excused herself. The two men watched her walk away. Roy filled in some of the blanks of Brand's questions. "There is one club where Cartwright likes to visit. I believe his girlfriend works there. Like I said. I'll have to make some calls.

To my understanding, he spends a lot of time there, and usually with only one other guy in tow. The problem is that the guy is a giant, a guy by the name of Bakker. Don Bakker." Roy lifted the bottle of beer to his mouth. "Hell. This Bakker makes me look average. I can't imagine Cartwright needing anyone else tagging along."

"What does the big guy look like?" Brand asked. Roy described the man. Brand nodded. The big man sounded like the same fellow Brand watched at the casino the night he met the gambling truck driver. If it was the same man, the term big somehow fell short in describing the giant.

"Where's the club?" Brand inquired. He would figure a way around the big man when and if the time arose. Had to be the same man, the Apostles couldn't possibly have two men of that stature in their club, could they? At least he hoped not.

Roy wrote the name of the club and address on a napkin, sliding the paper across the table.

"When he shows at the club, I'm not sure, but I can ask around in the morning for you. Cartwright's habits may have changed with the outbreak of trouble, but I doubt it. So far, we seem to be the ones on the defensive." Roy added.

"You have a name for Cartwright's girlfriend?"

"Not off hand. I'll get it for you when we return to the acreage." The two men dropped the discussion as Susan walked back toward the table. The next few hours, the three talked about anything but the fight that was raging between the two big outlaw gangs in the city.

With the meal complete and a collection of empty cerveza bottles, Roy suggested that they leave. The earlier clientele had finished their meals and left, the interior all but deserted except for Roy's table and the staff.

"We could drive back to the acreage and grab a few items then find a place for the night," Roy mentioned. Brand agreed. He had no place to be and he was hesitant to leave Susan. The Colombians had abducted her dad, and after the shootout, Roy's home now lacked the security he had hoped, leaving him reluctant to place Susan in further danger.

While Roy was talking with the manager, Brand escorted Susan to the door.

"Meet you in the car." Brand told Roy as they left him. When the pair was almost at the door, Susan stopped.

"I forgot my purse." She started and spun back toward the table. Brand waited inside the door for her.

Having taken care of the bill, Roy met Brand at the door.

"I'll wait for you outside," he said patting Brand on the shoulder as he squeezed past in the tight entrance and stepped onto the sidewalk. The front door closed leaving Brand standing in the lobby waiting for Susan.

The restaurant door vibrated and shook. Brand flinched, turning in curiosity to stare at the loud disturbance. His mind raced as he tried to place the popping sound and the rapid drumming happening on the street side of the wooden door, the explosions dulled by the thick material's cladding the outside wall of the building.

The Wolves Of Satan

Wonder changed to confusion as a feeling of dread crept over Brand, a realization borne by the familiar sound of gunfire. His mind reeled, the brutal realization sending mixed thoughts. He reached for the door handle. A flood of emotions swirled at the continued reverberations of bullets played a macabre melody against the restaurant door.

The sound began the second Roy stepped from view. Dropping low, Brand slid the door open. A sliver of streetlight reflected in his eyes highlighting Roy sprawled on the sidewalk; his brother's head visible inches from the entrance. Brand pushed further onto the sidewalk desperately reaching for the collar of Roy's jacket. Crouched low to the ground, he clamped his hands under Roy's armpits in an effort to drag the larger man back into the relative safety of the restaurant.

Bullets whined off concrete and thudded into the stucco finish of the building's exterior. Roy's men, the ones waiting with the SUV's down from the entrance, scrambled to return fire. Brand hesitated, his sight reaching beyond the prone figure of his brother, sweeping the street. He paused long enough to witness unfamiliar cars crawling down the avenue, darks shadows hanging from the windows, spits of exploding gunpowder erupting from the procession.

Swinging a foot, he braced the door open. Sweat creased his forehead while the muscles in his arms strained as inch by inch he wormed his wounded brother back inside the safety of the restaurant's lobby.

Minutes passed. All around the darkness exploded. Echoing blasts of gunfire and the high-pitched whine of bullets shrieked through the night air, the tiny lead projectiles indiscriminate as they thudded and chewed up everything in their path.

Then, as quick as the shooting started, it stopped. From within the restaurant, the revving of powerful engines could be heard, the unmistakable squawk of rubber tires spinning rapidly on dry asphalt vibrated into the restaurant. The noise of the escaping vehicles chased by the sporadic bursts of friendly gunfire.

Blood oozed from wounds high on Roy's body, the thick liquid soaking into the large man's coat. Brand peeled away his brother's coat and shirt. A flack jacket layered beneath his brother's shirt covered the upper body. The vest had protected the chest, but as Brand checked further, he noticed at least one bullet that went into the meaty part of Roy's shoulder close to his neck, the blood leaking out in pulses.

Looking around, he hollered at the wait staff to grab towels. For what seemed an often-repeated phrase of late, he hollered! "Call an ambulance!" Susan knelt by his side offering to help. The door to the street burst open. Roy's men ran into the building. Each man stopping mouth open as they saw their leader lying in a pool of his own blood.

Grabbing a handful of towels, Brand fought to stop the hemorrhaging wounds. With the worst of the bleeding stemmed, he switched spots with one of Roy's men, instructing the biker to keep pressure on the wounds until an ambulance arrived.

Standing up, Brand stared aimlessly at the pool of blood spreading under his brother. Darkness washed over him as he stood in the restaurant's lobby and looked down at the pale colour of Roy's face and the red mounds of torn flesh and leaking wounds that pushed the large man ever closer to death's doorstep.

Brand added Roy's life to the toll extracted by the Colombians and the escalating drug war and then subtracted what little he had left to loose if he didn't brace the rising tide. So far the equation favoured the enemy.

The Wolves Of Satan

The attempt on his brother's life destroyed the final straw of decency locked deep within his soul. Drawn into this dispute by the shootings at his house, he had since witnessed his friends killed, harassed and abducted, and now his brother lay at the edge of life in the lobby of some non-descript restaurant.

Brand stepped away from the group gathered around Roy and found a bathroom. Anger oozed from his pores as he washed Roy's blood off his hands. He returned to the entrance and demanded the keys for one of the SUV's parked out front. He had matters to attend to he replied in answer to inquiries. Turning with the keys, Susan grabbed his arm.

"I'm going with you." She said. The grim look on her face eliminated the need for discussion.

"You're not going to be safe where I'm going." Brand shook her off.

"Where am I going to be safe?" She screamed in his face, her grip tightening. Brand thought quickly.

"I'll take you back to the acreage. You grab what you need and I'll find a place where you'll be out of sight." He promised through clenched teeth, barely managing to contain the rising anger threatening to consume his soul. He spun and stormed out of the restaurant, covered the distance to the vehicle in a few long strides and climbed behind the wheel.

Susan's footsteps rang off the concrete sidewalk as she ran to match his stride. With a yank she wrenched the passenger door open, jumped into the seat across from Brand and barely had time to close the door before Brand put the car into drive and stomped on the gas pedal.

Richard Cozicar

Chapter 42

Brand paced in the hall, battling down an impatience brought on by a want to exact hurt on those responsible for the cowardly attacks on his friends and family. He made tight turns in the hallway while Susan moved around her bedroom collecting her things in a suitcase.

Noticing she was ready, Brand moved into the room to carry her luggage. Motioning Susan ahead, a piece of paper lying on the carpet just inside the doorway caught his attention. He knelt down and picked it up. The rumpled paper, Susan's used airline ticket, had fallen to the floor in her rush to pack.

Brand snatched it off the floor and turned to place it on a dresser. His eyes swept across the cities displayed in the destination and arrival column. Vancouver to Calgary typed in bold letters across the top line. He'd wrongly presumed she still lived in the Maritimes. When did she move to the west coast? He shrugged away his misunderstanding. Placing the paper on top the dresser, he stepped from the room, Susan's suitcase gripped in his hand.

Throwing the luggage in the back of the SUV, Brand dug around for his phone, swiped down the screen, located his contact list and dialled Detective O'Brien's number. Brand began speaking the second the detective answered.

"O'Brien, this is Coldstream. I'll take your deal, but I need you to do a couple of things for me."

"Hold on. That's not how this works." O'Brien balked at Brand's words.

The Wolves Of Satan

"That's exactly how this is going to work. Roy Thundercloud was shot outside the Mescalles restaurant this evening. I don't know which hospital they have taken him to yet, but I'm sure you can find out. I want guards posted outside his room…and I have a witness for you to protect."

"I'm not a babysitter." Detective O'Brien started.

"You want my help to shut these guys down, that's my buy-in. What is your address," Brand talked over the detective's objections, "I'm in a hurry."

"Yeah. Sure. Alright." The detective dropped his protests providing an address.

"We'll be there shortly." Brand ended the call.

"I'm not going to sit in protective custody…I want to stay with you." Susan protested. Brand looked at her and shook his head.

"What I have to do, I can't have you tagging along." He said putting an end to the discussion as he raced through the city toward Detective O'Brien's residence.

The rest of the ride to the detective's home passed quietly. After Roy's shooting, Brand left the restaurant with varying thoughts on what course of action he'd be best to take. Vengeful ideas of taking the fight to the Cartel, hurting them and their pet bikers badly for the toll they exacted, and with a touch of luck added bring Jerry out of the mess alive. A short list of possibilities circled his mind. Reviewing the possibilities of each scenario, distracting while driving.

Brand nearly sped by O'Brien's address, spotting the detective at the last minute, Detective O'Brien stood on the sidewalk in front of his house. Brand swerved into the oncoming lane, parking illegally along the curb in the tree-lined neighbourhood. He jumped from the cab and without a greeting, circled the black SUV and grabbed Susan's suitcase, leading her to the sidewalk, the pair stopping on the road in front of the detective.

"Take good care of her." He said as he turned to leave.

"What are you planning to do?" O'Brien called from behind.

Brand stopped with his back to the detective.

"Probably better that I don't tell you. I'll find the guy running the Cartel, the one you haven't been able to identify."

Brand turned around as O'Brien took a step toward him. "I asked for your help, but I need to know what you have planned." O'Brien stared into Brands eyes. "I can't have you recklessly running around adding fuel to problem."

"Too late for that." Brand replied then held his hands toward the detective. "You can arrest me on that trumped-up murder charge or get the hell out of my way." He dared O'Brien. Brand waited for the man to decide then left the detective and Jerry's daughter standing on the sidewalk as he climbed back into the SUV.

Cranking the steering wheel 180 degrees, the SUV changed directions in the narrow street. Brand pressed the gas pedal. The 8-cylinder engine surged as the vehicle straightened and he headed for the southern outskirts of the city. Traffic was light as he threaded his way across miles of city before hooking up with the Deerfoot for the final stretch of the trip.

The subsiding of adrenaline and the ease of his rage allowed his mind to refocus. A spark of an idea flamed into a workable strategy as he tossed it over in his head. The constant drum of the truck's tires comforting as the SUV rumbled over barren city streets. He needed to meet the Manager, the leader of the

Apostles and he decided against waiting until the man was alone.

At this time of the night and after the ambush on Roy, Brand counted on the Manager to be holed up at the Apostles clubhouse, maybe slightly off guard with the attack that rendered his rival leader incapacitated for at least a short while. With a bit of haste, he planned on taking advantage of the Apostles brief triumph to confront the Manager on his home turf.

The big son of a bitch who hung around with Cartwright was a problem all its own. Brand considered himself tough, but the guy was a giant and in no fantasy did Brand see himself being victorious if he came up against the man.

He mulled over different angles to deal with Cartwright's bodyguard, but in the end, his thoughts kept arriving at the simplest solution, one of survival. The urge to pack a gun and shoot the bastard or any other biker who stood in the way, fitted with his anger. Pay back for the carnage left behind by the recent attacks, reduce the enemies numbers. But the lawman from Brand's past wrestled away the thoughts. Killing out of angst wasn't his style.

He merged onto Deerfoot Trail and put pressure on the gas pedal. Time was of an essence if he had hopes of accomplishing what he set out to do. Surprise and stupidity were the only two things he had as an ally at the moment, and the longer he waited to implement his plan, the less chance of surprise.

Twenty minutes later he signalled off the highway for a dirt road and drove Roy's Black SUV onto the gravel path leading to the same Quonset he had visited a couple of days earlier when driving a stolen tractor-trailer containing a shipment of the Cartel's illegal cargo.

In the shadows of the late hour, men slowly emerged into the glow of the head lights and watched the SUV roll into the back quarters of the hidden building, an array of weapons pointed at the vehicle. Brand shifted the truck into park, left the engine running with the high beams lighting the property and the building.

Sitting in the SUV's cab, he watched as armed men filtered from the cover of the bush rimming the yard. Brand fished in his pocket removing his cigarettes, his eyes busy scanning the building and the growing number of men. He took his time lighting a cigarette then slowly opened the door and emerged. His hands held high so he wasn't accidentally shot before the bikers realized whom he was.

Brand kept his hands in the air and closed the SUV's door with his foot before walking toward the men. One of the bikers advanced to meet Brand, the barrel of his rifle levelled at chest height.

"That's far enough." The biker warned. Brand stopped. Just his luck, in the darkness, none of Roy's men could recognize him.

"I'm Roy's brother." Brand called out and sidestepped into the light flowing from the front of the SUV. "Put the guns down before somebody gets hurt. Roy's been shot." He added, doubting that the men hadn't already heard.

The bikers guarding the Quonset snuck glances at each other, confused with Brand's appearance. The standoff continued in the yard until a door on the side of the building opened and another man walked outside, his eyes looking over the commotion, stopping when he saw Brand.

Little Abe, Roy's second in command. Abe had been with Roy since the conception of the Wolves of Satan and had fought side by side with Roy as the gang grew in notoriety.

Little Abe's real name was Jesse, but his striking resemblance to Abe Lincoln, mostly due to the man growing his facial hair to resemble the late president. The first part of his nickname little was a misnomer. Little Abe was three times the size of the original. Abe Lincoln on steroids. Jesse grew into the name and was never without the facial hair the original Abe made famous.

He walked past the line of bikers surrounding the vehicle; recognition dawned on the man's face changing his features as he drew closer to Brand.

"Put your gun's away." He shouted into the night air and walked closer. "We received word of the attempt on Roy." Little Abe said. "So, what brings you here?"

Brand related the shooting at the restaurant; then he switched to the reason for his visit. "I came to take the tractor-trailer, the one containing the stolen drugs. Is it still here?"

"Yep. It's inside." Little Abe motioned with his head. "What do you need that for?" The biker asked suspiciously. Brand traded glances with the bikers guarding the Quonset.

"I'm going to trade it for information."

"I don't know about that. I would have to clear this with Roy."

"Roy is in the hospital. I don't think he'd give a rats ass right about now."

"Well. We'll have to wait."

"When I leave, I will be taking the truck and trailer. I am a long way past waiting." Brand challenged. "This isn't a request.

Richard Cozicar

So either you help me or try to stop me." He followed the lights of the truck and stepped past the line of men toward the building. His first look inside was directly at the 18-wheeler. The tractor looked like it hadn't moved since the night that Brand had parked it in the Quonset.

Once inside, the armed Wolves spread around Brand. The confused men glancing from the late night visitor to Little Abe, guns ready. Turning to Little Abe, Brand broke the standoff. "Is there a place we can talk?"

The biker pointed across the building to an office crammed under a set of stairs. Brand walked ahead of Little Abe. When the two entered the room, Brand closed the door.

"Abe. I need the truck and I'd rather not create more troubles for you." Brand stated. He briefly outlined the basics of his revenge attempt. Brand left his words for Roy's lieutenant to ponder switching to another pressing matter.

"Roy filed me in on conversations he's been holding with the leaders of some non affiliated biker clans. Any chance you know their names."

"Most of them." Little Abe replied.

"Do you have the phone numbers to go with the names?"

The biker shrugged, then went to the desk and fished around for a notebook. The two men began by calling associated chapters of the Wolves. To the crew leaders Roy had mentioned, the men explained the current situation. Roy's offers to the men left on the table for those who pledged to help in the battle.

Finishing his calls, Brand left Abe behind in the office. He detoured toward a bench filled with tools. He glanced over the

294

random wrenches and automotive paraphernalia spread on the counter.

The bulky head of a tire iron poked out among the assortment. Brand dug the large wrench free and hefted it in his hand. Not exactly the kind of metal he wished for going into battle but the tire iron could even the advantage if he ran across the huge Apostle muscle, Don Bakker.

"Open the big doors." He requested as he climbed into the cab. His eyes dropped to the steering column. Fortunately, the keys were still in the ignition. Little Abe climbed up the side of the truck and spoke through the window.

"You let me know when you find the assholes who shot Roy?"

"Count on it." Brand replied.

"You gonna need some help?"

Brand thought about the request. "No. Better I do this alone. Things could go sideways pretty easily. You stay in touch with the Calvary. Keep on them, make sure they ride with lots of manpower."

Abe climbed down and hollered for the overhead door to open. Brand twisted the key in the ignition. The big engine rumbled to life. Columns of black exhaust lifted into the air. Brand shifted into reverse, nodded toward Little Abe and backed the truck out into the night.

Chapter 43

On the top floor of the Millennium Casino, Quintin Rojas stood, his head bowed in front of his boss. The subject of a heated conversation between the two men was the shooting of Roy Thundercloud earlier that evening.

"We had to act fast. He left the acreage with Coldstream and a few men." Rojas replied. "When the guys saw him leave the restaurant, they opened fire." Quintin Rojas searched for the words to explain his actions. "You wanted the Wolves spirits broken. Thundercloud is the head of the pack. We took him out."

Rojas' boss stared at his underling, disappointment in his eyes. "Still. You should have cleared the attack with me. Your rash decision may make the Wolves dig in their heels in harder." The boss chastised. "Shore ain't gonna help our cause." He paused then conceded the fact that there was no undoing the shooting of the Wolves leader.

The Cartel boss changed subjects. The open shooting of Roy Thundercloud caused a need to accelerate his plans. "How many men do we have in the city? Cartwright's bikers and our men from the coast, I mean?"

"The Manager has probably pulled in a couple hundred of his bikers and wannabes from across the mountains...his *vagabundo*, together with our men. I think we have plenty of manpower." Rojas did the calculations as he spoke. "Thundercloud's Wolves have been depleted. His men either shot up or arrested. The remainder are said to be laying low. I have reports that only a few were sighted, and these are mainly protecting his establishments. None of his men have been found operating the streets the past couple of days."

"I have a bad feeling." Rojas' boss interrupted. "Something doesn't feel right. I never expected the Wolves to run at the first sign of a fight. Still, we are gaining ground, but we have to be careful. One wrong move could expose us." The boss sighed with disappointment. "With Thundercloud out of commission, now is the time to flood his territory and run the Wolves out of town."

A clock somewhere in the confines of the office ticked its steady rhythm as the two men became lost in thought planning the looming conclusion in the war against the Wolves of Satan.

"Notify the men. I want them ready to move on the Wolves territory before the week is done. Ratchet up the pressure against all of the Wolves establishments that remain operating. I want them shut down and Thundercloud's men driven from the streets. Don't give the orphaned Wolves a chance to think or plan. They'll be disorganized with their leader out of the picture. Push our advantage. The longer we prolong their demise, the better the chance that that big Indian will pull something together."

The Moreno boss steered the conversation away from the evening's troubles. "Any word on my phone or what Coldstream is up to? I was hoping the fool would get lucky and find the damn thing. What, with the threat you're holding over him?" Rojas' boss stated.

A smile grew on Rojas' face. "I haven't heard back from the man since I made the call to Thundercloud. Coldstream left the restaurant after the shooting and we lost him. Could be he's not the tough hombre you think he is, and if the phone is not recovered, so be it? Soon it won't matter."

A fist slammed the desk rattling the surface and making Rojas step back.

"I CARE!" His boss screamed. "I have spent years building my cover. My attempts to remain anonymous, well, it's made running this Cartel a lot easier. I move around with out looking over my shoulder. The anonymity has allowed me to cross borders freely and undetected." The boss paused. The anger on his face resided as he fought to regain control of his anger. "... Because of that, I've made a nice life in this city, and free of suspicion, I've built my business right under the nose of the law. I like the fact that I don't have to worry about the cops or some low life rival trying to end my life." He calmed down. "I shouldn't have to explain..."

"Find the FUCKING phone." The boss leaned on the desk inches from Rojas' face. Through clenched teeth, he spoke. "I should never have dropped my guard and let that phoney fishing guide get so close; then he would never have had the opportunity to blindside me.

But he was smart. Not for a second did I suspected Halperson of being an undercover narc. Not until my phone went missing."

The boss took a deep breath then slowly let the air escape his lips. "Unfortunately, the man is dead, and you have yet to recover the only proof of my involvement. So squeeze Coldstream harder. In his day, he was a top-notch investigator. Make him do our work for us. Convince him of the urgency regarding my situation." The Moreno Cartel boss glared at his subordinate. "And do it quickly! When the phone is in my hands, you are free to deal with the man however you like."

Chapter 44

Brand turned off the gravel road onto Highway 2. The quiet of night disturbed as the truck's engine rumbled. At the bridge crossing the Bow River, Brand found his mind drifting. A scattering of moonlight reflected off the current in the water. Thoughts emerged of better days floating the river, of drift boats and fly lines, fleeing Rainbows and bullish Brown trout. Brand pushed the distracting memories away. Shaking his head, he tried to refocus on the highway and the task lying ahead.

The multi-lanes of the busy thoroughfare were free of traffic at the late hour by the time 18-wheeler crossed into the city limits. The journey before him a rash decision brought on by a mixture of anger and revenge. Struggling to hold his emotions in check, Brand stared out the truck's windshield, his thoughts in disarray. The Cartel, the Apostles encroachment on Roy's territory, and the loss and injuries to his friends all fought for priority in his mind. The only way to ease the cries of the suffering and change the direction of the future was to do something drastic. Time had come to go on the offensive.

There was much he needed to learn, and the urgency of collecting the information from someone at the top of the organization. He knew too little about the Colombian calling the shots for the rogue bikers. Where the man lived, who he surrounded himself with and if Rojas was holed up at the casino, what type of protection would stand in Brand's way? How to get to the Cartel was the problem.

An alternative solution would be to flush out the Apostles top man, the Manager. His whereabouts were unknown to Brand and with Roy temporarily out of the picture, finding the Manager's location fuelled his late night drive. Brand would begin the search with the simplest means, the most obvious starting point; a clubhouse in a northwest community Calgary.

*****

The city was dark as any major metropolitan centre could be at this late hour. Lighting a cigarette, Brand guided the truck across the deserted streets, angling for the western edge of town. He was thankful for the lack of traffic due to distracted thoughts and the skills required to manoeuver this train of wheels through miles of city streets.

Blocks from the biker clubhouse, Brand brought the truck to a stop and shut off the engine. The loud, rumbling motor an unwanted disturbance in the peaceful neighbourhood. He climbed down from the cab, crushed his cigarette under foot, scanned his surroundings then, clinging to the shadows, walked a couple of blocks down the street toward the fenced off compound.

Across the road from the enclosed yard, he leaned against a wall and studied the place. The driveway leading onto the property was clear of vehicles, but the height of the gate and fence blocked his view of yard inside. The sidewalk in front of the compound, deserted.

Brand slowly swung his head, his vision following the divided asphalt road in both directions as they led away from the clubhouse. A side road, a half block down and opposite the gate, ended in a t-intersection. Brand wished he had a better view of the property inside the confines of the fence. He rejected the thought of scaling the top of the fence for a look.

The Wolves Of Satan

Good chance cameras were planted around the property to notify the occupants holed up inside of unwanted attention.

He shrugged off the concern, forcing doubt away. If anything lay in his way, the worst obstacles to be encountered would likely be a scattering of motorbikes littering the lawn between the perimeter and the house. Hopefully not too many, he found himself thinking as he walked back to the truck.

Sitting behind the wheel, he chain-smoked another cigarette and reviewed the consequences of his actions. What he was about to do was reckless, but he was past the moment of giving a shit.

The truck roared to life at the turn of the key. Brand placed his hand on the gear selector, shifting the transmission into low gear. Columns of black diesel smoke mixed with the darkness of night surrounding the cab. With pressure on the gas pedal, the truck lumbered away from the curb.

The big rig rolled slowly past the clubhouse. Brand pressed easy on the gas, aware of the loud echo of the exhaust stacks in the quiet of night. At the corner, he turned wide. Two hands played the wheel, steering the rig onto an adjoining road then back around the block until the tractor-trailer lined up on the street ending with the t intersection. Brand's gaze momentarily passed over the passenger's seat. The crowbar from the Quonset sat waiting.

Throwing his cigarette out the window, he pressed the gas and worked the gears. The rig gathered speed. Forcefully working the clutch and gas pedal simultaneously, he pushed the protesting engine. One hand shifted through the lower gears with the rhythm of the motor's rpm's, building momentum. His left hand gripping the oversized steering wheel as the truck and trailer rolled closer to the gate protecting the Apostles clubhouse.

The truck's engine screamed while the rpm's climbed. The big rig lurching forward with each gear change, 18 rubber wheels hissing on the pavement, gathering speed.

At the intersection, Brand swung the truck close to the curb, straightening the truck's path to the tall metal gate.

The speedometer flashed 60 km as the truck crossed the street and rolled up onto the curb. The screech of tearing metal exploded into the night as the rig's chrome bumper pushed past the gate. The truck lurched and swayed, the powerful machine crushing abandoned motorbikes under its large rubber tires.

The seatbelt caught, holding Brand tight against the seat. He ignored the whine of crushed metal and bone crushing jolts as he pushed the truck over the row of bikes, the speed nearing seventy, only inches from the wall of the clubhouse.

Bracing for the impact, Brand watched the front window of the house dissolve into shards and the vinyl siding on the buildings exterior wall give way. Brand crushed the gas pedal to the floor. Startled silhouettes danced behind the flapping curtains covering the shattered picture window.

The impact from the collision of the tractor-trailer meeting with the frame of the house whipped Brand forward. His forehead glanced off the steering wheel before momentum snapped his upper body back into the cushioned backrest, the straps of the seatbelt biting into his shoulder pinning him tight to the fabric of the seat, the rigid straps unforgiving.

Brand cursed from anger and the new found pain. His fist smacked the wheel in retaliation for the whack on his forehead.

A shower of glass and wood preceded the grill of the truck as it came to rest a cabs length into the house. The front roof sagged dangerously, feet above the nose of the tractor, the buildings wooden supports shattered.

Brand shook his head to clear the cobwebs. A sharp pain radiated in his shoulder and chest from the restraint of the seatbelt, the discomfort melting as rage coursed through his veins. He searched for the tire iron on the passenger seat. The sudden stop tossing the metal bar onto the floor of the cab. He fought to release the seatbelt's grip, reaching over the centre console. With the reassuring feel of the hefty metal bar in his hand, he kicked open the driver's door.

Semi-darkness surrounded the cab of the truck and the destroyed front room of the clubhouse. Electrical wires ripped from their wooden supports sparked around the wreckage. A theatre of horror lit by a failing power system greeted his arrival.

Steam from the truck's radiator hissed into the room, seeping from under the twisted engine cover, the sweet odour of overheated coolant mingling with dust and the flickering house lights. Into the obscure gloom, Brand carefully stepped from the truck's running board onto what remained of the main floor.

The undercarriage of the big truck stopped to rest on broken floorboards and torn carpeting. The front wheels sunken below the subfloor and framing, hanging down in the basement. Broken, jagged edges of plywood and joists protruded upwards, the furniture in the room upended and scattered.

Moans rose from the wreckage. Brand warily moved across the damaged floor, pulling aside disrupted furniture and chunks of building materials to check on the condition of injured men. Each face he studied carefully in the twinkling lights. A hand full of men laid spread throughout the room tangled in the mess of furniture and lumber.

Working his way around the carnage, he moved toward the back of the house. The Manager wasn't among any of the injured at the front of the house. Shoving a couch that dared block his path to the hallway, he strained his eyes, peering through the dust and intermittent lighting.

A door at the back of the house opened. A man stumbled into the hall. Even in the poor lighting, Brand spotted blood covering the man's head. The man's face and exposed upper body coated with dust. The man staggered away from the room, extended a massive arm to steady his body, swayed, and then swung his head to peer down the hall, his eyes locking on Brand. The giant of a man, the Manager's right-hand, Don Bakker stood scowling at Brand. A deep growl emanated from Bakker's heaving chest

Brand cursed under his breath. Of all the people to remain on his feet, it had to be the giant. Just his luck, he thought. The way the man supported his body against the wall, the man's unsteady demeanour and the blood flowing from a wound on Bakker's head alluded to the possibility of a serious injury, which, coupled with the unbridled rage coursing through Brand's body, steeled his resolve.

Doubts of facing the giant faded. The thoughts chased by an adrenaline fed anger bubbling to the surface. Days of angst and frustration pushed logical reasoning from Brand's mind. His eyes narrowed as he stared back at the giant. His hand tightened around the metal bar. The iron bar smashed against the wall as both a warning and a starting point.

"I'm here for Cartwright." Brand yelled at the giant. "Tell me where your boss is, and I'll let you walk away."

A glint of light reflected off the man's teeth. Bakker's mouth opened in a malevolent grin. The giant grunted at Brand's offer, kicked debris aside and advanced. To meet the guy in the tight confines of the hallway wasn't the way Brand had expected this evening to go, but it was too late now. Fear and common sense disappeared replaced by the unbridled desire to hurt anyone standing in his way.

Brand's nostrils flared as he waited while Bakker closed the gap. When the giant was in striking distance, Brand feigned a swing at the man's head with the tire iron. Bakker's head lifted as his eyes followed the path of the tire iron, the man raising a massive arm to block the threat. With Bakker's attention drawn to the flight of the bar, Brand shifted his weight onto his back leg and lashed out. Bakker might be immense, but a man was a man.

The toe of Brand's boot connected with the crotch of the giant, the kick vicious enough to make the man bellow in pain before doubling over. Brand's knuckled fingers shot upward into the soft flesh of the biker's throat. He quickly followed the fist with an elbow to the side of the man's head.

Bakker lashed out with the back of his hand. The power of his fist knocked Brand backward. Brand scrambled through the pain of the blow and broken furniture littering the floor to regain his footing. Bakker shook off Brand's attack, a mask of fury twisting the giant's features. Brand raised the tire iron and rushed the large man. Between the bar and his fist, Brand delivered a flurry of blows to the giant's head and body. Bakker's movements grew slow from his injuries. Brand continued his assault, determined not to quit until the man was lying on the floor.

Bakker stood solid as Brand's attempts struck the big man. Finally, unable resist the assault, Bakker sagged against the wall and slid down to a sitting position. Grasping the tire iron in both hands, Brand pressed the bar against the man's throat choking Bakker's air supply.

Richard Cozicar

Brand leaned close to the giant's ear and repeated his question.

"Where is Cartwright?" Brand asked. Bakker's reply came in the form of a fist to the side of Brand's head. Brand straightened from the impact. He took a step back, his feet tangling with the litter spread across the floor. He stumbled, the tire iron flying from his hand. Brand scrambled over the scattered furniture at the mouth of the hall to regain his balance.

A shower of small explosions rattled his brain. Darkness began edging the fringes of his consciousness. Shaking his head violently, he fought to regain his senses. Bent over the floor, he watched his opponent rise.

Bakker used a wall for support, inching his body upward on wobbly legs, the man's head covered in blood. The biker took a threatening step forward.

Brand sprang from the floor. The sole of his foot aimed at Bakker's knee. The force of his weight buckled the giant's kneecap at a sickening angle. Brand followed the kick with a leap, hurtling feet first into Bakker's chest, the impact driving the massive man over. Bakker's head thudded into a doorjamb. The man sagged against the wooden frame then slowly slid to the floor.

With the biker down, Brand stepped close, delivering several more blows, ending the man's ability to continue the fight. With bruised knuckles and gulping mouthfuls of air to feed his searing lungs, he stopped. Don Bakker lay collapsed on the floor; his back slumped against the wall, blood running down his battered face onto his chest.

"One last time." Brand said in between rasping breaths. "Where's your boss?"

Chapter 45

San Diego, the boss of the Devils Disciples, an offshoot of the much larger Wolves Of Satan, sat staring at his phone. He had just concluded a call with the leader of the Grave Runners, an American crew operating south of the Canadian border, in the state of Montana. The two had been trading calls since the news of Roy Thundercloud's ambush.

Both, San Diego's Disciples and the Grave Runners from Montana were small in comparison to the Wolves of Satan group in Alberta, but factoring the men spread across western Canada and down into the bordering states, the two bands numbered well into the hundreds.

Shortly after the call ended, the Disciples gathered at their clubhouse in Regina. The Saskatchewan motorcycle gang fired up their bikes and headed west down Highway One for the Alberta border. The plan agreed upon called for them to meet up with the Grave Runners at a small bedroom community twenty minutes east of Calgary. Once joined, the two groups of bikers would ride into the city together.

The Desperados out of Ontario ran an excess of illegal activities throughout an enormous portion of the western part of that province and across the provincial boundary into Manitoba. The Desperados were a couple of days into their trip west before Roy's shooting occurred. The Desperados leaders were bargained into the looming turf war in Calgary by Roy Thundercloud and had agreed to throw their lot behind the Wolves.

Their help in the war traded for favours from the Wolves. Improved underground lanes to move product and guaranteed protection of cargo as it passed from the Pacific Ocean east over the mountains and across the prairies to Ontario. A decent payoff for their part in assisting the Wolves to remove the Columbian backed Apostles. The cooperation between the Desperados and the Wolves would open a nation of possibilities for both clubs.

Calgary was a hard three-day ride west, but the Desperados had no plans on delaying and missing the fun that was certain to erupt in Cow town.

Most of the gangs Roy had brought into talks already worked under an uneasy truce with the Wolves. All managed to maintain working conditions with each other with the Wolves being an integral part of the drug pipeline from the Orient and South America suppliers

Word of the building war in the Albertan city had echoed across the prairies and farther east. The separate gangs set their differences aside, any resentment of fellow groups stifled with the truce Roy Thundercloud proposed. Each group's leader knew Roy Thundercloud, at least by reputation, and respected him enough to ride to his aide.

The smaller gangs had already begun to feel the ripples in their operations caused by the Apostles and the Moreno Cartel. While joining forces, the growing biker syndicate brought new rules for those partaking in the illegal underground business along with the will to control the illicit drugs flowing from the Pacific inland. Word spread quickly about the new consortium's power and the disregard for competition. While mounting the war against the Wolves in Alberta, fingers of the Cartel/Apostles venture already had begun its march to gain control over the other provinces.

The Wolves Of Satan

With the Apostles being backed by the Colombians, the only path open to the smaller biker gangs was to tow the line or be steamrolled by the growing juggernaut. Backing the Wolves was the better, and more favourable option left open for the Eastern gangs who were determined to remain independent.

Early the next morning in Edmonton, the Crypt Riders of the North motored south down Highway 2 with plans of hooking up with more of their members along the way. They left the Albertan capitol in the early hours of sunrise, their expected arrival time in Calgary, early that morning.

Two days before Roy fell victim to the hail of bullets at the restaurant, the Lower East End Posse gathered with the West Coast Reapers in Kamloops and together they rode toward the City of Calgary. A war was brewing, and these two groups were allied with the Apostles and backed by the Colombian Cartel. Local police forces and RCMP detachments along the way followed the bike gang's movements as they headed east across the province.

Once the gang's destination was determined, phone calls poured into the Calgary Police Headquarters warning of the incoming invasion. Police forces along the way stood aside as the few hundred bikers rode. The riders were careful not to break the law, and as the numbers increased while they headed east, the spattering of law enforcement grew less likely to challenge the growing ranks of criminals and had little stomach to harass the bike gangs.

Meeting at an Apostle hang out west of Calgary, the members of the East End Posse and the Reapers drank and partied with the host Apostles and a smattering of Cartel underlings before receiving instructions concerning their expected actions. The next day the hunt was on for any, and all associates tied to the Wolves. Businesses managed by the Wolves came under attack.

Rojas and Cartwright decided to end the turf war before the Wolves were able to bring in reinforcements to swell their ranks. The night, after the attack on Thundercloud's acreage, two cars of Colombian gunmen were sent to deal with the Wolves' leader.

By the time the local cops got wind of the attacks, the deeds were complete. Wolves' members were hunted. Nightclubs and other businesses of illegal repute were swarmed, some burned to the ground. For two long days, the Wolves of Satan were tracked and dealt with, the surge by the Moreno Cartel culminated with the shooting of Roy Thundercloud.

The combined forces of the Colombian drug Cartel and the outlaw Apostles bikers were on the verge of claiming another major city with undisputed rights of running the burgeoning market of underground trades.

The city of Calgary had blossomed into a world-class centre for the past number of years, which meant a lot of young, affluent people living in its limits. The perfect scenario was unfolding for the growing drug and gambling trade to flourish.

The Cartel wanted to expand east from the coast, and with the Apostles providing muscle and insight, the only thing standing in the way was the Wolves of Satan…and a fishing guide.

*****

The morning after the shooting of Roy Thundercloud, the rumble of bike engines rattled a small city east of Calgary. The Devils Disciples flooded the parking lot of a local eatery when they arrived in town. The roar of the bikes could be heard in the restaurant before the first metal two-wheeler crossed into the parking lot.

Nervous early morning diners peeked warily through the slits of the restaurant's blinds and into the rising sunlight. Mumbles of disbelief interrupted family meals as tentacles of uneasiness and fear settled over the breakfast crowd. Parents with young children pushed aside partly eaten plates of pancakes and eggs, called for their bills and slipped from the restaurant as quickly and as meekly as was humanly possible.

San Diego sat with his men. Grim smiles streaked their faces as they rested on leather bike seats, smoking and watching the scared families with amusement while the parking lot emptied. He and his men waited. The Runners were to join them shortly. After breakfast, they would ride as a group to meet Thundercloud's men.

Chapter 46

Brand stood on the outside of the damaged building looking back up at the Apostles clubhouse. The front half of the truck lodged inside the building. Intermitted flashes of light reflecting off the metal frame of the damaged cab. Brand lifted a cigarette to his lips, flicked his lighter then scrolled his phone screen for Detective O'Brien's contact number.

"O'Brien." A tired, annoyed voice answered.

"I got a tip for you." Brand replied. "Wake up the uniforms at the station and send a couple of squad cars to the Apostles compound." Brand rattled off the address. "An 18-wheeler is parked halfway into their clubhouse." Brand listened to the detective curse across the phone line. Cutting O'Brien off before he asked the wrong questions, Brand added as an afterthought. "You better send an ambulance or two along with the patrol cars." Brand told the detective. "Warn your men to be cautious when they enter the premises. There's a big man inside and when he wakes he's probably going to pissed."

Before hanging up, Brand said. "Detective, you might want to take the time to make an appearance. A trailer full of evidence is attached to the back of the semi tractor. Check amongst the pallets of produce. I'm certain you'll find that the product in the trailer matches the stuff on the streets the Apostles peddle." He ended the call not waiting for O'Brien to waste time asking needless questions.

Walking across the yard, Brand sorted through the damaged bikes. Some escaped the path of the 18-wheeler's tires. He walked to one leaning to the side of the clubhouse, the motorcycle still drivable. He stood the bike up and pulled the ignition wires loose. Before climbing onto the bike he took a gun, he recovered from inside the house and shoved it into the back waist of his jeans, slipping his coat over and spun the bike around heading away from the crash scene, his destination north of the Apostles clubhouse.

It had taken Brand time to pry the Manager's whereabouts out of Bakker but eventually, the giant of a man succumbed to Brand's charms. James Cartwright was at a sleepover at his girlfriend's apartment. The friend's place was in the northwest part of town, one of the fast-growing, new subdivisions in the expanding city.

Brand felt the wind tug at his hair as he left the Bowness area, turned onto Shaganappi Trail, and wound his way through the deserted city streets toward the far reaches of the north end.

Leaving the bike in an alley, he walked up to the apartment's entrance and studied the buildings security system. The front door was locked, and he couldn't count on many people leaving or entering at this hour if the morning.

Avoiding the buzzer to Cartwright's girlfriend's apartment, Brand randomly pressed buttons hoping for a half asleep or otherwise non-caring resident to grant him entry without any questions. A few annoyed and suspicious patrons refused his attempts, tired, curious voices asked who he was and reminded him of the late hour. Several failed beckoning rings passed before the buzzer on the front door notified him that the door was now unlatched. He quickly seized the door handle and entered the main building.

Walking through the deserted hallways, he stopped at the elevator, pushed the up button and waited for a ride to the fifth floor. Turning left in the upper corridor, he paused in front of the apartment number Bakker had given him. Had the big man lied? A few moments of pondering the truthfulness of the information, he pulled his lockset out of his pocket and quietly let himself into the dark unit.

Standing motionless behind the closed door, he breathed shallow, allowing time for his senses to warn him of unwelcome movements. When he was satisfied that his entry went undetected, he moved about the apartment searching for the bedroom, his final destination. Again he remained immobile, his hand on the doorknob, his ears strained for sounds of activity from the other side of the door.

Brand retrieved the gun from behind his back, pushed the door inward and stood silhouetted in the doorway as he studied the layout. His eyes adjusted to the dim light seeping past the window blinds from the streetlights outside the building. Two dark lumps lay among the shadows on the bed, the bigger of the two bundles hopefully the Apostles leader; the man lost in sleep while his snoring disturbed the otherwise silent room.

In two long strides, Brand reached for the prone form lying in bed and with his left hand clutched the man's t-shirt in his fist, his right hand holding the gun at Cartwright's head. The Manager's eyes snapped open, his pupils expanding at the sight of the gun in his face.

The biker started to yell, and Brand smacked the butt of his gun into the side of the man's face.

"Quiet." He growled. With the gun remaining tight to Cartwright's face, Brand slowly pulled the man into a sitting position before easing his grasp on the t-shirt. Brand took a step back. The barrel of the pistol unwavering, pointed at the Manager's head. The commotion in the room woke up the apartment's owner. The woman startled awake, her eyes zeroing in on the gun and then up at Brand. A scream burst from her lungs.

The Wolves Of Satan

"Shut her up, or I swear I will." Brand warned. The Manager turned his attention away from the gun and with a few sharp commands quieted his girlfriend.

"Grab a sheet and tie her up." Brand instructed the Manager. "Not too tight though. She's so damn skinny I don't want her to die of hunger before she can get loose. Quickly," Brand urged. " We're in a hurry."

Standing back to give the Manager room to complete his task, Brand waited impatiently. With the woman bound, Brand spoke. "Find your clothes. You're coming with me."

Brand had thought about questioning Cartwright in the apartment but changed his mind. Too many variables to consider and then the problem of containing the man once he had his questions answered created another problem. He didn't view the girl as a threat, he doubted she had no idea who he was, and if she was aware of what line of work her boyfriend was involved in, that ruled out the possibility of her running to the police, at least for the time being.

With his gun held at the Cartwright's back, Brand escorted the man out of the building and over to a part of the building dark in shadows as he surveyed the street.

"What do you drive?" Brand asked. The two riding away from the premises on the stolen bike, awkward, he realized.

"My truck," Cartwright answered pointing past the building toward the visitor parking.

"Lead the way." Brand nudged with the tip of the gun; the barrel pressed tight to Cartwright's back. The hard metal of the handgun digging into flesh made the biker wince.

Chapter 47

Relaying directions to the south of the city and back to the acreage with the Quonset, the two men rode silently. James Cartwright, his eyes focused on the road, occasionally stole glances at his captor. Maybe the fuss about the fishing guide had some merit, he thought. In his mind, he chastised himself for underestimating the man's abilities and until he had a chance to escape he had to suffer from his mistake.

Brand sat stoically, nursing the pain radiating throughout his beaten and battered body. His eyes tilted in the direction of the brooding Manager. The two men, each wary of the other's reputation, traveled uneasy on the journey across the city.

The clock in the pickup read four thirty a.m. The adrenaline that built during the evening and powered Brand's quest quickly began fading. He struggled to keep his eyes open, and his mind focused on the man driving the vehicle.

Quarter after five, the two pulled off the highway and drove the last few minutes on the gravel road, past the bush line and into the yard housing the Quonset. Brand told Cartwright to stop. He waited. Past heavy eyelids he watched as the rifle-toting guards materialized from around the building. The yard lit up by the truck's headlights.

"Turn off the truck and hand me the keys." Brand commanded. "If you step out of this truck the men you see are more than likely going to shoot you and I can't allow that to happen quite yet." He said as he climbed out of the passenger side, his hands held high in the air. He waited for Roy's men to approach.

The Wolves Of Satan

Little Abe, the same biker who had approached Brand the last time he showed up at the Quonset, moved cautiously toward Cartwright's truck, his automatic rifle held with both hands covering the unknown vehicle. Noticing Brand, he lowered the gun.

"Jesus…you keep showing up like this you are going to get yourself shot."

"Yeah…I know…next time I'll call ahead." Brand dropped his arms and walked around the truck yanking open the driver's door. He grabbed the back of Cartwright's collar and pulled the leader of the rival Apostles out into the open.

At the sight of the Manager, Little Abe raised his gun back up. "What the hell?" He exclaimed. "Why would you bring that asshole here? What's going on?" Abe took a step back, his gun covering Brand and the rival biker.

"Whoa. Slow down cowboy." Brand tightened his grip on Cartwright's collar and led the man toward the big metal building. "I needed someplace to have a private conversation. I'll need somebody to watch over this fine gentleman until I have more time to deal with him."

The bikers guarding the building looked at each other. Angry words floated across the yard.

"Because of this asshole, a lot of our friends are in the hospital. His buddies have hunted our guys and destroyed businesses, so what makes you think that we won't kill the man?" One of the guards asked.

"Some nerve." Another angry voice cut through the night air. "Who do you think you are? Waltz in here like you own the place and think we'll be happy to entertain this bugger! Not fucking likely!"

"I don't know man." Anger coloured Little Abe's face as he separated from the other men. "Letting you take the truck was one thing…but this is going too far."

Brand yanked on Cartwright's collar. He ignored the protests dragging the Apostles leader toward the door of the Quonset, the disgruntled bikers begrudgingly moving out of his path.

"I highly doubt his asshole has enough authority to call the shots." Brand defended his actions. "I don't think he had much say in organizing the attacks. A small potato like him, he does what the Colombians tell him to do, I suspect." Brand said over his shoulder. "They wouldn't trust this coward any more than you do."

Inside the building, Brand marched his captive to a post in the centre of the room. He glanced around spotting a length of chain lying to the side.

"Pass me that and a lock." He pointed. Brand handed the Manager an end of the chain. "Hold this and keep your arms by your sides," he instructed. Brand let the links slide through his hands as he walked circles. The chain tightened as he wound it from the Mangers waist up to the man's shoulders. Tugging at the metal rope, he fed the pin of a lock between two links snapping the chain shut.

He paused a moment eyeing his work then looked around at the bikers. Brand read the disgust and hatred on their faces.

"Go back to what you were doing. No one lays a finger on this man." Brand turned, nodded to Little Abe and motioned toward the office. A couple of bikers followed the two.

"I hope you know what you're doing. You're not making any friends around here." Little Abe commented. "What's next?"

The Wolves Of Satan

One of the straggling bikers piped up. "What in the hell happened to your face?" The man asked. "Looks like you went a few rounds with the bumper of a truck."

Brand let a tired smile move his lips. "Worst part is that the damn truck fought back. Any coffee around this place." He asked digging his pack of smokes free. After the long night, he felt his muscles relax. Pain and fatigue seeped into his conscious as tension drained away. He accepted the coffee, enjoying the effects of the cigarette.

The ringing of his phone interrupted his short respite. He glanced at the time and then the phone number before answering, a few minutes after six. The number he didn't recognize.

A soft female voice filtered into his ear.

"Is this Mr. Coldstream?" The woman asked tentatively.

"Yeah. Who's this?"

"My parents said you visited the store the other day asking about a phone."

"You're parents...what store?" Brand's overtired mind wrestled to make sense of the caller's words.

"I'm sorry." The female apologized. "My name is Yen Lee. My parents own Lee's Groceries in Montgomery. They told me you came to the store asking about Dave Halperson and a phone that was missing."

Her words cut through the fog in Brand's brain. He sat up, the weariness weighing down his body all but forgotten.

"Yeah...yes, I was." He responded suddenly alert. "Do you know anything about Dave or the phone?"

The girl hesitated. In a barely audible voice, she answered.

"Dave was special to me. A few days before he died, he came to me and begged me to hide a phone. He wouldn't tell me why. Said I would be safer not knowing." Brand waited. The young lady choked back a tear. "That was the last time I talked to him." She continued. "I hid it away and honestly; I had forgotten about it until you walked into the store and talked to my parents."

"Where are you now?" Brand asked. He had the keys to Cartwright's truck in his hand and was crossing the floor as he talked.

"The same place you met my parents. We live on the second floor. We have an apartment above the store."

"I'm on my way. A friend's life depends on it." He was about to end the call. "You haven't told anyone else about this phone, have you?" He had to ask.

"No. As I said, I'd forgotten about it until now."

At the Quonset door, he stopped and called out to Abe.

"I need Cartwright alive." He said pointing to the Apostles tied to the post. "Something important has come up. I'll be back as fast as possible." As an afterthought, he added. "Promise me you'll keep your guys from killing him." Brand left without hearing Little Abe's response.

Chapter 48

Traffic into the city had increased significantly by the time Brand picked up the freeway that flowed into town. Rush hour was well under way. His fingers tapped an anonymous rhythm on the truck's steering wheel while he moulded with the northbound traffic as it crawled, 3 lanes wide, toward the centre of the city.

Forty-five minutes later he pulled into the strip mall. Closed signs greeted him from shuttered windows of businesses yet to open for the workday. A hand full of vehicles sat scattered randomly in the lot. Owners and employees, early to work, preparing for the new day, their vehicles mixed with cars abandoned after a night of too many drinks at the corner pub.

Brand wedged the truck into a stall a business down from the grocery store. The lights inside the building were off, the door locked, a neon sign read closed. Under the red bulbs a sign displaying the hours of operation.

He stood gazing up at the front of the building. Brand lit a cigarette. Standing on the pavement, he pulled the phone from his pocket. Swiping through the array of screens, he stopped on the call log and hit redial. The number from Lee's daughter's recent call front and centre on the list. Before the call connected, a moving curtain on the second floor caught his attention. A small face framed by straight black hair peered down at him. Her head backlit by the apartment lights.

Brand raised his phone in greeting and shrugged. The woman raised her hand to her ear.

"Are you Dave's friend," she asked.

Brand nodded his head. "Yes," he replied.

"Give me a minute," she said.

Brand crossed the sidewalk closer to the store's entrance. Muffled footsteps grew louder as they approached the door. Metal slid on metal as the door locks were released before the glass and steel frame opened a crack.

"Mr. Coldstream." The same face from the second-floor window enquired. Brand pocketed his phone and took a step, stopping close to the opening.

"Yes." He acknowledged. "Brand. You can call me Brand." He said and smiled with what he hoped was a reassuring gesture. "Nice to meet you." He faltered, thoughts of young Dave ran through his mind. Sad that he never knew Dave had a girlfriend and embarrassed to meet the girl under these circumstances. His mood darkened. Some friend he had been.

Brand followed the girl to the back of the crowded convenience store. A back room stuffed with boxed grocery items, trays of goods and a hollowed out space containing an overburdened desk. Yen Lee looked up into Brand's face. Spent teardrops glistened at the edge of her eyes. Her words came out sadly.

"Dave mentioned your name often." Yen Lee started. "He enjoyed the fishing and the friendship." Lee turned her face away. In a shaky, tear-filled voice she told Brand about her relationship with Dave. The young woman's story drifted at times. She smiled at the couple's happy memories and then talked quieter, choking back the pain of her loss.

Brand felt the fatigue return, swamping his body. He pushed against the lack of sleep and politely listened. The rage over the young guides death fuelling the familiar anger he had been holding at bay for the past several days.

The Wolves Of Satan

"I am sorry to burden you, Mr. Coldstream," she apologized. Yen Lee squeezed past Brand in the tight confines. She slid a stack of boxes aside revealing wooden shelves. Standing on her toes, she stretched and reached a hand, her fingers exploring at the back of a rack.

Yen Lee twisted and dropped back to flat feet. She faced Brand. Her fingers wrapped tightly around a device as big as her hand. She raised the phone in his direction.

"I hope this helps you," she said.

Brand nodded. "It will. Believe me."

Palming the phone, he held the power button. A warning flashed on the blank screen and a red line told of the lack of battery power. He hid his disappointment. The answer to so many questions nestled in his palm but unable to access them. The need to recharge the battery before he could comb through the stored videos and his chance to review the pictures that cost one friend his life and another kidnapped by the Cartel.

"Maybe one day we can meet for a coffee and share happier memories of Dave." He suggested.

Brand stuck the phone in his pocket and thanked the young lady. He wound through the crowded grocery aisles and into the morning sunshine.

One hand on the truck's door handle, his phone rang again. He thought about ignoring the ringing nuisance. He was dead tired and still had lots of work to do before he had a chance to rest. On the third ring, he accepted the call. Susan was on the other end.

"Can you pick me up?" She pleaded. "Detective O'Brien hadn't returned home since your call last night, and I'm afraid to be here alone."

Rubbing his face, Brand stood beside the truck mulling over her request. She was probably safe enough at the detective's house.

"Fine." He said. "I'm not that far away. See you in a few." He hung up and climbed into the truck. The Quonset where he drove Cartwright would also be safe enough, he figured. Roy's men guarded the place continuously. They may be able to keep an eye on her as well, he supposed.

Back in the yard surrounding the Quonset, Brand went through the now-familiar routine of waiting for the guards to do their thing. He was in no mood for these games any longer, but he wouldn't blame the bikers for being cautious. Not after the war that was being waged by the their rivals over the last few days.

Men appeared at the edge of the bushes. A lone biker, gun held chest high and aimed at the cab of the truck, left his post and warily moved forward.

Recognizing Brand, the guard signalled to the other men watching the property. The man nodded and waved Brand through. The truck rolled the last several feet before Brand slid the selector into park and removed the key.

Stepping out of the truck, Brand forced his sagging eyelids open. His legs unsteady, his body faltering from equal amounts of fatigue and spent adrenaline, waited by the nose of the truck for Susan to climb from the cab. He motioned Susan ahead as the two walked past armed men.

Crossing the threshold into the metal building, Susan pulled up short at the sight of the leader of the Apostles chained to a post in the middle of the building. Her hesitation was slight. She recovered quickly and continued further inside. Brand noticed her pause and chalked it up to jitters then put it out of his mind.

"There's possibly a pot of brewed coffee in the office," he pointed her toward the open door. "I'll be along in a minute." Brand strayed to the centre of the building. The day's activities transformed the building. The squeal of air wrenches and compressors rattled. The smell of auto paint tainted the air as men climbed among a variety of vehicles in different stages of repair. Fenders and various auto parts littered the floors. The tone in the Quonset muted. The men were murmuring amongst themselves.

"The boys treating you all right?" Brand stopped, facing the Manager. Cartwright glowered back. Brand studied the biker's face. Red rimmed eyes half concealed behind drooping eyelids. The man struggled against the chains holding him upright against the post.

"You look tired," Brand commented. "Me too. You might as well grab a few winks. We can talk later." Brand was operating on little sleep and knew that if he didn't find a place to lie down soon, he'd hit a wall of fatigue and be rendered useless.

Walking out of the office, steaming mug of coffee in hand, Brand tracked down Little Abe. "Is there a place I can crash? Somewhere out of the way to grab a few hours of sleep?"

Little Abe pointed to the second level.

"Second room on the right has a couch. I'll make sure you're not disturbed," Abe promised.

*****

Richard Cozicar

The roar of bike engines entered his subconscious bleeding into his troubled dreams. He was on a bike being chased by a band of demons. The demons morphed into the Colombians…then the scene switched to his friends chasing down the highway after him.

The nightmare jumped from the highway to alleys filled with rot, buildings crumbling all around. A wall of brick stopped Brand's escape. Behind Brand, his friends gestured at him accusatorily, their heads replaced by white skulls as flames burned in place of their eyes….

He sat up, his eyes snapping open, the bizarre images disappearing but the rattle of bike engines remained loud, seeping into the building, slowly rising to the still room in the loft he had sought refuge in a short while ago.

Brand's hands rose to his head. A headache drummed his brain while pain and throbbing wracked his weary body.

Outside the massive metal structure, a loud resonating roar vibrated the building. Shaking the cobwebs of sleep away, Brand swung his feet to the floor and stretched before leaving the couch and walked to a small window in the loft. He stood to the side of the window; his fingers peeling the dusty curtain aside.

Gazing outside, he peered down into the yard searching for the source of the noise that had woken him from his dreams. An army of motorbikes filled the gravel lot outside. The loud mufflers of the bikes unable to restrict the throaty rattle thrown off by the powerful engines. The group of unknown bikers straddling the loud, metal horses sported a variety of patches and colours.

The Wolves Of Satan

He dug in his pocket for his phone to check on the time. He pulled two out. In his tired state, he had forgotten to charge the phone Yen Lee had surrendered. Turning his attention back to his phone, he hit the button and swore, early afternoon already.

Looking back out the window, Brand studied the leather vests and jackets adorned with unfamiliar gang colours and patches. None of the badges resembled the Wolves but in the same breath, not Apostle colours either. The arrivals filled the space between the trees bordering the yard and the building. Noises rose from the lower floor seeping into the loft. Loud, excited talking. The combined sound of many footsteps moving about on the concrete floor below.

Remaining by the window, he spotted Little Abe and an entourage of Wolves walk into sight from somewhere near the Quonset. The Wolves men spread apart, crossing the short distance from the building to challenge the rival bikers.

To Brand's tired eyes, the meeting outside the window was tension filled. His hand went to his side searching for a gun. Were these new riders part of the Apostles and did they discover the location of the Quonset or...no, he realized. The new arrivals would not have ridden in peacefully. Instead, the men would have raced into the yard with guns ablaze if they were intent on attacking.

Still, he hung by the window watching the proceedings. The gathering outside seemed friendly enough, and the men who rode into the yard were obviously the bikers Roy had been recruiting.

Brand left the room and climbed the stairs. He spotted Susan walking from the centre of the room back toward the office.

"I'm not sure what to do with you?" Brand confessed to James Cartwright as he crossed the floor. "I can't imagine that my threats or even a good beating would convince you to tell me what I want to know." He continued as he walked a circle around the Manager. Cartwright followed Brand's movements. The Apostles sagged against the chains holding him in a standing position.

"And frankly. I'm too tired to care." Brand added. "I will tell you what I am prepared to do though." He stopped in front of Cartwright locking eyes with the man. "I need to know where your Colombian buddies are holding my friend. Tell me, and I will guarantee that the Wolves will not touch you."

He stopped and listened to the sound of the unrestrained motorcycle engines thunder out of exhaust pipes and filter into the massive room.

"That roar you hear. That is your personal hell coming to pay you a visit. The days of you and your Cartel friends are over."

Brand walked to the office, dragged a chair back and sat in front of the Manager. He remained silent letting the other man consider his options. The obtrusive racket of bike engines growing unbearably loud, the roar flooding into the confines of the building echoing off the metal walls. Brand raised his voice to be heard over the wall of noise.

"I'll give you another minute," he shouted, "after that I am walking outside and the men in the yard can do with you as they wish. I think the lot of them will jump at the chance to vent their anger after what your men have put their friends and colleagues through."

James Cartwright returned Brand's stare. Fear pulled at the defiant expression on the Manager's face. His features sagged as he imagined the horror awaiting him beyond the building's walls. Brand watched Cartwright struggle. Loyalty to his men and the Colombians or the prospect of a short future, one he presumably would like to avoid.

The biker broke his silence.

"Sure, what the hell. I'm tired of the Cartel boys and their shit anyways. You can guarantee me that these guys aren't going to cut me to pieces or leave me lying in a ditch with a bullet in the brain?"

"I can persuade them to let you live if you cooperate."

"The shooting of Thundercloud was never my idea," Cartwright confessed. "That slime ball, Rojas. He wanted to repay you for the stolen drugs and the destruction of our warehouse."

"Ya, ya whatever. Where's my friend, the old fishing guide? Where can I find him?"

"That I can't help you with, but I can tell you that Rojas and his men occupy the top floor of the casino. It's their home base whenever they're in town." Cartwright struggled with his dilemma. "They could be holding your friend there; I rarely set foot on that floor."

Chapter 49

The leaders of the newly arrived gangs swung off their bikes and approached Roy's men. A few minutes of conversation were followed by handshakes. The opening of the door interrupted Brand's conversation. Little Abe led the unknown bikers into the building. The ear-shattering din of revving engines died off returning the acreage to an eerie silence.

Brand gave the Manager a final look then walked over to Little Abe.

"This is San Diego," Abe introduced the Disciples leader, standing next to Diego, Abe motioned to Harv Greely, the man leading the Montana Grave Runners. The three men were already planning the demise of the Wolves rivals.

"Those fuckers won't know what hit them." San Diego growled. "The boys and I can use the challenge. We'll help drive those losers over the mountains and all the way to the coast."

Little Abe laughingly agreed. "Those that will be able to run…by the time the night is over, most will only be able to crawl or be carried away." He focused on Brand and explained what the extra manpower would mean in putting a stop to the Cartels siege of the city.

The mood inside the Quonset changed. The Wolves gang members, who only a short time earlier, were looking up at a war from the losing end, breathed a sigh of relief. Although Roy's men stood tall in the face of the advancing Apostles, their attitudes strengthened at the addition to their depleted ranks.

The Wolves Of Satan

From the back of the Quonset, cartwheels scraped across the worn concrete floor. Loud voices quieted as everyone looked in search of the interruption. Cases of beer towered from a rickety cart, loaded from a back room and offered as a sign of friendship. The sight of the wobbling beer cart drew hoots and yells of encouragement.

Brand glanced around the room at the mingling of tough men sporting the various colours of gang symbols. He noted the change in atmosphere. The sight of the wagon loaded with beer helped smooth tensions among the newly introduced bikers, as it rolled from the far end of the room. The quiet, reflective mood of the Wolves from minutes earlier changed to a lightened, celebratory feeling.

The pungent smell of burning weed wafted into the air mingling with the sound of opening beer cans and loud cheers of approval. The members of the various gangs grew boisterous as they settled into a sense of ease with the each other.

Standing to the side, Brand half listened as the bikers drank beer and plotted to return the city to the Wolves. Shouted questions rang throughout the building. Each group receiving separate orders of who and how many men would be employed to attack chosen Apostles hangouts.

Susan appeared. Her features etched with concern as she scanned the leagues of men. Strangers sporting vests and jackets stitched with colourful patches denoting unfamiliar emblems of the different gangs flooded the interior of the room. Pushing through the growing crowd, she crossed the floor and stood by Brand's side. The two stood quietly, mesmerized, as the melding alliance of bikers argued over details. The air interrupted at times by loud displays of anger toward their now common enemy.

Brand took Susan's hand and pulled her away from the mob of boisterous bikers and back toward the office leaving the door open. He began searching the desk and drawers. The ravaging pain haunting his body after days of abuse begged for a reprieve. He rifled through drawers filled with receipts and notebooks, pens and envelopes.

"What did Cartwright tell you?" Susan asked. "Is he privy to the Colombians inner workings? What do they plan on doing? Did he identify the leader of the Moreno Cartel?" Susan bombarded Brand with questions. Her words betrayed her curiosity, the tone of her voice bordering on panic.

Brand half listened to her questions. His mind occupied. His joints ached, the blood vessels in his head sparked with each beat of his heart. If only…the second drawer down, on the left side of the desk rewarded his effort and fortified his belief in human behaviour. Nine times out of ten, in drawers of an office desk, you would find a bottle of pills.

Facts were facts. The same held true for other traits. When people were nervous, they let their guard slip. No matter the façade they presented, certain mannerisms were hard to disguise. These ruminations flashed across his consciousness in between the jolts of pain throbbing in his skull.

Relief for the headache came in the form of a bottle of painkillers. The key to understanding the Cartels weakness came in the philosophical quest to find something that he knew lay waiting for discovery. Brand popped the lid off the pill bottle and dumped two tablets into his palm. Tossing the plastic container back into the drawer, he turned his search to the side of the office. A collection of liquor bottles sat on a shelf.

Glancing up, he noticed Susan sneak another troubled look out the office door toward the bound Apostles leader. She quickly pulled her gaze back inside the office when she saw him turn in her direction. What if his approach to the shootings and the Colombian's actions were from the wrong perspective? Could he be overlooking the obvious because of personal bias? In amongst the throbbing pulse in his brain, a new train of thought presented itself. Despite himself, a flicker of a smile touched his lips. In the midst of a raging headache, a moment of absolute clarity. He knew what he had to do.

Brand squeezed past Susan, his hand gripping a bottle of amber whiskey. Spinning the cap lose, he tossed the pills into his mouth then tilted the glass bottle of whiskey, washing the pain medicine down his throat with a promise of the whiskey chaser speeding up the medication. Out of the corner of his eye, he studied Susan as she stole another furtive glance in Cartwright's direction.

The pills slid toward his stomach, the whiskey burned the back of his throat. Brand shook his head bracing against the raw burn of the potent liquid. The scattered pieces of a troubling puzzle slowly locked together.

Brand set the bottle back on the shelf and turned to Susan. Briefly, he explained how he intended to free her father. The plan was risky but possible. The war was going to end tonight, he assured her.

"Cartwright." He said pointing to the Apostles chained in the centre of the room. "He figures there's a chance that the Colombians may be holding your dad at the Millennium Casino. The gambling house perched on the western outskirts of the city," he clarified. "Apostles run, but under the control of the Colombians." Brand paused, wondering how much of his plan he should reveal. "The top floor is strictly Cartel inhabited, he told me."

"Has that man seen dad?" She asked apprehensively. Fingers in her raised hand pointed to the man tied in the middle of the milling bikers. With a worried expression, she glanced at Brand and then out of the office at the Manager.

Brand shook his head in response "No. Cartwright said he hasn't been up to that floor for weeks but thinks it's entirely possible that your dad could be a prisoner there. It's all I've got to go on for now," he shrugged. "Slightly better than nothing." He said in way of an apology. Studying her face, his words conveyed the poor feelings he suffered for not having a better answer.

"I'm going to the Casino take a look later tonight." He looked past Susan at the fusion of bikers who continued loudly plotting. "I can't wait. If these guys clash with the Apostles, your dad could become a casualty. I won't allow that." He promised.

"Take me with you." She pleaded.

"No. My idea is too dangerous. I could very well be walking into a trap."

"The casino will be crowded. Surely the men at the Casino wouldn't try anything with so many witnesses around." Reasoning with him, Susan added. "I can blend in on the gaming floor. I should be safe among the crowds."

Studying her, Brand pretended to turn the idea over in his head before finally giving in to her request.

"We'll leave when it gets dark. It'll be harder to spot us on camera when we arrive. Grab your things. I need to make a quick call, and then we'll head into town and grab a bite to eat."

The Wolves Of Satan

Brand excused himself and showed Susan out of the office. Closing the door, he locked out the loud, rowdy talking of the bikers.

*****

"...Yeah. I'm going in tonight. Will that give you enough time to set up?" He listened briefly to an answer, and before he ended the call, he added. "Be sure to apologize to Sarah for me, will you. I've been pretty busy." He hesitated. "Tell her I'll call as soon as this is over."

Grabbing a piece of paper from the desk, he scribbled a brief note and left the office. He scanned the mob of bikers gathered in the Quonset, crossing the warehouse floor when he located Little Abe. Brand pulled Abe aside, and turning his back to shield his movements he stuck the note in the bikers vest pocket.

"Read this after I leave." He instructed Little Abe then quickly sketched out his plans for the evening. "Something I've got to check out at the Millennium," he finished the conversation when Susan joined the two men.

With Susan at his side, the two walked away from the bikers and the Quonset for Cartwright's truck.

Chapter 50

The discussions among the newly formed group of outlaw bikers dragged on into the early evening hours. Plans were made then changed and changed again. Each gang considered equal among the others so delegating orders became heated at times.

Around the supper hour, the Crypt Riders from the Northern part of the province rode into the already crowded lot of the Wolves metal building. Close on the heels of the parade of outlaws came a small police presence. Singletary squad cars followed the caravan of roaring motorbikes. Officers watched as groups of bikers turned off the secondary highway. A long line of rattling machines and dusty riders flowed out of sight disappearing onto the grassy entrance of a yard. The police cars remained on the shoulder of the secondary road unable to enter the private land. The pairs of uniforms bided their time in idling patrol cars broadcasting updates to their superiors, recording plate numbers and staring at a narrow view offered of the yard between breaks in the shielding bushes.

The recent arrival of a large number of riders wearing unfamiliar colours and entering the city proper caused concern for the cops in charge of keeping law and order in the greater Calgary area. The bikers had so far broken no rules. Keeping an eye on the gathering, while showing a police presence was the only action available.

Joining in on the plans for a raid against the Apostles faction, the Crypt Riders became impatient.

"We didn't drive all this way to sit around drinking beer and cackle like a bunch of old ladies." Matt Henley, the frontman of the Crypts gang shouted while urging his fellow compatriots to action.

"What about the cops sitting outside." Asked a junior member. "They're waiting for us to move."

"Not enough of them to bother with." Little Abe responded. "When we leave, we leave in small groups. The cops can't follow all of us. We join up again once we're closer to our targets."

As dark began descending, the men crowded in the building set the beer aside and fuelled by the booze and drugs, focused on the long night ahead. Little Abe began dispatching small units of riders away from the Quonset. Sets of four or six men mounted bikes, drove off the property and re-entered the highway, turning toward the city.

After a number of the men left, Abe motioned to San Diego of the Devils Disciples, Harv Greely from the Grave Runners and Henley of the Crypts.

"Mount up." He said. "The cops know who I am. When we leave, I'm sure that the uniforms posted out front will follow." He raised his voice and spoke over the dying noise from the remaining men. "Give us a twenty-minute head start and then ride to your assignments."

Abe gave final instructions to the men who would leave the premises last.

"Remove what you can and then burn the building to the ground. After tonight, the police will return with warrants to search the place."

The police assigned with spying on the gathering, sat in their cars, thumbs on car mikes, reporting as the bikers slowly filed out of the Quonset. Every few minutes a small group of men climbed on their bikes and left the area. Updates were issued across police channels and back to central dispatch. The police hierarchy, well aware of the trouble heading into the city, sat with no legal cause to stop the bikers. All the law enforcement in the area could do was prepare for a battle they knew was soon to happen.

The leaders of the separate outlaw gangs rode together out of the yard with Little Abe in the lead. The four men wheeled onto the secondary road past the idling squad cars. Recognition of Little Abe had the desired effect. The officers watching the acreage rammed the squad cars into gear and followed the men north.

A grim smile etched Little Abe's face as he led the procession away from the Quonset allowing the largest part of bikers to leave unhindered. He motored into the city lights and wove among the evening traffic to the northeast quadrant of the city. Abe rolled his bike into a hospital parking lot. The same hospital that Roy Thundercloud currently occupied a bed, recovering from the gunshot wounds a night earlier.

Little Abe dismounted. He glanced past the vehicles filling the lot, his smile growing as he spied the squad cars roll to a stop at the entrance to the hospital grounds. With the police forces eyes focused on him, the next part of the plan now had a chance to unfold.

Hanging his helmet on the bike handlebars, Abe led the visiting bikers into the hospital. Before the attack on the Apostles could begin, a visit to the bed-ridden leader of the Wolves in a show of respect.

*****

The Wolves Of Satan

At a strip club in the mid-Northwest of the city, half a dozen Apostles leaned against their bikes smoking and talking. The conversation ending abruptly as one by one their heads swivelled, their voices drowned out by the sound of rumbling motorcycles turning into the parking lot.

The upside to wearing biker colours: the insignias alerted others who you rode for and warned them to leave you alone. The downside: everyone knew which gang you rode with. The approaching band of bikers carried colours unknown to the Apostles. The colours the new riders wore were from 3 provinces east. The Desperados motorcycle gang out of Ontario, the Desperados gang's colours and insignia soon to be introduced to the local boys.

The bikers wearing the Apostles colours pushed upright off the bike seats, unfinished cigarettes flung to the ground. The men eyed the approaching riders, uncertain of the newcomer's intentions. The new squad rode up to the hometown bikers. The leader of the group stopped in front of the Calgary squad. Straddling his machine, he removed his helmet and sat on his bike. A grim face scanned the confused men.

The man shouted at the Apostles over the rumble of his bike's engine.

"This your establishment?" He asked.

The club member closet to the man stepped forward.

"Names Ike. You're on Apostles turf friend." He braced the man with more confidence than he was feeling.

The Desperado's leader smiled back. "Ike is it. Good to meet you. I'm John Harvey." The frontman for the Desperados returned the greeting. He motioned with his head signalling his intentions. Men, dusty from the long ride, rolled their loud bikes past the leader surrounding the Apostles. Kickstands dug into the gravelled lot while the newcomers dismounted. The rattle of chains and the glitter of street lights reflected off lengths of metal pipes freed from saddlebags sent a wave of fear through the small group of Apostles.

"How many men are inside?" Harvey asked the biker named Ike. Ike gulped down his nervousness. The question was rhetoric. The number of men outside and the number of bikes they stood clustered beside were equal in number."

Harvey eyed the man. "Do you have a phone, Ike?" The Apostles patted his pocket.

"Pull it out," Harvey commanded. "I want you to send a message to your clan. Choose the number you dial carefully. You'll only get one chance." John Harvey waited while the Ike fumbled the phone from his pocket.

"What message?" Ike asked.

"Tell whoever answers to listen to your words very carefully and then spread the message through your organization." Harvey lit a cigarette while Ike dialled his phone." Harvey listened as Ike spoke to his contact. "Tell them; the Apostles run in this city is over. Warn your compadrès that any who choose not to put this city skyline in their bikes rear view mirrors within the hour will... Well, let's just say they will understand my message very soon."

John Harvey motioned to his men. "Some of you to head into the club. Empty it out before burn it down." Harvey sat on his bike. He listened to the sound of kickstands digging into the ground and the crunch of footsteps. He studied the puzzled Apostles, never letting his eyes stray from the men in front of him.

The Wolves Of Satan

The Apostles bikers watched with wide eyes as a several of the Desperados climbed the stairs to the entrance of the strip club.

When the Desperados left an hour later, frantic emergency calls from shocked bystanders who happened onto the scene summoned the police. Volleys signifying the escalation of the inevitable war began. The unconscious Apostles bikers littered the parking lot of the strip club. The six men wearing the hometown colours were severely beaten and left as a warning of the long night to come.

The Desperados herded patrons and staff out into the parking lot before the trashing the interior and then tossing cocktails of flaming rags stuffed in bottles of liquor across the empty business. Smoke rose slowly from the interior of the club. Not a three-alarm blaze yet, but the flammable material lining the club's walls and floors would fuel the fire into one.

As the evening wore on, the merging of the Desperados and Little Abe and his posse, tore a path of destruction against clubs and bars tied to the Apostles and protected by the Colombians. In the path of the cleansing, bikers associated with the Apostles colours fell in their wake.

Those who survived the run-ins with the Wolves and who could move were stripped of their colours and warned to leave the city while they were still able to ride. The next time around, the disenfranchised bikers would be lucky if a bad beating was all they received.

The Apostles/ Colombian faction started the war. On this night, the Wolves and their new allies were determined to end it. By morning the city would be the turf of the Apostles or the Wolves of Satan. The days of the city split between the two rival bike gangs drew to an explosive end.

Chapter 51

Parking at the Millennium Casino was at the minimum. Brand slowly rolled the truck past double rows of vehicles, weaving from one end of the multi-acre lot to the other. He searched for an open stall with regards to the proximity of the casino's security cameras located throughout the lot. He chose to park the truck at the very edge of the vast parking compound. There the cameras were spaced farther apart due to the distance from the building. Closer to the main entrance and the grounds immediately around the building perimeter the cameras overlapped in their coverage.

Chances of being recognized or watched were probably slim; still, Brand took the precaution. Advancing thoughtfully, wanting the element of surprise on his side a while longer. Rifling through the back seat, he found a tattered ball cap and adjusted it to his head.

"You're not going to stay in the truck if I ask, are you." He wasted the words on Susan. He knew what her answer would be but made one last attempt to keep her out of a possibly soon to be a dangerous situation.

She shook her head in response and together they wove their way past the myriad of automobiles, each step shortening the distance to the main doors of the casino entrance. Susan's movements quiet and slow, Brand, cautious and alert. His eyes darting over and around the lines of cars and trucks, eager to detect the tell-tale signs of their presence tracked by the enemies in the casino. He walked on an indirect path, weaving among the lines of vehicles abandoned in the massive parking lot, his route chosen to avoid the security cameras.

The Wolves Of Satan

While part of his brain kept busy moving forward for an undetected approach to the building, in the back of his mind, he sifted through the little information he acquired and reviewed the layout of the casino and it's Colombian owners. Aware of the small amount of knowledge he possessed on the two, he ventured onward with little to no preconceived plan of slipping past security and gaining entrance to the top floor of the building. The best he could hope for was to adjust quickly to the way the events unfolded and act accordingly.

The purpose of his visit was to gain access to the top floor of the building and once there, find his old friend, if Jerry was indeed there. One step at a time, he cautioned. First order of business was to cross to the building without allowing the men staring at the video feeds from the security cameras sprinkled across the massive parking lot to identify him. Next, pass security at the front door then enter the gaming rooms and from there access the elevators.

Neither of these two steps should present much of a problem, he considered. An organization like the Cartel probably had a long list of people plotting against them. He couldn't be all that important in the overall scheme of things. Thoughts of bringing a gun on this mission had crossed his mind, but the security guards and metal detectors at the entrance made that more of a hassle then he needed. If he had to shoot his way into the Millennium, the possibility of bypassing the buildings layers of security would be impossible.

Once inside, he could get his hands on a firearm. On his previous visit to the Millennium, he noted that the security guards all carried hidden side arms. He banked on his abilities to convince one of security personnel to lend him a gun. Not the greatest of tactics but certainly doable.

The gun part of the plan was minor compared to gaining access to the elevator and the trip to the fifth floor and into the

Cartel's den. James Cartwright had provided a mental map of the casino layout from the front doors to the elevators and up. The opening of the elevator doors on the top floor gave him the most worry. That part was a little more open to interpretation. All the planning was usually worthless in a situation like this. Too many variables, too many unknown moving pieces to choreograph once the shooting started.

Steps from the entrance he tugged the ball cap lower on his forehead and put his arm through Susan's. As a couple, the two climbed the pebbled concrete steps. Arm in arm they walked between towering concrete pillars. The reflection of their approaching bodies growing clearer in the polished glass of the entrance as they drew nearer to the sliding glass doors. Their mirrored images almost life-sized by the time the double doors slid open, welcoming them into the casino lobby. The pair walked up to a set of heavy wooden doors, the only barrier remaining between them and the lights and bells of the gambling floor.

Letting go of Susan's arm, Brand pulled on the wooden doors and gestured for Susan to enter first. An atmosphere of excitement poured into the opening. Raised voices belaying the happy anticipation found in gambling establishments joined the clanging of one-armed bandits underscored by piped music. The palpable din was overwhelming to the senses.

Guards posted at the entrance eyed the pair as they crossed into the jubilant confines concealed inside the walls of the gaming room. The men smiled at Susan as she stopped. A quick wave of a portable wand and the men waved Susan onto the floor; then the guards turned their attention to Brand. Brand's facial features appeared relaxed. Casually, he studied the guard's expressions. If the two were expecting him to show, the men revealed little.

344

The Wolves Of Satan

The burly men watching the entrance eyed him from head to toe. He hesitated briefly before taking a step closer to the screening area. Nodding, he strode up to the guards. One man motioned him closer; the other stood to the side, neither was inclined to talk.

The guard with the scanner motioned for Brand to raise his arms then proceeded to wave the detector the length of Brand's body. Susan stood beside the second guard. The bulk of the man's body hiding Susan's much smaller frame. At the edge of his vision, Brand noticed Susan's partially hidden hand move near the guard's pocket.

The guard's eyes flashed in her direction then locked back into a bored expression. The man stood unmoving. His heavily muscled arms stretched the fabric of his suit jacket and folded across a massive chest. The man stood poised, ready to assist his partner should trouble ensue.

Trained, competent pros, the pair dressed the part in matching black suits. These men were different from the guards Brand had encountered on his first visit to the casino. At that time, the security was looser. Poorly disguised bikers with small man syndrome, big egos matched with bodies pumped up at some gym, brawn with little brain.

In the short time between visits, he was surprised at the change of attitude...or was he. The Apostles who fronted the Colombians operation were now being phased out. Well, the classier sides of the business anyways. Brand imagined that the bikers would be kept around for the dirty, gutter aspects involved. The sewer dealings in back alleys and crack houses that would require the well-dressed Cartel to muddy their hands.

The security guard waved him on, ending his musings. He put his arm through Susan's and strolled around the gaming floor. His head swivelled as he studied the layout and the bodies of gamblers and staff alike. Gathering new information, processing what he saw and readjusting his fly by the seat of his pants plan. He was inside, unchallenged, so a gun and an elevator ride to the top floor, undetected, were next on the list.

Arm in arm, the pair wandered the floor of the gaming room. Cameras were spotted as well as the routine of the casino security. The two walked, unhurried, as Brand scouted for an area where the multitude of cameras would be blind and allow him an opportunity to disarm one of the floor security team. What he needed was a distraction, some event that would garner a guard's attention, but not be disruptive enough to draw the interest of everyone else on the floor.

Near a small alcove away from the main pool of gambling activities, Brand stopped. His back to a guard stationed close to the chosen spot. Susan faced away from him gazing over the room. On a whim, Brand grabbed Susan inappropriately. Surprised, Susan let out an involuntary shriek and turned to face him, her face reddening from the assault. Anger flashed across her face. She raised her hand and with an open palm and swung.

Brand felt the sting of Susan's blow. A sharp retort rang from the harsh contact of her palm on his cheek. The crack echoed loud in the corner of the floor, but yards away the sound was swallowed by the loud din of the busy gamblers and the bells and whistles at the centre of the room. Susan's slap loud enough to grab the attention of a nearby guard and force the man to prevent the situation from escalating.

"You okay Ma'am?" The guard asked shoving past Brand to check on Susan. Moving his body slightly, blocking the guard from the view on the casino floor, Brand raised an elbow and drove it into the side of the guard's head. The man turned. A stunned, uncomprehending look on the guards face challenged

Brand before the man stumbled and fell back into the alcove. Brand followed the man down, his actions swift, disabling the guard before the man had a chance to raise a hand or an alarm.

From the time spent walking the floor, Brand had little trouble discovering where the guards carried their firearms. His hands quickly searched the man, retrieving the hidden weapon and removing a casino security card pinned to a lanyard around the man's neck. Remaining bent over the guard, he inspected the gun, checking the chamber and the clip of bullets.

In a deft move, he stood, turned and simultaneously tucked the gun into the back waistband of his pants. Straightening his coat, he grabbed Susan's hand and led the way across the room to a bank of elevators directly across the crowded floor.

Now came the pressure. How long until the discovery of the prone guard and the rest of security notified? And would the security card get them to the top floor? These thoughts flashed through Brand's mind while he pressed the elevator button and waited.

A bump brought his focus back to the presence. Susan straightened and apologized. Brand felt her hand slide the newly captured gun from under his coat. In that instant, he knew he didn't need the security card to gain access to the top floor. Susan's actions guaranteed his meeting with the Colombian, Rojas.

He sensed Susan take a step back. He pictured her using both hands to raise the weapon at his head. His intuition proved correct by the metallic click as the hammer cocked into firing position. Slowly turning his head, he stared into the black hole of the barrel.

Chapter 52

"You don't seem overly surprised," Susan said motioning Brand into the elevator. Standing diagonally across from Brand, she risked a glance at the panel using her elbow to press the button for the fifth floor. The gun held with both hands level at his chest. She studied his face, unsettled by his calm demeanour.

"This story could have ended on a happier note if you would have cooperated?"

Brand remained quiet. His hand lifted to the front of his jacket. He reached into his pocket. His fingers brushed the power button on the cell phone nestled against his cigarette package.

"Hey," Susan waved the gun in warning.

Brand slipped the cigarette package into view. He flipped open the cover and released one of the tightly rolled sticks from the foil, his other hand lifting a lighter.

"You can't smoke in here." Susan said. The irony of her holding a gun pointed at him while at the same time admonishing him for crime of smoking in a public space lost on her. He drew on the cigarette sucking the smoke deep into his lungs then slowly let the wisps of smoke escape past his pressed lips. A slight jerk of the elevator signalled the start of its climb upwards. Brand's silence began wearing on Susan's nerves.

"Say something," she anxiously commanded.

The neutral look on his face told her all she needed to know. Brand looked down into Susan's eyes. Fear of the unknown tinged their edges. He lifted the cigarette back to his mouth. The less she understood of his motives, the better the chance of he had of succeeding.

Brand briefly tussled with the notion of relieving Susan of the gun. While he bent over the guard, he purposely sheltered his movements from her, emptying the bullets from the magazine and stashing them on the fallen man. The gun she held served only as a prop.

He was a bit surprised by her need to reveal her loyalties so quickly, and he could quite easily wrestle the gun away from her, but he needed access to the top floor. Her method was safer than following through with his deception and possibly the need to avoid the rush of bullets when the doors opened on the top floor.

He had been slow to figure things out at first. The tiny fragments of puzzle pieces too small at first to lead to any conclusion. Over the following days, the scraps of information started to connect and fill in the blank spaces. Random thoughts merged and slowly worked together to reveal a broader picture.

When the shooting had taken place at his house, he balked at the detective's theory for the late-night visit by the unknown gunmen. A mistaken drug deal, a wrong address, no reason to think otherwise. The continued pressure by the Cartel, though, that part never made sense and got him thinking.

A young guide shot dead in his house, his other friend wounded. Susan attacked at her dad's house and a lost cell phone the Cartel was desperate to get back. Why.

Suddenly things started to, not add up. Young Dave, an undercover cop, sticking close to Old Jerry. The half-assed attempt on Susan, at her dad's house, an insider in Roy's organization leaking information to the Apostles allowing the rivals to stay one-step ahead.

The attack at Roy's acreage, the rival gunmen satisfied with taking pot shots at the house instead of attempting to overwhelm Roy's men and enter the building. If they were intent on grabbing Susan, which he presumed was the reason for the attack, then why the lack of effort. A poorly executed ruse used to deflect attention away from the person in Roy's company responsible for leaking information?

And finally, the airline ticket he found lying on the floor of Susan's room. Susan had flown in from the west coast not from the east like he assumed. When he stopped to think about her arrival, she had shown up at the hospital in a swift fashion. If she had departed the Maritimes immediately after being informed of Jerry's condition, a good portion of the day would have passed before she visited the hospital. If the flight included in a layover in Toronto, it would have been evening by the time she set foot in Calgary.

Susan's hesitation when she saw James Cartwright at the Quonset. That's when he started rethinking the pieces of the puzzle. He still maintained a glimmer of doubt on her part until she grabbed the gun. Now the doubt was removed, but he did get an invitation to the fifth floor. He had wondered how the story would unfold and when her façade would drop.

He stood watching her, his face devoid of emotion. He dropped the burning cigarette. Watched it fall and bounce on the carpeted floor. Tracking the smoldering remains with his foot, he squashed the burning tobacco out. By the time he raised his head, the elevator had bounced and settled. The doors slid open. Four men, dressed in the same attire as the guards on the casino floor, were waiting, automatic rifles pointed at the elevator.

"You notified the guards at the entrance," he confirmed, remembering the glimpse of her hand when she moved it near the man's pocket while he stood under the scrutiny of the second guard. Susan glared up at him and used the tip of the pistol to motion him from the elevator. He stepped past the waiting gunmen and walked across a short foyer and through an open set of double doors.

Moving straight ahead, Brand noted the office's interior. The room was big but not overly. Along the wall from the French doors, a second door farther to his right. A set of chairs set with a small table rested against the side exterior wall. Windows flanked the chairs offering a view overlooking the lights of the parking lot and then, what Brand imagined, during daylight hours, a clear line of sight to the Rocky Mountains that rose to the sky an hour west of the city.

Opposite the windows, to his left, pictures hung on the wall leading to the back of the room and a stand-up bar in front of a mirrored wall filled the corner. Two men followed him into the room, and he spotted only two more armed men flanking a much smaller man. The trio back of centre, standing behind a decorative piece of furniture centring the room.

"Mr. Coldstream." A heavily accented voice called to him. Brand focused on the man. Standing behind a polished wooden desk was a slight man with medium length, slicked-back hair and a tanned complexion. Brand walked further into the room, the gunmen from the hallway, trailing close behind.

"Have a seat." The words beckoned to him from behind the desk. Brand slid a stuffed leather chair, stepped around and sat down, his eyes remaining on the Colombian.

Quintin Rojas stood behind the desk, watched Brand cross into the room and once Brand was seated, the Colombian lowered into his chair.

"What a welcome surprise." The Colombian sneered at his guest.

Richard Cozicar

"You must be Rojas?" Brand commented. "The Moreno Cartel's number two man."

"It is fitting that you would show up here after the problems you've caused." The Colombian paused, scowling at Brand. "Did you think you would be allowed to walk in here without us knowing?" Rojas averted his eyes from Brand and sought out Susan. "We've been keeping tabs on you for some time now." He added smiling.

Brand followed the Colombian's gaze, his gaze also stopping on Susan.

"So it seems." Brand agreed. "Some days it's tough to separate your friends from your enemies." He declared. His stare fixed on Susan's face. "Although that does explain a lot."

"Do you take us for buffoons." The Colombians voice grew louder, more exasperated. "What. You think you could steal our merchandise and destroy our property and yet remain out of our reach." Rojas' face reddened by the reminder of the Cartels lost shipment of drugs and the money lost because of this man. He started to anger all over again.

"Hey, asshole." Brand replied. "You sent gunmen to my house. They shot my friends or don't you recall... well I suppose only one was my friend as it turns out.

A few ounces of drugs and a couple of dollars should be the least of your worry." Brand threatened. "Count yourself lucky if I don't climb across this desk and rip your head off and stuff it up your ass for what your piss ant Cartel did." Brand struggled to stay seated as rage replaced caution. The gunmen standing behind his chair took a step closer. One put his hand on Brand's shoulder pressing him tight into the chair to prevent him from going through with the threat.

The Wolves Of Satan

Rojas waved his men back and sat studying Brand.

"We could have used a man like you." Rojas shook his head as if the thought saddened him. "But I see it would not have worked out...you and us. Tell me, with all the effort to come up here; you did bring the phone to trade for your friend?"

Brand smiled. The phone. He had all but forgotten about it after plugging it in to charge back in the loft. The events from the afternoon occupied his mind. He forgot to check the video and see if it contained the identity of the Moreno Cartel's boss. Suddenly, the phone didn't seem to matter, he supposed. The Colombian boss's identity was no longer anonymous to him.

A cold smile crept on Brand's face. He looked Rojas' in the eyes.

"You know, I actually forgot about the phone. I guess it doesn't make a difference...I don't believe I have a friend here to trade it for, now do I. In fact, I would go as far to say that I don't even have a stake in this stupid turf war any longer." He waited and let Rojas digest his words before calling the Moreno Cartel's boss out.

"Isn't that true, Jerry," He said, his raised voice causing the words to reverberate inside the room.

Chapter 53

A door somewhere outside of Brand's view opened. The talking ceased. Brand remained staring forward. The whispered breathing from the others in the room replaced Rojas' words. Soon, the hushed tread of shoes on carpet stepped closer from the opening door.

Rojas looked past Brand. The Cartel underboss' gaze followed the sound of the open door. Brand ignored the temptation to turn and look, his sight instead focused on the mirrored wall behind the corner bar. The silencing presence of an older man with carefully groomed grey hair and a perfectly tailored suit strode deeper into the office, the man's image growing larger in the mirror. Pale green eyes studied Brand's face from the reflection.

Brand stared straight ahead, his eyes shifting from the mirror to the distracted Rojas. Footsteps preceded the man as he walked over to the desk. Brand listening to the soft footfalls on the carpet as the steps drew closer. The final link of understanding earlier in the day still left him reeling from shock as the newcomer stepped into his sight. Three men crossed into his vision. Two armed men and the leader of the Moreno Cartel.

"You get around my friend. That's for damn shore." The old fishing guide said as he waited for Rojas to vacate the chair.

"It pains me that we have to meet again under these circumstances." Jerry confessed to Brand. The Cartel boss took the vacated chair behind the big polished wood desk. Absently his hand swept at some imaginable dust on the desk's surface.

Brand held his reply, but his eyes remained locked on Jerry's face. He reassessed the man sitting on the other side of the desk, a man whom Brand had regarded as a close friend. For the past several years Jerry's act of being an old, down on his luck, drunk, fishing guide, fooled him. Boy, he sure read that book wrong, Brand admitted.

The men sat across from each other re-evaluating what they now saw. One looking for the entire world as a well to do businessman who had things under control, the other staring back with a look of deep contempt.

The man running the Moreno Cartel ended the stalemate.

"Sorry it has to come to this my friend." Jerry Kartman glanced from Brand to his daughter. "For what it was worth. I did enjoy our time on the water and our impromptu bullshit sessions." "Long before my life took this path, I honestly relished the days I spent guiding back home."

"Back home as in Nova Scotia or back home in some South American country?" Brand spat out refusing to merrily go down memory lane. "Did you ever live in the Maritimes or was that all part of your cover?"

"No. I am originally from Halifax…" Jerry looked up at the ceiling as the long forgotten memories poured back into his conscious. "That is where Susan was born. Before I divorced her mother. The name was different back then, mind you. I feel I at least owe you an explanation." He continued.

"Spare me." Brand stopped him. "I really haven't got time for your shit."

Jerry looked back at his friend, his face reddening from the auditory slap.

"I believe that this may be all the time you have left, so don't be in a hurry to throw it away. When I'm done speaking, I will have no reason to keep you alive. In fact, quite the opposite, I can't let you live, knowing what you now know." Jerry added with no more emotion than if he was ordering a meal.

"Back in the Maritimes when I was a lot younger and after several bouts on the wrong side of the law, I was given the option of jail or joining the army. Obviously the army won out." Jerry launched into his life story. Brand took the opportunity to survey the room. Mentally placing every piece of furniture, committing the room's layout to memory. He placed the guards, deciding which men he should deal with first, which ones presented the path of least resistance and his best chance of appropriating a gun and maybe walking out of this office alive.

"My string of bad luck followed me into the army and how shall I say...I had to part company ahead of a court martial. Do you know how many opportunities wait ex military in those shithole South American countries? The ruling governments are happy to employ mercenaries. The Cartels are always on the look for employees who don't mind blood on their hands and even the American government was more than happy to ignore my misforgivings as long as I was willing to work as a hired gun. Hell, the Americans sought me out and recruited me."

Brand noted the movements of the others in the room, especially Rojas. The Colombian was the wild card. He stood to the side and remained wary to every movement, in comparison to the guards who had started to relax while Jerry droned on.

"I did contract jobs for different agencies for a while, but the longer I remained in the area the more I grew to admire the Cartels. They commanded respect with fear, lived in the big mansions high above everyone else. THEY told the government officials and the police what to do and when. And money. Jesus…they had money, so much so that they could wipe their asses with it. So I made a decision right then and there, I tell you. I wanted what they had. The respect, the women, the money."

The guards flanking Jerry relaxed; their guns held loosely in their hands. Brand turned his head slightly and caught the reflection of the two guards stationed directly behind him. These two were also becoming less attentive.

Still, Rojas watched like an eagle. Susan had wondered over toward the windows, the gun she had removed from Brand, lying unattended on the side bar. Useless, he noted, since he removed the bullets earlier.

"I put in my time being an errand boy for the Moreno boys. Biding my time until I gained the trust of the two brothers who ran the Cartel. One afternoon, as luck would have it, I found myself alone with the Moreno's. By this time my friend Quintin and several others in the Cartel's employ had become tired of the brothers. There I stood. All I had to do was remove the brothers and bingo…I inherited my very own drug operation.

The first problem to arise was the fact that I'm obviously not Colombian. People in that country are suspicious of outsiders. I knew I couldn't control the men if they knew a foreigner was running the operation so I convinced Rojas to pose as the new boss. I ran the business from the shadows.

Things worked better then I hoped. I was able to travel and move about undetected. I had it all, the respect, the big mansion, I even sent for Susan. She came and lived with me, but then the other organizations began putting the heat to us…well, we figured we'd set up shop back in this country away from their tentacles.

And it was working beautifully until that nosey kid came along hiring on at the fly shop. Just another snot nosed fishing guide." Jerry paused and shook his head. "The kid was good. I will have to give him credit. All the while we hung around, I never once suspected him for an undercover narc.

Hell. I couldn't believe my good fortune when I found out you were retired and guiding in the city, the best agent to ever work for the Canadian government. Your reputation certainly precedes you, by the way. The great Brand Coldstream.

So here I was. Running my new venture in the relative safety of my home country and right under your nose. Perfect. I stuck close. I thought that if the law ever became suspicious of an old fly guide making numerous trips back and forth from the coast, my association with you would deflect any suspicions."

Brand kept scanning the room tracking the others movements. While Jerry talked, he found a clock mounted across the room and checked the time. Jerry noticed the clock, stopped his auditory then stared at Brand and scowled.

"Am I keeping you from an important appointment? Have you got some place to go?" Jerry snapped. Brand shrugged away the question and motioned the old guide to carry on as he stifled a yawn.

Jerry sat quiet staring at his prisoner, trying to read his old friend's mind and figure out what the man had up his sleeve. He turned and looked at each of his guards checking on their positions. After a brief time he delved back into his story. The man in front of him had no options as far as he could see.

"When I discovered my phone missing, I thought at first that maybe I did get sloppy and misplace it while we were drinking. Then I got to thinking…you know…in my business it pays to be paranoid." He stopped and smiled. "What's that saying…just because you're paranoid doesn't mean they're not out to get you." An uneasy laugh burst from the old guide's mouth.

"I had spent years religiously hiding my identity and then my phone goes missing. That phone contains some compromising pictures for a man in my position. Video of me doing business with some very prominent business associates. Men who I've had the good fortune to convince to help my cause because of the videos and suddenly all that was in jeopardy because some snot nosed kid steals my phone.

The more I thought about that, the more paranoid I became." Jerry stood up and left his desk walking over to the bar in the corner. The room remained quiet as he mixed a drink then slowly returned to his chair.

"I suddenly started to wonder if you weren't involved with the kid. You with your background in law enforcement, I mean. What was a guy to think?"

Brand started tapping his foot in impatience. A few more minutes, he reminded himself, were all he needed if his plan were to actually work. He needed Jerry to keep talking.

"So why bother with the façade of being a fishing guide? Hell, we spent rain days tying flies and drinking?" Brand asked.

"Well that part was genius." The old guide bragged. "Under that guise, I was free to travel back and forth to my warehouse and keep an eye on things with out anyone questioning my movements. To the men at the warehouse I was only another down and out bum tricked into carrying the drugs. I mean…really, who was going to question an old man pulling a drift boat down the highway?

And why. Guides in this section of the country are always traveling between provinces, guiding the rivers in between. This area is famous for the fishing." Jerry stopped and smiled pleased with the plan that allowed him to run his operation in the open with nobody the wiser. Then his face changed from a pleasing smile to an outright scowl.

"Which unfortunately brings us back to the current problem. You, my friend." Jerry scowled deeper as if he was struggling with a problem that had no pleasant options left but the inevitable. "My phone. Do you have it or not?"

Brand pulled his phone from his front pocket. Holding Jerry's gaze, he slid his thumb over the screen activating the power, surreptitiously sending a prearranged message. He gently set the device on the desk. Careful to lay it face down hiding the glowing screen. He gave the phone a nudge toward his one time friend. The phone obviously different then the one he expected, his eyes returned to Brand's face. The Cartel boss failed to notice the lit phone screen.

"Sorry to disappoint you, but this is the only one I have on me." Brand shrugged. "One thing bothers me about the night Dave died." He hoped to keep the focus away from the transmitting phone. "Did you pull a gun on Dave first or did he realize you discovered what he was doing and cornered you?"

"Ah." Jerry's hand involuntarily touched his chest where the bullets entered. ""That was most unlucky for me. When my men busted into your house, out of nowhere, a gun appears in Dave's hand. That, I did not expect."

The Wolves Of Satan

Jerry's eyes lost focus as he relived the moment. Brand watched the man wince as he ran his hand over the healing bullet wounds.

"I couldn't let Dave shoot my men so I pulled out my own gun. I rushed my shot, missing the young bugger. He shot through his surprise. His first bullet caught me near the shoulder. His second came damn close to my heart. Almost ending me.

You were supposed to be there." A flash of hate passed across Jerry's face. "I had convinced myself that Dave and you were working together to take me down. I couldn't allow that so I arranged for those men to visit the house and eliminate you both.

Easy enough to explain to the cops, a drug deal gone sour. Nothing the cops haven't come across before. I even had a cache of drugs in my truck to plant on the scene."

Jerry stoked his chin. A sad smile moved his lips. "Dave packing a gun to our drinking party. Who'd have thought?"

Coming out of his brief reverie, Jerry focused back on Brand. "Alright then. I hope I answered all your questions. Won't matter though. Seems that your time has run out." He turned to look at Rojas.

"Quinton…" the old guide started to say when the lights in the office flickered off and then back on. Questioningly, he looked around the room. The overhead bulbs blinked a second time. The room was again plunged into darkness. A couple heartbeats passed before the brightness returned. The promise of light also brought an ear piercing assault. Fire alarms screamed a warning. The high-pitched squeal added to the confusion. Mixed in with the alarms unnerving whine came a louder, underlining rancorous rumble, an un-muffled roar that emanated

361

from outside the building and rose up the five floors, reverberating in the closed confines of the office.

"What the...?" Jerry exclaimed. "Get security on the phone and see what in the hell is going on." He issued the order to the men standing in the room.

Quinton Rojas ignored his boss. Strange sounds outside the building drew him toward the large office windows. Puzzled, he gazed down into the parking lot five stories below. Bobbing, solitary headlamps distinguished rows of thundering motorbikes as the machines rolled off the adjoining streets and turned onto the casino grounds. The bikers began flooding the lanes between parked vehicles, weaving their way toward the base of the building.

The individual engines combining with each other to compile a symphony of deep growling undercurrents that vibrated the structure of the casino.

Rojas remained by the window. Casino patrons rushed out the exit doors and into the cool night air, the stampede driven to panic by the screeching alarms blasting through the building.

The second lapse in the room's lighting foretold a predetermined signal for Brand to advance his plans. He pressed his eyelids closed and breathed deeply, calming his heart, preparing for the chaos to come. His pupils slowly adjusted to the lack of light, his ears sorting through the stuttered movements of the Cartel members in the office.

"Holy shit!" The Colombian, Rojas, exclaimed as the lights in the office went out a third time and remained off.

Chapter 54

Before the generators in the sub basement had a chance to switch on and power the emergency lighting, Brand planted his feet firmly, his body tensed and ready.

Launching out of the chair, he dove across the large wooden desk, his leap, one of faith, a complete trust of his memory as to where the gunmen in the room stood. In the cover of the unexpected darkness, Brand's shoulder contacted the soft midsection of the guard standing on the old guide's left. The momentum from his jump carried the two men back toward the bar in the corner of the office.

Taking advantage of the element of surprise, Brand smashed an elbow into the side of the man's head, dazing the guard. His other hand fought against the guard's grasp, both men wrestling for the guard's handgun. A second slice with an elbow, Brand felt the guard's tight grip loosen. Brand wrenched the gun free and rolled off the stunned man. With his back tight to the corner bar, he waited motionless, bent low to the floor.

He tracked the others by shouts of disbelief and scurrying feet. Scrambling to his feet, he indiscriminately sent a double tap of bullets traveling in the direction of the desk. Faint silhouettes moved in the tight confines of the office. With no friends in the space, he fired freely, tracking the movements of shadowy figures as they were highlighted by the weak infusion of light filtering through the office windows.

Scrambling footsteps on carpet and the exhalation of breath betrayed the people scurrying in the room. He strained to detect the faintest of sounds from the others. The escalating thunder rolling off the poorly muffled bike engines converging in the parking lot climbed the buildings five stories, entered through the glass windows, the roar beating against the interior walls of the upper office, wiping out all other sounds in the room.

Brand squeezed tighter into a corner created by the bar. With shallow breaths, he systematically scanned the room's interior for living shadows.

The advantage was now his. He had no worries about who he shot, a disadvantage for the Cartel men hunting him. A fleeting shadow crept along a perpendicular wall. He fired and moved, the flash from the gun barrel exposing his position. A startled grunt told him that his bullet wasn't wasted. A surge of bullets replied and slapped into the wooden bar. Splintering wood and shattering glass exploded outward.

He stuck low to the floor scurrying over splinters and glass. His shoulders brushed a chair lying on its side nearer the middle of the room. The chair he dove from minutes earlier. Extending his hand, he felt in the darkness for the side of the desk.

The intensity of bike engines increased throwing up a wall of overwhelming sound. The deafening noise rendered his hearing useless. Taking a risk, he rose up from behind the shelter of the desk and sprayed a round of bullets into the far walls. The guns hammer clicking loudly as it hit an empty chamber.

Cursing he ducked back below the top of the desk. Trails of light passed overhead as a volley of bullets gouged the desk and potted the wall behind. Thinking quickly he reviewed his options. The safety of shelter was limited. He recalled Susan setting a gun on top the bar after they entered the room, a tinge of regret for removing the gun's ammunition a curse.

How hard had he hit the first guard he took down? Would the man still be unconscious beside the only other form of shelter in the room?

The Wolves Of Satan

Taking a couple deep breaths, he steadied himself then dove the short distance from the desk. The unmistakeable feel of cloth-covered flesh greeted him along with a growing wetness. Brand sniffed the air. The tangy, metallic odour of fresh blood mixed with the stinging smoke of spent bullets. The guard caught the brunt of the searching gunfire meant for Brand.

His hand dropped back to the guard. Wet fingers felt along the body. His hand stopped at the familiar touch of hardened plastic. With an increased sense of desperation, he fumbled with the fabric of the unconscious guard's jacket, his fingers clawing for the opening to the coats inner pocket.

Deftly, he slid a thumb across the top of the cartridge holder tracing the tapered metal of a casing. Brand hefted the weight of the body and squeezed between the man's bulk and the edge of the bar. He ripped the spent magazine free of the gun and rammed the full one in its place.

Peering over the shoulder of the downed guard, he searched the darkened room for the remainder of Jerry's men. At least two were wounded, he figured. That would still leave two guards, Rojas, Jerry and Susan. Susan he discounted because she had left the gun when they entered the room.

He would have to concentrate on Rojas and the other two guards. And Jerry. The old guide had claimed he was ex-military. That set the odds at four to one. All the men, he counted as dangerous and if he lay hidden, the four had the chance to flank his position.

He slid up the wall, his back pressed tight alongside the bar. For a second he focused on the side of the desk facing him. The shadows were unbroken. He fired past the desk hoping for a lucky shot. The wall of noise engulfing the room grew in pitch. His senses overloaded.

Shoving away from the downed guard, he tumbled across the floor. His roll stopped when his shoes contacted the hard material of the desk. With his head tight to the floor he watched, his haggard breathing loud in his ears. Was it his imagination or…a change in the near complete blackness…a foot shifted a short distance away.

From his awkward position, he twisted, bringing the gun inline with the opening under the desk. Brand squeezed the trigger. The bullet found its mark. Even with the numbing sounds of the bikes engines flooding the room, he heard a surprised cry of pain. Then he felt, rather than heard, a thud rattle the top of the desk. Another presence loomed out of the dark. Brand fired up into the mass, the bullet sending the body toppling back.

Brand flipped onto his feet. He braced his hands and lifted the desk. The room shook when the wooden edge slammed hard into the floor. The desk now rested on its side. His actions eliminated the very opening he had just used. From the far wall, bullets tore into the solid desk.

The acrid smoke from the gunpowder that drifted through the closed room thickened. Each breath burned and tears flooded his burning eyes.

The roar of the motorbike engines peaked and then the brain numbing chaos eased. Brand found the sudden absence of the uproar unnerving. In front and to the side he heard the rub of hinges. A door opened then slammed shut.

Who or how many went through the door. He had no way of knowing, but gambling on the others leaving could prove fatal, that thought was quickly replaced by another. Whoever left by the side door now posed an even greater problem? What if that door led into the hallway and back to the main office door?

Brand slid around to the side of the desk putting his back toward the bar. The first guard he knocked out. The bullets that found the guards body, were they fatal? Would the man wake and pose a further threat? He strained the limits of his sight searching the darkness across the room looking for shadows that didn't belong.

While his attention focused on the far wall, the office door flew open and bullets stung the frame of the desk. The spot he had seconds earlier vacated. Closely following the flurry of shots fired from the door, a shadow moved from the side of the room and rushed forward, a second flash of exploding gunpowder marking the shooter's positions.

Rolling toward the advancing shadow, Brand fired just above the flare of the exposed gun barrel, aiming for the mass of the person squeezing the trigger. The first of his bullets missed and shattered a window. In a sweeping motion, he pivoted and fired over the top of the overturned desk in the direction of the office door while he leapt back.

The wall of the office met him, stopping his retreat. He bounced off. Dropping to his knees, he waited. His vision temporarily blinded by the flash of gunfire. A primitive scream broke through the brief silence. A shadow lifted from the floor and rushed. Bracing against the wall, Brand straightened to meet the challenge.

One of the guards charged the short distance; the man's hand held in the air, an empty gun wielded as a club. Brand ducked under the weapon driving a fist square into the man's mid section. Foul air washed over Brand as the breath erupted in a blast from the guard's mouth. The man staggered back. Brand braced for another rush realizing that he was exposed to the rest of the room.

A second body rushed him. Brand lowered his gun and fired. The attackers momentum carried into Brand. He struggled to overcome the crush of Rojas' body as blows were delivered at his head. Using his gun as a club, Brand swung upward, stunning the Colombian with a strike to the man's jaw. Using his empty hand, he followed the guns arc with a fist to the Colombian's body. His efforts stopped the forward momentum and drove the man back.

While Rojas shrugged off the assault, he fought to gain his footing, tripping over the sprawling guard. The unexpected collision sent him careening in the direction of the broken window. With impeded vision, Brand watched the blending of shadows and silhouettes dance in the weak glow of lighting from outside the room. As if in slow motion, Brand saw Rojas' macabre dance to gain his balance while being entwined with guards attempt to rise from the floor.

The combination sent the small Colombian teetering through the window shattered minutes earlier by the stray shot of Brand's gun. A short pause followed by a harrowing scream as Quinton Rojas body toppled through the opening in the shattered window, five stories above ground. The small man held briefly by the shards of glass jutting from the window frame.

Another man rose to his feet, turned at the sound of the underboss's terrified scream then clutched desperately to catch hold of falling man's coat, the flimsy fabric slipping out of his grasp.

Taking advantage of the distraction, Brand fired point blank into the guard, once, twice, then the hammer clicked on a dry cylinder. The man crumpled to the ground.

The Wolves Of Satan

A breeze blew into the room, the roar from the motorbikes climbed in decibels, rising up to reach the fifth floor and rushing into the room through the opening. In the room, Brand stood motionless, his senses alert for further attacks. A door slammed followed by the sound of retreating footsteps, the noise in the hallway growing faint, a body or bodies beating a hasty retreat from the room.

The cry of sirens made Brand glance back toward the broken pane of glass. Emergency vehicles, their lights flashing and horns blaring, started to mix into the blend of fire alarms and motorcycles.

Chapter 55

Brand remained standing, his eyes staring into the darkness. The flickering preceded the casinos emergency lighting being brought on line. When the lights filled the room, he searched for Jerry or Susan. The pair had escaped the confined shooting in the room. He wandered the top floor of the casino looking for the two.

By the time he climbed the stairs down to the main floor of the casino, the lighting had been restored. Stepping into the main gaming room, he searched again for the familiar faces of the old guide and his daughter. Conceded the two had disappeared, his eyes were drawn to the seas of outlaw bikers and police. The room was trashed. Slot machines smashed and ripped from their stands, gaming tables overturned. The litter in the room spread around the standing bodies.

Several of the casino's security either sprawled on the floor or standing in a group watched over by bikers wearing a variety of colours and patches, none bearing the Apostles colours.

The whine of the fire alarms still echoed throughout the building warning the buildings occupants of a fire that had yet to happen. Brand wove his way through the carnage toward the entrance doors, his movements lost amongst the surging throngs of police and warring bikers.

Before walking outside, he caught sight of Little Abe standing among a group of bikers bracing a squad of cops. Abe looked in his direction and nodded. Brand walked unchallenged past the entrance doors. He removed the ball cap from his head and tossed it to the ground on his way to Cartwright's truck. The one he parked at the edge of the lot hours earlier.

The Wolves Of Satan

At the bottom of the steps he picked up company. Detective O'Brien fell into stride with him. The two walked without a word, the chaos of the casino falling behind.

"Care to tell me what happened back there?" The detective spoke.

"I guess the house doesn't always win." Brand commented and stopped mid step, looking the detective in the face. "You should be able to uncover more than enough evidence against the Cartel on the fifth floor. I left the doors open." He added and continued walking. The detective watched him walk away then spun and returned to the mayhem of the casino.

The cars and trucks that had filled the parking lot earlier were replaced by a crush of motorbikes and police vehicles, the flash of blue and red strobes from the cars adding a surreal layer of light to the surrounding lot.

Pulling his cigarettes from his pocket Brand selected one from the pack, stuck it in his mouth and lit it. Turning to face the casino and the scurry of activity, he said a silent prayer that he had seen the last of the turf war in the city.

*****

Entering the hospital proved a lot easier than his entry into the casino. Careful to avoid detection from the nurses on staff, he found his way to the hospital room Roy occupied. Light and sound from the small overhead TV in Roy's room greeted him as he brushed aside the privacy curtain separating the room from the hallway.

Roy looked up as he entered the room.

"Quite the late night viewing." His foster brother said as Brand pulled a chair close to the bed and sat down.

"Yeah. The whole world is going crazy, apparently." Brand replied to his brother's comment. "How you doing?" He asked Roy.

"I've been better," Roy touched the dressing on his wounds. "But I'll live. Tell me what the news channels can't?" Roy urged.

Brand flossed over the events leading up to the night's visit at the casino. How he pieced together the identity of the boss for the Moreno Cartel and the deception against them by Jerry's daughter.

The two chatted in between watching breaking news stories. The city's news stations running non-stop coverage of the outbreak of the gang war menacing the city. The stations switching between live broadcasts from a spate of nightclubs where fights had broken out among rival bike gangs. With every report, the Apostles motorcycle gang appeared to be on the short side of the battles.

The coverage at the Millennium Casino garnered most of the brothers' attention as the reporter's interviews of the police and witnesses slowly told a story of the shootings and violence that had transpired earlier that evening.

"Exactly what were you thinking walking in there alone?" Roy asked about Brands venture into the den of the enemy.

"I wasn't alone, per say." Brand confessed. "Do you remember Brent Gallows? He was one of the guys in my unit when I served with CSIS. We've stayed in contact since I retired.

Brent's done pretty well for himself. He owns a private security firm. Does contract work for the government now a days. I contacted Brent before I left the Quonset on my way to the casino. He employs some of very talented computer techs."

Brand strayed from his story. "A few years back I met a woman while working with Brent. Her name is Sarah. I've been seeing her since. She's moved to town." Brand's mind drifted at the thought of seeing Sarah again. "When you're on your feet, we will have to get together so the two of you can meet."

Brand dragged his mind back to his story. "I told him of my plan and asked him to hack the Casino's security. Nothing complicated. On my signal, he had his people shut down the power in the building and provide some appropriate music." Brand smiled. "If you call fire alarms music. The distraction provided me with an opportunity to disrupt the Cartel's plans.

When I left the Quonset, I slipped Little Abe a note explaining what I had planned and when it was to happen. I asked him to bring the boys to the party." Brand looked at his brother and winked. "What could have possibly gone wrong?"

Brand gazed down at his injured brother. His eyes took in the bandages covering Roy's chest. "I'm sorry," he said. "Susan fooled me. Played me for a fool. Because of our friendship, she planted herself in our lives and relayed our plans and positions back to the Cartel. I should have caught on sooner. You damn near lost your life because of her deception." He shook his head blaming his unbiased trust of Jerry's daughter for Roy's injuries.

News cameras at the casino kept a live feed going as they followed officers escorting a number of leather clad bikers to waiting vehicles for a drive to the downtown police headquarters.

Cutting to another camera, one of the city's police Captain's were explaining to the reporters about the casino being used as the headquarters of a Colombian Cartel and how the building was being combed for evidence as they spoke. Evidence they would be sharing with federal prosecutors bringing an end to the Cartel's reign of drugs and violence that had followed them to the city.

After the Captain gave his statement he introduced Detective Darcy O'Brien of the RCMP drug and gang division. O'Brien was introduced as the man who had been working hand in hand with the Calgary City Police Service in an effort to halt the Cartel's expansion into the city.

The detective started his interview by telling the reporter the head of the Cartel was dead. His death caused by a fall from the fifth floor of the casino. From there Detective O'Brien launched into a brief summary of the evenings events.

"Son of a bitch." Brand growled under his breath at the detective's statement about the Cartels boss, then Brand remembered the phone he had left at the Quonset.

"I guess the detective will have a nice surprise waiting for him once I give him the phone." Brand told Roy of the phone Dave gave to Yen Lee.

"Once their faces are made public you know that Jerry and Susan will have no where to run." Roy pointed out. "Even if they manage to slip out of the country, where can they turn? His Cartel is shattered. I don't think he'll be able to return to Colombia and rebuild. Not with his identity made public."

The two spent the next couple hours talking and commenting on the breaking news stories.

The Wolves Of Satan

"It was good to see you again." Roy declared. "I know you've never approved of my choice of work," Roy admitted. "Things aren't always what they seem. In a way I do a service for the city. Sure we run illegal joints and dabble in the drug trade but we're not all that bad.

I've got a loose understanding with the city cops. They restrict their pursuit of the Wolves and in exchange, we monitor the underside of the city. We have strict rules. I make certain neither my boys nor anyone else preys on innocent people. We keep the seedy underbelly away from the law abiding public. The Cartel began to change that." Roy watched Brand's face as he struggled to ease his brother's moral dilemma concerning Roy's outlaw life.

"I know it doesn't change your opinion," Roy shrugged. "It sure was good to see you."

Brand stood and put a hand on Roy's shoulder. "Things change, people change," he said. "When Sara gets back to town, I'll give you a call. The two of you will get along fine."

In the wee hours of the morning Brand bid his brother farewell, the days and weeks leading up to this reunion catching up to him. He left the room. A week of adrenaline highs and lows settled on his shoulders. His mind and body tired beyond belief.

Chapter 56

"…Yeah me too." He answered softly. "I'll see you tomorrow morning at the airport." He disconnected the call and climbed out of the truck. Standing on the street, he faced his house.

In the stark glow of the streetlights, the house stood abandoned. Grounding out his cigarette, he crossed the sidewalk and unlocked the door, hesitating in the doorway. Running his hand along the wall, he flicked the switch for the hall lights and sauntered down the short hallway to the open kitchen, dinning room area.

With the rest of the lights turned on, he stood and surveyed the mess left from the shootings of a couple of weeks before. The police crime scene tape had been removed and the police had their cleaning contractors in to remove the blood and aftermath of the gunfight. The rest of the mess was left for him to deal with.

Grabbing a glass out of the cupboard, the rye from the freezer, and the Pepsi from the fridge, Brand poured a drink then ambled around the counter and stood by the table staring down at the very spot he had sat that rainy Friday night before the shootings started.

Feathers, thread and other tying materials the three friends had been using lay scattered across the table, all mixed together. His vice still had the beginnings of the fly clamped in its grip.

Brand bent close to the vise and using his forearm, swept aside the clutter crowding the clamped hook. Taking a long swallow of rye, he placed the glass in the clearing on the table then picked through the pile of material lumped together to his side, his eyes searching for a clear, thin plastic bag containing strands of peacock herl.

Plucking a few strands with his left hand, he pinned the fibres tight against the metal shank of the size 14 hook. Gripping the hanging bobbin in his right hand, he wound several wraps of black thread around the feathers locking them in place before collecting the tips of the feathers in his fingers and winding them forward to form the body of the fly.

Richard Cozicar

Read on for a preview of the next Brand Coldstream novel....

The Wrong Side Of Too Late

A Brand Coldstream Mission Files

The Wrong Side Of Too Late

Prologue I

November 16, 2003

Frank Kursen glared annoyingly at the second hand on his watch. The clench of his jaw and the furrow of his brow implied the inanimate object was somehow responsible for the late hour that found him still occupying the chair behind his office desk. The face of the watch taunting him as it persistently ticked off wasted seconds.

The Senior Fund Manager sat hunched over the organized desktop regarding the expensive Swiss timepiece; a watch Frank's employer had given him as a reward for 15 years of dedicated service.

Through bored eyes he studied the watch; first the superb workmanship then focusing on the inlaid jewels and finally his gaze returned to the obstinate second hand as it lazily swept around the face of the watch counting off the seconds as they added up to minutes.

His evening appointment was late. Frank sighed and leaned back in the chair looking blankly at the door opposite his desk while his mind drifted. He longed to be enjoying the confines of a secluded private men's club than sitting at his desk late in the evening awaiting a client. His thoughts already at the club, a comfortable chair, a glass of brandy and a fine Cuban cigar while he discussed the world's problems with like wise members.

The club and its exclusiveness had been his habit for the past 7 years. The membership was very restricted and highly sought after. An exclusive membership at the Free Republic broadcast to the world that the members stood amongst the top financial and powerful people in the country.

Not to mention the guarded privacy his fellow members enjoyed along with the special privileges the club made available. From there the world was your oyster and more.

Rubbing shoulders with billionaires, industrial titans and the countries most influential politicians had been Frank's dream since he'd first become aware of the club's existence years earlier. At that time he was only a junior fund manager but a man about to make his climb to the top of the business.

In order to qualify for consideration by the exclusive club, Frank had to be personally nominated by a standing member before being subjected to a lengthy screening process. During the early stages he and his career were vetted and permitted limited liberties before an arduous internship that lasted years before he was finally accepted and anointed a full time membership.

To Frank, the wait had been worth it. The club's privileges, both legal and some more adept to the grey area of the law, were far beyond even what he could have hoped and tonight he relished the thought of taking advantage of the clubs exclusive itinerary once again.

With planned foresight he had called his wife and using the excuse of a late night at the office faked disappointment in not being able to return to his palatial estate this evening but instead he would stay in the city and sleep at the club.

The Wrong Side Of Too Late

The second hand on his watch continued crawling around, his impatience growing. The client had wanted to meet with Frank and Frank only but wouldn't agree to meet until early evening.

Frank had no choice but to agree. The client was an important man in his own right. A Sudanese national with close ties to the Sudanese government and an enterprising, international industrialist who owned a very impressive portfolio, a combination that fit well with that of Frank's firm. The board members running the firm insisted Frank make every effort to acquire the man's business.

Frank was head of the division within the Canadian Banking giant and over saw the majority of international clients and business. The Canadian banking industry was cut throat at this level, all the major banks fighting each other tooth and nail for the foreign investments flowing into the country. Plus this meant another feather in his cap as the client had personally requested Frank handle his investment. An opening on the banks board of directors was now vacant along with the title of CFO and rumoured to be filled soon. Frank's name had been tossed around as a possible candidate.

As Frank thought of this he smiled. The second hand on his watch could be ignored; he had the rest of his life to enjoy evenings at the club, maybe even arriving there one day soon as a bank director. At least now he wouldn't be lying to his wife, he chuckled…he actually was going to be working late.

*****

The intercom to his office rang. His secretary Sheila who had so graciously agreed to stay late rang again and then her voice carried through the system announcing the arrival of the Sudanese businessman.

"A Mr. Suleyman Obi to see you, Mr. Kursen." In all the years Sheila had worked as his secretary, Frank never remembered a day when she was anything but professional and although she was a little older than he preferred, there was something about her legs he just loved. I'll have to take her out for supper one of these evenings and maybe a little raise in pay so she can buy some nice outfits, he thought before answering her call.

"Please show Mr. Obi in, Miss Vond." He replied then removed his finger from the button and stood up to prepare to meet his guest. The heavy oak door to his office was eased open and Sheila stepped aside allowing the smartly dressed Sudanese businessman to enter.

Frank Kursen stepped around his desk and extended a hand to greet Suleyman Obi. Over his clients shoulder Kursen looked at his secretary.

"That will be all for this evening Sheila. Why don't you call it a night?" He dismissed her then turned his attention back to the visitor.

"How very nice to meet you Mr. Suleyman." Frank said releasing the man's hand and directing him to a chair in front of the imposing mahogany desk. He waited for the man to take a seat and find a spot to set his briefcase beside the chair. "A drink perhaps before we get started?" He asked as he stood by his desk.

"Yes. A nice scotch if you happen to have one." The Sudanese said with a knowing smile.

The Wrong Side Of Too Late

Pouring a drink for himself, also, the banker returned to his desk placing the scotch down in front of his guest.

"Merci." The businessman offered, as he tasted his drink. "Thank you for seeing me at this late hour Mr. Kursen." The African drawled in a thickly accented English.

"Frank. Call me Frank, Mr. Obi." The banker replied. "Your time is valuable and our bank prides itself in going the extra mile for our customers, so no problem at all."

"Now. How can I help you?" The banker oozed with charm. Charm learned with countless years in the banking industry and honed with repeated frequency.

The Sudanese businessman lifted the offered glass to his lips, sipped the aged whiskey, swished the amber liquid in his mouth letting the flavour escape and warm the back of his throat before setting the glass on the desk. Obi locked eyes with the banker, the smile lighting the African's face melting to a cold, threatening mask.

"It is not bank business I am here for, Frank. Well, not business beneficial to your directors anyway." Suleyman's words monotone, scraped free of emotions. " What I need from you are the passwords to open your banks vaulted accounts."

Richard Cozicar

Prologue II

The banker leaned back in his stuffed chair, cocking his head to change the view of the man sitting across his desk. The smile on the banker's face, polite, as he kept his eyes fixed on the African's face, expecting a smile to return in the sharing of this joke. As Suleyman's eyes completed the change from friendly to not joking, Kursen bolted back upright.

"You are not joking...are you?" Kursen exclaimed. His mood switched to anger. "What the hell is this? Some sorry attempt at a shake down?" The banker's voice grew cold. Business hours were over. "Get the hell out of my office." He uttered through clenched teeth with all the indignation he could muster. His hand lifted. A stretched finger pointed toward the door. "Leave now before I call the buildings security and have you thrown out." His fist pounded his desk as an exclamation point.

The African lifted his briefcase onto his lap. "You may want to calm down, Mr. Kursen...Frank." The man added with an exaggerated accent before proceeding to flip open the leather briefcase.

"What...you got a god damn gun in there? Is that it? You plan on threatening me?" The banker stared at the open case, his finger poised over an alarm button located on the underside of his desk.

"No. Something much more harmful to you." Suleyman Obi slid a manila envelope out of the briefcase and without a word held it out for the senior bank director. When the banker refused to accept the envelope, the man from Sudan dropped the envelope flat on the desktop.

The Wrong Side Of Too Late

"You will want to open that." Suleyman Obi left little room for argument as he held the bankers attention. When Frank refused to touch the envelope the African hollered at him. "Open it...open the envelope now!"

Pulling his hand away from the alarm buzzer, Kursen picked the envelope up in both hands and slowly lifted the tab, reluctantly peering inside. To his relief, little pieces of stiff paper were stuffed inside. The fingers of his right hand dug the rectangular papers out and held them in front of his eyes.

After a quick glance, he threw the pieces onto his desk. "What the hell are you trying to pull, what is this shit." His eyes flicked up to the African's face then were drawn back to the small pieces of paper, glossy paper...light cardboard actually. He continued staring at the photos lying in disarray on the surface of his desk.

He started to sputter again when Obi stopped him.

"Your private club, the Free Republic, the hideaway where you go to live out your perverted fantasies, they should be more careful, wouldn't you agree Frank. I have a stack of interesting videos of you preforming there. These photos are stills taken from the videos. Shameful, don't you think."

"I...I have no idea what you are talking about...I have nothing to do with these photos, they certainly have nothing to do with me." The banker stammered in a non-convincing tone. His normally red face drained to a ghastly white, his fingers fighting to release the knot on his tie, which he found was now suddenly choking.

"Well, alright then. I suppose if I send them to the police and your family...maybe a few copies to the banks directors, you won't really care. Am I right." The Sudanese businessman's lips curled into sick, evil smile.

Frank thought as quickly as his shocked brain would allow. After a brief internal fight he swung toward the pc on the far corner of his desk and typed furiously. When he finished, he hit the print button and sat deathly still as the printer hummed and purred as it laid down in ink, numbers that were the most guarded commodity in the bank.

Passwords that opened the door to billions upon billions of dollars the bank either owned or kept under tight computer lock and key for their customers along with names of private accounts, bonds and numerous other banking details.

Suleyman Obi stood up, walked to the printer and pausing to study the pages briefly, neatly placed them in his briefcase. Closing the lid and snapping the locks he rose from his chair.

The African businessman drew another packet of pictures from his briefcase. These he withdrew slowly from the envelope and methodically placed them in front of the dazed banker. Captured in the photos were the banker's wife and daughter. With an unspoken threat, Suleyman Obi turned to leave.

"You will not tell anyone that you provided me with the passwords? Forget what I look like and forget that I was here. After my associates relieve your institution of the fees we charge for our continued silence I will contact you and hand you the videos ending our association.

You're leaking of the passwords will probably be discovered and you will surely be fired not long from now but I presume jail for embezzlement will suit you better than the jail time you would serve for your actions on these videos." The businessman tapped the photos. "We can reach your family at anytime we choose. Think of that before you try any heroics."

The Wrong Side Of Too Late

Suleyman Obi looked down upon the defeated banker. "No need to stand Frank, I can let myself out." Suleyman said hoisting the glass of scotch to his mouth, draining the smooth, aged liquid.

Prologue III

Frank Kursen sat at his desk. His head supported by his hands as he stared down at the pictures spread across the surface. How, he kept asking himself. How was it possible that someone was able to video his escapade's while inside the walls of the Free Republic? The club prided itself in its member's privacy and anonymity. Totally secure, he was promised.

His future stood in front of him in ruins. The club, the shoulder rubbing with prominent peers, the distress he could picture his family facing and the long jail term that loomed ahead of him flashed across his mind like scenes from a horror movie. Why had he been so smug, so willing to delve into his deepest fantasies?

Through clouded eyes he stared at the pictures of adolescent boys and girls he had indulged in while thinking he was invulnerable. The naked, sexual fantasies he led himself to believe he had a right to enjoy suddenly coming back to haunt and crush him.

As the hours passed, he remained sitting at his desk like a statue, his mind wrought with despair and the fear of being exposed. The clock ticked forward. A ringing phone sliced through the haze that had settled over him.

Startled by the interruption he was transported back to the present. Lethargically he reached for the ringing annoyance. The receiver slipped in his sweaty hands falling against the desk before he snatched it and placed the phone to his ear.

"He...hello?" He felt the words stumble out of his parched throat.

"Mr. Kursen." His drivers voice traveled the phone line. "Are you all right sir?"

"Shit." Kursen mumbled. He had forgotten that he told his driver to stand by and take him to the club when the meeting was concluded. Fighting to gain some sort of control over his despair, he cleared his throat.

"Jurgenson. Sorry. I got caught up with work. I'll be right down." Kursen stood up and on legs unsteady from carrying the weight of his burdens he left his office, his briefcase deserted beside his desk, his overcoat forgotten by the door as he passed.

Dishevelled and downtrodden he arrived at his car. His dreams of the club and his excitement of the evening dashed, he told his driver to drive him back to his estate out of the city.

For the next two weeks Kursen moped around his house. His wife worried by his mood but after repeated assurances by her husband that everything was all right she left well enough alone.

On the afternoon nearing the end of the second week Kursen received a call from the directors of his bank. An emergency meeting of the board was called for the following morning and he was subtly told that missing it was not an option.

That morning Frank Kursen decided against calling his driver and instead drove his own car into the city. Minutes before the 9 a.m. meeting he climbed into the elevator in the parkade and rode it to the tenth floor were he then forced his distressed body into the banks boardroom.

Several board members were already seated and peered at him with what he perceived were troubled looks as he walked pass them. He had tried to pull himself together before leaving his house but even with a force of determination, he had failed miserably.

His eyes bloodshot from lack of sleep. His face yellowed and gaunt caused by the stress of his gloomy future.

Trying to put on an outward air of confidence that he didn't feel, he nodded and delivered what he thought was a smile as he met the member's eyes. Eventually the million-mile walk across the room ended as he reached his chair, the hair on the back of his neck bristled as his guilty mind was certain that the others in the room were staring at him with contempt, knowing of his betrayal.

The banks CEO walked into the room and took his place at the head of the table. The CEO's face etched deep with worry as he waited for his coffee to be poured before addressing the seated members.

Chief Executive Officer John Rissdale cleared his throat then waited for the room to grow silent.

"Fellow board members." He welcomed in a booming voice. "Today we meet under very troubling times." The CEO paused for effect. "It has been brought to my attention that late yesterday evening our bank came under the attack of hackers, a most heinous crime has been perpetrated against our fine institution." Again the head of one of Canada's largest banks waited, his flair for drama being used to its fullest.

The Wrong Side Of Too Late

"The CFO of our Asian division called me personally after he discovered that just under half a billion dollars was removed from our banks electronic treasury and transferred to... who knows where." Rissdale slowly looked over at each disbelieving face at the table before proceeding.

"Our security staff has been notified and after several hours of digging and following the money have notified me that this theft has been going on for days and no alarms were triggered because the thief's apparently have access to our classified codes."

"How and where they got the codes is still a mystery but I have informed the RCMP frauds division and from what I was recently told, CSIS is also now involved. The few trails our security have found so far lead beyond this countries borders." The CEO lifted his coffee and tasted it while again letting his eyes roam over the people seated at the table.

Several of the members squirmed under his scrutiny. The CEO knew that once the police were involved a lot of the members had secrets that may be uncovered during a thorough investigation.

Enjoying his moment, the CEO set his cup down with a bang.

"There are only a few in this company trusted with those passwords, the majority of you are in this room." Again his gaze lingered on each and every person seated around the boardroom table "The thief's accomplice will be routed out soon enough and in my opinion should be prosecuted to the laws fullest extent, the bank will not lend a finger of support."

Finished with the brief meeting the CEO stood and stormed out of the room followed by a bewildered and ragged trail of board members. Frank Kursen sat staring at the table in front of him. The CEO's words adding one more level of despair to an all ready deep abyss of inconsolable self-pity he carried to meeting. Momentarily shrugging off the feeling, Frank rose from his chair and joined the trek out of the boardroom not wanting to be the last and add to the suspicions of the other members.

Small groups of people gathered in the hallway whispering to each other about the news of the missing money. Frank passed the groups, avoiding eye contact with the others as he moved toward the elevator. His mood deepened as he rode the elevator down past the floor his office was straight down to the parkade.

Somewhat relieved that he wasn't singled out, he knew his time was short. With the police and Canada's main security agency investigating the bank's loss, discovery of his actions would come to light, and then what. Time in federal prison as an accomplice for his surrendering of the secure passwords or come clean and spend time in prison as a pedophile.

The cloud of darkness looming over him pressed down. His natural 6 feet of height lessened by the slouching of his body as he trudged out of the elevator into the parkade a defeated man, his mind on the verge of deserting him. How would he possibly come out of this with any semblance of respect?

On his short walk to his car his phone rang, on the end of the line, the very man who had started this descent into hell.

"You have done a good job of keeping our agreement quiet, Frank." The African lauded. "Meet me tonight and I will return the videos to you. Your problems will be soon come to an end." A short list of instructions followed.

The Wrong Side Of Too Late

Frank stared at the phone in his hand once the call was over. Did he dare let himself believe that the man would be true to his word?

Chapter 1

The wall disappeared. Brand found himself struggling to gain his balance, his feet precariously placed on the ledge of the building, the jumble of sounds from the street twenty floors below rising up to meet him. He could feel the fingers of the hand that gripped his coat start to slip, the fabric of his jacket slowly sliding through the fingers tight grip.

He tore free of the hand holding him back. His arms flailed, panic rose as he fought to remain balanced on the tin ledge. Then from out of nowhere a second hand shot toward him. In the palm of the out stretched hand a phone rang. Suspended over the buildings edge he stared in bewilderment at the offering. The phone continued ringing. The shrilling tone filled the recesses of his brain.

The surreal scene faded as the dim light of the room eased into his consciousness. Blinking awake, Brand slipped from under the warm arm draped over his shoulder and grabbing the extension phone from the nightstand, he swung his feet out of bed and padded out of the room, stopping at the doorway.

His voice still groggy from sleep, he whispered into the receiver.

"Hello." He choked out.

"Coldstream. We've got another dead banker." Russ Parnell, the Assistant Director of Intelligence for the Canadian Security Intelligence Service, stated matter of factly. "I want everyone in the office by six."

"Uh. Yeah. No problem." Brand replied shaking off the cobwebs of his interrupted sleep. He peered at the alarm clock perched beside the bed. The glowing L.E.D. numbers displayed on the clock read 4:25 A.M.

"I haven't been able to reach agent Stone." The A.D. added with a touch of sarcasm. "If you know where to find her, relay this message?"

A smile crept into Brand's voice as his eyes passed from the clock and rested on the body outlined under the covers of his bed. "I will be sure to pass on the message boss. See you at six." He disconnected the call and crossed back into the bedroom.

"Who was that?" Came the sultry voice from under the blankets.

"A.D. Parnell. He wants everyone in the office, shortly." Brand sat on the edge of the bed. "Another banker died."

Agent Stone sat up, holding a blanket draped around the front of her naked body.

"Race you to the shower." She teased and threw the blanket over Brand's head.

*****

Brand waited for Agent Stone to precede him out of the elevator before joining her. He switched his coffee to his other hand, the large paper cup of black coffee still burning hot even with the added cardboard sleeve. The two CSIS agents treaded down the carpet to the end of the fifth floor hallway, the wooden double doors of the boardroom yawning open in front of them.

Agent Brent Gallows greeted the pair at the doorway. A smile lit his face in greeting.

"Morning kids. Nice to see you could make it." He laughed. "What. Only one coffee." He pointed to Brand's hand as he stepped into the hallway.

"Jesus Brent. Kind of earlier to be leading an assault on a fortune five hundred company isn't it." Brand quipped as he watched his fellow agent stride closer. Quarter to six in the morning and his friend was dressed in an impeccably stylish suit. Brent's clean shaven, angular face framed by a nest of red hair. The agent's head perched above the suits collar on a long reedy neck.

Brand had to raise his eyes slightly to gaze into his friends face. Brent standing inches taller then Brand's own six feet.

"Where you off to? I thought the meeting was about to start?"

"Forgot some papers in my office, I'll be right back." Brent replied and then let his eyes linger on Agent Rebecca Stone. Brand felt a flash of jealousy wash over him. Even dressed in an agency approved drab blue skirt with a white blouse and matching blazer, Rebecca's beauty radiated. Her reddish blond hair pulled back and tied behind her head. A set of emerald green eyes set in an exquisitely sculptured face.

"You had better watch yourself." Brand chided. "Agent Stone is likely to run you in for gawking with an open mouth."

Brent Gallows smile grew bigger. He winked at the couple and resumed his hasty retreat to his office.

Stepping through the open double doors, Brand's eyes scanned over the agents already gathered in the boardroom. At the end of the table farthest from the door sat one of the oldest members of the unit and also the shortest.

The Wrong Side Of Too Late

Juan Carlos sat with one hand holding a paper cup of coffee, his other hand turning pages of a file parked in front of him. The elderly agent squirmed uncomfortably in the stiff shirt and kakis all agents were required to wear.

Even after spending the last two years with this specialized CSIS unit, the ex- warrant officer still preferred the military fatigues he had grown accustomed to during his years of service.

Brand's eyes traveled next to Agent Winthrop. Gary Winthrop glanced up from the table and with a nod and acknowledged Brand and Rebecca's presence; a serious expression gripped the man's face.

Winthrop's height and physique closely matched Brand's own at around six feet and slightly less than Brand's two hundred pounds. Unlike Brand, Gary Winthrop sported a moustache that draped around his mouth and thick eyebrows shading his eyes. Where Brand's hair was medium brown and shoulder length, Agent Winthrop's was dark brown and tightly curled, a throw back to the seventies.

The last agent in the room sat with his back to the door. Agent Brennan Dumaire's head of short black hair was bent forward as he studied a stack of papers spread on the table in front of him. Still in his early twenties, Dumaire hailed from a small Quebec town nestled just the other side of the Ontario border. The young Frenchman had signed with the Agency shortly after completing basic training with the Royal Canadian Mounted Police.

Dumaire stood four inches over six feet and dwarfed the other members with his two hundred and forty pounds. A size and build more suited for the gridiron than the delicate field of Intelligence.

Brand and Rebecca Stone pulled out seats alongside Agent Dumaire. The CSIS agents sat preoccupied with a silent unease waiting for the A.D. to enter the room and start the meeting.

The sound of voices made Brand turn his head. Agent Gallows chatted with Assistant Director Parnell as the two pulled the heavy wood doors shut before moving to their spots at the head of the table.

All the seated agents focused their attention on the Intelligence Agencies number two man. A.D. Parnell removed his suit jacket and hung it on the back of his chair before seating himself. The room remained quiet as the A.D. rolled up his shirtsleeves, a tactic he often resorted to before discussing serious business.

Chapter 2

"Fill them in." Assistant Director Parnell spoke to Agent Gallows then stared down the table at the other CSIS Agents as the report was read.

"London P.D. were called to the discovery of a body at the bottom of the Gerrard Street Bridge at 3 A.M. this morning. The body has been identified as one Frank Kursen, senior funds manager for the securities division of the Transnational Bank of Canada."

The local police were treating this as an apparent suicide but once the body was identified the RCMP fraud unit was notified. Mr. Kursen was a person of interest in an apparent bank fraud at the institution where he was employed. Coroner's report placed the body in the river for almost a week." Agent Gallows paused then leafed through the papers in his hand and read briefly from the dead bankers bio sheet provided to the Agency.

"Kursen was sixty-two years of age…married thirty plus years…one child, a twenty seven old daughter and has been employed with Transnational for the past fifteen years." He flipped back to the top page.

"You may recall that over the last six months two other senior bankers have turned up dead. This now makes three deaths associated with the same banks where large amounts of cash have digitally disappeared. The RCMP fraud unit has been investigating the breach's at the banks and their forensic hounds have found a trial that leads out of the country."

The agent sat down and glanced at his boss. A.D. Parnell took his time before addressing the room.

"I got a call a couple of hours ago from the Minister of Finance. He is very concerned over this latest bank heist. His thoughts are that this latest security breach will send tremours throughout the Canadian banking system and make foreign investors nervous about bringing their money into the country." The Assistant director looked up from the papers in his hand.

"Foreign traders invest a lot of money into our system and the consequences could end up costing the country billions. I have been instructed to assign more agents to help the Mounties with this investigation." The A.D.'s eyes stopped on Agent Carlos at the far end of the table.

"Juan. Have you had a chance to read the full report on banker Kursen?"

"Yes." The Latino agent replied. "It seems that Mr. Kursen was rising to the top of the Mounties suspect list. A very select few managers, several who have already been cleared by the fraud unit, knew of the banks secure passwords that were used to drain money from Transnational. It says here..." Agent Carlos reread parts of the report.

"The report was focusing more on Kursen as the investigation narrowed."

"That sounds very familiar to the stolen money transferred from the previous two banking institutions." A voice from the opposite side of the table joined the conversation interrupting Juan Carlos' report.

"You have something to add Agent Dumaire?" The Assistant Director piped up.

"Sorry sir. I was just thinking out loud." The junior agent apologized. "The pattern seems to be emerging. The thefts closely follow the first two bank jobs." Undaunted the young agent explained his observation. " The first two banks are also being investigated for inside jobs. Both systems opened with secure bank codes followed by the suicides of two of their high level funds managers."

"You're a regular Sherlock Holmes." Russ Parnell commented drawing smirks from the other agents seated at the table. "But that does seem to be the consensus the RCMP fraud unit is working on."

The director turned serious. "I want everyone to set aside your current assignments. For the time being we will be assisting the Mounties in an effort to stem the bleeding of our financial system. We need to find out who and why our banks are being targeted."

"The first two suicides were investigated separately by the local police. The bank frauds were never reported until recently, the banks handled their own in house investigations. The RCMP fraud unit has been notified and will continue leading the investigation into the three bank heists, but as of now, we have will three different attachments dealing with the investigation into the suicides and the RCMP fraud squad searching for the missing funds.

What I want you to do is coordinate the info from the suicides and the bank jobs bringing the investigations together under the same umbrella. The RCMP forensic team is certain the stolen money was funnelled out of the country..." The A.D. stopped. "Let's find out where and by who.

Gallows. I want you and Winthrop to hook up with the fraud unit's money hounds. If we can find out where the money trail stops we can work backwards from there." The director turned his attention to Agent Carlos.

"Juan. You and Miss Stone re-interview the banker's widows. See if anything jumps out. Something the local cops might have missed or deemed unimportant."

"Coldstream. You take young Mr. Holmes with you and head to Transnational. The Mounties have arranged a meeting with the CEO at Transnational at ten this morning.

I want you to sit in on the interview and then also work backwards. I will set up meetings for you with the first two banks. See if any of the deceased men altered their habits before they killed themselves. Anything that would hint of their alleged betrayals to their employers."

Brand nudged Dumaire.

"Grab a copy of the reports young Sherlock. It's too early for any bankers to be at work. We might as well have breakfast while we familiarize ourselves with the files."

"I want all of you back here by five. Make sure you have something new to report." The director drummed his fingers on the table speaking loudly over the chatter in the room. "We need results   and   I   want   them   quick."

The Wrong Side Of Too Late

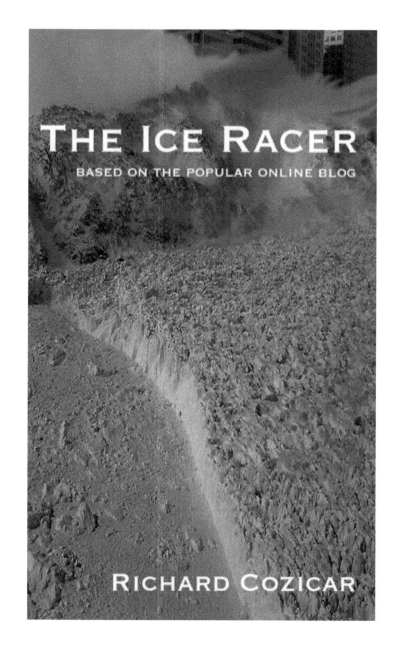

THE ICE RACER

BASED ON THE POPULAR ONLINE BLOG

RICHARD COZICAR

The 23rd century. The third planet from the sun is now a revolving, uninhabitable sphere of ice, void of sunlight. Volcanic ash clouds the skies and the air, toxic.

A small, isolated cluster of earth's surviving population labours in caves deep beneath the expanding ice cap. Ice Racer, Mike Ryan, is among the brave few who dare venture to the frozen surface in search of supplies to sustain the city's struggling inhabitants.

In a vast cavern, stories below the surface, exists the City of Adams Mountain, and a civilization long thought extinct. Stranded and alone, a chance discovery reveals a paradise unlike anything Ryan could have imagined.

The prophets ruling Adams Mountain are intent on keeping their shiny city and its existence hidden from the outside world. For Mike Ryan, the newly discovered paradise holds dire consequences for unsolicited visitors.

A rebellious young woman, a free thinker among a society of followers, aids the young hero on his quest to escape the clutches of the prophets and return to the ice caves of his home.

Traversing the sub-Arctic temperatures and unrelenting storms sweeping the dead planet may mean certain death. Will the journey home, past rivers of molten lava and through a forgotten civilization ruled by tyrants prove even deadlier?

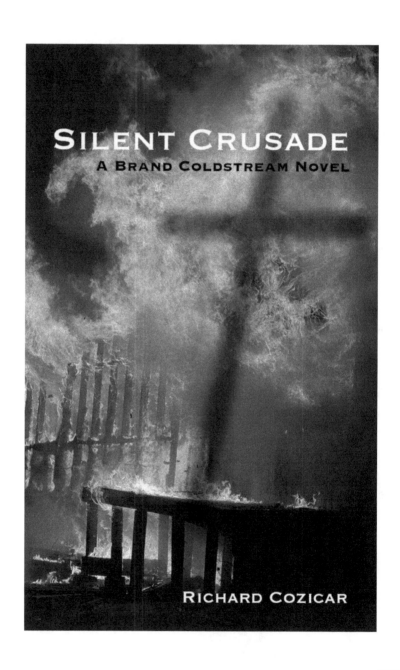

SILENT CRUSADE

A BRAND COLDSTREAM NOVEL

RICHARD COZICAR

The end of a weeklong fishing trip and Brand Coldstream is rested and ready to head back to the business of the bustling city and the arms of his girlfriend, Sara Monahan.

As he leaves the peace and seclusion of the outdoors, his world slowly unravels. Repeated attempts to contact Sara on his flight back to civilization go unheeded. Disappointment is replaced by concern when the retired CSIS agent discovers Sara's house empty, her whereabouts unknown.

Instincts bred from years of working for Canada's premier intelligence agency send Brand on a desperate search for his missing girlfriend. Brand quickly discovers that her disappearance may be the tip of the iceberg in a centuries-old feud between two rival factions.

What connection does the kidnapping of a computer researcher and a secret Cabal have in common? And what part could Sara possibly play in the developing plot? The trail of the abduction leads Brand on a cross border mystery that puts him in the middle of a religious war, a battle waged in the deep shadows and corporate boardrooms.

In a plot so devious, can the world survive the consequences as the religious battle draws to a close? Only one man has what it takes to straddle the fine line of the law in order to stop the sworn enemies from destroying each other and world peace.

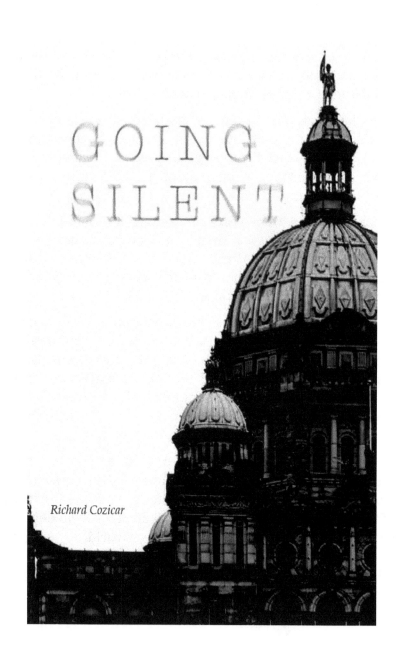

GOING
SILENT

Richard Cozicar

Retired CSIS operative turned fishing guide Brand Coldstream is forced back into action when he narrowly survives an attempt on his life. Not knowing who to trust, Brand is forced underground as he investigates his would-be assassins and their connection to his old unit and their last big operation, which ended under very suspicious circumstances.

From North Vancouver to the shipping ports of Montreal, Going Silent is an exciting, modern thriller that follows Coldstream as he works to uncover a conspiracy that goes back longer, and up higher, than he ever imagined.

About the Author

A Canadian author in the Mystery Thriller genre. Skilled carpenter and avid fly fisher. Collector of music, movies, books, and all things Elvis.

Contact Information:

Twitter: @RichardCozicar

www.facebook.com/RichardCozicar

richardcozicar@gmail.com

www.richardcozicar.com

CPSIA information can be obtained
at www.ICGtesting.com
Printed in the USA
LVHW050830300623
750050LV00005B/16/J